ZitrO Publications

This is a work of fiction. Any character references or likenesses to persons living or dead are completely coincidental. Actual people and places have been added to give the story a sense of reality.

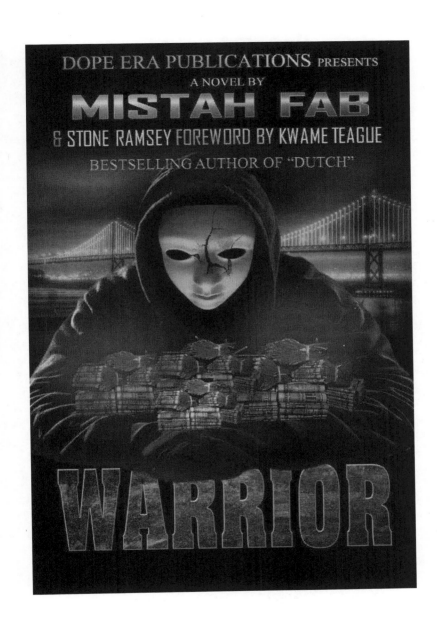

DOPE ERA PUBLICATIONS PRESENTS
A NOVEL BY
MISTAH FAB
& STONE RAMSEY FOREWORD BY KWAME TEAGUE
BESTSELLING AUTHOR OF "DUTCH"

WARRIOR

Foreword

I am one of the pioneers of this urban lit game. Someone who was there when only books that got sold were out of the trunks of cars. When no one believed it could be done. We did it. Just like Hip Hop in the early days, what got noticed were good writers. Men and women who could describe a steak so well you could taste it, or describe a pussy so good you feel it.

We were that good.

Then the game exploded and all the haters and naysayers became Mr./Mrs. Me Too. Everybody had a story to sell, but no story to tell. They bit styles, style plots, bootlegged the masters and drove the game straight into the ground.

Massive meltdown......

Now, we have the leftovers. Mediocre at best. But look deeper, because shine even brighter when surrounded by nothing as black coal. The next generation of voices are emerging, and once again, they are that good.

Stone Ramsey is one of those voices.

The Bay area has always been known for its own swag. Its slang, fluid and vivid. Stone brings that kind of voice to the urban lit game. He can make you laugh or cry, but bottom line, he makes you feel every word.

Take it from Dutch. I am who I say I am. The truth, therefore the truth I speak.

Stone Ramsey is the truth too and every fuckin' word is WRITTEN IN STONE."

Dutch aka Kwame Teague
(Author of the best-selling "Dutch" series).

ACKNOWLEDGEMENTS
MISTAH FAB

Everybody has a warrior in them somewhere
Life is about finding your inner strengths and flexing on the
world, I thank my mother for always instilling in me that no
matter what life throws at you do something with it,
Life gives you lemons make a juice bar, gives you peanuts
turn into George Washington Carver, when they attempt to
stab you
Take the knives and cut your own lane out
Basically never accept what you don't want agree with...
Many highways are taken in this life
I'm grateful for the freeway I've drove
Blessed to be in position to create outlets
If you guys don't take anything from me
Take this!!!
DO WHAT YOU WANT IN LIFE
BE HISTORIC, LEGENDARY & GREAT
LEAVE YOUR MARK!!!!!
Love you Libby
And Stone, thank you for the opportunity.

Mistah Fab

Acknowledgements
Stone Ramsey

S/O FROM THE TOP TO THE BOTTOM OF SEMCITY.
KENZO, MY BROTHER FROM ANOTHER MOTHER.
DAMEFAME, FAME, RELL, TAY-TAY, PHILTHY-RICH,
FLYAZZD-MO, TACO, SIRQUAN, RICK, HAMMY, WAYNE
GORDON, BEAUTIFUL, PRETTY MARV, RIP DADA, RIP
RELL-MO, BIG MO, LOGAN, RIP CURT, RIP CHOPPA-KEN,
RIP JODY, MONE, PRETTY REESE, HUB, GLEN, SHAWN
UPSHAW, GALEN. BANKMONEY ENT. MALLY-MAL, B.O.T.,
HYPH
(if i forgot anybody, I'll get you on the next one).
S/O TO BH THA GREAT & DEVIN HANEY, MAC PRINCE, B-
MACK, G.O.V., LEV BERLAK, YAMVO TEAGUE, R.I.P. TUFF
THA GOON, RIP THA JACKA. STEVIE JOE, MOZZY, DRU-
DOWN, THA LUNIZ, KEAKDASNEAK, RIP EKLIPZE, T-LUNI,
BREAKING BREAD/FAMILY ENT., WISEGUYS,
GOODFELLAS, THE DRAGONS, E-40, B-LEGIT, SKULLY G,
ZITRO PUBLICATIONS, KWAME TEAGUE, GODFATHER
HUNTER, AND ALL THE OTHER GREAT WRITERS. THANK
YOU DORIE FOR YOUR ASSISTANCE ON THIS PROJECT.
MY COUSINS, TOO MANY TO NAME.... NENE, SANDRA,
ANDRE, KIM, AUNTIE PAULA, KISHA .... MOMS, YOU
KNOW I LOVE YOU. POPS... PRESTON GORDON...., I
HOPE YOU'RE PROUD OF ME.... MY SONS, SEAN &
PRESTON. DANNI & GABBY.
AND, LAST BUT NOT LEAST,
MY LOVELY WIFE, ANGEL....

Stone Ramsey

Prologue

"Kenzo, where you know this dude from?" Preston asked, his eyes probing his best friend's face.

"Dude, I tol' you already."

"Tell me again."

"Look, bruh, if you ain't got the heart, you ain't got to start!" snapped Kenzo, stuffing his hands in his hoodie, storming off.

Preston watched his ace-boom, and alter-ego saunter off. He huffed, and shot a glance up into the sky before walking briskly, catching up to Kenzo.

"I'm just sayin' though, Zo, I ain't—"

Kenzo's pirouette cut Preston's complaint off in mid-sentence. Kenzo's face was chopped and screwed; his eyes were fiery with frustration.

Clearly vexed, he spat, "P, it's ugly out here, man! Ain't no fuckin' jobs worth my while, cuz I'll be damn if I flip a fuckin' burger! Moms done kick'd my dawg azz out again. Man, even my fat bitch dissin' me. Blood, I got to get it how I live! And P, whenever you get to askin' eight million questions, I know you ain't wit' it."

There he was, listening to the OG break down the schematics to him and Kenzo. Afterwards, they watched the movie *Heat*, starring Robert De Niro and Val Kilmer, repeatedly until they were all zooted with adrenaline, ready to get rich or die trying.

What the fuck else am I 'posed to do? Preston thought.

On the morning of the heist, Preston and Kenzo's hearts were thumping; dressed in all black, they leaned back in the stolen Dodge Charger in the parking lot of the bank. They sat, watching the clouds finally concede, and the sun break over the buildings surrounding them to chew on the morning dew. Lyfe Jennings' "Stick Up Kid", subbed at a low volume on repeat. Kenzo stroked the Browning 9mm as though it was a puppy and mouthed the lyrics.

"I be robbin' these niggas..."

Laser focused, Preston watched the unsuspecting bank employees make their way to the bank's entrance, clutching Starbucks coffee cups in one hand, and keys in the other.

For most, it was just another nine to five day in the rat race. For the two young men, it was do or die, or both. Kenzo slunk down further in the driver's seat as a bank employee walked by, too close for comfort. Kenzo glanced at his watch and they both peered towards the bank, watching the employees file in.

"You ready, P? This is it!"

Preston was deep in thought. He thought about how ashamed he was coming home broke night after night, and the pathetic look, Marie, his girlfriend, tried unsuccessfully to mask. He remembered how they were forced to hide their car three blocks away from their apartment, in a cat and mouse game with the repo agency. He couldn't even hustle in the 'hood, because not only was it hotter than a firecracker, with at least five different police agencies patrolling every five minutes, but to make matters even worse, law enforcement officials had filed a restraining order on him and several crew members. That meant that if he so much as stepped one foot in the 'hood, he'd go directly to jail.

This shit is crazy, how in the fuck am I 'posed to survive?

"I said, is you ready, niggah? Don't get cold feet on me now, Blood!" hissed Kenzo.

Preston chambered his Glock.

Click Clack!

"Dead the reverse psychology niggah, let's go get this doe!" Preston shot, snapping out his daydream.

"That's my niggah, but you got to admit, I know how to get you fired up."

"Nah, Blood, the only thing got me fired up is this economy!"

"Well then, let's go economize."

With that, they pulled their fitted caps down low, and pushed out the car, as Lyfe Jennings crooned, "*I'm doin' bad y'all....*"

The bank employees were just performing their first transactions. Only four patrons had entered its doors from the minute they opened. As planned, two feet before entering the bank, they slid on half masks and entered the banking institution.

Once inside, Kenzo tossed the unarmed, sixty-year-old security guard on the ground, and announced to the stunned patrons in a booming voice, "Everybody down, now! Prone the fuck out, and arms out in front of you!" They did so immediately. Kenzo kicked the security guard in the ass and ordered him to lie down, next to the other proned-out customers.

On cue, Preston leapt the counter like a cheetah, duffel bag slung over his shoulder, shouting, "Step away from the counter, don't try nothin' slick, and keep your fuckin' hands high!" Quickly, his eyes panned in search of his target. "You!" he pointed, "Bank manager! Come on, you know the drill!"

The OG had already identified the bank manager, and explained to them that she would have the key to the vault around her neck. She stepped forward, shaking as though she had Parkinson's disease. Preston spun her around and yanked her hair back, and boomed, "Okay, the rest of y'all move to the lobby, single file! One slick move and she gets it! Understand?"

Terrified beyond belief, they trembled as they walked off, with a unison of nods. One employee pissed his trousers and as they hurried to the lobby, he left a trail of urine. "Please don't kill me!" he pleaded.

Preston glanced at his watch and quickly whispered in the bank manager's ear, "I'm not gonna hurt you. Just open the vault, give me the money. No dye packets. No tracking devices. Got it?"

She nodded.

"Let's move."

Meanwhile, Kenzo had the lobby secured. His eyes zipped over the prone patrons and employees. "Ladies and gentlemen," barked Kenzo, "This is a bank robbery. Don't make it any more than that. This muthafucka is insured, your money is not in jeopardy. Do not, I repeat, do not try to be a hero or shero. Stay calm and we'll be gone in seconds. But if a muthafucka move, dey gets it! Comprende?"

He waved his firearm, as they nodded and squirmed.

In the vault, Preston bent each stack of money before he dropped it in the duffel bag, recalling what the OG had repeatedly drilled them on how the dye packs and tracking devices were hidden in the money stacks that did not bend.

"If it don't bend, it don't spend," Preston recalled the OG's rhyme of admonishment.

"Hurry up! Fifties and hundreds only!"

She nodded, hands trembling.

Kenzo glanced at his watch. "Time!"

The bank manager handed Preston one last stack, which he threw in the duffel bag and pushed her out the vault.

"Lay down out there with everybody else!"

They ran out the bank into the already running Charger. Kenzo raced out the parking lot, while Preston frantically searched through the money stacks, looking for a tracking device. Kenzo wheeled around block after block, speeding to their secondary car, his eyes snapping towards the rearview every second.

"Found it!" yelped Preston, tossing the device out the window.

Kenzo smiled, and slowed the Charger, but his smile crashed and burned when he saw the blue lights dancing in the rearview.

"Shit, we got company!"

"Fuck!" spat Preston, seeing the patrol car two blocks away, but closing on them fast.

"Bust on 'em, P!"

"Nah, man, it ain't that type of party!"

"Fuck it, scary ass niggah, I ain't goin' to jail!" raged Kenzo, reaching for his gun.

Preston thought quickly. He knew Kenzo would gun them down without a second thought.

"Look niggah, next block, jump out with the money and I'm gon' take 'em on a ride."

They passed the secondary car and watched the OG slink down in his seat. Kenzo hit the next corner, and without thinking twice, he braked and jumped out. Preston threw him the duffel bag. Instead of driving forward, Preston put the car in reverse and jammed his foot on the gas, before yanking the wheel expertly causing the car to spin 180 degrees. Almost sliding into the pursuing patrol car, at the last second, Preston started regaining control and peeling off, tires screeching, rear end fish tailing. The Charger sped off again, leaving the patrol car in smoke. Preston slid around another corner, and ran several stop signs. He glanced in the rearview and caught a glimpse of several additional cop cars joining the chase. His heart beat wildly and he was ready to bail out before the ghetto bird came hovering, because he knew it would be over then. He banged his fist on the dashboard.

"Damn! Damn!" he exclaimed as he ran another stop sign.

At that moment, he was blindsided by an unmarked police car. The driver's side window exploded, the door crumpled like an aluminum can, and unexpectedly, the airbag burst from the steering wheel, punching his face like a blow from Tyson.

He faded to black...

"Never seen a niggah diggin' in the ashtray", crooned Lyfe Jennings.

****

NINE MONTHS LATER...

"All rise!" shouted the bailiff.

Once the courtroom was seated, the Honorable Judge Peter Jensen announced, "Preston Gordon, you are hereby sentenced to the California Department of Corrections and Rehabilitation for the sum of ten years," and without further ado he banged his gavel, causing Preston's heart to jump in his chest.

His eyes watered as he twisted his neck to look at Marie and his sister, both of whom were teary eyed. His nephew threw up a peace sign bravely. Preston smiled pretentiously, turned around slowly and felt compelled to put his head down. However, his conscience spoke to him, *keep ya head up, don't let 'em see you weak, cuz then they'll get weak.*

Seeing his confliction, his lawyer patted him on his back and whispered, "Do the time; don't let the time do you."

Chapter 1

Eight and a half years later...

Beads of sweat rolled down his face, stinging his eyes. His muscles contorted and flexed as he jogged in place in his cell, creating a puddle of sweat below him. His muscles burned from his toes up to his neck, yet they drank his adrenaline and loped beneath his skin like a high performance engine underneath a hood. He took a deep breath and pushed on, pushing to the limit. Burpees were one of the most strenuous exercise routines employed by prisoners; it is a vigorous confluence of aerobic and anaerobic exercises, involving jogging in place then mounting the ground into a pushup and snapping both knees forward once the pushup is completed. This is done repeatedly, non-stop, in one motion, according to the burpee count. Then it's back up, jogging in place, preparing for the next set. Prisoners use this routine for strength and stamina. This exercise is what that Preston mastered, working his body like a crazed machine; this exercise helped him block out the pain of freedom denied. *Dorado* (Latin for I shall survive) was his watchword, and with a ritualized cadence that could be faintly heard outside his cell, he pushed himself.

> *"Push, pull, stride*
> *Souljahs on the rise*
> *One, two, three UN-I-TY*
> *Fighting for EQUAL-I-TY*
> *Through these walls*

Freedom calls
Can't stop, won't stop
Chin up, chest out, spirit SOARING
Mind ROARING..."

He caught a movement in his peripheral, and thrust himself off the floor, stepping back away from the cell bars. Even though he was locked behind the bars, he wasn't safe from the threat of boiling hot baby oil, mixed with a caustic substance to be thrown into his cell. This was prison and anything could happen, and he had seen it happen, which is why he stayed on constant guard. At 6' 0" and 209 pounds, he was a beast of a ripped and chiseled Afrikan god. His abs creased and formed an impressive eight-pack that flared up into a "V", melting into cobra-like wings. His chest was superbly muscular, complemented by cuts and indentations that were the envy of the prison workout pit. A handsome face the color of wild honey, and a set of light brown, piercing eyes, containing uncanny holding properties, capped this off. He braced himself as the movement came closer.

"Don't spear me, Shaka Zulu, it ain't nobody but the Squeak here."

Preston relaxed. Squeak was a cool dude who buzzed around him so much initially; he wasn't feeling him at first, but now he looked forward to seeing Squeak. Squeak put his head on the cell bars as though he was utterly helpless.

"Man, we need to talk," mumbled Squeak. "I been humiliated once again."

Squeak was a hilarious character whose antics reminded Preston of a young Chris Tucker, because no matter how serious his demeanor was, everything he said came out funny.

"What happened now, Squeak?"

"What do you mean, what happened? What always happens? Heat Miser!" said Squeak, lips poked and eyes narrowed.

Preston chuckled.

Squeak's baby's mama had a severe case of halitosis, but Squeak couldn't bring himself to tell her. He turned his face and pressed it close to the cell bars. "P, feel my face, it's burning."

"Man," he said in between feverish laughter, "I'm not finna feel ya face, dawg."

"Nah man, I'm serious, P, I can't feel my goddamn face! All day long, it was blowing all up in here." Squeak moved his hand in a circular motion, inches from the side of his face.

Preston couldn't contain the balls of laughter bouncing in his stomach; he had to get it all out. "Ho-how hot was it, Squeak?"

Squeak turned up his nose and pinched his lips together. "Man, it was vicious, it was ferocious, it was volcanic!" In mid-sentence, he switched to his imitation British voice. "It was hotter than a jolly rotten, rip roaring, pungent, flame barreling from the innards of the devil's arse."

Squeak grinned at Preston ecstatically.

With one hand on his stomach, holding back cramps of laughter, he shooed Squeak away. "Go on, man, get up out of here so I can finish working out."

"Working out!" replied Squeak incredulously. "Knock it off, P, ya goin' home tomorrow; it ain't nothin' you can do to improve what ya already got. Man...you just being greedy."

"Call it what you want, but lil mama gon' melt like hot butter over breakfast toast when she see this Maserati body," quipped Preston flexing, pecs rippling.

"Yeah, well, me myself, I'm leaving my girl. I ain't got to take this shit, P, I'm a good man," said Squeak, mildly ranting and pounding on his chest with his fist. "Oprah even said it herself. 'All the good men are in prison.' You think women like them stick-up-the-booty ass niggahs like ol' Steadson?"

"It's Steadman."

"Well, whateva the name he calls himself, Oprah don't want that niggah." He changed his voice to an aggressive gravelly tone and stuck his chest out. "They want a niggah to take charge! That niggah look so soft, he probably can't even fart loud. He probably be walking around shooting silencers, ssss, ssss.'"

"Squeak, you crazy," chuckled Preston.

"Man, I'm serious, P, women like catz with swag. Look at Jay-Z and Beyoncé, or Obama and Michelle. You know what? When I get out, I'm goin' after Gail."

Preston mounted the floor in pushup position, returning to his workout. "Shit, you better leave Gail alone, Oprah will have you assassinated."

"What?" piped Squeak, "Man, I'll fuck Gail so good, when I'm through, she'll jump out the window and go slap the shit out of Oprah."

Preston fell flat on his stomach in hysterics. He jabbed his index finger. "Get out of here Squeak. Now!"

Squeak shoved his hands inside his prison jacket, stenciled with the word "PRISONER" on the back in large letters. He turned around to leave, but hesitated and turned back around.

"Aye P."

"'Sup, Squeak?" grunted Preston in the middle of a pushup.

"Man I really came by here to say goodbye and wish you luck, cuz I ain't gonna bother you tomorrow, cuz I know everybody gon' be sayin' they fake ass good-byes. But Blood, on the reals, I just wanna let you know dat it's been a pleasure to be around you," croaked Squeak, all his other words knotted up in his throat.

Squeak's sentiments grabbed Preston like a sad blues melody. He closed his eyes and let the gale of Squeak's words wash over him. He pulled himself up off the floor, wiped his hands on his sweatpants, and stuck his hand out the cell bars. They shook hands, energies merged. Squeak's eyes welled up, causing Preston's eyes to water. "I'mma miss you, P."

"I'mma miss you too, Squeak."

Squeak bit his lip to keep it from trembling and pushed off down the tier, never looking back. Preston watched him leave, his eyes zeroing in on the word "PRISONER" on Squeak's jacket. He caught a tear before it could descend, down his face. Squeak had a life sentence...he was never getting out of prison.

Chapter 2

In a surreal, dream-like manner, the prison gates cracked, and it was a feeling he could only describe as being hatched out of a raw egg of slime and ignorance into a world of uncertainty. Yet, like a newborn colt, with each step he gained confidence. All the while, he made sure not to look back at the prison gates. Not once! He told absolutely no one on the streets he was coming home six months early. His rationale was that he came to prison on his own, and he should leave in his own way. In other words, he'd gotten himself into trouble, and he should walk away from that trouble on his own two feet. Knowledge of self, fend for self, and self-sustainability was the preponderant, if not the core factors, creating the construct of his evolution into consciousness.

He leaned up against the wall outside the Greyhound station in Imperial, California, the city that housed him for almost eight years in the bowels of Centinela State Prison, a piece of shit penitentiary located 26 miles southeast of Los Angeles. He set the grab bag containing two painstakingly typed manuscripts he'd penned, a Bible filled with quotes and maxims from intellectual giants of the ages scribed in the back notes, and his favorite novel, *Yadadamean:BayBizness* by author STONE RAMSEY next to him. Then he turned to browse his reflection in the bus station's window. He smiled vainly at his handsome face. No doubt, he was *fresh to def*, despite the prison issue khakis.

"It ain't what you wear, but how you wear it," he reminded himself, with a wink.

Over the years, he'd mastered the art of grooming his hair and goatee. Which is why, on this day, his hair was stylishly fashioned into a silk-like ebony beehive of shiny waves spiraling madly, yet symmetrically throughout his hair, highlighted by a blended taper and a razor crisp line. Posted at the hem of the prison issue khakis were a pair of coke white Air Force 1's fresh out the box, and shielding his eyes from the California sun was a pair of chic Ray-Ban shades, a parting gift from Squeak. Satisfied, he adjusted the Koss earphones on his head so that they fit snugly on his ears, and bobbed his head to Lauryn Hill's smooth voice crooning, "*Tell him...*"

He took a deep breath. The air was fresh and invigorating. The day was beautiful as the ebullient blue skies punched the clouds. Every so often, he lifted his shades, allowing his eyes to feast on the world around him. In prison, the world was stinking, drab, and redundant. Today the vibrant colors, aromas, and unrestricted activity awed his senses. An adolescent part of him felt the urge to shout, "I'm back, muthafuckas!"

Instead, he broke out into a Mona Lisa-like grin. His bus pulled in and he was the first passenger onboard. He nodded coolly at the leather-skinned bus driver and made his way to the back of the bus, calmly snagging a window seat, sitting his bag at his feet. He watched the remaining passengers file in, quickly tallying that he was the only African-American, everyone else was either Mexican or white; which was fine by him for Lauryn Hill's sultry voice was the only conversation he required. Just as the front doors hissed, signaling that they were prepared for takeoff, a latte-colored woman with a duffel bag slung over her shoulder and a baby in her arms, scampered up the bus steps, clearly out of breath.

"You barely made it, young lady," said the bus driver.

"I know, thank you for not leaving," she replied sweetly, catching her breath.

Preston stretched his neck to take an instinctive peek at her figure.

"Damn!" he said into his fist, because she was nothing but sweet hips and curves. His thoughts quickly turned elsewhere. It was all about his fiancée, Marie. Yet, before he could lose himself in those visions, lo and behold, she stopped at his seat. He forced himself to look straight ahead to prevent reckless eyeballing; something most prisoners conditioned themselves to do to cure any unnecessary accusations that were routinely lodged by female staff, mostly the ugly ones.

At that moment, she pretentiously cleared her throat. "A-hem."

He lifted his shades and their eyes danced for a millisecond. She smacked her lips, bugged out her eyes, and glanced down at her bag.

"Oh, my bad, ma'am," he said reaching for her bag and placing it in the baggage compartment above him.

"Thank you, but, I hope I don't look old enough to be your mother," she snapped icily.

He disregarded her attitude, re-seated himself and smiled at the adorable little girl cooing and giggling in her arms. The resemblance was just striking; it was obvious that they were mother and daughter.

"My bad again, this isn't starting off too good, huh?"

She looked him up and down and rolled her eyes. He put his headphones back on and muttered under his breath, "So much for being a lady-killer."

"Excuse me!"

He ignored her and rearranged the headphones back on his head and zoned out; he was in for a long ride back to Oakland.

About an hour or so later, as he combed over his latest manuscript, which he'd tentatively called *Truality* (a phrase he'd coined that was a combination of the two words, true reality) for the umpteenth time, he was jolted out of his zone by a sharp pull at his headphones.

Man, I know this br... he caught himself and was melted by the little cinnamon ball of a baby girl giggling, still reaching for his headphones. She had the most intoxicating pair of cognac-colored eyes, and two cute baby teeth waved at him above her bottom lip, as she smiled like a Gerber diva.

"Stop it, Gabby," she admonished the baby, pulling her away from him.

The adorable baby girl poked out her bottom lip, balled her face up, and fired up her tear engine.

Preston winced before cooing in his best baby talk rendition, "Awwww, pretty girl don't cry, 'kay?"

Instantly, she sniffed back her tears and held out her hands for him to pick her up. His eyes dipped swiftly towards the baby's mother. She smiled and nodded her head. Preston lifted her into his arms and bounced her on his lap.

"You lil flirt, you," teased the mother playfully as Gabby giggled and toyed with his earphones.

Within minutes, she was sound asleep and the mother reclaimed her daughter. Preston's shirt was spotted with baby spittle.

"You better let me clean that."

"Nah, don't trip, it's good."

"So how long did you do?"

He looked at her, surprised. "Is it that obvious?"

She nodded. "It's the clothes, plus my baby's—" she corrected herself, and continued, " I mean, my daughter's father is in Centinela, too. As a matter of fact we just had a conjugal visit."

Preston looked her up and down. "Shouldn't you be glowing right now?"

"Humph, prison is not a romantic rendezvous. I couldn't wait to get my baby out of there, it felt so soulless."

"I see your point. What's your husband's name?"

"Greg, they call him Gangsta, though. You know him?"

Preston tried his best not to show his disgust, but he couldn't stand the dude. The cat was a wannabe rapper and a high-powered coward.

"Yeah, I know him in passing," said Preston, trying to mask his disdain.

No wonder why she couldn't wait to break wide, it's him and the prison!

"It's okay, nobody likes him but Gabby."

Preston's eyes narrowed. "What about you?" he asked.

She turned her head and it spoke volumes. For a few minutes, it was an uncomfortable silence. Finally, she said, "That song you keep playing by Lauryn Hill, is one of my favorite songs."

"Yeah, it's one of mines too, actually it's the glue that keeps me and my girl bonded."

"How so?" she asked inquisitively.

He reached into his bag and retrieved his Bible.

"First Corinthians thirteen…as a matter of fact, put these on and I'll hold the Bible for you, and you can see for yourself."

He slipped the headphones on in a way that wouldn't mess her hair up, held the Good Book open, and watched as she mouthed the words, matching the lyrics to the verses.

"Wow, I never knew that song was based on that chapter!" she said awestruck.

"Well yeah, when me and my girl struggle, we use that chapter and song as a point of reference," he said casually.

"Thank you."

"Don't trip."

While the baby slept peacefully and the bus ambled up the highway, they became lost in conversation and he ended up practically telling her his life story. She listened intently, encouraging him on, asking thoughtful questions that gave cause to extended explanations. He described how he'd been on his own since the age of fifteen, when his mother abandoned him in the juvenile hall system after he was arrested for stealing a car. That she remarried and moved out of state, and the caseworkers had no choice but to place him in a group home. He explained that this led him to be shuffled in and out of the system, bouncing to various group homes until he turned eighteen.

"What about your father?" she asked, gently and compassionately.

"My father is a truck driver, who stays on the road and basically lives in his truck, but I can say, he sent me money any time I asked, without delay."

"I see," she said softly. "But what made you rob a bank? I mean, that's a long way from stealing cars."

He paused for a second to gather his thoughts, before replying. "You know, it was a combination of things, but for the most part, I was just frustrated with being broke. I tried working and hustling, hustling and working, and wasn't shit workin'. My back was against the wall; that's the only way I can describe it. You feel me?"

"I guess," she shrugged.

It was another pregnant silence, before she asked, "Didn't you ever think about going back to school or learning some sort of skill to, you know, like give yourself better choices?"

"Honestly, nah, I never thought about that. I wasn't taught or trained to think like that."

"What?" she stated in disbelief.

"I mean I always felt like school was like a mass babysitting corporation, created specifically to keep me from doing what I felt like doing."

"Yeah, like getting in trouble."

"True, but I don't recall one teacher who sat me down and broke down the bigger picture."

"You got to do that on your own."

"You're right, but it's helpful to have an example. I mean, aren't you gonna set an example for your daughter, or are you gonna tell her to learn on her own?"

"How long did you do?" she asked, changing subjects.

"Eight and a half years."

"Wow. If you don't mind me asking, what did you do with your time?"

He explained that he read voraciously.

"What, K'wan?" she said sarcastically.

"Naw, Dostoyevsky, George Jackson, Tolstoy, Nietzsche, among others. I studied economics, microeconomics, macroeconomics, and small business, small business management," he replied, ticking the fields of economics off his fingers.

"I'm impressed."

"Don't be, 'cause I still got my work cut out for me."

"So what are you gonna do?"

He blew air through his teeth and said, "What am I gonna do? I'm gon' do a lot of things, but for starters, I'm gonna publish a couple novels I penned."

With doe-like eyes she said, "Are you serious…you wrote not one, but two books?"

"I'm as serious as a Russian."

She looked at him inquisitively, as if weighing him with a new scale and asked, "What made you decide to change the way you once thought?"

"That's an easy one there. I was reading this book titled *The Life and Crimes of Don King,* and all through the book, the author was trying his best to make Don King look like a scoundrel, but all it did was make me realize how remarkable a dude Don King is, at least from my standpoint."

She sucked her tongue and remarked, "What's so remarkable about cheating people out they money?"

"The same thang that's remarkable about me doing eight and a half years for one bank. When Wall Street stole billions from investors, causing millions to go into foreclosure, and don't do one goddamn day in jail. Or how 'bout a single mother in Ohio who gets caught lying about where she stayed, so her kids can go to a better school district is sentenced to ten days in jail for fraud. But these people who have every conceivable social advantage, fleece the country of their hard earned homes and retirement, and get bailed out and I don't mean out of jail."

"What does that got to do with Don King?"

"That's just it, when he does it, he's a villain. But when they do it, it's an honest mistake. You see, promoters had been taking advantage of fighters for decades, but they were all white, so it was all right. You see, I just left a prison where a multitude of inmates are doing life sentences for a ten-dollar rock of cocaine, or a burglary, or a stolen credit card. Life! And as I was reading about Don King, he stated he read a book called *The Meditations of Marcus Aurelius*. He went on to say reading about Rome made him want to read whatever he could get his hands on, and when he came out of prison, he saw a bigger horizon, a richer imagination, and a more complex self-image. Basically what he was saying was, 'I figured out how you people do it, and you can only do it in America. You just gotta play by the rules...'"

The baby's stirring interrupted their discourse, just as they entered Oakland.

"Hey sleepyhead," she smiled as Gabby rubbed sleep out her eyes, and pulled at her mother's shirt.

"Excuse me, I hope you don't mind."

Before he realized what was going on, in a flash of motion, she discreetly fished out a voluptuous coconut-sized breast and fed her daughter, who suckled happily.

****

At the Greyhound station in downtown Oakland, he once again helped her with her bags.

"Thank you for everything and I enjoyed our conversation, um...umm...that's a damn shame. I didn't even get your name," she said, shaking her head.

"Preston, and yours?"

"Precious. It was nice meeting you, Preston."

"Same here."

"Hold her for one second."

He took the baby out her arms, and she wrote down her phone number.

"Here, call me and I'll tell you my story," she said seductively.

She retrieved the baby as he looked at the number and attempted to give it back.

"Hey look, I don't break up happy homes, you got a—"

She turned around while he was in mid-sentence and walked towards the cabstand. Over her shoulder she said, "Play the lottery with those numbers then."

Chapter 3

It was almost six o'clock when the cab driver pulled in front of Marie's residence in San Leandro, California; a small city on the eastern border of Oakland. He paid his fare and descended from the cab, grinning all the way. He had dreamed of this moment a million times. Suddenly another wave of surrealism washed over him.

Déjà vu or stage fright, he thought, but couldn't quite put his finger on it; whatever it was, ensued in slow stills and frames.

He shook it off and glanced up into the sky; the sun had just begun to set casting its scarlet makeup and residue across the horizon. He became aware of a light wind nipping at his ears and his nose, as his eyes inhaled every detail and nuance of the world before him, including the well-kept apartment complex. According to Marie, it housed hot coochie single mothers and well-to-do hood rats. The apartment complex was gated and walled off, surrounded by large trees; anxiously he made his way to the complex's call box and located the four-digit listing for Marie's unit. His heart quickened, spurring butterflies in his stomach to go "ape-donkey". He took a deep breath; he had waited eight and a half years for this moment. During those years, their relationship had been challenged relentlessly, far from being a pie in the sky, and was, in fact, often littered with peaks and troughs. Like most convicts clutching onto a relationship as such, he was forced to make psyche-slicing sacrifices that in any other instance, they wouldn't even think about considering, let alone acquiescing. Yet for Preston, it had boiled down to two relative principals: loyalty or faithfulness. In the real world, he would have demanded both of Marie, but prison was a sub-existence where certain elements just couldn't exist for an extended period of time. Therefore, he decided to cement their union in the auspices of loyalty; overstanding that eight and a half years of celibacy was a difficult burden for any woman to carry. In prison, he'd even posed the subject of fidelity to a respected elder by the name of Heshima, and was quickly chided (OG's are routinely harsh and pessimistic when it comes to women and long distance relationships).

"A pussy is a muscle and it will be exercised, and a relationship centered solely on the waist down is surely, a waste."

With these factors in mind, he made great pains to build the heart and soul of their union, suppressing the thoughts of Marie entertaining other men, with a dynamic force of unconditional love that blew the doors off lust and instant gratification. Albeit, it was truly excruciating accepting such realities, yet he loved Marie enough to make those sacrifices; *after all, she wasn't the one who got caught robbing a bank!* However, despite all sacrifices, he made sure this yielding's were not evidence that he was getting soft, and didn't hesitate to stand on his square, *hard in the paint!* He'd come to learn that the same thing it took to attract Marie; was the same thing it took to maintain this attraction. In other words, although he had matured into consciousness and by all means, a man of reason; he was still a man and there are just some things no man should ever compromise. Nor would he ever become guilty of being or becoming a wuss for the sake of their union, because this was anti-seductive to Marie, something they both knew. Therefore, because of the depths of his love, Marie's heart had no choice but to bow down and recognize this insurmountable magnetic pull. As evidence, for the last two years, she hadn't missed not a visit; tearing down the prison gates every chance she got to visit him, eagerly anticipating his release, so he assumed.

He was snapped out of his indecision to buzz Marie's unit and the fog of his thoughts, by the motion of a resident leaving out the pedestrian gate; before she could close the gate, he brushed past her.

"Hey! Excuse me!" she snapped.

"Pardon me, ma'am," he said over his shoulder, but kept it movin'.

Within seconds, he was at Marie's front door and as he put his ear against it; the sound of a bass-laden rap song subbed from somewhere in the apartment. He licked his fingertip, swiped his eyebrows, and smoothed down his goatee. He gave the door a fast knock before instinctively twisting the doorknob. It was unlocked; he let himself in.

"Slippin'," he muttered to himself, shaking his head.

The unmistakable aroma of chicken and marijuana flooded his nostrils. Alarms went off in his head, and his eyes lowered to slits; Marie didn't smoke herb. He dropped his bag and pushed through the small hallway. Marie's thirteen-year-old daughter, Dannielle, was the first to see him. Her eyes widened, and her hand flew to her mouth.

"Daddy?" she whispered through her fingers.

Dannielle was a baby when he and Marie first met. Her father had been gunned down in a shootout with a rival drug gang while Marie was pregnant with Dannielle, and so it was, he became the only father she had ever known. Dannielle's eyes swung warily towards the living room. He followed her eyes. On the couch, a young cat no more than twenty-one sat erect, clutching a control panel of a video game, his fingers frantically engaging its various buttons. He was caught up in a gamer's frenzy and hadn't noticed Preston's presence. A blunt burned in the ashtray next to him. At that moment, Marie walked out the room wearing form fitting boy shorts and a Pittsburgh Steelers t-shirt.

"Dannielle, I thought I heard some—" Preston's presence caused her jaw to drop. His eyes arrested hers, and she dropped her head.

"Marie, who in the hell is that on the couch? You better pray it's your nephew!" said Preston, slow and deliberate.

She could only stutter, "Ba-ba-baby, uh-uh-uh..."

The youngster, now aware of Preston's existence, stood up. Quickly Preston sized him up; at least six feet, medium build, long dreads and hip-hop clothes. *GOON.*

"Nigga, I ain't her nephew, that's fo' damn sho'," he quipped mockingly.

In the streets, especially in a volatile environment, it is absolutely imperative for a souljah to discern if his adversary is armed; in a flashpoint, a failure to misjudge this rule of thumb can and has been fatal. The fine hairs stood up on the back of Preston's neck; the tone and demeanor of the youngster piqued Preston's instincts and he surmised that the young cat was indeed strapped. Preston showed no fear as he eased and inched close as he could.

"Is that right, kid? Well check this out, you had your fun, now it's time to get your little video games and kick rocks!" said Preston, still moving furtively closer to the youngster, watching his hands closely.

"You need to let her tell me that, niggah!" said the youngster, his hand creeping towards his waistband.

"Unt-uhn, dude, you gotta go!" spat the ever outspoken Dannielle.

"Stay out my business, lil girl!'

"Careful, careful," Preston counseled this goon, still easing as close as possible.

As much as he loved Marie, he'd be damned to get himself killed over a bitch, *no siree,* but if the youngster gave him an opening, he'd take a calculated risk out of necessity, not out of emotions, because becoming too spooked or submissive often fed an attack, as opposed to neutralizing one.

Finally, Marie spoke. "Rico, I think you should leave now."

However, her delivery lacked the necessary conviction or coercion.

"What bitch? I thought...Hell naw, you wasn't saying that—" Suddenly, something flew towards him. He ducked his head, but not in enough time before the flowerpot bust upside his head, shattering in several pieces as the cloud of dirt mushroomed around his face and neck.

"Ahhh shit!" he screamed, stunned.

"Niggah, don't be calling my mama out her name!" screamed Dannielle, after creaming him with the flowerpot.

This was all the diversion Preston needed; he sprang on the youngster like a wild bull.

"Preston, no!" screamed Marie.

Rico's reflexes were amazingly fast; he recovered and pivoted, whipped out the .380 and without a second thought, fired.

POP! POP!

Preston could only dip his head slightly; he saw the sparks flying out the barrel and felt the heat of the bullets passing his face.

"Aaahh!" he groaned and grimaced, as he was hit. However, before Rico could get off another shot, Preston rushed him to the ground. Rico immediately began slamming the gun upside Preston's head. That's where he made his mistake.

"Aaahh, muthafucka!" Preston raged. Blood poured from his head, but before he could score another blow, Preston clamped his large hands around Rico's wrists like a bear trap, then twisted and beat his gun hand against the coffee table, repeatedly. Surprisingly, Rico was strong; he almost reversed Preston's mount and nearly wrenched loose, but ultimately he was no match for Preston's fury and brute strength. It was like a pigeon battling a falcon. Preston easily subdued Rico, knocking his gun at least five feet away from their scuffle. Next, Preston wrest Rico's arms into submission and snaked his legs around Rico's legs, forcing them to split in a way that Rico couldn't use his legs for leverage, while Preston climbed into a mounted position. Then, Preston whipped his head back and viciously head-butted Rico repeatedly as Rico winced and crumbled with each smashing, bone-jarring whack. Rapidly, Rico's resistance began to wane and Preston unleashed a flurry of murderous blows to Rico's unprotected face; swiftly followed by a staccato of savage elbow strikes. Blood exploded from Rico's pulverized face and tears rolled out the corners of his eyes as his head dribbled off the ground like a basketball. Now each blow became deliberate and smashing. Nose, eye sockets, and teeth collapsed underneath Preston's brutal strikes. Rico tried to scream, but could only muster a death gurgle.

"Stop! Please! Preston, you're killing him!" screamed Marie frantically.

It was then that Preston's nose caught a whiff of a sharp, pungent odor, and he realized Rico had shit himself. In one motion, Preston jumped to his feet and dragged Rico up, pushed him down the hall and out the door. Rico staggered away in a trail of shit, piss, blood and shame.

"Fuck wrong with you, Re-Re!"

Instantly she submitted, dropping to her knees, clamping on to his legs.

"I'm sorry, Preston, it wasn't nothin', daddy," she whimpered.

"What you mean it wasn't nothin'? You got that lil punk in our house roun' my daughter, carryin' guns and shit!"

"P-P-Preston, I know, I fuck'd up. I-I-I don't know what to say."

Dannielle assessed the scene in total awe of her father's vicious demolishing of her mother's boy-toy. She hurried into the bathroom and returned.

"Dad, you're bleeding kinda bad," said Dannielle, softly dabbing a wet towel on the side of his head.

Although Dannielle was trying to defuse his fury, it was still lively and sanguine.

In the heat of battle, he had dismissed the reality of being hit.

I must have been just skinned by the bullets, he thought, grabbing the towel, pressing it against the side of his head.

"Dannielle, go get me a shirt!" he ordered, ripping off the bloodstained khaki shirt.

Dannielle scurried off and was back with a shirt in seconds. "Damn Daddy, you hecka buff," said Dannielle, admiring his ripped and bulging muscles straining his wife beater.

Marie rose from the ground and attempted to hug him. He spun from her in disgust, grabbed his bag and bailed out the door, slamming the door so hard the hinges shivered and screamed.

Marie ran to the door and squawked, "Preston! Preston!"

She turned around and was about to collapse to the ground until she noticed the soiled floor.

"Dannielle, bring me a bucket of water, now! "

Thirty minutes later, after shooing away the police and nosy neighbors, she lay sprawled on her bed confused and ashamed. Next to her sat Dannielle, whispering into her cell phone.

"Tee-Tee, how come my daddy popp'd up out the blue, and come beat the doo-doo out my mama lil friend?" she giggled. "No girl, real dookey!"

"Dannielle, what I tell you 'bout puttin' my business in the streets?"

"But Mama," she protested, "he like, doo-doo'd on himself. I can't hold it in, I'ma 'bout to bust."

"Get off the phone, Dannielle!"

Dannielle clicked her tongue. "Dang Mama, I'll call you back, Tee-Tee."

"As a matter of fact, Dannielle, get your jacket and let's go."

"Where we goin', Mama?"

"I'm goin' to find my man!"

She quickly dressed and the hurried out the door.

Chapter 4

The bleeding slowed to a trickle, but the side of his head throbbed and his ears still rang. He held the towel against the gash on the side of his head, and walked briskly in no particular direction underneath the cloudless and moonlit sky. As he pushed into the night and in the face of a biting wind, the skin around his eyes tightened. His body was cold, yet inside the residue of pain and resentment had him steamed and heated. The wind began to water his eyes; he spun and put the wind at his back. With his bag in one hand and the towel pressed against his head with the other, he mumbled belligerently.

"For eight and a half fuckin' years I sat in prison, holdin' my tongue while C.O.'s heckled me with their eyes like I was their dope, packaged in a cell, and *all* I had to counter that reality was a bullshit vision of love and loyalty! I can't believe I fell for that shit!" He bit his lip and snarled, almost howling. "I'm a fool! A sucka! No, better yet, I'm a dope!" he ranted. "Aaahhh!" he screamed and slung his bag in the air. "This is some bullshit, man..."

He dropped to one knee and shook his fist at the stars. His emotions collided like two rams in battle, and his bottom lip trembled. "Is this what you had planned for me? Is that all you got?" he screamed into the sky.

At that moment, a squad car banked the corner in a slow predatory crawl. Instantly he froze, his eyes locking in on the cop car and the fine hairs on the back of his neck stirred. He rose to his feet. "Aw, God, naw, man. I didn't mean dat shit like dat," he pled through a whisper.

In one lithe motion, he snatched up his bag and walked in the direction of the approaching squad car. He knew if he turned the other way, it would instantly become an open invitation to get jacked. At the same time, he realized he still had the pistol in his bag.

Fuck! He brooded inwardly, just as the squad car eased up next to him. The officer's cold and edgy blue eyes raked over him. His insides squirmed, but he managed to nod his head at the cop, whose eyes narrowed while involuntarily returning a nod as he kept going. Preston exhaled a giant wind of relief, glad that the cop didn't notice his head wound.

"Do *not* look back," he counseled himself, but couldn't help it; glancing over his shoulder, sure enough the officer flipped a bitch.

"Shit!" He walked a little faster before his nerve broke and he broke into a sprint. He heard the distinctive revving of the high performance engine, singing its highest note.

VVVVRRRROOOOMMMM!

He ran full speed with the wind at his back, dropping the towel as he hit the first residential corner like a track star, his Air Force 1's stitching the sidewalk, lugging the bag like a football. Quickly, he scampered into the parking garage of an apartment complex and ducked behind a car. He opened the bag; his hands were shaking like a man with palsy, but swiftly, he grabbed the gun and looked around for somewhere to throw it, but thought better and stuck it on the back tire of the car. The cop car cruised by, whipping his spotlight here and there, before pulling off. With his heart beating wildly, Preston went on the move again, running the opposite direction. He got about a half a block away when two squad cars came out of nowhere, with officers bursting from the passenger seats, guns drawn in a classic two-hand gun stance.

"Put the bag down and get on the ground, motherfucker!" screamed the one cop.

"Hit the ground, dirtbag!" yelled the other simultaneously, overlapping themselves.

"Yagottabekiddingme!" hissed Preston.

"Down, motherfucker! Down!"

He knew if he made one false move, these high energy, corn-fed cops would body bag him with no hesitation. Slowly he got down, hands up, palms out. They approached, screaming and ranting garbled expletives. One cop kicked the bag away from him, while his partner tried to kick him in his face. Preston anticipated the routine and turned his face just in time, but the officer's foot landed just above the gash. He shuddered in pain, almost passing out. Another boot flashed again, this time rocking his groin area.

"Aaahhh! I'm down, Officer." His head began to bleed down his face, pooling in his ear.

"What the fuck you running for, motherfucker? Breaking into cars, huh?"

Preston did his damndest to dig his head in the concrete. Next, a boot went to his exposed ribs, practically lifting him off the ground; it knocked the wind from him. He felt a knee on his neck and felt himself being cuffed and roughly lifted off the ground by his cuffs. The pain was excruciating.

THA-FUCK! his mind screamed, but nothing came out, because he was still out of wind. He was tossed against the car, immediately his head was slammed on the hood of the car.

"Spread 'em, dipshit!" yelled the cop, kicking his legs viciously in opposite directions.

"I said spread 'em!" screamed the cop, once again palming Preston's head and slamming it down brutally on the hood.

Preston could only wince as the hood bent underneath his face, and he could feel the warmth of the engine and the blood oozing down his cheek.

"Got any fuckin' needles on you, scumbag?"

The cop slammed a fist into Preston's side when he didn't answer fast enough.

"Ooooofhhh," coughed Preston.

"Speak up, punk, I can't hear you!" The cop yelled so close to Preston's face, he could smell the gum, fighting the coffee on his breath; the cop's voice rang in his ear like a horn.

Preston bit his lip, anticipating another face slam as he desperately gasped for air.

"I said do you got any fuckin' needles on you?!"

"N-No sir", he wheezed, finally catching his breath; he tasted blood in his mouth, entering from his cheek.

Roughly, the officer ran his hand through Preston's pockets, and then thrust his pants down to his knees, exposing Preston's genitals, examining his briefs.

"Any dope on ya dirtbag?"

"No," spat Preston, thoroughly humiliated. The officer gruffly pulled his pants back on his hips, jacking the underwear up Preston's buttocks.

"Hey Jim, cool it, he's bleeding all over ya!" admonished his partner.

"Who gives a fuck? What's in the bag?" he replied harshly over his shoulder.

At that moment, he envisioned himself blasting a bullet through the cop's cranium.

"Uh, just some fuckin' typed up crap...probably some kinda trash rap, uh, let's see here," he continued, "sunglasses, a few letters and a CD player."

"Well, look around will ya; he had to have tossed something."

Preston prayed like hell that they didn't backtrack and find the pistol. Meanwhile, the cop meticulously swept his flashlight up and down the block, kicking at bags, through grass, and searching under cars.

"Hey Jake, it's clear."

Jake spun Preston around violently. His beady eyes plowed over him.

"What the fuck you run for?"

Preston was too battered and frustrated to lie. He squinted his eyes and thought about spittin' in the cop's face, but quickly reshuffled his thoughts, thinkin', *don't let your pride be your guide.* He took a deep breath through his nostrils and replied, "Man, fuckin' instincts, a'ight! That's why I fuckin' ran. Furthermore, I'm having the worst fuckin' day of my life, man. I just did a bid and come home and my girl got some young punk in the house."

Jake glanced at his partner in a millisecond as their eyes spoke and they adjourned.

Preston began to feel woozy; he leaned back on the squad car, barely able to stand. The remaining cops appeared.

"What we got?" snapped the senior officer, authoritatively.

"Says he just got out and found his girl with another dude; he's clean...nothin' on him," replied Jake.

"Nothin' but a lot of blood, you got some writing to do tonight, Niccitinni."

From the car and walkie-talkies, the radio dispatcher suddenly squawked, "One Adam Twelve, One Adam Twelve...We have an officer down! All available units respond!"

"Oh shit! Let's go. Cut him loose Nicchitini!" yelped the senior officer.

"Looks like it's your lucky day, *my nigger*; or is it niggah?" mocked the cop as he hurriedly uncuffed Preston. "Me, myself," he continued, "Personally, I like nigger, has a better ring to it." He laughed over his shoulder and sped off like a demon in the night. Preston spat the metallic taste of blood in the direction the cops peeled off, and abruptly sat

down Indian-style right where he stood, and glanced up at
the stars.

Chapter 5

Steam clouded around her curvaceous mahogany body like London fog. Jetting needles of pore opening hot water spilled down her body in a million, high-pressure aqua kisses. Eyes closed, she opened her full lips, allowing the water to rain into her mouth before spitting it out. The water massaged her nipples to points, and she became aware of a spreading tingle between her thighs. She stepped back and let liquid needles dribble down her vulva valley.

"Ummm," she moaned as she touched her pearl, "oooh." Her legs trembled and twitched spasmodically. "Damn, sista girl got a situation here," she mused. She thought she was gon' get broke off a lil sumthin' sumthin' tonight, but once again, the sex peaked nowhere near her breakpoint. As it stood, her orgasm count for the month was bankrupt. "I guess if you want something done, ya gotta do it yourself," she whispered into the groove she felt throbbing like a soft hum, vibrating from lips of fur. She caressed her pearl again, the source of the velvet purr; then cupped her firm and lively voluptuous breasts and cooed, "How y'all feeling tonight? Had fun?" Her nipples shrank. She clicked her tongue. "That bad, huh?"

"Tamala!" bellowed her company from the living room.

"Yeah, what's up, hun?"

"Uh, I think you need to come out, you have a visitor."

"A visitor…what the hell?"

"Who is it, Kevin? It's the middle of the night!"

"It's...He says he's your brother."

"My brother," she muttered to herself. A light bulb flashed in her head.

"Preston?" she yelled over the shower water.

"Uh-yeah," answered Kevin, in a tone of curiosity and a tinge of unease.

"Oh my God!" she shrieked. Her heart beat excitedly. "Okay, I'll be right out!"

Within seconds, she appeared in her spacious living room, still ruffling a towel through her hair. When she saw his battered face, she gave a deep gasp and wailed, "Preston wh-what happened?"

He flashed a handsome smile, decorated with a deep dimple in his left cheek. "I ran into some slight turbulence on my way back from hell," he half moaned.

She scurried across the plush carpet to embrace him, completely disregarding the fact that she had on an eat-your-heart-out porn star kimono. Squeezing him like a pillow she said, "Bruh, how you gon' come to my house in the middle of the night, lookin' like you just got jumped in a gang?"

"Had nowhere else to go."

"Let me see,", she said, peering at his wounds.

He couldn't help but notice that her breasts were on the verge of spilling out the kimono.

"Uh, like, sis...you should like, put on something a lil more decent, ya know?"

"To hell with that. Kevin, can you get the first aid kit out the bathroom for me and some ice?"

Like natural enemies in a chance encounter, cop smelled convict, convict smelled cop. Kevin's grey-blue eyes met Preston's and became poisonous. Preston's lip curled to a snarl.

"Kevin!"

He slipped off reluctantly, ice-grilling Preston all the way, before returning with the items requested. Tamala escorted Preston into the kitchen and doctored on his cuts and bruises. Preston sat, encapsulated in her feminine and fragranced aroma. Her tender touch and silky probes swallowed most of the throbbing he'd been experiencing. Soon, she had him clean and patched up.

"Preston, it doesn't look like you'll need stitches, but it's a bad gash, maybe you should go to the hospital?"

"Naw, I'm good, sis. Can I ask you a question?"

"Preston, I already know what—"

He cut her off. "Um, sis, since um, when did you start doin' honkeys?"

"Preston, please don't go there, okay? Here, put this ice on that swelling."

"I mean, but..." he replied, pressing the makeshift ice pack against his head.

"But nothin', Preston. I'm grown, I'm a college graduate, and a professional, and most importantly, I'm not shallow. Love is love, it don't matter what color the package comes in."

He glanced at her hands. "Sis, I don't see any rocks on your fingers."

"What does that got to do with it, Preston?"

"I mean, sis, you just literally went into deep waters, just to explain why you sleeping with that fake ass, Brad Pitt honkey in there, but you can't validate it."

"Preston, I don't have to validate my personal business," she snapped, hand on her hip, sharp shooting each word.

He sat the ice bag on the kitchen counter, clutched her wrist, and tipped her chin up to look into her honey brown eyes.

"Yeah, you're grown, yeah you graduated, and I'm proud of you, and even though you're a D.A., you're still my sister. So it's never personal with us, cuz when you boil it all down to the essentials, it's family."

He held her eyes captive until they dipped and swam away, and his words cooked on her. Her entire body relaxed and she softened her voice to a calm register.

"Okay, Preston, let's not fight. I haven't seen you in over eight years. Can we talk about something else, like what you're gonna do now that you're home?"

He nodded before replying, "You really are a D.A., huh? See how quick you threw me out that space? I feel sorry for the defendants on your caseload."

As they walked back into the living room, suddenly, Preston's eyes nabbed Kevin, crouched over his bag. "Aye, what the fuck are you doing?" spat Preston, snatching his bag from Kevin.

Instantly, they were nose to nose. Preston's eyes chewed Kevin's all-American mug; cleft chin, perfect nose, close cropped blond hair, and five o'clock shadow. Kevin's thin lips cracked a sneer without breaking eye contact and snickered, "I'm a cop, I couldn't help myself."

"Correction, you're a crooked cop, but I don't give a fuck if you're Jesus, punk, stay out my shit!" Preston growled.

Although they were about the same height, Preston had him by about ten pounds give or take. However, he knew the type; one of those white boys you'd have to kill, 'cause he'd keep coming and coming.

"What are you gonna do about it? Looks like you've already got your ass beat, but I don't mind sloppy seconds," said Kevin.

"The last episode the pigs had me outnumbered, but this little piggy, I'll beat the brakes off!" snapped Preston, bobbing his head, emphasizing his threat, fists clenched at his sides.

Kevin stepped closer, and now they were chest to chest. "Oh yeah, what's stoppin' ya?"

"Kevin! Preston! That's enough, stop it!" screamed Tamala, stepping between the two would-be combatants. "Kevin, I think you should leave!"

"What? Tamala, th-this," he stuttered, "scum, comes in—"

"Watch yo mouth, cracker!"

"Please Kevin, I'll call you tomorrow, just leave, okay?" He grabbed his jacket and twisted his torso in a way that Preston could see his sidearm.

"That shit don't scare me, Charlie Sheen! Get yo punk ass out!" he yelled over Tamala's head.

"Preston, stop it!"

Kevin shot him a deadly glare, before storming red-faced out the door, enraged.

Chapter 6

"Oooh, oooh, Kenzo! Oooooh Kenzo, shit!" screamed Ramona, flailing her head from side to side, legs spread, hands underneath her knees.

Arms out, palms down, Kenzo watched Ramona's huge breasts jiggle and flop before him, as he nailed her pussy to the mattress with long, deep strokes.

"Oooh daddy, make dis pussy cum, 'kay? Beat it up!" whimpered Ramona, as her face contorted into the shivering signals of climax.

"Yeeeaaah, take dat dick!" rasped Kenzo, his buttocks bunched and clenched as he piped her pussy out.

"Oooh I'm cu-cummin' Zo…oooh!" Her lips formed a wrinkled 'O', her eyes rolled to the back of her head, and she shuddered.

Damn, thought Kenzo, *Ramona tosses the freakiest fuck faces on the planet.* "Open them legs wider, take dis dick!"

"'Kay, okay, daddy," moaned Ramona, pussy milking at his dick.

He felt his leg shaking and he sped up his strokes. She glanced up to see his bottom lip trembling, and pulled her legs almost behind her head.

"Get it, daddy, get this pussy!"

It was nothin' but pussy and titties in front of him. Ramona's breasts were so huge; as they flopped, they hid her face. "Ooooh shit girl, here it cum!"

"Bust it on me, daddy."

He pulled his massive member out her moist shell. It gave way with a wet plop.

"Oooh," she purred and shuddered.

In successive spasms, he splashed his semen atop her quivering breasts. Ramona rubbed at it like lotion, before reaching out at his glistening shaft in slow, sensual strokes, coaxing his penis to spray its remains.

"Oooh yeah, daddy."

He was still squirting when she looked up into his lust-filled eyes and cooed, "That was a fat one, daddy."

He collapsed on top of her; she felt his heart beat wildly on her breasts.

"Damn daddy, you be beatin' my shit up!" she whispered in his ear, and pecked him on his forehead.

When his heart rate returned to normal, they faced each other. He leaned on his elbow, resting his head in his hand. He kissed her soft lips, and she returned the gesture.

"So lil mama, is it good or what?"

She smiled and kissed his lips again.

"It's always good."

Instantly his face turned to stone. "I ain't talkin' 'bout dat! You know what I'm talkin' 'bout, ma," he said sternly.

She clicked her tongue and attempted to turn around. He held her still with an iron grip on her shoulders.

"You turning your back on me, ma?" he growled icily.

She put her head down. "No," she muttered gloomily.

Placing his hand under her chin, he penetrated her eyes, studying her face. His voice was set at an authoritarian croon. "Look ma, I tell you all the time; time and time again, don't no bitch come before you. You are my queen, and I'm yo' king! But I ain't no square. I'm playin' this game the only way I know how, and you knew this when you got with me! Right?"

She nodded her head.

"Now peep, there are certain situations that neither you nor I can afford to be in. You know this right?"

She blinked and nodded her head again.

"And I never lie to you, do I? I always keep it one hunnit, feel me?"

She was quiet. His eyes narrowed and he frowned.

"Do I lie to you?"

She shook her head slowly.

"Now you know niggahs out there is grimy, back stabbers, and triple cross artists, right?"

"Yes."

"Then why take a risk when I can send a bitch!"

She rolled her eyes. Kenzo was a skilled street thespian and a cold playa; he knew that his game had to cook on Ramona and he knew her well enough to know she wasn't biting on the first take.

"You see, ma, your problem is that sometimes you see yourself as the bitch. So when I say 'send a bitch', you get offended." He pressed his index finger against her head. "What you got to get into your skull is that you're the queen, not the bitch."

"How do I know you not tellin' dem other bitches this same shit?"

He made a show of breathing hard out his nose. She winced.

"Baby," he said, as though his patience was waning, "didn't you just agree with me that I never lie to you?"

"Yes."

"Then how can you doubt me?"

"I don't."

"Oh, so you just don't believe me?"

"I didn't say that."

"So what is you sayin'?"

She bit her lip and looked the other way.

"Ramona, get up and go get my chessboard," he ordered.

Obediently, she tossed the blanket aside and walked across the room. He watched her ass wiggle.

Ramona didn't possess a big ole dooky booty, but it wasn't flat. Besides, her humongous breasts more than made up for the difference. She returned and set the pieces in the correct spots, with the exception of mistakenly placing the black queen and king on the wrong squares.

"Baby, remember white to your right, queen always on its color."

Quickly she shifted the queen and king in the correct positions.

His eyes combed her body. She had a roll or two she was extremely self-conscious of, and a few stretch marks; she wasn't perfect, but she was perfectly loyal. Beauty fades, but loyalty, if appreciated, lasts forever. "What I always say, Mona, about dis game?"

"Chess is the game of life and the way of life, and you got to always stay ten steps ahead of the game, but most importantly, play your position."

He kissed her on the cheek and twisted her nipples.

"That's right, boo."

"Stop daddy," she giggled.

Right then, he knew his game was cookin', but to him it wasn't really a game, it was more so his philosophy.

"Now look at my chest."

She eyed the design of king and queen chess pieces tattooed on his pectoral muscle, both of their names inscribed at the base of the respective pieces.

"Who name is that?" he questioned, tapping his finger on the queen piece on his chest.

"Mines."

"Then how can you think like a bitch?"

He pointed at the chessboard. "Mona, what's them little pieces called?"

"Pawns."

"And, pawns are—"

"Sacrificed and expandable," she finished his sentence.

"Ramona, the pawn is the bitch, not the queen! You just proved to me that you know this in theory. Now why can't you see it in real life?" His eyes probed her face.

She looked away.

"You know why, Mona? Cuz you think it's a game!" He licked his finger and rubbed it vigorously against the tattoo.

"Baby, that ain't comin' off. This is a statement; this is a brand. This ain't no goddamn game!"

She bit her lip again as his eyes held hers.

"Those punk ass pawns can't get no money head on; it can only attack the side, and in most cases. one square at a time. But the queen—"

"Can go anywhere, cuz she's the strongest piece on the board," she said, eyes now on the chessboard.

"Now that's what the fuck I'm talkin' 'bout, Mona. Act like you know!" he exhorted.

She smiled

"Come here, baby."

She melted into his body.

Husky and intimately, he said, "Baby what you got to realize is that it's me and you, king and queen, against the world. Me and you against them bitches! Not me and them bitches against you. Feel me? Do you see a pawn on my chest?"

She shook her head, no.

"Look, the bitch ain't got no kids, she gon' help around the house, and she gon' bust checks, play doe, boost, strip, whateva she got to do to pull her own weight. Furthermore, she will be instructed to answer to you and she will, as long as you don't abuse your position as the queen of our castle. That means you got to be fair and compassionate; after all, she gon' be eatin' yo' goodies too," he quipped.

"How long she gon' be here?"

"Shiiit, until she blows up; you know nothing last forever but us."

There was a pregnant silence, but Kenzo heard her thoughts loud and clear.

"And stop worryin' 'bout what the fuck Felicia and Keisha gon' say! Cuz dey niggahs out here fuckin' everything movin' and got what? Three or four kids same age as theirs, and like two or three more on the way. Plus blacken' dey eyes up every other month! Why? Cuz dey livin' a lie! And they not real enough to bring it to the table. My life is real. This shit is the truth, either accept it or reject it," he paused and let his thoughts drop like an anchor in her brain. "Mona, Felicia and Keisha are either fightin' some young bitches, or walkin' 'roun da house with streaks on dey eyes, boo-hooing cuz dey ain't seen they mans in days. Am I right?"

She nodded with a slight smirk on her face.

"Then why should you give a dry fuck what dey think, when dey rockin' black eyes and sad faces, while you rockin' diamonds, *"kaplinkle"*, and rockin' yo' pussy on my bitch face?"

"I thought you said she gon' be my bitch too!"

"In a way she is, Mona, but I don't want you to look at it like that, cuz then it will be animosity, as opposed to order. She's your subordinate; you're the queen. You got to remember she ain't on your level, but at the same time, like I said, you got to be fair and compassionate, so for the most part, you got to look at her as part of the family."

She clicked her tongue. "That bitch ain't my family."

"Okay, now when the bitch payin' for your diamonds, and new clothes, plus suckin' yo' pearl and all dat shit, you can't be grateful?"

"Yeah, I guess."

"Then that's all I'm askin'."

Ramona cocked her head to the side in deep thought, before folding her arms across her big titties. "She betta not be ugly either!" she pouted.

Chapter 7

Kenzo pushed the metallic gray 2011 Dodge Challenger SRT8, through the boulevards like a wild bully past a schoolyard of wimps. The 6.1 Hemi engine swallowed the high-octane fuel and growled at a muscular purr, before being interrupted of its insatiable thirst by a traffic light. To Kenzo's left sat a driver with large mirrored windows. He lowered his tint and shoved his Tom Ford shades atop his head to glance at his reflection. The Forgiato Inferno with gray inserts crouched on Pirelli tires, gleaming majestically against the Challenger's super clear coat and black racing stripes. Vainly, he nodded at his mirrored image.

"*If I ain't a hotboy then wadoyacalldat?*" he chimed and flashed a megawatt smile.

Traffic behind him blasted their horns at him. The light had changed. He snapped his head back towards traffic.

"At ease, fleas! Can a niggah shine one time?"

His eyes darted in the rearview mirror, mouth slightly agape; the crushed diamonds in his gold grill sparkled. 'Kaplinkle'. No cops. His head panned the streets, he hit on the brakes with one foot, and stomped on the gas pedal with the other. Instantly, the high performance rear end, kicked and both tires spun furiously, peeling mad rubber. A cloud of smoke mushroomed from beneath the screaming tires, while the rear end of the Challenger swayed like a stripper in a slow dance.

"Now *that h* what I call showing my ass," said Kenzo snidely, while expertly shifting the B&M shift kit into gear, fishtailing forward, speakers quaking savagely, pumping Yukmouth out the interior and custom audio enclosure trunk set up.

Four songs later, he pulled to a stop in front of his Aunt Paula's, lightweight scolding himself for pullin' the stunt at a traffic light. At twenty-eight years of age, it was somewhat immature. "But," he mused, "I've been making so many grown man moves, I'm entitled to a bit of fun here and there, naw mean? Plus, I'm legit; at the most, they got action at givin' me a ticket."

Thoughts turned toward the business at hand. His new work was waiting for him inside his aunt's and he was amped about moving her into KING ESTATES, which is the title he had given the duplex he owned. Prophet, the OG, has schooled him to the fact that all kings had a castle and all castles should have a name to give it life. Although it was only a duplex, it was his first step towards acquiring a bigger castle. In the meantime, he and Ramona stayed in one unit and rented out the connecting unit to an elderly couple who were never late on their rent, and who had an active interest in horticulture. The happy little couple kept the property's lawn neat and trimmed, with an array of beautiful flowers decorating the perimeter. Kenzo had come a long way from the impetuous young man in the past...

When Preston was arrested, the very first task the OG put to order was getting Preston private counsel. The caper had amassed over two hundred thousand and Preston's attorney fees came off the top. The OG had spent twenty years in the feds and he was now forty-eight years old. He looked sixty, due to his failing health issues with diabetes and hepatitis. The money burned holes in their pockets and Prophet and Kenzo blew fast money. Prophet had done some time in jail; he tried to live life as if it was no tomorrow, and Kenzo didn't mind helping. Together, the men tore through, trips to Vegas, clothes, women, jewelry, and cars. Prophet did everything, but hard drugs. When they were down to their last grand, Prophet pulled Kenzo to the side and said, "Youngin', in some ways, I purposely helped you to blow through your doe as a lesson, cuz you'll never truly appreciate having big money until you had it and lost it. Feel me?"

Kenzo nodded his head, mind shuffling. He had tremendous respect for Prophet and in many ways, they'd developed a father and son relationship.

"Now, peep, youngin'. I've showed ya how to get money and blow it, now I'm finna teach ya how to get money, appreciate it, and grow it. From now on, we gon' play this game the way it's s'pose to be played."

"What we gon' do now, OG?"

"We gon' get it how we live!"

Within weeks, another bank heist ensued, providing one hundred and eighty-nine thousand dollars. This time, they moved the money, not allowing the money to move them. At the time, their headquarters was a warehouse Prophet leased near Oakland's Estuary. It was bare, except for two futons, a boom box, a desktop PC and a small fridge. This was their bat-cave and when they left the mouth of the cave, they left hungry and thirsty for the money. Prophet guided their push led by five composition books, containing meticulous notes and designs on a multitude of hustles he learned from criminal masterminds he'd run across in the federal prison system, and the various fields of organized crime he'd studied. Inscribed in the notebooks were how-to instructions and contact information written in his own shorthand code on: money laundering, counterfeit, drugs, escort services, insurance scams, real estate, and credit card fraud. Anything and everything except violence scrawled across the pages. Prophet's mantra was, *"When violence starts, money stops."*

They sat on the money for two weeks, letting it cool. During that time, Prophet schooled Kenzo.

"First things first, youngin', we got to get totally legit and play this game by the book, ya dig?" said Prophet, his eyes piercing and holding. Kenzo nodded. Prophet had a captivating presence and his oratory skills were magnetic. Every time he spoke, Kenzo was compelled to lean forward. Prophet continued.

"What we got to do now is get our FICO scores up above seven hundred."

"Fike-da-fuck-wha?"

"Youngin', don't make simplicity complex, the P gon' break this shit down as we go, but just picture a FICO score being the equivalent of a batting average in baseball. The higher ya average, the mo' doe you got access to."

"But why we need credit when we got cash?"

"Cuz this long range game don't work like dat. You see, them clear people judge you by your title and your reputation, and just cuz you rich, don't mean you wealthy, plus we need good credit to BOP'M."

"BOP'M?" Kenzo's eyebrows cinched.

"Yeah, Blow Other People's Money!"

"Aww, yeeaah...I like the sound of that, but how we s'pose to do that, Prophet?" asked Kenzo, scratching his head.

"Simple, we gon' lay our traps."

"Now you poppin' some 'ism I can relate to."

"What you think Young Jeezy, Kanye, and them catz doin' with their doe, Kenzo? What you think Baby be tellin' Lil Weezy?"

"Talk dat shit, OG!" Kenzo exclaimed, eyes wide, leaning forward.

Prophet made a steeple with his fingers, peering over them, he said, "In America, nor anywhere else in the world, will they cast pearls to the so-called swine. The rich get richer and the members of the rat race finish last and never get enough cheese, unless it's government cheese! Either you'll be a pawn or a king, a hoe or a pimp. That title is yours for the taking and if you want to be somebody in America, the best way to get a title worth noting is to become a landlord."

"Land-lord," Kenzo stated slowly, cracking the word like a walnut, digging Prophet's meaning out. He rubbed his hands together. "Oh yeeaah, I get it, a king owns the land, and it's his —"

"Kingdom," said Prophet, finishing Kenzo's thoughts.

"Fuck yeah, P, now that I think about it, when I was young when the landlord came around, Moms would treat that chump with more respect than she would treat Pops!"

"That's cuz he was lord of the land! And peep, youngin', the only way you can buy property legitimately is by making sure you got your credit history on point and game tight."

"How do I do that?"

"You just simply invest in yourself and build your credit rating. I got you youngin'; we gon' do this shit together. I got it all written down right here." He tapped the notebook with his fingers. "But while we're doing that, we got to hustle hard, and that's all right here, too."

From that moment on, the duo hustled hard; dabbling in just about everything. Prophet's contacts were the once in a lifetime connects street niggahs dream about. A Chinese connect dropped truckloads of knockoff Air Force 1's and Jordans so good in quality, only a company manufacturer could tell the difference. On any given day, the warehouse would be stuffed from the floor to the ceiling with shoes, fitted caps, sweat suits, and tees. Goods were moved on eBay, Craigslist, Facebook, and other sites. Others were dumped in bulk to swap meet and flea market vendors. Stacks of dead-on counterfeit bills were provided, compliments of Prophet's Nigerian connection, twenty cents on the dollar in hundred grand loaves. In turn, draped in jewels, and shrouded in an array of alias names, the two shrewd hustlers mixed the play doe with real doe and sought out suckas out of town. Once a sucka was identified, great measures were taken to ensure the mark wasn't a narc. Afterwards, they bought all the drugs they could get: x-pills, cocaine, heroin, crystal meth. You name it; they bought it and vanished like smoke. The *game* loved them, 'cause they always had dope at bargain prices. Their hustle was fast, furious, and ferocious.

In the end of the third year of monsta hustlin', Prophet hired a staff of ten, including an accountant and an MBA and formed a Limited Liability Corporation; under its umbrella were a janitorial service, a towing company, and an entertainment division. When it was all said and done, the duo held corporate accounts, loads of credit, and personal and business FICO scores of 760, respectively. However, it was bittersweet; unexpectedly, Prophet slipped into a diabetic coma and never regained consciousness. He left everything to Kenzo, because he had nobody else.

Chapter 8

Strolling into Aunt Paula's two-story Victorian house, he was immediately besieged by the always present, yet pleasing aroma of soul food and potpourri. This female dominated household produced a motley hive of stinging and contrasting personalities, with Aunt Paula being the de facto "Queen Bee". He could hear them upstairs buzzin' and buggin' as usual. *Prolly givin' each other advice on how to run a man off*, he thought, as he pushed into the living room.

Out the corner of his eye, he caught the twins, his bad ass little cousins, bent in mischievous crouches on either side of his Uncle Ervin, while he was posted on the couch deep inside a drunken nod, drool hanging from his mouth. Barely containing their impish giggles, the twins were tickling Ervin's ears and face with a string and a feather.

"Y'all betta stop that shit, fo' he wake up and go dummy on y'all," chuckled Kenzo. He couldn't help but giggle and watch; as a kid, he used to do the same shit to Ervin.

Both bebe kids cupped their mouths, snickering feverishly, paying Kenzo no mind, continuing their knavish foolery. Suddenly, Uncle Ervin's head jerked out his slow nod and he slapped at the crawlings on his face, smearing a red substance across his face in the process. The boys had put ketchup in Ervin's hands.

"Aww, hell to-the-naw, these lil niggahs took it to a whole 'nother level," laughed Kenzo into his fist.

Uncle Ervin was now wide awake and furious, but unfortunately for him, he was still quite drunk. Lookin' like a bloodied Herman Monster, he raged, "I'ma get y'all bad asses!"

The twins crept as close as they could to Ervin, and with rascally smirks twisted into their faces they jested, just above a whisper, "You ain't gon' do shit!" then took off in different directions like jackrabbits.

"You lil bastards!" shouted Uncle Ervin and gave chase, but fell face first with a loud boom over the coffee table.

Kenzo doubled over in laughter.

"What the hell's goin' on down there!" somebody yelled.

"I know y'all ain't running in my damn house again!"

"Mama! Mama! Uncle Ervin's havin' flashbacks again!" screamed one badass twin.

"He tryin' to get us, Mama!" chimed his brother.

"Ervin, leave them damn kids alone! I don' tol' you now!" yelled Aunt Paula, their voices getting closer. Soon the women held their positions around the living room.

Ervin got up and stumbled towards the bathroom, muttering to himself. Aunt Paula tossed her brother a look of disdain. "Niggah, I don' tol' ya 'bout dat shit."

He grumbled something incoherent under his breath. Kenzo shook his head. Ole Ervin was these man-eaters' punching bag. The twins dashed back inside the house and attached themselves to Aunt Paula's legs. She rubbed their heads.

"Y'all leave Uncle Ervin alone," she chided.

"Aunt—"

"Ssshhh, I don't wanna hear it," she snapped, then focused her attention on Kenzo.

"Well, well, look what the wind done blew in, y'all."

"Ole Pimpin' Ken himself, humph," quipped another.

"'Sup playa?"

"Ay wassup, Sharonda, where Cocoa at?" replied Kenzo, in an attempt to deflect all eyes on him, but flashing a play-boyish grin. Sharonda was his favorite cousin and partner in crime; she primed all his chicks for his 'ism.

"Boy, I know you ain't ignoring A.P.", said Aunt Paula, raising her hooded lips and rolling her neck. At fifty-five, Aunt Paula still looked, felt, and acted as if she was in her thirties. "You betta come give A.P. some sugar."

"That's right Mama, check him, he think he's all that", piped one of her daughters.

"Hush up, heffa, let A.P. handle dis."

Under a spell only a seasoned woman can cast, Kenzo blushed and shuffled over to his auntie and she hugged him, pressing her huge, Chaka Kahn sized breasts against him.

"'Sup, Aunt Paula?"

"Nephew, you know wassup, family love and don't you ever forget dat." As usual, he melted like butter on a hot ear of corn.

"Look at dat niggah, y'all. I don't see how dem broads be fallin' fo dat niggah's game, look how lame he look."

That was all it took for Kenzo to snap out of Aunt Paula's charms. "Detra, I know you ain't talking?"

"Ding, ding, ding, it's on y'all. Sharonda hurry up, go get the popcorn!" cackled Donna, Sharonda's twin sister. Twins ran crazy in their family.

Detra was Aunt Paula's oldest daughter, and Kenzo's archrival. Much to her credit, she was thick like Niecy Nash in the ass, with bangin' hips and pretty face to match, but when she opened her mouth, all hell broke loose.

"And what niggah! Yeah I'm talkin'. Last time I checked, I was De-to-the-tra," popped Detra, resting her arm on her ridiculously wide hip, rolling her neck, eyes bugged.

"Okay, let's see here," Kenzo said, ticking points off his fingers. "First baby daddy, deadbeat. Second baby daddy, dope fiend. Third baby daddy, gay. I'd really watch what I said if my vajayjay was so busted that a niggah would rather..." He made hilarious neck and hand gesticulations simulating oral sex, and then continued, "Than snuggle up with me."

"Oh no, he di'int," said Sharonda, hand over her mouth, barely holding onto her laughter.

Detra's eyes swam towards Sharonda and thought she broke their secret woman's alliance, before recovering and firing back. "Niggah, that shit was always in him, all y'all niggahs got some ole down low shit goin' on. Shiiit, I wouldn't be surprised if you came out the closet next."

71

"Ooooooh!" exhorted the ladies of the house.

"Okay. Okay. Watch dat cussin' in A.P.'s house!" warned Aunt Paula.

Unperturbed, Kenzo spat, "So I guess you didn't see ya first baby daddy was a bum, and the second one a crackhead; that was on the low-low too, huh? And for the record, the only thing comin' out my closet is *this*," he emptied both pockets, but kept his eyes focused on Detra. Two softball-sized bankrolls bounced onto the carpet.

"Oh man!" piped the twins and scrambled after the money rolls.

"Give me that damn money!" said Aunt Paula, snatching the money out the twins' hands, thrusting the rolls into her breasts.

"Awww man."

Detra clicked her tongue. "Niggah, money don't mean nothin', I got mines. I'm holdin' down two jobs, got my own house with the Lexus parked in the garage. I can't help it if it ain't no good out here and you niggahs is all duds."

"O-kaaayyy!" Somebody gave her a high five.

"If niggahs is a bunch of duds, then y'all got to be the dud machines, cuz we come from y'all. Problem is, since y'all got it so easy out here, y'all make it seem like we ain't shit, and y'all don't got to listen or be submissive. Y'all want to be the man and the woman, and keep niggahs as pets, rather than men. And deep down, ya really don't wanna niggahs to shine, cuz then you'd have too much competition; so you'd rather have a dope fiend or a deadbeat, cuz he'd haf to depend on ya."

"Easy niggah? You think it's easy, watching you dumb ass niggahs star on *Cops* or *America's Most Dumbest Criminals*! You think it's easy, goin' to see you niggahs behind a Plexiglas window, or behind some bars, lookin' like animals? You think it's easy workin' two jobs, cuz you niggahs can't seem to figure out this society and would rather sell dope and blame it on the white man when ya get caught? Niggah pleeezzze. And hell nah, ya damn right, I'm not 'bout to be sub shit and definitely not submissive, like yo' dumbass broads."

"Oooooh," all eyes dipped towards Cocoa entering the room; she'd been upstairs braiding Detra's daughter's hair. She rolled her eyes at Detra, who bugged her eyes out and rolled her neck back at Cocoa like "And yeah I said it."

"First Peter, Chapter Three." He knew this passage by heart, one of the many verses Prophet made him commit to memory. "Wives, in the same way be submissive to your husbands, so that if any of them do not believe the word, they may be won over without words by the behavior of their wives."

"And!"

"Y'all want to act like ya believe in God, but interpret the word the way you see fit. You see, Detra, you know what a real man looks like, that's why you challenge me all the time, cuz deep down inside, you know that if you ever met a niggah like me, you'd break that independent woman bullshit down and play yo' position as beta to my alpha. But you'd rather have a chump at home and pay to watch Denzel. Ya man should lead ya, not need ya."

73

"What-evvaa niggah, it ain't no good men out here and if there is, they're already taken."

"Share."

"You got me messed up if you think I'm 'bout to share a man."

"You gon' do it anyway, might as well keep it real with yo' self."

"Why? So I can get played like ya playin' Cocoa and Ramona?"

"See, that's just it. I ain't playin' nobody. I'm bein' up front wit' mines. It is what it is. I ain't made this shit up either. King Solomon had seven hundred wives and three hundred concubines, and I betcha he didn't lie to none of 'em."

"Niggah, what dat got to do with you?" said Detra, cocking her head to the side, eyebrows furrowed.

"I'm not a playa, I'm a king! Playas play a game with their women and their women play along, slap boxing with the truth, while backing up into a sinkhole of lies. Me, I'm gon' keep it one hunnit with mines. She can either accept it or reject it. As a matter of fact, monogamy is a European custom. In Africa—"

"Unt-unh niggah, you besta go on somewhere wit' dat oom-foo-foo shit," said Detra, waving her hand. "We in America, not Africa!"

"Ali bomaye, Ali bomaye," chimed the twins, who'd just recently watched a film clip of Muhammad Ali.

"Y'all get ya asses upstairs!"

"Awwww man, it was just getting good," whined one twin.

"What I say?" scolded Aunt Paula, pushing his shoulder. They scampered off chanting, "Ali bomaye, Ali bomaye," leaving the living room in a ball of laughter.

"Bad ass lil niggahs…can't wait 'til Shari come get dey ass," hissed Aunt Paula.

"So, um, like I was sayin', Detra, if you can't find you a good man, ya might as well piece up on one."

"Whateva niggah, I'll get a white boy, fo' I do some shit like that."

All the women rolled their necks and looked at each other like Detra was crazy.

"Uh-huh, that's exactly what they want you to do; swirl, so you can swirl away your glorious heritage. I'm out of here, gon' stay on my king shit and let you tend to yo' battle of the bums."

"Here baby," said Aunt Paula, handing him back his bankroll, before she politely slipped a few bills off the top. "You know A.P. needs some groceries."

She winked her eye at him and he kissed her on the cheek. He spun towards Cocoa, and said, "You ready?"

She nodded and followed behind him obediently.

"That boy's a pimp, I tell ya!" howled Uncle Ervin from the hallway. The women turned on him.

"Shut yo' drunk ass up!"

Once they were in the car, Kenzo turned to his young tender; she was twenty-one, smooth cocoa butter complexion, full lips, honey brown eyes, and a body that made old men wish for younger days. He reached into the glove box. "Close your eyes." She did what she was told. That's what he liked about her; no nagging, no questioning, just straight up down for her dude. "A'ight open." Her eyes flew open excitedly. She put her hand over her chest and sucked in air.

"What's this for, Kenzo?" she stammered enthusiastically.

Inside was a gold necklace with a diamond-encrusted letter "P" hanging from it.

"It's beautiful, but what does the "P" stand for?"

"It stands for Princess. I have a queen already, but I don't have a princess," he said smoothly.

"Awwww baby," she cooed and he helped her put it on, then kissed her forehead, and reached for her chin, tilting her head to meet his piercing gaze.

"Look boo, you see that shit you heard in there?" She bit her lip. "Well, ya gon' hear that shit all the time. People ain't gon' understand how we rockin', they gon' pass judgment, make all kinds of way out comments; but at the end of the day, they gon' be living a lie and we gon' be living the truth," he paused and let his 'ism boil on her. "Now my question is can you stand the rain?"

She batted her eyelashes and replied, "Daddy, it's like you said in there, a bitch gon' be sharing either way, so why not keep it one hunnit? As long as you make me happy, I'm gon' be happy, and whatever you love, I'm gon' love. It's gon' be hard tryin' not to be jealous, I ain't gon' lie, but the way I see it...I'd rather lay in truth with a real niggah, than live in a lie with a lame."

"That's what's up, ma."

He put the car in gear. The sound system rumbled an Isley Bros. hit song, *Voyage of Atlantis*. It was a song Prophet hipped him to about a man with two women. Prophet always preached to Kenzo that they weren't like average niggahs, but that they were cut from a different cloth: the cloth of Solomon.

"I'll always come back to you..." crooned Ron Isley.

As he slid in and out of lanes, he felt Cocoa's eyes crawling over his profile, he lowered his eyes to slits and his face melted into his movie star gaze. His mind shuffled and contemplated what the "P" on the necklace really stood for. *Pawn.* The "P" was something that would remind Ramona of Cocoa's position.

Am I lying? He questioned himself. *Nah, not really, cuz all chess players know that if a pawn makes it to the other side, they can be anything they choose to be, including a queen. It's in the game.*

Chapter 9

"But, fairytales don't always come trueee..."

Aaron Hall's vocals crooned through the speakers, the volume cranked up so high that the bass vibrated the apartment's walls continuously, in a seductive amplified throb. Unfortunately, for the apartment complex, it was three in the morning. The neighbors beat the walls in protest, but Marie was too far gone to care. She sipped on her pineapple Cîroc and slipped into a separate mind state, desperately attempting to escape or untangle the dilemma she now faced. Whichever came first was fine with her, as long as it eased the pain in her heart.

For the moment, her eyes were all cried out, but on the plate of her mind's eye, the innards of her scandalous and self-admitted stupidity were wet, rank, and on full display. Her conscience circled her folly like a fat boy on a cupcake.

"How could I have been that damn lax and foolish, lettin' my lil boy toy hang out up under me like some love sick puppy?" she admonished herself. "Yeah, I had fun playing with his mind, and yeah, he could nail my coochie out all night if I let him. But no man on God's green earth moves me to the degree Preston does."

Just thinking about the pain that etched Preston's face caused her to throw back a gulp of the sweet concoction. As the smooth warmth of the alcohol rushed down her throat, she shuddered before bursting into violent sobs; her torment came in waves, each stronger than the next. Soon the weight of her sorrow pressed her head onto her chest as each tear felt like an ocean coming out of her eyes.

"Mama. Mama!" called Dannielle, outside Marie's bedroom.

Marie tumbled deeper into her disorder. Suddenly her mind swung and she wondered where Preston could be. After he charged out the house, she'd combed the streets around the neighborhood and went everywhere she thought he might have gone, but no one had heard hide nor hair from him.

"Mama, for real, the manager is at the door! You got to turn the music down! Please, Mama!" pleaded Dannielle.

Marie offered no response.

"Dang," Dannielle groaned, clicking her tongue and stomping her foot in despair, then quickly went back to tinker with the lock on her mother's door, with a butter knife.

Click.

The door gave way and she pushed into her mother's room. Marie was clearly inebriated and the room was in shambles.

"Mama?"

Food and alcohol products were haphazardly strewn across the bed and floor. The only items that had any sort of order to them were numerous bottles of prescription pills. Suddenly, Dannielle's heartbeat raced. Her eyes snapped towards Marie, and she rushed over to the nightstand.

"Mama, did you take all—" she grabbed the pill bottles in mid-sentence. Most of them were full or almost full; she exhaled in relief. "Aw, heck naw, Mama, this ain't da business."

Although only thirteen, Dannielle was extremely mature for her age, both physically and mentally. Oftentimes, she and Marie subtly traded the dynamics and nature of parent-child psychologies between themselves. Many times, they behaved more so like sisters, especially when Marie became depressed or mentally drained.

Dannielle went to work quickly, retrieving the remote and lowering the volume; then apologizing to the irate manager, before stashing the pills and pouring the alcohol down the kitchen sink. Marie barely noticed her daughter, and continued to weep silently, rocking back and forth in a sitting position.

With everything sufficiently neutralized, Dannielle eased back into her mother's room and gently slid behind her mother and massaged her shoulders. "Mama," she said soothingly, "it's gon' be alright. He's just hurt, but you know Daddy don't love nothin' in this world more than you. Can't nothin' come between you guys, y'all the Barack and Michele of the hood."

Marie began to relax as Dannielle's therapeutic fingers worked on her neck and shoulders. Dannielle paused for a second to hand Marie some tissue. "Here Mama, wipe your face."

Slowly, Marie managed to pull herself together; she accepted the tissue and blew her nose.

"Thank you, baby," she sniffled, "I just don't know what I'd do without you, but I just feel like I played myself, you know." She sniffled again and wiped her nose.

"Mama, we all make mistakes...ain't nobody perfect."

"He is, Dannielle, he's perfect for me, c-cuz he loves me with every fiber of his being. You don't understand right now and I don't expect you to, but one day, trust me, if you're fortunate enough, you'll feel the ethereal."

"Ethereal? Mama, what does that mean?"

"See I learned that word from your daddy. It means something heavenly or spiritual-like. But like I was saying, Dannielle, when you feel it, you'll remember this day, cuz baby, th-that man loves me, loves us! So hard I-I can feel it in my DNA."

"Well Mama, if he loves us that much, then he should be able to forgive you once he's calmed down and I know he is."

"Th-that's just it, Dannielle, even if he does forgive me, it's hard for me to forgive myself...I-I don't think I even deserve to be loved like that," croaked Marie, fighting back tears. "I just feel like I betrayed the greatest love of all," sighed Marie, before thinking out loud, "But why didn't he just tell me he was coming home?"

****

"But why didn't you just tell her you was coming home?"

"Tamala, maybe I should have, but if you're loyal to somebody, I mean if you really love somebody, you don't need to be warned, you just 'posed to always be ready! I mean, there was times when she just popp'd up to visit me while I was in prison and I had no idea she was comin'. But you know what? I was always ready; had an extra set of pants and a shirt exclusively for visiting, creased to the max, hanging up in my cell. All I had to do was jump in the shower, and...BAM! Within minutes, I'd show up in the visiting room, 'so fresh and so clean'," he said, chuckling singsong like.

"That's different, Preston, come on now."

He arched his eyebrow in protest.

"How so? I could have been in the visiting room with another broad, gettin' my mack on, but I wasn't."

Tamala didn't encroach on his reasoning, she couldn't.

"I'm just sayin', T, I'm not stupid; I know women have needs, but you don't 'pose to bring that shit to the house. Not in front of Dannielle. What kind of example is that? So I feel like she compromised not only my trust, but also her integrity as a mother."

Once again, she made no attempt to counter his argument and logic.

"So, um, what are you gonna do, Preston? Are you just gonna walk away, turn your back on all the days your love shined brightly, because of one dark day? Or will you give her a chance to redeem herself?"

Preston shrugged and stared up at the ceiling. He bit his lip and said, "I really don't know, T."

"Well, until you figure it out, you're welcome to stay here; in the meantime, let me fix you something to eat, unless you want to go out for breakfast?"

Fresh and fueled by the birds chirping majestically outside her comfortable home in Oakland's Diamond District, and the hot latté she'd been sipping on, her hair was pulled back in a tight bun as she buzzed around him in an over-sized Oakland Raiders jersey.

"You sure your bust me down James Bond boy scout won't mind?"

She clicked her tongue. "Boooyyyy, forget you!"

She bounced toward the kitchen, and although the jersey was baggy and curtained at her knees, her ample bottom was visibly active beneath, and he had to tear his eyes away.

"Are you hungry or what?" she called over her shoulder.

"Can you still make those scrumptious omelets? Or does Billy Ray Cyrus only eat Grey Poupon?"

He heard her giggling in the kitchen. "Preston, you gotta to make up your mind, is he Charlie Sheen, Brad Pitt, James Bond, or—"

"He is a white boy; it don't matter, it's all the same," snapped Preston.

"Can we please talk about something else?"

"Like what, T? Like how big your ears were when you was a little girl?"

Instinctively, she glanced at her ears in the reflection of a mirror. "My ears were never big, Preston, and I was never a little girl. I was always all woman."

"Yeah right, let you tell it. Aye, but if you don't mind, I'd like to take a shower and clean up. I don't want to be smellin' like roadkill while I'm eating."

"Go ahead. Towels are in the linen closet and there's a new toothbrush in the medicine cabinet."

"Damn, I was gon' use yours then scrub my butt with it and put it back on the rack," joked Preston.

"Uggggh, boy, don't be playin' wit' me like that," shrieked Tamala, before bursting into feverish giggles. "Preston, do you remember you did that to Lester Lang?"

"And you came up with that song afterwards? It was sooooo funny!"

"Yep."

"I now pronounce you, Lester Lang, half the distance between a fart and a shit stain!" The harmony of the verse was delivered in a southern twang, ala Anthony Hamilton.

Both of them broke into raucous laughter.

"I fixed his ass didn't I, T?"

"You sure did, Preston."

Preston and Tamala met in a group home in Fairfield, California, a small town about forty minutes from Oakland. Although they weren't biologically sister and brother, the dynamics of their relationship was just as deep and compelling...

84

Tamala's parents were killed in a car accident when she was five years old. Afterwards, she was forced to stay with a succession of relatives who had neither the time, love, nor resources to properly care for the then shy, skinny, and traumatized little girl who sucked her thumb compulsively. To make matters even worse, one of the aunt's boyfriends took advantage of Tamala and forced her to suck his penis, whenever her aunt was either passed out drunk, or running the streets. He made it seem like a secret game they shared with one another. He would even whip her if she didn't comply. Terrified and ashamed, she told no one, but because of this violation of her innocence, she began to wet the bed.

Still every chance he got...

One night, he pushed Tamala's eleven-year-old head beneath the blanket; while he feigned half sleep on the couch watching television, he forced Tamala's head to bob up and down. Her aunt woke suddenly and caught him red-handed, but he claimed he was sleep and he thought he was dreaming. Her aunt bought his act; hook, line, and sinker. The next morning, she called CPS and Tamala became a ward of the state and a victim of the ghetto.

She was twelve years old when she was escorted inside the group home by a frog-faced social worker. Preston was the first person she saw. She was instantly smitten. He had her at hello. Unfortunately, all the other kids tormented her because she wet the bed. However, it was Preston who put a stop to their cruel teasing and cured her from bed wetting. All it took was love. He was fifteen and had been hustlin' all his life and even in the group home, he *always had a pocket full of money. Tired of smellin' Tamala's urine lingering or catching her trying to hide her sheets, he began to reward her every time she successfully went through the night without wetting the bed. He bought her barrettes for her hair, candy, dolls, stuffed animals; he'd even went so far as to bribe the other girls housed in the group home to make sure her hair was whipped and styled. She began to look forward to him warning her not to drink any liquids before she went to sleep, and sometimes he even woke her up in the middle of the night to urge her to use the bathroom before she went to sleep. Preston became Tamala's hero; she followed him around everywhere he went, sucking her thumb like it was her last meal. He'd even broken her out of that habit. She'd do anything to win his approval.*

The following year when Preston ran away, she cried the entire day. That night she ran away and convinced an old man to give her ride to Oakland. Miraculously, she made it to Oakland safely and even more miraculous, she found Preston that same night. As luck would have it, Preston's Aunt Paula moved to Oakland from Louisiana to teach African American studies at Merritt College. She took them both in and eventually adopted Tamala, but Preston continued wild out in the streets. On the flip side, it was under Paula's tutelage that Tamala began to excel academically. As it turned out, while Preston was sentenced to prison, Tamala went away to college and went on to earn a law degree. After passing the bar exam on her first try, she decided to work inside Alameda County's District Attorney's office; not to throw the book at criminals, but to be as compassionate as possible with young black women and men, and also to lock away child molesters and pedophiles. However, her 'save the world naïveté' was choked by the gripping machinations of law and order and the furious pace of the rat race. Within the span of three years, she went from overtly opposing the policies within the District Attorney's office and privately despising white people, to becoming a rising star in the DA's office. This came on the strength of a string of phenomenal guilty verdicts in several high profile cases; all of which ironically, were against young black men. Moreover, even more ironic, was the fact that she was now dating a white detective.

Chapter 10

"You're not fully clean, unless you're Zestfully clean," Preston grinned after singing the familiar jingle aloud. Stepping out the bathroom, towel around his waist, he strolled into the living room; evident above the towel was the years of push-ups, pull-ups, and intense calisthenics as his chiseled pectoral muscles and washboard stomach flexed and rippled with each step.

"Aye, T, check it out," Preston called into the kitchen.

"Hold up, I'm putting your plate in the microwave," piped Tamala, as she entered the living room. "You was taking so long, I thought you shriveled up into—"

She stopped dead in her tracks, and her mouth dropped when she saw him standing there half-naked. "Boy, put some clothes on!" It came out more like a moan, rather than an order. She tried to keep her eyes from slowly crawling down his body. Unconsciously, she licked her lips, blood rushed to her cheeks as her eyes feasted on the eye-popping print, bulging beneath the thick, forest green towel. It was obvious that he was hung like a horse.

Conscious of the effect his presence and physique had on her, he flashed his billion-dollar dimple, made his chest muscles dance and sucked in his abs; they rocked into granite slabs. He shot her a dreamy pose and replied, "Close ya mouth and put some lotion on my back; you act like you ain't never seen a Maybach body."

In a spell-like trance, she gravitated towards Preston like iron filings to a magnet. Her unmistakable attraction created a throbbing arousal within him, his manhood stretched and rose. So not to reveal his growing erection, he offered his back. Her body heat proceeded before her like warm sun rays, and beads of sweat formed on his forehead. Tamala applied a liberal amount of lotion into her trembling palms and massaged it into the large muscles of his back; his pores drank greedily.

"Damn, T, that shit feels good," he said, closing his eyes.

She inched closer to him; her nipples began to bud as she chased the lotion in small circles with her thumbs.

"Get up here by my neck, Tamala," he urged softly.

"You're too tall; you got to lay down for me to do it."

"Well, come on." He pulled her by her hand into the bedroom, and she offered no resistance. He lay across her bed and dropped his head in his arms in front of him. Slowly and sensually, she massaged his smooth, wide, muscular back as he squirmed pleasurably beneath her.

Admiring his body, Tamala said, "Preston, I don't ever remember your back being this wide, what was they feeding you in there?"

"T, the muscles you see come from carrying the body of ignorance for years and years. Now be quiet, cuz ya missing spots and messing up my concentration."

She clicked her tongue. "Boy puleeze, and don't think I'm gon' be doin' this all morning." She bit her lip.

"Sshhh," he admonished, closing his eyes, enjoying the pleasure of her fingers melting in between his muscles.

"Does it feel that good, Preston?"

"Hell yeah try going almost nine years without being touched like this."

"Well, since you said it like that, I'm really finna put it on you," she purred and straddled his lower back, her hands working expertly across his neck and shoulders. "How you like that, huh?" she teased.

"Ummmm-hmmm, keep it coming," he moaned.

She applied more lotion to his back.

"Sssssss, right there, girl!" he responded, sucking air through his teeth.

"Preston, you puttin' too much on it; it doesn't feel that good."

"What?" He flipped over on his back and the towel fell to the side, exposing his long, cucumber-sized penis, stretching and towering before her. "Wanna bet?" he asked; his eyes full with lust.

"Oh my God," she whispered. Within seconds, she was stark naked, lowering herself gingerly onto his elongated meat missile; timidly, she circled her nether lips with the bulbous mushroomed head of his massive erection, before easing down on its girth. A moan escaped her throat. "Oooohh..." she bit her lip and whimpered. "You're huge!" She was extremely wet, yet she still had difficulty accommodating his width. He raised his hips to help her adjust on his penis. "Ssss, no, Preston. Don't move, let me do it," she panted. She eased down, inch by inch. He watched closely as her pussy lips slid over the stretched skin and veins of his large penis. "Ooohh," she moaned, throwing her head back and tapping her stomach. "Preston, I can feel you way up here!" she said, shuddering on top of him and caressing her stomach.

He locked his large hands around her wrists and gingerly, guided his swollen member upwards. Her cantaloupe-shaped breasts were erotically decorated with large areolas and her nipples jutted forth. He lathered her nipples with his tongue, coaxing her hips to join his.

"Sssss Preston. You're too big!" she panted, but leaned forward, feeding his mouth the ripe fruits of her breasts. She began to gyrate on top of him, creating her own rhythm. Tamala gasped when he met her rhythm with his own thrusts.

"Yeah, there you go, there you go!" he urged.

He released her wrists to caress and knead her shapely buttocks, guiding her cheeks onto his throbbing penis repeatedly. She shivered on top of him and her hips began to tremble and curl with each stroke he served. Her breath sawed and rasped in her throat. Tamala adjusted her body so that she was now squatting on his penis and boldly bouncing up and down. Sweat ran between the cleavage of her titties and rained on his chest. She fucked him like a porn star, titties bouncing erotically.

"Get dat dick then, girl, get it," he moaned, while watching his long dick shoot in and out her wet vagina.

"Oooh, you see it? Oooh shit..." she panted and rode him wantonly.

He latched onto her and pulled her into his thrusts.

Oooh yeah, oooh yeah, right there!" Tamala screamed.

Wet smacking sounds emitted from her honey hole, again, and again.

"Oooh Preston, you hear that...you tearing it up!" she whimpered.

His hips shot forward over, and over again, while he fucked her as though his life depended on it. Unable to take that position anymore, she got off her haunches to straddle him. Preston reached behind him, parting her buttocks until they were spread wide to their limits, then pistoned his member in and out, stuffing her pussy to the hilt. Her eyes rolled into the back of her head, and she rubbed her stomach indicating that he was that deep in her.

"Preston!" she whimpered, "it feels like you 'bout to come out my mouth. Oooh God, it's good!" she screamed again, enduring the sweet pain.

He began to stab upwards unmercifully again, and again. Tamala's titties flopped wildly. She placed her hands on his chest for balance and grinded into an intense, earth shattering orgasm, and then another one followed it.

"Oooh Preston. Oooh daddy!" She screamed and convulsed violently. "I'm coming!" She yelled.

Afterwards, her lips puckered and trembled into a lewd fuck face and she collapsed on his chest as she came again...

****

It was well into the afternoon before they were finally drained and satiated. Tamala's head rested on his chest, while she caressed his penis underneath the comforter.

"This thing is monstrous," she cooed in awe.

"I see you enjoyed yourself," he replied confidently, running his fingers through her hair.

"Whew, it was incredibly and deliciously taboo-like," she said, pulling his now semi-hard penis from beneath the comforter and gave it a quick peck. It throbbed in her hand and came to life again. Tamala fondled, stretched, and jacked it in amazement. She even went so far as to measure him with her hands. Finally, she lay across his lap, studying his penis while stroking him. She took him in her mouth, just to see how much she could take before gagging. She bobbed her head up and down, gagging about halfway down. She pulled it out to examine it again. "This is just a work of art", she mumbled.

"Are you done playing with my dick, Tamala? Or would you like to hold it while I piss?"

She looked up at his face. "Can I?" she replied, dead serious.

"Tamala, let my dick go, please," he said, rising up out the bed, heading towards the bathroom. She followed. "Tamala, you better back up, I got gas."

"Ughh." She stopped for a second, but continued on. He raised up the lid of the toilet and let forth a heavy stream of urine. She stood on the side and watched closely. Unconsciously, she began to suck her thumb. When he was just about done, she stepped behind him and reached around, grabbing his penis while peeking her head around his body.

"You got to milk it first, T," he said.

She did so.

"A'ight, now wag it," he ordered.

She wagged it, aiming towards the commode, missing badly. "My aim is all messed up, huh?"

"Yep, stick to pussies," he said and chuckled.

When he was through, he cleaned the toilet, washed his hands and within seconds, they were cuddled up again.

"You think I'm a freak, Preston?" she asked, caressing his chest.

"Nah, why you ask?"

"I don't know, but you do bring the freak out of me, though," she admitted, "But you know what?"

"What T?"

"I swear I always knew it was gonna be good."

"How you know?"

"Humph, a woman's intuition; I just knew," she said, speaking into his chest.

"T—"

"Sshh, be quiet, let me hear your heartbeat," she said, pressing her ear against his chest.

"How does it sound?"

"Strong," she replied.

"That's 'cause I have so much love to give."

"Is that right?"

"Yep."

"Well, the million-dollar question is, who you gon' give it to?" she posed.

"To whoever deserves it," he replied.

"Good answer," she said, snuggling back up against him, raking his chest gently with her fingernails.

"Preston?"

"Sup, T?"

"Do you still rap?"

"Nah, ma, I gave that corny shit up years ago."

She sprung up and swung a pillow at his face. He covered up just in time.

"Come on, T. What's all dat for?" he said, chuckling, flashing his dimple.

"Boy, you know why! I hitchhiked all the way to Oakland, and God knows what could have happened to me. But I was determined to bring you your rhyme book and you quit!" she yelled, eyes blazing.

He grabbed her in a bear hug. "I'm down, Tamala. That was back in the days."

"But you was so good though, Preston," she pouted. She clicked her tongue and continued, "I used to think that you was gonna be the greatest rapper alive," she said, her eyes drifting back down memory lane...

"I mean you used to have this crazy energy, like you was possessed by some kinda rhyme god. And you could go on and on without missing a beat," she recalled, rising to sit Indian style, with the blanket wrapped around her shoulders. He lay there naked, arms behind his head, watching her eyes comb over him. She licked her lips and continued, "And I remember dudes used to come to the group home to battle you, and you'd just slaughter them." She stopped to look in his eyes. "Do you remember what you used to always say to niggahs when they stepped to you?" she asked.

"Spit ya best shit, or keep my name out ya mouth," they said in unison.

Tamala's eyes lit up. "Oh my God, Preston, I remember it just like it was yesterday! Couldn't nobody see you, baby!" she exclaimed excitedly. "And when they would spit their best rhymes, I would always watch your eyes; they would be constantly movin' like this..." She moved her index finger in front of her face real fast. "Like they was takin' a million pictures," she said, reminiscing.

"They was, T; each picture was a thought, each thought became a punchline."

"And my heart would beat so fast and sometimes I'd get scared that one day somebody would be better than you," she said.

"Never, T!"

"I know...I know, cuz when they'd get through, you'd have that look on your face." Her eyes snapped towards his eyes. "Preston, make that face for me, puhleeze," she pleaded.

"T, I can't just make it like that or it would be fake. That shit is my game face. I got to be in a battle or something," he explained.

She pouted and rolled her eyes. "You could make it if you really wanted to, I know you can."

"Not."

"Anyways you'd flash your stinking dimple, and I mean you'd just eat 'em alive," she started laughing. "Preston, niggahs used to want to fight you when you'd get through."

"They really didn't want it, T."

"I know, I know, but still they'd be hella mad. Remember when you told that one dude something 'bout his rhymes stinks, but you could still give his bad breath a good rep? Oh my God, Preston, and then you told that other dude that his nose looked like a Volkswagen!" She cradled her stomach and tried to fight tears. "I kept tryin' to figure out for years what that word meant you rhymed with Volkswagen."

"Efil4zaggin, it's Niggaz 4 life spelled backwards."

"See what I mean, Preston, I thought you said something in German he couldn't understand, and that's why he wanted to fight."

"Nah, he wanted to fight, cuz his nose really looked like a Volkswagen."

They laughed together.

"You should have never stopped, that was your calling," said Tamala, with a melancholy expression. Suddenly her face beamed. "Do you know what my favorite song I used to love hearing you perform?"

"Of course, T, you'd beg me to spit it over and over, knowing damn well I hated spittin' the same songs."

"But it was my absolute favorite," she whined, lips pursed, face frowning. "I betcha don't even remember it no more."

Preston made a show of blowing air out his mouth. "Here we go again."

"It's the one where you'd have all the kids in the house, singin' the chorus," she explained eagerly.

"I know, T."

"Say it for me, pleeeaaase," she begged.

"Nah, T, I don't rap no more."

She straddled him, her voluptuous breasts dangling deliciously in his face. Tamala rocked her hips back and forth and bent forward to kiss his chest. Instantly, she could feel him growing beneath her.

"Come on, Preston, do it for me," she purred.

"No, Incognito Piss Girl, T!" he teased, bursting with laughter.

"Aw hell naw. No you didn't call me that shit Lester Lang used to call me, 'fore you put doo-doo on his toothbrush. You wrong for that, but he used to call me something else, too."

"Pissy Missy Tamala, the Mattress Damaga," blurted out Preston in a sing-song fashion.

"Oooh, I hated when he'd call me that!" snarled Tamala, folding her arms across her chest. "Now you really got to make it up to me for bringing up those horrible memories."

He sat up to give himself room, and said, "A'ight T, I'm goin' to do it for you, just this once."

Tamala's face cracked into a bubbly smile.

"A-hem," he cleared his voice, and then began by pounding a beat on his chest and snapping his fingers. Tamala caught the rhythm and bobbed her head.

> *"Fell in love with this chick who said I was subpar.*
> *Broke my heart into a zillion pieces and has 'em in a*
>
> jar.
> *Said she'd give it back if I gave her a star*
> *So I styled every place*
> *And I shined up in space*
> *And the next time she seen me I just spit it in her face*
> *I'M A RAP STAR, BITCH!"*

Tamala bounced her head singing the chorus, "You already know, you already know."

When he was done, she dived on him and kissed his face all over in quick pecks.

"Stop T, come on now. I wanna ask you something," he said, moving his face out of reach of her lips.

"What?" she asked, looking deep into his eyes.

"T, why'd you like that song so much?"

"Cuz Preston, all the girls in the group home and at school loved that song, and we'd all wonder who the girl was that broke your heart. And I'd dream all the time that if you ever fell in love with me, I'd help you put your heart back together, a kiss at a time."

He smiled and she sang the chorus again. "You already know, you already know."

Chapter 11

It was never a doubt in anyone's mind that Kevin O'Reilly, Jr. would be a cop. He came from a family of cops. Almost every male in the O'Reilly clan joined either the armed forces or law enforcement; they were bred so. As a child, Kevin Jr.'s favorite game was cops and robbers, and of course, he was always the cop. The lone black kid on the block fought him to a draw after Kevin repeated what he heard his dad rant countless times. "Niggers should never be cops."

When the black kid's father, who was the track and field coach at the local college, confronted Kevin's father, Kevin Sr. apologized profusely and promised to have a long talk with Kevin. In his bedroom, Kevin Jr. pled to his father through watery eyes. "But Dad, he wanted to be the cop; you said niggers…" he covered his mouth, "I mean…blacks couldn't be cops, only the bad guys."

"I know, Kevin."

"Then he said that there are a lot of black cops on TV, and I tol' him what you tol' me, Dad; that it was just make up and that they're really white inside."

Kevin Sr. squatted on his knees and looked his son in the eyes.

"Son, like magicians, you never give your secrets away. That's how you stay a good cop. To keep from being a bad guy, you got to keep 'em sleep."

"But Dad—"

"Now son, I'm not punishing you for callin' him a nigger, I'm punishing you for giving away an O'Reilly secret."

Little Kevin bent his head in shame. "Can I still be a cop, Dad?" mumbled Kevin Jr. morosely.

"Sure ya can, you just got to practice your techniques," said Kevin Sr., running his fingers through his son's hair.

So on the day Kevin Jr. graduated from the police academy, it was of no surprise; he was born to be a cop. His only fault, according to kin, was that somehow Kevin incongruously preferred his women the same color he liked his coffee and suspects: black.

What started out as a junior high school crush on a coal black, middle-class girl at school who managed to turn the hormone-fueled Kevin out on a steady diet of blackberry pie, spiraled into an insatiable thirst for chocolate milk, and now Katy Perry could quench his sexual palate. Kevin had kissed a black girl and liked it. The O'Reilly's convinced themselves that it was just a phase and feigned indifference, but inside they were seething each time he brought home a black girl. Albeit they were all attractive, yet they were all eggplant black.

Only once did Kevin Sr. become undone at his son's romantic color code. It was during Kevin Jr.'s senior year in high school.

"Son do you plan to mongrelize this bloodline?"

"Cut the crap, Dad, I'm not a kid anymore."

Kevin Sr. stepped closer to his son. "Kevin, I don't want you bringing those people to our house!" bellowed Kevin Sr., in an Archie Bunkeresque-type voice.

"Screw you, Dad!" snapped the outraged boy.

In a flash of motion, Kevin Sr. knocked his only son to the ground, but just like an O'Reilly, he got back up and stood; eyes on fire, nose a bloody mess. Kevin Sr. promptly turned his back and stormed into his room. It was no use; Kevin Jr. was an O'Reilly and it was just hardwired in his genes to die or kill for something he loved or believed in. From that day forth, the O'Reilly's begrudgingly looked past their son's shades of romance.

Kevin O'Reilly was an excellent cop, so quite naturally he had already read everything in Tamala's personal file; he knew her high school GPA and her current FICO score. This was why he couldn't sleep when Tamala practically threw him out her house, in defense of scum who he was certain she wasn't related to. In fact, he knew Tamala's parents died in a car accident and she had no siblings. However, blacks always claimed some quasi-kinship; soul brotha this or soul sista that and he didn't want to seem inconsiderate towards Tamala's culture. Nevertheless, he knew it was bullshit. The minute the guy sauntered into the house Kevin knew he was rabble, like the type he'd arrested hundreds of times, however the guy had a different hum about him, but scum all the same. What piqued his senses was the way Tamala's eyes danced when she saw the guy. It was not a sibling gaze...

Early the following morning, he crept like morning dew on grass blades, against the side of Tamala's comfortable home, peeking in her window just in time to see Tamala's heart-shaped bottom impelled on her "so-called" brother's huge, pistoning cock. He was so close to the couple he could see her juices coating the guy's rock hard shaft. Kevin gawked hypnotically as Tamala shuddered, moaned, and tossed her head back in ecstasy, as her lover spread her buttocks wide and thrust his hips off the bed, furiously jamming his swollen member savagely up her quivering backside again and again. Kevin's breath fogged against the window; interestingly he became aroused, eyes fixed to the rolling, large testicles slapping lewdly off Tamala's gyrating buttocks. It felt eerie, as though the guy knew he was watching, and it took all his inner strength to tear his eyes away from the porn star penis ravishing Tamala.

Partly furious and partly aroused, he sped off in his car, skidding to a stop in an obscure inner city alleyway. Enraged, he slammed his fist against the dashboard and screamed incoherently. Layer by layer the rage subsided, swiftly replaced by a dark, creeping schizophrenia. He glanced into his rearview; his eyes were crazed, sweat streaked down his face. Suddenly, he reached for his sidearm. He pressed the barrel against his temple and squeezed his eyes shut. Then he thrust it under his chin and grit his teeth. Next, he slowly stuck the large Sig Sauer in his mouth and cocked it, but instead of yanking the trigger, he sucked on the barrel like a porn star, laughing and crying simultaneously...

East Oakland's International Boulevard, as usual, was buzzing with young hot prostitutes advertising their wares. Plenty of skin showing; whore skirts, hot pants, and high heels. Behind his aviator sunglasses, Kevin's hawk-like eyes surveyed the hoe stroll. Like a predator, he was looking for an easy kill. Not the prostitutes huddled together squawking, they were too seasoned, too unpredictable. He knew exactly what he was stalking; the fawn who stumbled off too far from the protective doe, and like death, it was always there waiting for him. Minutes after cruising the Blvd., he found his prey posted on the corner all by her lonesome, in a tight miniskirt and a matching halter top, barely holding her ripe young fruits.

There you go my fine, feathered friend. How do they say it in nigger vernacular; young, dumb and full of cum, thought Kevin, licking his lips.

He pulled to the curb in the nondescript Volvo and rolled down his window. "Hey darling, you got a sec?"

She folded her arms across her breasts, her eyes narrowed. "Not if you da po-leeze."

He sized her up quickly, maybe sixteen, runaway. He looked around to see if she had a two-bit pimp trailing her, before yanking down his trousers, revealing his privates. "Cops can't do that, now can they?"

She glanced at his stiff pecker and clicked her tongue. "How much ya spending?" she said apprehensively.

"That depends on how much you providing, chocolate."

She tilted a jet black, curvaceous hip to the side and sat her hand on it. "You sure ya not a cop?"

"Get the fuck in!" he snapped.

Her eyes widened and she stepped back away from the car; realizing his mistake he said, "Hey look, I'm sorry. I just don't want to get busted. Here." He shoved several bills at her. "You can have this for starters and more when we're done, okay?"

She glanced around before grabbing the money. "And you can't do me in the booty," she muttered.

If she was smart, she would have took the money and ran, but she'd been yelled at all night for not bringing in enough money by her "boyfriend" aka pimp, who was s'pose to be watching her back. She got in the car, but she never got out again...alive.

Chapter 12

Alameda County District Attorney's Office is just like another jagged tooth in the gargantuan mouth of America's criminal justice system. Within this system, some teeth are liberal, and others are right wing and yet, just as there are teeth designed specifically for holding, while others are designated for chewing, nonetheless it's all arranged to chomp down on the souls of the lower class caste. This system is crammed to the throat with African Americans, Hispanics, and those too poor to buy justice; insatiably chews crunches and swallows the ignorant in an unjust rhythm and harmoniously shits out justification.

Tamala sat at her cluttered desk, perusing the thick file off a murder case scheduled for trial in the coming weeks. It was a slam-dunk case: young black male, barely nineteen, emptied a full clip into the head and torso of his former childhood friend, before vomiting his guts out at the scene of the crime. Motive? Drug debt. The following day, his mother promptly parades him into the police station, with no lawyer and a full confession.

She reared back in her chair, and glanced outside the office window, observing the congested traffic of downtown Oakland. The streets of Oakland were mean, and dangerous.

When will it ever end? she thought.

"Senseless," she muttered to herself, closing the file, shaking her head in disgust. She'd offered him the only deal available: second-degree murder, twenty-five to life. But by then the jailhouse lawyers had gotten in his ear; she could imagine what they told him.

It don't matter if it's thirty seconds to life, in the State of California unless you have political ties like Fabian Nunez, a life sentence is exactly what it read. A life sentence! You'll never leave prison alive.

He turned it down and opted to go to trial. She didn't blame him. His defense? He was afraid for his life. Although the victim had a history of violence, he had no weapon; he was killed in cold blood. Thus, the assailant's defense wouldn't fly. She wouldn't let it.

She reached for her Starbucks latté, as she sipped her thoughts slipped inwards. *What about the cop who shot and fatally wounded Oscar Grant while he was handcuffed and unarmed, or what about the cop who gunned down Jodie McKinzie? How can we justify a killing and hand down leniency on one hand, yet prosecute an accused murderer who claims the same defense and pass down life sentences on the other? White man's justice, black man's grief.*

However, just as quick as she pondered the complexities of jurisprudence, she quickly reshuffled her thoughts. She'd let God sort it out, she had a job to do. The teeth off the criminal justice system wouldn't be getting a cavity on her watch.

Tamala may have been putty in Preston's hands; however, during working hours she was a pitbull in a skirt. It had to be so; she was under constant scrutiny by her predominately-Caucasian co-workers and superiors. Any sign of leniency towards African-American defendants was an instant red flag and she would be strategically demoted to misdemeanor case files. She was an exceptional attorney, but her ascendance up the ladder was fast-tracked, due to her ability to connect with the murder victims' families, coaxing the reluctant African-American family members and / or friends to testify. Something that was totally frowned upon in the hood moreover, dangerous.

The trial itself was a mere formality. The jury comprised of 85% Caucasian and a dash of color, would believe everything the prosecution presented as evidence, and look dubiously upon anything the defense presented. Minus a high-powered attorney equipped with: jury consultants, investigators and experts at his or her aid; ten times out of ten, Tamala would secure a guilty verdict. Sometimes it was bittersweet, and other times, the defendant deserved the sentence and some. Either way, she mused, "I'm just doing my job."

A quick knock and her door cracked. Cindy, a bubbly brunette, with an obsession for Trey Songz peeked her head in. "You busy?"

"Naw, what's up?

"Two things, first this..." Cindy broke into the Dougie dance.

"Go white girl, go white girl," cheered Tamala. Cindy had mad rhythm for a white girl.

She straightened up and resumed her professional bearings. "I got it though, huh Tamala?" she asked, her green eyes sparkling, starving for Tamala's praise.

"What? You killed it, girl." They high fived.

Cindy smiled and fiddled with her hair. Cindy was a lower level prosecutor that they'd never let anywhere near important cases involving black men. She loved black men with a passion.

"Hey, you got a visitor...says it's important."

This wasn't unusual for Tamala; one never knew when the witness you needed to provide that smoking gun woke up with a conscience. "Who is it? Never mind, send them in. Thanks."

"O-kayyy", said Cindy demurely and motioned towards the visitor.

Tamala stood up and smoothed her skirt down. Marie walked in briskly, lips in a sneer.

Cindy's eyes darted from face-to-face; somehow she felt the vibes. It was a woman thing. For a brief instant, Tamala's eyes became pointed arrows before forging a smile that was more of a smirk, desperately attempting to hide fangs. Cindy cast a curious glance at Tamala.

"Thank you, Cindy," said Tamala sternly, this was an office-wide choreographed cue to allow privacy.

"Have a seat." It was more so an order than invitation. Marie sucked her teeth.

"It's okay, I'll stand."

Tamala remained calm as possible. She sat down wishing like hell she had a cigarette, but since she gave up the habit, she reached into her desk for a pack of gum. "Can I offer you a piece?"

"I'm good."

"How can I help you?" said Tamala icily.

Marie's eyes glanced around Tamala's office, noticing the framed law degree, pictures of Tamala smiling next to the mayor, numerous press clippings.

"A-hem," Tamala feigned a cough, "did you come for any specific reason, other than to gawk at my office? I could give you a tour if you like."

Marie fixed her gaze on Tamala and studied her face coldly. Before Preston went to prison she'd accused him several times of sleeping with Tamala, but each time he'd deny it profusely. Yet Marie had never been truly convinced.

"Preston, I know when a bitch got eyes for my man!"

"Look Re-Re, Tamala is like my sister, she had issues when she was young and I helped her through them. If she has a little crush, it's harmless, it will go away; it has to. cuz you're all I need to get by..."

"Hello, are you okay or do you need a doctor or something?" said Tamala snidely.

Marie clicked her tongue, squinted her eyes and said, "Uh, I want to know if you've seen my man!"

"Excuse me!"

"Are you deaf or something? I said have you seen my man?" snapped Marie, folding her arms across her breasts and tapping her foot.

Tamala inhaled deeply, and exhaled sharply before glancing up at the ceiling and muttering, "Please Lord be with me," and signed a cross over her chest. Next, she snapped her eyes towards Marie's curling lips and rolling eyes. "Marie, as you can see, I've worked my ass off to get to where I'm at...so please don't bring that niggah shit to my job!"

"Niggah shit?" spat Marie incredulously, rolling her neck, arms akimbo.

"That's right, niggah shit. Whatever you did to your niggah ain't got nothing to do with me or my profession, so if you'll excuse me..."

"Wait a minute...how you know I did something to him?"

"What?" Tamala's eyes shuffled briefly. "That's beside the point, the point is that I'm not your watchdog and when Preston wants to see you, I'm sure he'll contact you...now if you don't mind—"

Marie's eyes crawled over Tamala's face. It was Tamala's expression, the way she said his name. It was written all over her face. "You nasty bitch! You fucked him, didn't you? You fucked my man!"

That was all she could stand. Tamala burst out her seat, hands bracing on her desk. "Bitch...who you calling a bitch? You fucked yourself, slut! Screwing some little boy, I ought to have you triflin' ass locked up. You st—"

The office door opened. Michael Golde, a senior prosecutor entered, his appraising eyes assessing the situation.

"Um, is everything okay?" he asked authoritatively.

"Yes, Michael, everything is under control," replied Tamala professionally.

His eyes dipped towards Marie. Marie bugged her eyes at him. He flashed a concerned glance at Tamala.

"Michael, it's okay," she assured him. Hesitantly, he nodded and backed out the door. Marie rolled her eyes at him as he departed.

"Humph, got these crackers backing you up, got they words in yo' mouth. Tramp, you ain't all that!" spat Marie as she turned to face Tamala.

"Got these crackers' words in my mouth?" repeated Tamala unbelievingly. She bit her lip to keep from screaming. She swallowed hard and fired, "Why you low budget, lazy hood rat! Whose words do you have in yo' mouth when you go beg these crackers for food stamps, huh? Whose words do you have in yo' mouth when you stand in line for nine hours for a Section 8 voucher? Answer that, you swap meet welfare thief!"

"What?"

"You heard me! Don't get mad at me, 'cause I studied hard and respected my body enough, not to let some mangy niggah skeet in me and turn me into Jerry Springer material. Don't get mad at me, 'cause I own and you rent!" Tamala rested one hand on her hip and waved her index finger at Marie. "Don't hate, skank, take notes!"

Tamala's insults found their mark and stung deeply. Marie's eyes watered and she gulped noisily, but she stood her ground.

"Tamala, just 'cause you went to law school, you think you better than me?"

"No, smarter!" Tamala smirked Marie winced.

"Okay Tamala," said Marie, gathering herself, "let's say you are smart enough to do the white man's dirty work for him; and you studied hard to make sure people rot in prison. I'm happy for you. And yeah, I got pregnant and shit, but I graduated though. Nevertheless, it don't make me no lesser woman in my eyes, 'cause my daughter is my pride and joy and I wouldn't change that for nothing. Cuz while that funky piece of paper on your wall gives you access to these crackers, my daughter is evidence of the gift of life in me, and it ain't nothin' you can say that can make me feel bad about that."

"Okay fine," Tamala said and shrugged, "you're fertile." She clapped softly. "Congratulations. Do you want a Nobel Peace Prize? Or would you like me to issue a warrant for your deadbeat baby's daddy? In the meantime, don't come into my office and try to turn your slut-tacular actions into the 'white man this and the white man that'. You triflin', lazy ass hood rats always yappin' that white man shit, but quick to go down to his offices and apply for his crumbs. Hmmph."

"Tsss…Tamala, you know what? When yo' lil ugly oompa loompa lookin' ass—"

"Oompa loompa?" retorted Tamala, screwing her face up, tossing her hair back vainly.

"Yeah. Oompa to-the-fuck-loompa! Ass useta come around all goo-goo eyed, sniffin' my man's nuts. I knew you'd be a problem one day. But then he made me feel sorry for you when he told me how you useta sleep on the floor with towels stuffed in between yo' legs so you wouldn't pee the bed. Or how your uncle came in your mouth so much that it stained your teeth yellow; and how even after they caught y'all, you'd still suck your thumb and wait by the door, hoping he'd come back."

"That's preposterous, it didn't happen like that!" Tamala protested meekly, utterly embarrassed.

"Oh yes it did, bitch. I know all about you."

Tamala thrust her hand in her desk and came up with a canister. Marie thought she was about to get maced, and backed away. It was only air freshener. Tamala sprayed it in an arc above her head.

"Alright, that's enough of this bullshit. Air out, skank, or I'll have you escorted out."

Chapter 13

"Brandon J. Square extraordinaire?" mocked Preston, "what kind of handle is that?"

"It's a handle that keeps me out of jail to chase the tail," replied Brandon with exaggerated flair.

Brandon was Tamala's sorority sister's little brother, and she'd asked him to take Preston to purchase some odds and ends, and to see his parole agent. Brandon, affectionately known by friends and family as B.J., was her go-to guy for things of this nature. She also used him to issue subpoenas to women who were uncooperative, they never suspected him when he showed up at their door. B.J. was a loquacious, tall, debonair young man in his early twenties, rockin' that pretty boy swag; always fresh to def, sporting a megawatt smile, putting one in the mind of Cam Newton.

"Izzatright?" quipped Preston, as they trudged towards the Apple computer store to purchase a cell phone. Tamala insisted that he get an iPhone, citing the multitude of apps that would assist him in his writing endeavors. B.J. continued to articulate his squareness.

"Man, it's like this. I ain't no goon or gangster, never have been, straight up. But I ain't no punk or no nerd. I'll knuckle up with the best of 'em, but if a niggah pull out a gun, I'm gonna break dat shit down and accept a beat down; it ain't worth it, ya know. Played b-ball all through high school and was on my way to UNLV until I blew out my knee. 'Kay, now I like flashy things, like fine women, clothes, fast cars, just like the next man, but I ain't 'bout to go to jail tryna get 'em."

"A'ight so how does all that make you square extraordinaire?"

"Simple, cuz my square game is out of this world!" B.J. popped his imaginary collar, gave it a little twist, wiggled his fingers for special effects and said, "Stardust," comically.

Preston smiled and shook his head at B.J.'s humor; he was beginning to grow on him.

"You see, bruh, I'm king of the squares, cuz I know the rules of engagement; I know a goon when I see one, and I'm smart enough to rep the squares."

"Rules?"

"Yes, rules; you should know my nig that it's a formula to everything in life."

"Spit it."

"Spit what?"

"The rules."

"A'ight, you think I'm bullshittin', huh? Okay, rule number one: anything above a misdemeanor shall miss my demeanor."

"Riiight," chuckled Preston, "That's a good one."

"Okay, rule number two: don't ever; ever, ever, ever fuck with chain snatchers or wrastlers."

"Huh? Ya losin' me, kid."

Just in front of the Apple computer store, B.J. stopped and waved at a cutie pie eyeing them, before turning his attention back to Preston.

"Bruh-Bruh, a chain snatcher is code name for the weasel type cat who's always into some lowkey slick shit. and he's like a chameleon and you never see it coming, but as soon as you let him in ya circle, he's gon' cause a diversion, have you lookin' one way, then he'll snatch ya chain and disappear the other way."

"And the chain is like symbolic in terms."

"Right, bruh, you got it."

"Okay that makes sense, but what 'bout this wrastler, do you mean, like, wrestler?"

"Yeah, exactly, one of them Magilla Gorilla type niggahs, always tryin' to test a niggah, bullying, hatin' on a playa; a cat who uses violence to solve all his issues. Man, them is the most in-securest niggahs in the world. They take everything the wrong way, and the minute ya try to reason wit 'em, they take that as a sign of weakness."

"My nig, you kind of sharp for a square. Chain snatchers and wrestlers. Ha-ha," Preston barked a laugh, "you ain't lying. As a matter of fact, I know quite a few wrestlers; you can't even take them catz around no broads, cuz if they don't get no play, they'll cause a scene."

"Exactly, that's why I just work my square extraordinaire game: I got a network of squares, we got our low risk hustles, a misdemeanor scam here and there. Plus, I got a little carpet cleaning company. I stay lookin' good, and smellin' good, keep a couple of square chicks lining my pockets and man, I'm happy and most of all, free. Shiiit, I stay on my square," said B.J., poppin' his collar emphatically.

Preston examined B.J.'s face and nodded his head. "Eloquently put, I'll have to chamber that philosophy."

"You would want to...don't let these catz out here trick you into throwing rocks at the penitentiary; but look, enough of me, what's up with you and Tamala?"

"That's G-14 classified."

"Like that?"

"It don't matter anyway," said B.J. as they walked into the store, "she ain't never let a niggah use her credit card; as a matter of fact, she ain't let a niggah do nothin' with her lately...if ya know what I mean."

"Swirl?"

"Exactly."

He purchased the iPhone, with B.J. more excited than he was, eagerly illustrating the impressive array of gadgets, numerous apps and functions. Next, Preston went to see his parole agent, who promptly ordered him to empty his pockets. Luckily, he had B.J. hold Tamala's credit card just before entering the office. The balding, needle-nosed, pompous white dude read Preston the parole riot act, before demanding a urine sample. He couldn't wait to get out the parole agent's office; even the air was oppressive.

Don't hate me cuz I'm beautiful, thought Preston.

As the thin-lipped parole agent rambled on, Preston cussed him out in his head. When he got back in the car with B.J., he exhaled sharply. B.J. shook his head and pulled off in silence, giving Preston a chance to calm his nerves and gather himself.

B.J. whipped the Paul Newman blue, mint condition, '99 Lexus G.S. 300, sittin' on 20's through the avenues as Preston finally emerged from his funk.

"Man, this is a nice ride B.J., and it still rides smooth for it to be an older model!"

"Thanks, it useta be Pop's, but he gave it to me right after I graduated."

"What he do, upgrade to a Benz?"

"Naw, he bought a Honda Accord."

"Honda Accord?" said Preston, eyebrows raised.

"Yep, that's why I keep it in mint condition; to show my appreciation, cuz Pops sacrificed so I could shine."

"That's what's up…you got a good old man."

"Shiiit, you betta not let him hear you call him old."

"Oh, he still think he got handles?"

"Bruh, Pops still a beast."

"That's what I'm talkin' 'bout then…real G's don't die they multiply," jibed Preston.

"Aye, but peep bruh; I've been chauffeuring you around all day, now I need my herbs and spices."

Preston registered B.J.'s meaning and instantly frowned and barked, "Bruh, don't take me through no dope turf! Drop-me-the-fuck-off!"

"Man, if you don't knock it off maine! Brandon J. Square extraordinaire don't go on no dope turfs, I ain't 'bout to get my car jacked or towed off. Kick back, ya wit' da kid."

Preston cast a conspiratorial glance at B.J. and muttered, "A'ight now, Kickback Kid."

At that moment, straight ahead of them, three scantily dressed women danced like wild, seductive sirens in front of a well-kept two-story apartment complex. From the back, they looked like the Pussycat Dolls in the hood. Preston's eyes immediately locked on the shortest of the trio. She had an elephantine, yet curvaceous backside that she was swayin', shakin', and droppin'. Preston grabbed his crotch and said, "God-deezzam, look at the shitter on dat critter."

B.J. pulled to a halt across the street with one hand on the steering wheel, and the other shaking a bag of O.G. Kush pinched between his fingers, he said, "Yeah maine, see, I got the herbs. I just needed the spices."

He nodded his head towards the girls who were still dancing, oblivious to B.J. and Preston. B.J. honked the horn and two of them spun out their dance steps and looked in their direction. They were a'ight, surmised Preston, but his eyes were on the thick one, when she finally turned around, Preston jumped back ala Smokey in *Friday*. She might have a bangin' body, but she had the face of a Rottweiler.

"Aw naw, dawg. I knew it was too good to be true...pull off fo' she bite us, man!"

B.J. laughed so hard, he damn near choked. "Ki-kick back blood, you ain't never heard of the Nevil Devils?"

"Hell naw, I..." he stopped in mid-sentence, as his eyes whipped towards the street sign ahead of them. Sure enough, it read, "Nevil Street".

"Well, I'll be god dammed," he snickered. He'd heard about the fabulously promiscuous sisters from Nevil Street all through the prison system; legend had it that they were freaky as hell, closest thing to porn queens. Hence the name, Nevil Devils.

All three girls waved enthusiastically for B.J. to get out the car.

"You only live once, bruh, you coming?"

"Man, I can't believe this shit," said Preston, ascending from the vehicle. *Fuck it. I've been in the fuckin' ground for the last eight years, might as well live one time,* he thought.

They crossed the street and the ladies fawned over B.J. as though he was a rock star. Preston scanned the women; one had big lips, the other had big tits, and the short, hound-faced one, who was now eye fucking him, had more ass than Serena Williams scrunched into a barely 5-foot frame. She bit her fingernail, fluttered her eyelashes and cawed, "Wee way wat? He woot."

Preston screwed up his face. "Whadafuck?"

"Be cool, blood, she's deaf."

"Man, fuck dat shit. I'm out!" Preston snapped and pushed towards the car.

"Awww, that's fucked up B.J.," snapped Big Lips.

"Yeah niggah, you ain't all dat!" fired Big Tits.

Preston spun around to pop off a slick retort, only to see the deaf chick's head in her palms engaging in violent sobs. His heart melted. He glanced at B.J., who just shrugged, then back at the two girls who were mean muggin' him.

"You know what y'all, my bad. It's just been a long day."

"Well, you ain't gotta take it out on her," chimed the sisters.

It was apparent that Big Lips was the de facto leader of the trio. Preston's eyes swept over her glossed down, giant, soup cooler lips in awe. *Them things is vicious*, he mused inwardly, and for some reason he became horny as hell.

The deaf chick peeked above her hands. Although she was absolutely homely, much to her credit, she had an enchanting set of innocent eyes. She thrust her tiny hands on her bangin' hips, jutting out her bottom lip and garbled, "Woo wean."

Preston's eyebrows pinched.

"She said you're mean," interpreted Big Lips.

"No, I'm not." He went to hug her, but she turned her back; consequently, her ample backside bumped into his groin. Instantly he swelled.

She felt him, whipped her head over shoulder, and then glanced at Big Lips before giggling out, "Wonwey."

Big Lips clucked her tongue. "You hella nasty, bitch." She rolled her eyes at Preston, "She said you got a donkey dick."

All three girls giggled feverishly, and eyed him wantonly.

B.J. stepped to Big Lips and ran his hand across her ass, she purred. Big Tits straightened her back to make her boobs pop out even more.

"So B.J.," she cooed, "is we gon' kick it or what, cuz I know you got that piff, and you know we need some drank."

"Yeah baby, give her some money to get some drank," said Big Lips, now all over B.J.

B.J. nodded his head at Preston, he said, "It's up to my boy."

While they held their breath waiting for Preston's reply, he caught a glimpse of the tiny hearing device in Big Butt's ear. He damn near broke wide, but eventually gave in, figuring you only live once.

Big Tits collected some ends from B.J. and scurried off to the liquor store, while Preston and B.J. followed her sisters up the stairs. Preston's eyes were locked on Big Butt's juicy, jiggling backside as she climbed the steps. He rubbed his dick and whispered to B.J., "You got some condoms?"

"Always. Aye, how you like lil mama's DSL's?"

"DSL's? Fuck is that?"

"Dick suckin' lips."

"Aww niggah, yo' square ass got funnies fo' days, huh?" chuckled Preston into his fist.

The living room was dim and dingy, and Goapele's hit song, "Closer to My Dreams" pumped out the house speakers. Preston loved that song; it was so ethereal; you could almost see clouds coming out the speakers.

The Nevil Devils slammed back a few glasses of cognac and the freak fest was in full effect. The air was thick with hemp fog, and all three ladies were tipsy and dro'd out the game. On the couch directly in front of Preston was B.J., sprawled out, legs spread, head thrown back, howling like aa demented dog; his hand was guiding Big Lip's dome down repeatedly on his erect phallus. Her lips were amazing. She milked, suckled, suctioned, slurped and gulped down B.J.'s penis to the balls, in a lewd, yet sensual rhythm. Every few seconds, her tongue would flash across his dick like a lizard. Preston had never seen anything like it. Their eyes met. Unintentionally, he licked his lips. Spurred by his obvious lust she put on a show, her head bobbed frantically, like a mad oilrig.

"Oooh...shiit, girl...hit that thang," rasped B.J.

"Damn Londa, you killin' it, bitch," panted Big Tits, posted next to them, legs gapped wide, rubbin' her exposed pearl. Her breasts were large and firm, topped with ripe, beefy, blackberry-like nipples. She bit her lip, closed her eyes and flicked her finger rapidly around her clitoris.

Not to be outdone, Big Butt came out her clothes, wearing a dental floss sized thong. She positioned herself right in front of Preston's line of vision, palms down, on all fours and gyrated her body, so that her ass cheeks clapped loudly.

Smack, smack, smack.

She glanced behind at him, eyes of a freak, puckering her lips; she shook her tail feather from side to side and it wobbled; then she made it clap again, even louder.

SMACK! SMACK! SMACK!

A heady musk floated from the wobbling cheeks. Preston was out his clothes with Godspeed, dick spearing the air.

"Ummmm Humph, that niggah do got donkey," gasped Big Tits, now assisting her sister ravaging B.J.'s dick. They both gawked back at Preston's massive erection with wet lips.

Big Butt came out her thong and lay down on her back, spread eagle, and before him was the bushiest pussy he'd ever seen in his life.

"Shiiit!" hissed Preston in disbelief.

"Way wy woo wak werwey," cooed Big Butt.

"What?"

"She said, 'That's my throwback jersey'," giggled Big Lips, running her head back down in a synchronized suck down of B.J.'s long dick.

B.J. squirmed and moaned out, "Ooooh damn, oooh get my balls, too."

When it was all said and done, Preston and B.J. ran through a 6-pack of Magnums, nailing all three girls in the process. B.J. dropped Preston off in front of Tamala's house, thoroughly drained in the wee hours of the night.

Tamala swung the door open before he could even knock. She had fire in her eyes and smoke coming out her nose and ears. As he walked by her, she wrinkled her nose.

"Phew! You smell like a bucket of busted ass!"

He threw his bags on the couch; he didn't have the energy to argue or the gall to lie. "Don't blame it on me; blame it on Brandon J. Square extraordinaire."

She clicked her tongue in disgust. "We need to talk!"

"Speak on it."

"First of all, your fuckin' hood rat came to my office, lookin' for you."

"And?"

"And!" Tamala yelled, piqued at his casualness. "The hussy was disrespectful and caused a scene!"

"Tamala, you slept with her man. She must have seen it on your face. Y'all got a sixth sense 'bout shit like that."

"Preston, don't give me that bullshit, I'm not a little girl anymore. Besides, that's not even the biggest issue."

"Okay, what is?"

"This!" screamed Tamala, pulling out the 9mm, holding it with a pencil stuck in the barrel. The gravity of his carelessness now creased his face.

"T, you know damn well I forgot about that damn thing. I apologize."

"I don't care, Preston! You can't jeopardize my job bringin' shit like this to my house!"

"Jeopardize yo' job, T, ain't nobody gon' search yo' house."

"That's not the point, Preston. First, it's guns, next thing you know, it will be drugs. I'm a District Attorney, not just a hood rat."

"Are you serious, T? I think you're over exaggerating."

"Leave my house, Preston."

"What?"

"Leave my house now!" yelled Tamala, tears streaming down her face.

"Ta—"

"Now Preston!" she snapped, pointing towards the front door.

Chapter 14

"Please allow me to introduce myself. My name is Sir JoyPain. Middle name Sunshine. Last name Rain," mumbled Preston solemnly, and then flopped on the motel bed. He blew out a long air of frustration, before glancing above him. It was a cheap "fuck me baby" motel with mirrors on the ceiling. He removed his shirt and flexed. His muscles rippled and rocked. He smiled, but then his thoughts turned inwards. It had been an eventful last couple of days; like sunshine and rain. However, he wasn't in prison, for that reason alone, he could smile through the joy and pain...

He read somewhere that it was two layers of California: gold mines, Hollywood, Beverly Hills, Disneyland, Silicon Valley, surrounded by blue skies, palm trees, the aroma of gardenia, jasmine magnolia and tax cuts for the rich. In the underbelly off this opulence lies roach and rat infested ghettos, a deficient public school system, encased by a prison industrial complex that imprisoned its minorities at an astronomical and alarming rate. Two contrasting worlds. Two separate realities. Dreams fulfilled or dreams fantasized—one state.

The O.G. ST-1 had taught him in prison, "You don't have to have one state of mind, and don't listen to niggahs who are out of their damned minds". He chuckled at the memory of ST-1's dialogues; he could hear it now just like it was yesterday...

"P.G., it ain't gon' be easy out there, it's gonna be challenges and it ain't always gonna turn out like you think.

It's always gonna be the element of thee unknown; that's why you have to prepare for all the possibles and all the probables; expect the unexpected. It's always the things we can't see and / or the things we don't wanna see that sidetracks or blindsides us, but if you stay focused on the big picture, yet cognizant of the details you'll have leverage on all the sheep and the oppressor."

"And the big picture is?"

Feigning irritation, frown lines creased the O.G.'s face. "Come on P.G., I know you pay attention. You know this shit back and forth. You prolly can even teach this shit. Cuz ya bug the shit out of me pickin' my brain."

Preston flashed the dimple and replied, "ST-1, come on now, my dude, you know I pay attention. I just never tire if hearing you spit it so fluently."

"Young niggah, I done tol' you about tryna masturbate my ego."

Preston smiled cuz regardless of what the O.G. said, he was a sucka for compliments and he truly loved to teach.

"I'm gon' do this fo' you one mo' again, young gun." He began. "'Kay now, the big picture is that you're in the richest economy on the planet, there are absolutely no opportunities, nowhere in the known world, like there are here in America. And yeah, the system is imperfect, it's a multitude of bigotry, racism...Shiiit, matter of fact, it's all types of isms and schisms pervading this country, but it's all just to distract you from getting your slice off the cake and convince you to chase the crumbs, feel me?"

Preston nodded; all ears.

"A'ight, peep this quote by Benjamin Franklin, the niggah whose face is on the hundred-dollar bill. The United States Constitution doesn't guarantee happiness, only the pursuit of it. You got to catch it yourself."

He became silent while the game he was boiling bubbled in Preston's mind. His eyes rolled across Preston's face before he continued. "In other words he was sayin' if you want to get it, whatever your definition of happiness is, we ain't gin' give it to you, you got to get it yaself, but it's here for you to get! Yet niggahs be whining and complaining 'bout this country, but people in Mexico, Cuba, Haiti, China, all over the world, die tryna get over here to get the opportunities that we take for granted, or don't take advantage of."

"Such as?"

"Such as...oh, you want to hear me preach today, huh?"

"Man ST-1, I go home soon...I want yo' words to be etched on my brain, cuz you spit that real, big bruh."

The O.G. cocked his head, and then smiled. "Young gun, you good. I give you that, but I know you want it, that's why I spill it on you. But as I was saying..."

"Such as..." Preston reminded him.

"Such as starting your own business. In some countries, all businesses are run and supervised by the state and you got to get permits to open businesses, permits they don't issue out unless you somebody important, or have enough money to bribe them out one. Or some countries...if you start a business and it fails, that's it! You can never do it

again. And jobs. Man, they working for a dollar a day and lucky to get that. That's why it ain't no jobs for poor people in America, cuz poorer people are begging to do the work for pennies on the dollar. Nonetheless, this is the land of milk and honey, if you see the big picture."

"But it's tricks to distract you, right?"

"You damn right; it's trickeration and distractions...we in prison, ain't we?"

Preston's head swept the prison yard then turned to face the O.G. and said, "Yep, it looks like a prison to me."

"Don't make it ya coffin."

Preston screwed his eyes tight and winced. The O.G. studied his young pupil.

"You know you always wince when I say that."

"Yeah, I can't help it."

"Youngsta, I just don't want these idiots to trick you out ya life with all that bullshit they be on. You're a leader...these other catz is pied pipers, they just sound good. Like Ole Reverend Al Sharpton; you see in that book I gave you, The Life and Crimes of Don King, you see how easy he turned snitch?"

Yeah, ST-1, he wore a wire and everything for the feds on Don King."

"You see, young man, these clear people will let suckas like that rat lead, even run for president cuz they know they can keep their hand in his back, but he's the first niggah people yell for when they get discriminated against."

"Tssss...that's like yellin' fo' a public defender when you got a murder beef," said Preston.

"Yep, they both still work for the man. So you just got to be able to see shit for what it is, and not for what it seems to be, and the only way to do that is to educate yourself. Every great leader there ever was, was educated at one point or another. He just didn't wake up one day intelligent. Feel me?"

Preston nodded.

"And when ya educated, in other words, enlightened; you can and will miss the distractions, e.g. drugs, alcohol, the bullshit on TV, and the pied pipers, cuz that's the shit they use to lull us to sleep with. And not just no bullshit certificate from some damn bullshit paper mill that gives you the opportunity to come work for the oppressors. I'm talkin' 'bout studying economics, understanding guns and butter, and how to make your money grow in ya sleep. I mean, P, I ain't mad at the young catz that got to sell drugs. I just get mad that they give it all back to the clear people. Cuz I mean behind every great fortune, there was most likely even a greater crime. For instance, we celebrate Columbus Day, and that mothafucka was a mass murderer, he slaughtered the Indians in mass. I can go on and on 'bout the Kennedys, Rockefellers, Rothchilds, Bushes, and Wall Street. But the bottom line is, it's all about money, ain't a damn thing funny, and when you educate yourself on economics, you have a better chance to decide yo' own fate."

"Follow the yellow brick road."

"Follow the leader. Follow the blueprints of catz that's eating like Daymond John, 50 Cent, and Jay Z; those dudes are the big picture."

"Cuz when you got money and power you make the rules; when you don't got it you follow the rules!" said Preston.

"You mothafuckin' right, and don't ever let nobody tell you anything different. Did I not show you this in all the studies we've done on the great empires, Rome for example?"

Preston nodded.

"Well, that's what this country patterns itself after...we are in New Rome. We are not going back to Africa! We're not gonna overthrow this country! It's just not gonna happen. The best thing we can do is inherit this country's rights and privileges, and the way you do that is get the mothafuckin' money and the power. Bullshit ain't nothin'!!"

"When in Rome, do as the Romans do."

"That's wassup, P, don't get tricked out yo' life and rot in these prisons, whining and complaining, cuz don't nobody give a fuck 'bout that bullshit. 'Kay, now you got those books I read typed up, right?"

"Yessiirrr."

"That's yo' product, P, move that shit like dope, use those social networks to market yourself; build a team and brand your game. Get you one of those iPads, stuff it with your creativity and the secret teachings of giants, past and present, stand on their shoulders and utilize today's technology to blast your game worldwide."

"Cuz being American is not only a nationality, but it's also a title."

133

"Right, Young G, didn't Paul yell out, 'I am a Roman citizen'?"

"That's what he did say."

"A'ight, cuz membership has its privileges. Feel me?"

"I wouldn't be in ya face if I didn't, bruh-bruh."

"That's wassup, but look...what ya got to always remember when you tearing paper—"

"When violence starts, money stops," Preston said, cutting into ST-1's spiel.

"Yeah grasshopper, there it is."

"Okay O.G., last question?"

"Shoot."

"What about love... 'bout me and lil mama?"

The O.G. paused briefly, tapped his foot, looking away into the distance, he said, "You ask all the O.G.'s the same question, but it's a damn good question. But I'll tell you like Frankie Beverly said and leave it at that. 'Love can be bitter, love can be sweet, sometimes it's devotion, sometimes it's deceit'." He paused and turned to meet Preston's gaze. "Keep ya mind on ya money, and ya money on ya mind, love will find you if it's yours to find..."

Preston snapped back to reality and reviewed in his mind the events that had transpired over the last few days.

"Man, I'm not 'bout to feel guilty 'bout gettin' some pussy. Shiiit, I've been locked in a garbage can for almost a decade. Did they stop fuckin' when I got locked up? Hell-to-the-naw! Am I married? Negative. So don't get caught up in other people's emotions...stick to the plan, don't get distracted," he counseled himself.

His eyelids became heavy and he drifted in and out a slight slumber before suddenly giving in to the urge to call Marie. He dialed; it rang.

"Hello," a sleepy voice answered.

"Wassup Ma?" he said.

"Preston? Baby, where are you at?" said the voice, now wide awake.

"I'm safe in the cuts, don't trip."

"I'm comin'. We should talk, we can work things out..." her words stumbled over themselves.

He was silent.

"Preston?"

"'Sup Marie?"

"Say somethin'...say the word...whatever it is, I'll do it."

No reply.

"Preston..."

"'Sup?"

"Aren't you gon' say somethin'?"

Naw, not really."

"Then why'd you call?" she whined.

"Just to hear your voice, babe."

He heard her begin to sniffle, fighting back tears.

"I'm so..." tears squeezed out the corners of her eyes, and she whimpered.

"Re-Re," he said softly.

"Hmmm?" she responded, still sniffling.

"I'll always love you, ma."

"Wh-what does that s'pose to mean Pr-Preston, huh? You not fuckin' wit me no more?" she cried.

"I didn't say that."

"Or did you just call to torture me…to rub in my face the fact you fuckin' Ta—" The phone dropped, and he heard her sobbing in the background.

"Re-Re," he called. "Re-Re!" he called out, this time louder.

She blew her nose and fumbled with the phone before answering. "What Preston? You broke me down, are you happy?"

"Look Re-Re, don't twist the game, ma, you know the biz! I ain't that young punk you playin', feel me? Like I tol' you, I called to hear your voice, so miss me with the reversals," he snapped sternly. He could hear her mind reshuffle.

"Preston, I need you baby. I need to see you."

"You will."

"When?"

"Soon…look, I'm 'bout to lie down, this is my number, lock it in."

"No…I'm not hanging up Preston, not 'til we talk it out—"

He ended the call.

Chapter 15

"Well, well, well... Hmmph. If it ain't savoir-the-fuck-faire." Detra clicked her tongue and walked her eyes up and down Preston's body. He smiled and gave her a warm hug; her embrace was dry as sand.

She rolled her eyes and said, "Hmmph. I guess you think you baby Denzel now, huh?"

"Like that, Detra?"

She ignored him and yelled upstairs. "Mama! Yo' lil boy toy is here...the chicken has come home to roost."

Preston shook his head and stepped on in. Aunt Paula came sashaying down the stairs, as usual; she had an entourage in tow. Preston saw that she hadn't aged one bit. She had on skintight jeans, showcasing her thick thighs and hips, and her voluptuous mammaries were sitting high and mighty.

"Nut, is that you lil' daddy?" She opened her arms wide. "Come here boy and give A.P. that love," she said, real sugary like.

Preston blushed; happy he had on his shades so he could at least halfway look cool. Next thing he knew, he was being swarmed by her massive breasts as a light fragrance floated up from her cleavage. Surreptitiously, she fondled his johnson. He didn't move, yet he knew it was coming. Aunt Paula pushed him back, holding him at shoulder-length.

"Hmph...hmph...hmph. What a man, what a man, what a mighty good man. Shit, I knew you was gon' be fine, but day-yum," she caressed his chest and arm muscles, then grabbed his butt.

"Mama!" complained Detra.

"Girl, stay out of grown folks' business," Aunt Paula responded crisply, yet playfully.

Sharonda, Donna, and Five, watched from the sideline, snickering. Five was the youngest lady in the house and Aunt Paula's fifth and final child; hence the name, Five. She was only eleven when Preston was sentenced to prison, and she still held a serious crush on him. She slid between Aunt Paula and Preston, and hugged him tight. He shoved his glasses atop his head in disbelief.

"Sticks?" He called her Sticks, because she was all skin and bones as a kid.

She stepped back and double-clutched her curvaceous hips before poppin' one out to the side, resting her hand on it. He was flabbergasted.

"Yep, all me." She was a miniature Aunt Paula, only prettier and younger.

"Girl, if you don't get yo' triflin' ass somewhere," said Aunt Paula.

They all laughed and took turns huggin' him, before Aunt Paula wrestled him away.

"Why in the hell didn't you write, Nut? I coulda come up there and played like I was yo' mama and got us one of dos' conjugal visits."

"Mama, will you please stop embarrassing yourself?" said Detra.

"How in the Sam Hill can I embarrass myself, if I say what I mean in my own damn house? Girl, you better get wit da program."

"Hmmmph" Detra rolled her eyes. Aunt Paula returned the roll.

The twins ambled in from the backyard. Marcus, the youngest twin, had a noticeably effeminate gait; his eyes studied Preston's face curiously.

"A.P. who is dat?" he asked girlishly.

"Nunya."

"Who?"

"Nunya damn business! Now go on back out there and play. I don' tol you 'bout gettin' in grown folks' business," snapped Aunt Paula. Then she grabbed Preston's hand. Marcus rolled his eyes and walked back towards the back. All the women looked at one another, and each had the same thought.

"Come on upstairs, Nut, I wanna introduce you to somebody."

Preston followed. As he pushed up the stairs, Five winked at him salaciously. Detra gave him a stank look, before they all broke into conversation behind him. Aunt Paula's immense posterior swayed before him.

She got ole school ass like Michele Obama, he thought, then chuckled lightly.

She stopped and turned around, grinning mischievously.

"What you laughin' at boy?"

He smiled; he didn't have to say a word.

"Yeah, I still got it, huh?" She slapped her buttocks. "And it ain't no Lee-press-on ass, like these tramps be wearing nowadays. When I was comin; up, either ya had it or ya didn't. These hussies ain't got no shame today."

Preston laughed. Aunt Paula was something else.

Once inside her bedroom, Aunt Paula quickly locked the door behind them. Seated on her bed was a heavyset woman in her late thirties, he surmised, whose breasts, amazingly, dwarfed Aunt Paula's. She smiled; straight, coke white teeth, he noted. She was cappuccino-colored with a pretty face, and put him in the mind of Jill Scott.

"Girl," said Aunt Paula, sounding like a teenager, "this is Preston, but I call him Nut."

She shot him a freaky smile as if she stole the last cookie out the cookie jar.

"Nut, this is J'Neane; she's a writer. She writes dem freaky books like Zane."

J'Neane batted her eyelashes. He flashed the dimple. J'Neane smiled, shyly assessing him openly. Next, Aunt Paula closed in on him and fumbled with his belt buckle.

"Show her dat thang, Nut."

"Come on now, A.P. Stop playin'," he protested meekly.

"I ain't playin', boy. Now come on, I ain't seen it in a long time." She opened his pants and sat back down next to her friend, whose face was now painted with a curious expression.

"Pull it out, Nut," urged Aunt Paula, practically on the edge of her seat.

Hesitantly, he began to fidget with his boxers, when a knock on the door startled them. Preston buckled his pants as they glanced towards the door.

"Who is it?" yelled Aunt Paula.

"A.P., can we play with the Xbox?"

"Marcus, take yo' ass somewhere, boy!" yelled Aunt Paula. "I'm tellin' ya, dat lil niggah is a faggot; he know we doin' somethin'," she added under her breath.

"Dang, we cain't never do nothin'!" whined Marcus, storming off away from the door. Aunt Paula waited until she heard the footsteps fade and said, "A'ight now, Nut, show my friend dat thang...give her something to write about." She turned to J'Neane. "Girrrl, I couldn't give him no poonanny cuz him and my nephew was best friends, and if Kenzo would have found out, it would have liketa killed him. So I did the next best thang. I drug him up to this room and made him jack it off fo' me. Girrrrl, it was cum in the sky. Wooooo Wee! That's why I calls him Nut. Huh, Nut?"

He blushed.

"Paula you is just nasty", purred J'Neane, with a pronounced Southern accent.

Aunt Paula noticed Preston pussyfooting. She got up and fondled his privates. "You know A.P. ain't seen Nutzilla in soooo long," she cooed in his ear and sat back down with anxious eyes.

He lowered his boxers slowly and his huge penis flopped out and dangled. J'Neane's hands flew to her mouth and she reared back as if she'd been shot at.

"Oh my Gawd, it's damn near touchin' the ground, Paula."

"Woooo wee, that's a dick, girl, ain't it?" said Paula excitedly.

"Well, I'll say," giggled J'Neane as her cheeks flushed.

"J'Neane," Aunt Paula said and pointed, "look at dat damn vein. It looks like a garter snake." Aunt Paula put her hand on her heavy breasts.

"Whew shit…Nut, make it slap up against ya thighs like ya useta."

"Naw A.P., that's enough—"

She reached out and tugged at it, before slappin' it playfully. It swung and began to twitch and rock up. "Lawd haf mercy…a babyback dick clock. Wooo, I'm hypnotized already." Aunt Paula stretched her arms before her like Frankenstein's monster, rolling her eyes to the back of her head. Preston chuckled and decided to entertain them; he stroked his member until the head began to mushroom. "Hmmmph, hmmmph, hmmmph! J'Neane, have you ever seen anything like it?"

J'Neane's eyes were bugged as if she just had a hit of crack. The doorknob rattled. Preston slipped his dick back in his boxers and buckled.

"Can I help you?" called out Aunt Paula.

"Mama, Kenzo said he on his way and to tell Preston not to leave 'til he get here."

"Five, Nut ain't goin' no damn where no time soon!" Aunt Paula clicked her tongue. "Nosey ass wench."

"I'm just delivering the message...shoo!"

"Message deleted," said Aunt Paula.

"So um, J'Neane, how many books have you written so far?' asked Preston, trying to change subjects, but J'Neane was still basically speechless.

"See what good dick do, girl, ya stuck huh?" Aunt Paula clapped her hands together. "Panties in a knot, huh girl?" She laughed, then turned to Preston. "See Nut, she be writing all dem freaky books fantasizin', but when she see the monsta dick, Nutzilla, in real life...she freeze up and fall like a white lady in a scary movie." Aunt Paula slapped her thigh and laughed hysterically. "Wooo Lawd, J'Neane, you should see the look on yo' face, girl."

Slightly embarrassed, J'Neane looked away, with a sexy grin on her face. Finally, the color came back in her face; she cleared her throat and managed a reply. "I've penned six books so far," she said, fanning her face.

"Are they all urban erotica?"

"No, four are erotica...short stories. The other two are novels."

"And they're good and nasty, Nut. I read 'em all," interjected Aunt Paula.

Preston said, "Then we have something in common already. I've written two urban novels myself, but they're rough and definitely need editing."

Quite surprised, she replied, "Really? That's wonderful. You should know I also offer editing services at reasonable rates. I have a BA in journalism from LSU." She reached in her purse and fished out a business card. "Here, give me a call and I'll do a sample edit for you."

"Yeah, after she samples Nutzilla."

"Paula!"

"Okay, okay, just kiddin'; let's go downstairs fo' dem heffahs have a fit."

Preston let the women file out and followed. J'Neane was an Amazon, almost six feet, more than two hundred pounds all in the right places, and he noticed she moved gracefully.

Aunt Paula caught his attention and pointed at J'Neane. "Get her, she's a good woman."

"Paula, stop it."

"Girl, I'm just tryna fast track the inevitable."

Uncle Ervin was downstairs waiting on Aunt Paula in a dusty jumpsuit, surprisingly sober.

"Hey, up jumps the devil. Long time no see, young man."

"Wassup, Uncle Erv?"

"Uncle Erv betta get his dusty ass out my living room in them filthy clothes, dat's what's up with Uncle Erv."

"Yeah and afterwards, cuz Uncle Erv's been workin' hard 'round this house all day, he needs to get paid. I needs a sip-sip."

"Well, I got a tip-tip fo' ya...we'll talk 'bout yo' money after yo' skin takes a sip-sip of soap and water. Now go on now, Erv, out my living room."

Marcus tipped up to Preston, put his hand on his bony hip and stuck out the other.

"Can I have some money?"

"Marcus, what I tell you 'bout askin' people fo' money; he ain't got no money. Go outside and—"

"Uh-huh, he do...it's right there." He reached out and patted Preston's pocket, but what he'd touched wasn't a money lump. Shocked, he snatched his hand back as if he'd touched a hot stove.

"Somebody get me a damn belt, I'm whippin' this lil faggot's ass! Boy, what the hell's wrong wit' you?" spat Aunt Paula.

The boy began to tremble and burst into tears before tearing ass out the living room, screaming, "I ain't no faggot!"

"Well, ya betta stop walkin' around here switchin' like a girl and grabbin' on men's dicks, cuz dat's what faggots do!" Aunt Paula yelled after him.

"Maurice, go play wit yo' brother", said Sharonda. He immediately ran after his grief-stricken twin.

"That just don't make no damn sense," said Aunt Paula, shaking her head.

Preston watched Aunt Paula and he knew underneath all the cussin', she loved her grandsons and she was hurt deep by the tragedy behind their parents being missing from their lives. Barbara, the boys' mother, was Aunt Paula's second to oldest daughter. She was always withdrawn and quiet, in an odd way, and eccentric to boot. One day she'd come home early from work, only to find Big Marcus sexing some high yellow girl in their bed, the couple were goin' at it so tough, they didn't hear Barbara come in. Crazy Barbara as she came to be known, calmly boiled a pot of hot grease then stood over the two lovers and poured it over them. The grease was scalding hot and it melted Big Marcus's skin like plastic on fire. Big Marcus screamed to high heaven and without thinking jumped out the window. The high yellow girl got the rest of the hot grease, and she too belted out a blood-curdling scream while Barbara beat her with the scorching hot pot until the handle broke. Then she dialed 911 and waited for the police. The girl was grotesquely disfigured with third degree burns over her face, head and breasts. She also lost two fingers when the hot grease burned the meat off her fingers. She tried to block the savage blows of the pot and her fingers snapped off. She lost several teeth as well. Crime Scene Investigators had to scrape caked up skin off the pot. Big Marcus fared even worse. His head, neck, and back were hideously burned and to compound matters, he broke his legs in the fall out the window. Subsequently, he was in and out of mental hospitals before finally committing suicide. Crazy Barbara pled guilty and stoically accepted a twenty-five year to life sentence in California State Prison for women. Sadly, she learned she was pregnant and gave birth to the twins in prison, but refused to hold them.

"What's wrong wit' dat damn boy?"

"Mama, he just needs to be around some men that's all," offered Donna.

All at once, the women began to voice their opinions. Preston watched, amused. *Women sho' love talking*, he mused. He glanced around the room and caught J'Neane stealing glances his way, but also felt what he knew was Detra's probing eyes on his neck. The room was a buzz with chatter. Traditionally, this is how it had always been at Aunt Paula's, except now the participants were younger.

He was just about to reach for his cell phone to call Marie when Detra called out. "So, Preston, when you goin' back?"

He winced inwardly; he hated when people said that, because usually it was a police or a hater. He ignored her.

"You'll be back before the year is up, I betcha."

"Oh boy here we go," muttered Sharonda dejectedly.

"Detra, you need to let that shit go…why you gotsta pick at every man that comes here?"

Detra shrugged her shoulders.

"I'm just saying Mama, they always go back. That's they second home."

"She always got to start something, shooo!" grumbled Five, rolling her eyes at her big sister.

"Nobody care if you think that boy is all dat, Five! He ain't nothin' but a jailbird, like the rest of these niggahs."

The living room became deafly quiet. Preston seethed inside and fought to calm himself. He took a deep breath, and then said, "Damn Detra, if I didn't know better, you would think you wanted a niggah to go back or somethin', and if so, you should keep that hate aimed somewhere else and off my plate."

"Nah, I don't want to see you go back. I'd prefer that you man the fuck up and stop being the white man's bitch!"

"Ooooooh...no she didn't," exhorted Donna. Sharonda covered her mouth in disbelief.

"Detra!" snapped Aunt Paula.

"It's dem damn books Barbara sending her...she a feminazi now," Five mumbled under her breath, but Detra heard it.

"Naw, it ain't no damn books. It's these sorry ass niggahs out here." She pointed at Preston then started a heated diatribe. "No education. No vocation. White men got 'em scared to death. Police come; they run like roaches. When they get caught, they in the back of the police car cryin', pleadin' and snitchin'. Police gun 'em down in the streets. What they do? Cry and wear a funky ass RIP T-shirt! They just sorry, and got the nerve to call me a bitch and a hoe. Tssss...."

"What they s'pose to do Detra, huh?" fired Five emphatically.

"They s'pose to man the fuck up! Like the Black Panthers, them was some real men. Police couldn't come to the 'hood with that bullshit. They was on they ass like stunk on funk, following 'em 'round with cameras and guns, making sho' they was actually protecting and serving. Instead, nowadays they got these chumps abiding stay always from they own hood."

"And look at what happened to the Black Panthers, Detra," countered Aunt Paula.

"Yeah, one of these so-called D-Boys killed Huey P. Newton."

"It was way more to it than that, Detra; he was on drugs and robbing catz from what I heard."

"I don't give a damn if he was on dick and dynamite. He was a leader. Somebody should have protected him. How you gon' kill somebody who contributed so much to our people? You niggahs always doin' the white man's job fo' 'em. And you justify it by sayin' he was on drugs…niggah, you a sucka!"

"Detra, stop it now!"

"Nah, that's a'ight, A.P. Let her talk," said Preston.

"That's right, let me talk, cuz you ain't foolin' nobody prancing around here like a proud peacock when ya been in prison spreading ya ass cheeks for the white man. Answer me this. Out of all them times you bent over and spread your ass cheeks fo' dem crackers, how many times did you just flat out refuse to do it? Huh?"

The entire house looked at Preston. He was speechless.

"That's what I thought," her voice turned husky, "but you come in here," she walked back and forth; chin up, chest out, arms out imitating a buff male, "posturing like you all that and you've been lettin' the white man look up your ass for damn near a decade…and I'm s'pose to treat you like Nino-the-fuck-Brown? Niggah pa-leeze.!" She curled her lips and blew air. Tsssss. Her words stung hard and deep like sharp darts.

"Detra, you just need some dick girl". said Aunt Paula, trying to save his face.

"Nah, I can get some dick anywhere; I need a real man attached to it." She folded her arms across her chest and looked him up and down.

"You know what, Detra? What you say makes a lot of sense, cuz I never looked at it that way and I appreciate you bringin' it like that, cuz I needed to hear that raw and uncut just like you served it."

"Hmmph, that ain't all you need to hear!" she added.

"You know, Detra, once about a time we had the power, we had the knowledge. Africa—"

Niggah, don't you come in here talkin' dat Afrika Bambaataa shit!"

"Detra," he said calmly, "I let you speak and never interrupted you——"

"Yeah Detra, ley him say what he gotta say!" Five pleaded.

"Go ahead," she snarled, tapping her foot impatiently.

"Like I said, Africa is the cradle of civilization. We were the first to domesticate the animals, cultivate the land and record hieroglyphics; we knew about the mysteries of the sun, moon, and stars. We built pyramids that are still to this day a wonder of the world. In Egypt, we had a library five miles long bursting with knowledge of plants, animals, insects, astrology, medicine, and so on. People came from far and wide to study at our feet. The white man came and we civilized him and taught him the knowledge of self. But instead of using this knowledge for good, he used it to make weapons we had no defense for, 'cause we couldn't think that evilly. He was shrewd and cunning as he is evil. He has always been so—"

"What does that have to do with today, Preston?"

He continued. "When we were brought over here in shackles; men, women and child, they stripped us of our knowledge; gods, language, ancestry, body and belief. And any man who showed any signs of resistance was brutally slaughtered grotesquely and demonically; whipped, split in half while alive, burned alive, hanged, maimed, decapitated, dick cut off and shoved in orifices, women raped, babies sliced out stomachs, or slammed on the ground and stomped like bugs. You name it; these evil sons of bitches did it. So the minute we were born in this country, it was *you*," he pointed at Detra, "who taught us as a child to say…'Yessah Massa'. It was you, who begged us not to rebel, pleaded with us, 'cuz you knew the depths of the white man's evil. It was you, who had their babies and allowed their blond hair, blue-eyed children to suckle from your breast. And it was you who cleaned their houses, sewed their buttons on their clothes and wiped their asses—"

"Aw hell nah, niggah."

"Lemme finish!"

"Yeah Detra," said Five, now leaning forward on the couch chewing her fingernails. Preston scanned the living room. His eyes met with J'Neane's briefly before he spoke again. "And you were right when you begged us not to fight just yet, cuz in a head up battle with these crackers we'll never win, cuz they got our knowledge of self and replaced it with some bullshit. Furthermore, they're masters at war craft. That's what they live for. Every leader who has ever stood up to these devils, have been methodically assassinated, or rubbed out. Nat Turner, Toussaint L'overture, Marcus Garvey, Martin Luther King, Malcolm X, George L. Jackson, and so on. Any scholar will tell you that you cannot win by gunpoint or force alone with these people. They're entirely too shrewd and evil, they have too many weapons at their disposal: chemicals, poisons, toxins, germs, lasers, not to mention guns. They got shit you can't even imagine, Detra."

"So what the hell you gon' do...live on yo' knees? Why cain't you fight like the Palestinians or the Taliban?"

"Cuz I'ma mothafuckin' American! Didn't you say don't come with that Afrika Bambaataa shit? Besides, we were the ones who provided free labor, so this country could prosper. We fought in wars and contributed to the arts of this country. What the fuck I look like aiding the destruction of something we died and struggled so hard to survive in a country with the richest economy on the planet."

"So let me get this right, Preston. You give up. Are you satisfied being the white man's monkey?"

"You're misguided, Detra. I keep tellin' you that we can't win by just fighting physically. The only way we can rule this world again is if we inherit this country."

"Inherit this country. Niggah please. They ain't givin' this mothafucka up!"

"They have no choice. Ain't it a black president? Don't every other white dude you know love Eminem? Don't every white girl scream when Chris Brown dances? Imagine if all the thousands of men locked up in jail wake up out their slumber, educate themselves like Obama, started their own companies and raised their sons and daughters to do the same thing. Imagine if we bought property instead of tennis shoes and drugs. Imagine if we spent money solely with one another. That, Detra, would be a successful revolution, and we wouldn't lose a drop of blood. But those things take time, Detra, but we'll never get to that point if we hate each other."

Tears began to well up in Detra's eyes; her face was a mask of pain and confusion. Her bottom lip trembled as she croaked, "But can't you see, Preston, I don't hate y'all, I love y'all. I'm just tired of being hurt and dogged out."

Preston walked over and embraced her. She melted in his arms, bursting into tears. "It's gon' be alright Detra, we gon' get it together one day, one day soon." He kissed her forehead. It wasn't a dry eye in the room.

Chapter 16

"On Sitas bruh, you bet not hadda let none of day penitentiary shit stick on ya my niggah, cuz I'm tellin' ya right now, that bullshit don't work out here," said Kenzo behind a smirk, before embracing Preston; forearm to forearm, hands clenched tightly in steel-like grips, free hands clutching each other's backs. The energy flowing between them was intense and palpable. For several seconds, neither man released their grip.

"I missed you my, niggah," grunted Preston.

"Same here, bruh...you just don't know."

"Awww ain't dat sweet," called Aunt Paula from the upstairs window, overlooking the front yard. All the other ladies crowded the doorway; variations of smiles and happiness painted their expressions.

"'Sup A.P.?"

"Nothin' nephew, you just besta keep my lil man out of trouble, I know that much."

"You already know, Auntie."

The two men then waved at the ladies and rolled towards the Dodge Challenger and pulled off. Preston's eyes crawled over the car's console and interior; he put his fist to his lips and exclaimed in awe.

"Damn bruh, you got an iPad installed in this bitch, huh?"

"Fuck yeah, bruh-bruh the game is high tech nowadays! Niggahs is movin' and thinkin' at warp speeds;

only losers are out here winging it wit' ol' school beeper technology; and that's why they fuckin' losin'."

"Is this shit hard to operate, bruh? Shit looks like some *Star Trek* shit."

"Nah, bruh actually the operating system is fairly simple. You'll get the hang of it. It's yours anyway."

Preston's head pivoted, his eyebrows cinched.

"What's mines?"

"This whip and everything in it."

Preston turned his gaze straight ahead. Kenzo could hear his childhood friend's thoughts boom. Preston wrestled in his seat then said,

"Aye, blood, you don't owe a niggah nothin', knawmean?! I ain't did nothin' but what I was s'pose to do. Keep quiet, do my mothafuckin' time, walkin' slow and drinkin' a lot of water."

Suddenly, Kenzo skidded to a halt. Preston felt his heart quicken, and his testicles draw up, as their eyes collided.

"P, man, dead that bullshit! Niggahs ain't holdin' they water these days, you're the last of a dying breed. I mean you knocked down damn near a decade and ain't neva once asked me fo' shit. This here is the least I could do fo' you playboy."

Preston studied his comrade's face. Kenzo's nostrils flared, his eyes blazed with sincerity. They mugged each other, not for supremacy, but for camaraderie. In those few seconds bravado, trust, intellect, intuition and familiarity synergized; simultaneously each cracked a grin.

"And niggah, you betta not be boning Aunt Paula," quipped Kenzo.

"What? Getdafuckouttahere!"

"Yeah niggah," Kenzo said, putting the car in gear, nodding his head slightly, dipping his eyes at Preston conspiratorially. "I ain't stupid, cupid."

Preston shook his head and chuckled.

"As a matter of fact, you might as well drive and get used to this bitch."

"You ain't said nothin'."

They switched seats.

Cautious, initially, but quickly he reared in the car's power and wheeled through traffic confidently.

"So what you gon' do, bruh? I mean what you got up yo' sleeve now that ya out?"

"Zo, blood, I got a lot of shit I want to dabble in, but the first thing I wanna do is press up a couple of books I penned and move them shits, knawmean?"

"Is them shits good?"

"Man, my shit is fiya!"

Kenzo stroked his goatee, his face etched in deep thought.

"What they about?" asked Kenzo.

"'Bout a lot of shit, but basically I'm speakin' fo' niggahs who've been in the system and out here in the streets tryna figure this shit out and my novels, instead of preachin' to 'em, I help 'em see they way through it through characters they can relate to."

"That's wassup; I can see that, P. You've always had word play." Kenzo paused as if he was hit by a thought, then said, "P, if that's the case, you should like, record an album to go along with the book. That would be fuckin' ill!"

"Aw, niggah, you just want me to start back up rhymin' and shit."

"Yeah I do, but don't you think that would be a brilliant way to not only showcase both your talents but to cross promote and cross market yourself? I mean, I ain't read yo' book, but I ain't ran across a niggah hotter than you on the mic when you on ya shit, knawmean?"

"That rappin' shit is corny, blood."

"Look, P, it only became corny to us cuz we couldn't eat off day shit back in the days, and a starving rapper is like a pimp without a hoe. Just a niggah talkin' shit, knawmean? And yeah, these cheesy ass niggahs rappin' nowadays is corndogs and they skateboardin' and backpackin' and shit, but it's always gon' be street niggahs knawmean? And right now we got the scrilla, studio and technology to spit some real shit. I mean how you gon' speak fo' niggahs in the system and the streets if you don't voice yo' thoughts where they be at, cuz this hip-hop shit is where it's at."

"You shoulda been a fuckin' lawyer."

"I am; I appeal to bitches."

Preston croaked a laugh the triggered a rhyme session, where each matched the other's verse and rhyme.

"I'll peel ya bitch."

"I'll off, ya on switch."

"I'm fresh on da bricks."

"I got birds and cake mix."

"I spit goon tunes, they bend bars!"

"I got my money stacked so high my bitch can kiss the stars!"

"Ah niggah you been practicing," said Preston through a chuckle.

"Man, I tol' you I got a studio and some young hard hittas with beats in the clouds."

"Huh?"

"Tech talk, don't trip you'll catch on. But look where you stayin' at? Cuz like, you can't park this bitch on the sidewalk, knawmean, niggahs, breaking into shit like mad, nowadays."

Preston bit his lip, and said, "On some real shit, I don't even know blood."

"'Sup wit you and Marie?"

"Tssss...." Preston made a show of blowing air out his mouth as he stopped for a traffic light.

Kenzo desperately wanted to enlighten his comrade on the shit he'd been hearin' bout Marie, but he knew better than to be the bearer of bad news cuz niggahs tend to get mad at the messenger, and make excuses for the message.

"Well, bruh, I got some apartments where the studio is located, and you can occupy one of the empty units until you get on ya feet."

"Damn niggah. What, you been golfin' with Warren Buffet, my niggah? I see you invested ya doe wisely."

"Nah, P, actually I didn't. I blew through that shit, but it taught me how to appreciate money and make smart investments."

"I see," said Preston and pulled off as the light turned.

"Well blood whatever you want to do, I got you, but I hope you'll give this rap shit some thought. And here..." He passed Preston a knot of currency. "That's ten racks. That should help you publish ya books, or at least get started, knawmean?"

Preston held the money as though he was a trophy. It was the most he'd had to himself at one time. He was speechless.

"And don't think of no bozo, macho shit to say either, niggah! Here..." Kenzo grabbed the money and stuffed it in the glove compartment. "Just think of it as one of the car's features."

"I don't know what to say my niggah, knawmean?"

"Thank you would be just fine."

"One love, my niggah."

"It's nothin' to a boss! Aye and I'm serious about you boning A.P. too."

"Man, if you don't getdafuckouttahere..."

He dropped Kenzo back off at A.P.'s house and before he left, they kicked the bo-bo while Kenzo ran him through the car's features, specifically the iPad. Preston was blown away by the ingenuity of the device and the myriad of apps. Then finally, he was able to break loose from Five and pulled off, not before she kissed him dead in the mouth.

Oakland, California is a beautiful multi-cultural city and for the first time in his life, he viewed it as a tourist. So many things had changed: stores had closed only to be replaced by others. Apartments had been remodeled and whole neighborhoods had been re-gentrified. He made his way to Lake Merritt, the necklace of lights surrounding the water was breathtaking and couples strolled, while others jogged. He hit the I-580 freeway going eastbound, staying out the fast lane, and his head nodded to Musiq Soulchild. He exited on Seminary Avenue and pushed towards the Eastmont Mall. He had fond memories of the mall as a kid, especially when he'd sneak out the house and watch the sideshows, niggahs wildin' out, peelin' rubber, goin' dumb, but now the city had the streets all jacked the fuck up.

"No wonder why everybody's movin'"" he mused, "this ain't even the same."

Nevertheless, it still felt good to be free. He hit the freeway again and jetted towards Hayward, exiting on 164th Avenue and pulled behind a car, entering Marie's complex.

Perfect timing, he thought.

He slid into a stall facing Marie's apartment and then dialed her number; after a few rings she picked up.

"Hey babe," she sounded funny, somewhat disheveled. He was always in tune with her moods; that's what love does. When you love someone, the slightest eye blink can speak volumes.

"Aye wassup?" his reply was probing, to say the least.

"Um....I've been callin' all day."

160

"Yeah I know, but I'm just gettin' the hang of this phone, plus I've been handlin' some business."

"Hmmmph. I bet."

"But look, I'm on my way."

"When?"

Her voice was a little too high pitched, he told himself.

"'Bout thirty minutes. Why, you busy or somethin'?"

"Naw, just wanna get ready."

"Izat right?"

"Yeah."

"Aiiiight, see ya in a minute."

"'Kay babe, I love you."

"Love...yeah, I'll see you too."

He ended the call and waited. Two minutes later, her front door opened and the youngsta scurried out, his face still battered, and a bandaid under his eye. Preston's own face dropped and he felt like he'd been run over. He began to sweat and his heart thumped wildly. "Stupid bitch!" he ranted, enraged. He slammed his fist on the steering wheel in disgust, before sending a text message.

"LOOK OUT YO WINDOW!"

He saw the curtains move. He waved his hands, and he could see her hand cover her mouth. He fired off another text. "AND U WONDER Y WE CALL U BITCH!"

He pulled off slow, the Challenger's speakers pumpin' Lauryn Hill's "Ex-Factor.

BOOK II
ON TO THE NEXT ONE.....

Chapter 17

"Niggah, you know I don't smoke, so don't pass that shit my way no mo'!" barked Kenzo at his artist FreshKidd.

FreshKidd held the potent marijuana cloud in his lings, casually brushing off Kenzo's admonishment, then blew a feather of smoke in the air; his eyes sparkled and his face flashed a mischievous grin.

"Zo-ski," he teased, "bruh, what you got against this here cannabis? I mean the Most High made this shit to grow wild fo' niggahs like us can stay high and fly."

He drew on the blunt again; the spliff's cherry glowed, as he inhaled deeply.

FreshKidd got his lungs good and tight, and thumped ashes in an empty Patrón bottle, before barking off a few coughs. Gathering himself, he glanced at the blunt, making a show of holding the remaining cloud of smoke in his lungs, he croaked, "This shit is one step beyond bomb."

Kenzo shook his head. It was hard to remain upset with FreshKidd. He was one of those happy-go-lucky types: handsome, charming, and talented without trying, who assumed everything should just naturally go his way. Why? According to him, because he was born to be fly and after an hour in his presence, you'd forget all about your troubles and float away with him.

Watching them closely were Kenzo's uber producers, Drixxx and Kobain. Their talent was off the charts and he was convinced that they were the future of hip-hop. Drixxx was a rugged pretty boy, with cornflower blue eyes and wild blond hair hanging halfway down his back. He looked like a rock star, but was one hundred percent hip-hop. A former child prodigy gone rebel, he had ridiculous skills as a violinist, the bass guitar, acoustic guitar, and classical piano, all of which he channeled into hip-hop; creating extraordinary tracks. What made his beats unique was his penchant for stitching Jimi Hendrix guitar licks with horn stabs and organ chords, then magically infusing it with Doctor Dre-esque heavy bass laden kick drums. The shit was hypnotic. However, it was his sidekick Kobain's mixes and mastering process that twisted the confluence into a stupid dope beat. Kobain himself was a quiet, eccentric, bi-racial cat with hazel eyes and long reddish-blondish auburn colored dreads that he was always flinging out his face. He was so off key that Kenzo thought he might be a little touched. Nonetheless, no one could doubt his mastery of computer software and hardware. He could build anything you could imagine. Often times, Kobain would stay up for sometimes three straight days, taking apart some computer part or studio equipment. He'd even built a toy train that zoomed around the studio walls, behind a Plexiglas tunnel, as soon as a beat dropped; it even blew real marijuana smoke out the engine's valves and pipes, FreshKidd's suggestion of course, either way, the dude was vicious with his hands and imagination. He and Drixxx migrated down to Cali from Seattle together and Kenzo met the two young men at the Bay Area Music Producers' convention. Kenzo listened to a CD of their productions and immediately signed them to Liquid Beats, his production company.

At the time, FreshKidd was the hottest MC in the Bay Area, widely known for killin' shit on heavily circulated mixtapes. He signed FreshKidd and he turned out to be the perfect match for Mystic Soul Rock, Drixxx and Kobain's production title. Kenzo felt confident that that it was only a matter of time before they kicked in the door. However, he was prudently waiting to seize the moment because the music industry was in a challenging time and no one really knew how and where the game was gonna go once CD's were phased out. Yet he was able to drop a CD, showcasing FreshKidd just to test the waters, additionally now that Preston was home, he had other options in mind.

However, right now, his attention was focused on FreshKidd's shenanigans. FreshKidd was Polo down as usual, rockin' a pair of black, patent leather, Giuseppe Zanotti tennis shoes and a head full of silky curls, accentuated by a crisp razor line and ice pick sideburns. Kenzo grinned, displaying his diamond-laden grill, then said, "Ya know, FreshKidd, it was a time when ya boy caressed those same thoughts mentally, and I used to blow like a broke stove. But once I started gettin' these chips…" he paused and placed a wad of dead presidents on the table; the money fanned then the ends kicked up like the legs of a dead cockroach. His artist's eyes widened. Kenzo continued, "Then I learned that you got to keep proper maintenance on yo' cash flow or it will dry up."

His eyes panned the studio. "You see all this equipment in here? This shit didn't come out a box of Cracker Jacks; I had to jack crackers! No pun intended,

Drixxx," he added. "I literally had to throw rocks at the fuckin' penitentiary to build this shit you so easily blow dro in. And I never want to feel that fuckin' hopeless again. So I got to stay conscious, stay on my nickels: counting beans, mending seams, knawmean? Cuz keeping money is more important, than getting money."

"Zo-ski I hear ya, I hear ya. But what that gots ta do with this here hemp-tation?" said FreshKidd sarcastically, before blowing out a plume of hemp fog.

"As usual, that went over your head and under ya feet, so let me break this shit down to you so it can fit in ya bowl." He pointed at FreshKidd's head, and then said, "Ya see, FreshKidd, I got investments, ya dig? Which I call passive income."

FreshKidd's eyebrows arched, signaling he was lost.

"That basically means I get money while I'm sleeping and at my leisure, but not at my laziness. Shit like," he opened his arms wide, "this place and others, i.e. real estate, as well as vending routes, a diversified stock portfolio, and some mo' shit. But just cuz it's passive don't mean a niggah can disregard it. It's like cooking, if you don't check on ya dough, ya cookies will burn up on ya. And see that weed keeps a niggah lazy, laughin' wit da munchies; always forgettin' this and that. And most catz that smoke, start from the moment they wake up."

He turned his gaze exclusively towards FreshKidd, who smiled.

"So, while ya high, lackadaisical, feelin' good, stuffin' ya mouth with a giant burger; it's niggahs starvin' tryna cut you in the line, or out the line; it don't matter to them, as long as they take yo' position. Then ya got niggahs out here refocused, patrolling dey position, bar none. And I'm one of them niggahs."

Drixxx and Kobain glanced at FreshKidd. He shrugged unfazed.

"That's why you're the boss."

"Don't you forget it, either."

They laughed.

At that moment, the buzzer rang. Kobain hit the controls and the Swann security cameras flashed the front entrance on the monitor above them. It was Ramona and Cocoa. Kobain looked towards Kenzo.

"Buzz 'em in, Ko."

A moment later, Ramona pushed in with Cocoa in tow, both donning skintight jeans. Immediately, they made their way towards Kenzo and smothered him with kisses. He wiped his face.

"Awww, hell to-the-naw, y'all up to something coming here double teaming me, huh?"

Their eyes gleamed naughtily as Cocoa glanced at Ramona and they smiled. Ramona led off. "Baby, we just wanna go shoppin' and—"

"I knew it! Y'all ain't slick. How much?"

Ramona curved her fingers, forming a "C" as thick as a double cheeseburger, and said, "'Bout that much."

"Y'all got me fucked up!"

They pouted simultaneously, then Ramona nodded at Cocoa, who sashayed her thick ass over to him and handed over a large loaf of cash. He smiled and stroked his goatee.

"It ain't gon' hurt none, daddy, I've been bustin' moves fo' us," purred Cocoa.

The boys in the studio watched in sheer awe as Kenzo struggled to put the loaf in his pockets; he then handed the lovely ladies the wad of money languishing on the table.

"A'iiight here, and don't buy no shit ya just gon' leave decorating the closets."

"Daddy, you fo'got the Neo-soul fest is at the Concord Pavillion this weekend and we already got tickets," said Ramona.

"I ain't forgot nothin'!" he snapped.

"My bad, daddy, we just reminding you so it won't be no last minute stuff on our part," said Ramona, switching directions.

"That's wassup. Just make sure you get that lingerie I picked fo' y'all."

"Fa sho, daddy," said Ramona.

"But look y'all, we havin' a lil meeting...I'll be home in a minute."

"'Kay daddy", said Ramona and kissed him good-bye, then Cocoa followed suit.

"Bye FreshKidd," cooed Ramona. He blushed. She pinched his cheeks then said, "'Sup Ko and Drixxx."

Kobain nodded and Drixxx cast a goofy smile.

"A'iiight now, go on fo' these catz get all discombobulated."

They waved and were off. When the doors closed behind them, Kenzo ice grilled his face; he knew all eyes would be on him. Sure enough, the boys eyed him for a second until FreshKidd said, "How in the fuck do you do it? I mean, fuck, G, they ain't jealous of each other or nothin'."

"Yeah man, how do you do it?" Drixxx added.

"It's G-14 classified, my niggahs."

"Aw come on man," they chimed together.

Kenzo stroked his goatee. "The game is to be sold not told, so before I tell it, I'm under oath to sell it!" He stuck his hand out. "Hunnid dollars apiece and I'll give you the game."

"Awwww man, we're ya artists," whined Drixxx.

"I wouldn't care if you was my sons. If I don't charge you, you won't appreciate it. And I can't let the game gods down, so if you wanna hear it, cash me out."

Drixxx reluctantly handed over a hundred, and so did FreshKidd. Kobain just stared at him.

"That means you too, Yellowboybronze!"

Kobain made a weird ass face, folded his arms across his chest and looked up at the ceiling.

"Here Zo, I'll pay it for him, bro," said Drixxx.

Kenzo tucked away the money and cleared his throat. The boys leaned closer. "Now peep game and check play. First and foremost, ya gots ta have ya own spot. You can't be living with no chick and expect to call the shots, at least, the shots that count. Ya money and living arrangements gotsta be on point. Knawmean?"

They nodded.

"Then ya gotsta cop you that one chick, and she gotsta be the right one, not the *Ms. SuperindependentIdon'tneedanniggah* type chick. She ain't gon' do. It gotta be that one chick who's willing to follow yo' lead. You know, like that one chick you run into that's down to do anything to be with you, and it don't hurt if she's into other chicks, feel me? We all get one of those from time to time."

"Yeah I get them a lot, but I shake 'em," said FreshKidd.

"Then that's yo' bad! Those are the diamonds. I mean, why go chase after the ultra-high maintenance chicks and field all them goddamned headaches and BS that come with 'em? Knawmean!"

He paused and watched them soak his game up.

"Look at all those professional ball players, marrying these chicks, knowing damn well they gon' cheat. How can they not when you got super bad bitches on you in every fuckin' city? Then when they get caught, these chumps gotsta give up half they money and walk on eggshells just to see they kids, while Joe Blow is slam dunkin' her pussy in the house they bought. Fuck kinda shit is that? Knawmean?"

"You can say that again," Kobain mumbled. Drixxx and FreshKidd nodded in agreement. Kenzo popped his P's again.

"Look at the divorce rate 'round this bitch, fifty mothafuckin' percent! That means that America's widely accepted model for the purpose of bonding man with woman, only works half of the time. In other words, it's hit and miss. That said, I got to explore other options knawmean? Cuz ya see, after the cum and sweat dry up, after the honeymoon, ya got to have something else to hold ya together." He paused to correlate his thoughts, and then proceeded. "But look, I didn't mean to digress, so back to the main point. Ya got to have ya own spot, knawmean?"

They nodded.

"And you get that one chick that's down fo' whatever, right?"

Head nods all around.

"Okay, now you on point. But ya really gotsta love lil mama, and I mean she gotsta be one hundred percent convinced in yo' love."

"That's why ya get married, right?" said Drixxx quizzically.

"Hell naw! Why buy the damn cow, when ya get the milk fa free? Gettin' married is a whole 'nother level. And that's what them ball playas get it twisted."

They laughed.

"I'm serious though; you can show a woman you really care, without giving her one of yo' balls, knawmean?"

"Like what?" asked FreshKidd.

"Man, like you can get a tattoo, buy her some diamonds, take her someplace special. All the shit. But the worst thang you can do is enter an agreement ya know ya ain't gon' keep. Just think about it y'all. You, ya moms, pops and ya best man and her moms, pops, family get together with a representative of God and y'all make this vow, say oaths to do x, y, and z 'til death do you part. I mean, do you realize what kind of commitment that is?"

"Yeah one that works only half the time," said Kobain.

Everybody looked at him. He shrugged.

"Boy, you quiet as hell, but when you speak, you always say some real shit."

Kobain scowled and flung a couple dreads out his face. Kenzo just shook his head.

"Okay, so how do you get 'em to agree to stay together under one roof?" asked FreshKidd.

"The truth, that's how! Just like the Mormons, Muslims, and other religions that have a far better percentage rate than monogamy. Straight the fuck up. I come like this: 'Look lil mama, I'm gon' keep it one hunnid with you. I gots some work I want to bring into the family that will benefit the both of us. And instead of sneaking behind ya back, I'd rather bring it to the table, knawmean?'"

"That's it?" said FreshKidd incredulously.

"Nah, niggah that ain't it! Pump ya brakes and feel my flow. Now of course, she's gonna balk, squawk, and try to twist her way out of it. But ya gotta remember, she's in yo' shit, and she really loves you. So you got to reason with her, and allow yo' game to cook on her—"

"For instance?" interjected Drixxx.

"For instance, like, 'Look lil mama, first and foremost yo' know how a niggah was movin' when we got together, and these movements puts me in position to where I need assistance to get these chips out here, knawmean? But whatever I do, I do it fo the both of us. In other words, if a bitch is cashin' me out, she's cashin' you out. And as long as you overstand that it's me and you against a bitch, and not me and a bitch against you, you should never feel threatened or insecure 'bout no bitch. Knawmean, you're my queen.'"

"What happens when she says, 'If I'm your queen, why do we need anybody else'?" inquired FreshKidd.

"That's when you let her know that there are just some things queens are too valuable to participate in, and further, the chicks gon' be for her benefit as well and these are the type of perks that come with being my queen. But bottom line, you got to put ya foot down, ain't no way out! Yet at the same time, ya let her know that it's only a temporary arrangement. Which ya ain't lying, nothing is forever, but you tell lil mama if it ain't cool, you'll get rid of her. I mean, if they really ain't compatible, ya dig?"

"We with ya, maine," said FreshKidd.,

"Okay, listen close, cuz this is the most important."

They came closer. Kenzo sported an ultra-serious expression and glanced into each of his pupils' eyes. Only Kobain was halfway there, his mind was always working in a distant planet.

"This is real game I'm 'bout to drop, it might seem trivial, but once you analyze it, you'll realize the significance, but it prolly won't be 'til later in life, knawmean?"

They nodded.

"Peep, ya gotta understand that there is a natural hierarchy in women, just like in men. For example, you got the Alpha Male. The top dawg, then ya got the lieutenant, and then the private. Gold, silver, and bronze. Knawmean? Same thing with women, and you got to know what type of woman you got. Cuz she definitely knows her rank in a room full of women. But it's hard to figure out where the opposite sex ranks in the hierarchy, if you ain't lookin' fo' it."

"Why should you worry where ya girl ranks?" asked Drixxx curiously.

"Cuz if ya try to bring in a chick who's stronger mentally then yo' queen, she's gon' try to take over and it's gon' always be some bullshit. It's like bringing a bully into a room full of punks. He gon' take they lunch money the minute he peeps they steelo."

"Riiight," said FreshKidd, "she gon' try to take the queen position."

"Abso-fuckin-lutely! And see, a lot of times, we be so busy lookin' at the ass and tits that we neglect to see what's under the hood, knawmean? And ya can't have a chick coming in that can muscle ya queen out her position physically or mentally, or the arrangement won't last a day."

"So let me get this straight," quizzed Drixxx, "the chick that's coming into the castle has to be subservient to the queen?"

"Precisely."

"And how do you figure that out? I mean how you know if ya prospect is subservient?" posed FreshKidd.

"Observation...gauging whether she's the dominant female in her immediate group, family or friends. I mean ya just can't walk up to a chick and try to bring 'em home day one. It's a process of peeping her out. Does her friends and family kowtow to her or is she the flunky? Does she call the shots or get shots called on her?"

"Oh, I see!" exclaimed Drixxx.

"And it doesn't hurt if she's down on her luck, and of course into women, but definitely don't bring no bossy, independent, supreme, used up ass broad to ya castle."

FreshKidd began to rub his hands together then said, "The chain of command under the commander! That's what the fuck I'm talkin' 'bout maine."

Drixxx added, "But Zo, I'm not street like that. I don't run no game on a chick bro. It won't work with me."

"You'd be surprised, Drixxx. I mean, you're a handsome dude. No homo! And ya 'bout to be a star. Just be up front with yo' girl. You'd be surprised, I'm tellin' you."

"A'iiight. One last thing, Zo-ski. Like do you have problems, like, after she moves in?" asked FreshKidd.

"All the time, lil bruh. Always lil shit. That's why you got to lay down the law on ya new prospect comin' in. Fo' instance, ya queen always sits in the front seat with you, she always first at everything, and you can't ever mix it up. Cuz you don't want to blow ya queen, knawmean? And believe me, the new chick is gon' test ya pimpin', so ya got to always back ya queen's play."

"So where do you find the new chick?" asked Kobain.

"Shiiiit, she might just find you in these days and times. Or ya queen may find her. But all ya got to do is keep it one hunnid with every chick you meet, and yeah, a lot of 'em will pass, but you kept it one hunnid so she gon' respect your G. And once you know what to look for, your percentages will rise dramatically. Shit, the chick that passed might tell her friend and her friend will be like 'Where he at?' Knawmean? Just keep it one hunnit y'all and if the chick ain't wit' it, she can keep it movin'; but I guarantee somebody gon' bite. Ya see how I'm living..."

"That's wassup," they all chimed.

"Man...that was a hundred bucks well spent. I'm 'bout to write a song to that," said FreshKidd excitedly.

"Niggah, don't give this game away free!" snapped Kenzo.

"I ain't Zo-ski, they buying the song, knawmean?"

Kenzo chuckled. "I guess ya got me there. Kobain, run that new track. We got a new topic to write about."

Chapter 18

"Your background; it ain't squeaky clean, but sometimes we all got to swim upstream."
-"Long Walk" - Jill Scott

As he stood over her, his eyes kept drifting towards her tantalizing cleavage. J'Neane thumbed through the manuscript, carefully adjusting the Post-it notes she'd sprinkled throughout it. With every movement, her huge breasts shimmied. He forced himself to look away, and then said, "So um, what do you think? Trash it or shred it?"

She raised the glasses from her face; she was all business-like. Yet even in her reading glasses, she was as sexy as she wanted to be, which made her all the more attractive. Professional, intelligent, and sexy: *wifey material*!

"Preston," she said crisply, "this one is better than the first one."

Oh shit, I bombed, he thought.

"But can I tell you something that I and readers don't like?"

"Shoot."

"You do not have to over explain everything, let the story flow, and allow the characters to tell the story more than you. Understand?"

He winced inwardly.

Then she made eye contact and brightened. "But it's really good and I'm truly, truly impressed."

"Wh-what…you are?"

"Yes. In certain areas you really nailed it, and it's amazing how you channeled those emotions on paper."

He was flushed with relief.

"Did you ever finish high school?"

"Nah."

"Ever take a writing course?"

"Nah."

She exhaled sharply. "Ummph...ummph...umph, that just don't make no sense. You guys have so much talent!"

"So you're gonna edit it for me?"

"I certainly am."

"Cool," he said enthusiastically. "Aye look, whatever it cost, I got the money don't trip, as a matter of fact..." He pulled five crispy bills from his wallet. "Will five hundred be enough to start?"

She placed the bills on the desk.

"Look Preston, I'll do a copy and content edit on both books for fifteen hundred; far below my usual rates. But this isn't about the money; I just want to see you succeed, because reading your work gave me a closer look at your struggle..." J'Neane stood up and hugged him, and said warmly, "I'm just so proud of you, because so many men go to prison and become hardened." She released him and he saw that her eyes were misty.

He felt awkward; almost uncomfortable. He'd forgotten how it felt to be cared for on this level. He blushed like a kid.

She gazed into his eyes and said,

"When you become a writer, a good writer, you dive into your inner self and fish pearls of your innermost thoughts and reel them to life, and the way you articulate these thoughts, tells a lot about you as an individual. And it just amazes me that under the strain and oppression of having your freedom stripped away and being surrounded by so much hate, ignorance, and ill will, that you were able to be, and think so positively..."

He lowered his eyelids. "You know, J'Neane, I never even thought about it. I just knew I had a higher calling and prison wasn't a place I ever wanted to be again. So I lost myself in a dream of becoming a writer."

"I know it's palpable in the fabric of your writing..."

At that moment, Preston found himself zooming in on her lightly glazed full lips, and then her pretty almond shaped brown eyes. She noticed and primped her hair.

"What? Is something wrong?"

"Nah, it's..." he paused and took a deep breath, "it's just that I always envisioned somebody reading my work and not only enjoying it, but also understanding where I was coming from. I just never thought they'd be as caring and beautiful as you are."

She batted her eyes and placed her hand on her chest. "Oh flattery. Tell me more."

He pulled her close, hands caressing her soft curvaceous hips, and kissed her passionately. She went limp, before gently pushing him away.

"Whew. Stop that now, before it gets too hot in here," she said, fanning her face.

Suddenly a door slammed. A thump, and ruffling followed. "Mama!" yelled a female voice. "Whose car is that? It's hurtin' 'em out here."

"Excuse me," said J'Neane, and segued into motherhood.

"J'Nae, I'm busy right now, hon!" shouted J'Neane.

"Mama, Stephanie Tyler tried to step to me like she all that! Nobody want her ol' pootbutt boyfriend and his stink bomb breath!"

J'Neane and Preston exchanged glances then shook with laughter.

"Teenage tornado, a handful," whispered J'Neane, and then called out, "I have company, J'Nae."

"Oops, my bad."

Seconds later, J'Nae strutted in her mother's office, but stopped dead in her tracks when her eyes fell upon Preston.

"J'Nae honey, I'm with a client right now, okay? And pick up your mouth on the way out the door," she said sweetly, restraining her irritation. At fourteen, J'Nae was full-figured; all curves and hips. Like ta-dow!

She kissed her mother on both cheeks. J'Neane rolled her eyes.

"I love you, Mama."

"Love you, too."

J'Nae cut her eyes towards Preston.

"Mama, who is that?" she asked flirtatiously, head cocked, hands on hips.

"J'Nae," said J'Neane sternly, "don't make me get ignorant."

J'Nae sucked her teeth. "Dang Mama, you always bustin' me out, shoo!" said J'Nae and stomped out the room, mumbling something undecipherable under her breath.

J'Neane called out after her. "How 'bout you bustin' dem suds and dem books! Homework. Dishes. In no particular order, sweetie. Thanks."

Preston smiled, he loved the way black women worked their many hats with style, flair, and fortitude.

J'Neane winked her eye at Preston. "Okay now, where were we?"

"Uh, we were talkin' about the edit."

"Right. Now look, we'll meet every Friday to discuss the developments. In the meantime, you'll need to set up a Twitter and Facebook account. It's all about social media now; you'll need to develop a fan base and connect with readers."

"Yeah, I've been reading *Publisher's Weekly* and *Black Enterprise* and they all say that it's very important."

"Yes it is. But you'll have no problem, you're handsome and witty."

"Thank you."

"Oh, dammit," piped J'Neane, glancing at her watch.

"What's wrong?"

"I have a client scheduled in ten minutes and I haven't even looked at their material."

"Well, let me let you go then."

"Okay, I'll walk you to the car."

They proceeded through the living room. J'Nae had her homework spread out before her. She gave him a seductive wave. He smiled and threw up a deuce. Behind him, J'Neane scowled and J'Nae ducked her head back in her books.

At his car, he gave her a quick peck on her cheek and climbed in, and lowered the window.

"J'Neane, I appreciate you taking on this project; I know it needs work."

"Don't worry; it only needs minor cosmetic adjustments. Just watch how I polish it up and make the dialogue pop right off the pages. Trust me; I'm good at what I do."

He smiled into her eyes and said, "What else are you good at?"

"Wouldn't you like to know..." she purred and turned around and gave him her best sexy mama walk. At the last second, she glanced over her shoulder seductively. He made a show of biting his fist.

"Boyyy, please!" she said and waved him off.

He drove off with J'Neane heavy on his mind. *Now that's a real woman!*

Next, he activated the car's audio system and the instrumentals Kenzo gave him to write to pumped out the speakers. He bobbed his head; fingers strumming the steering wheel. The beat was crazy! The organ chords and guitar licks were mesmerizing. A euphoria-like sensation washed over him, creating something like a rebirth. It was all coming back. He started throwing rhymes in the air and they fell on the beat like snowflakes on Christmas. As he drove he freestyled, spittin' couplet after couplet, crushing his thoughts into dope verse after dope verse, followed by witty punchline after witty punchline. The beat stopped briefly, but he kept bustin' like a Tommy gun surging into the next beat. His adrenaline rushed through his veins like jet fuel, when he was done; he'd driven halfway across town without realizing. He glanced into the rearview mirror and thought; *maybe I will bless the mic again...*

Chapter 19

The summer breeze was just a slight tickle as the Cali sunshine flexed its golden muscles. J'Nae felt the warm sunrays on her latte-colored face, as she stepped outside her modest three-bedroom home in Oakland's middle class Fruitvale District. The block was adorned with well-kept homes of honest, hardworking, African-Americans and a sprinkle of Hispanics. Just a few blocks away resided several eyesore housing projects, whose residents frequently utilized J'Nae's street as a gateway to their drug dealing and knavishness, forcing the neighborhood to band together and stay alert.

J'Nae, dressed in her favorite pair of boy shorts, accentuating her young, glowing, shapely assets, bounced and shimmied towards their car to retrieve her mother's book bag from the trunk. Just as she twisted the key, a shout pierced the air.

"Hey blubber butt! Drop it like it's hot!"

She sucked her teeth. It wasn't anybody but Baby Ray, the neighborhood menace. She spun around and watched him in the street, poppin' wheelies with a snide smirk on his face. His crime partner was behind him, launching his dirt bike from the curb into the air before whirling his bike around, skidding impressively to a stop five feet away from J'Nae.

"Hi, J'Nae. Whatcha doin'?" he said, flashing a devilish smile.

"'Sup Carl, with yo' fine self."

He ate it up and blushed. Baby Ray came skidding his bike to a halt next to Carl, grinning impishly. J'Nae rolled her eyes. Baby Ray was eight years old and spoiled rotten. Mrs. Lacey, his grandmother, gave him everything he wanted and refused to believe he was capable of anything more than minor mischief. However, the boy was a fledgling terror, always trying to tag along with the rough project boys up the ways.

"Hey dooky-booty, make it clap," piped Baby Ray, elbows cocked out to the sides, ready to peddle off quickly at a second's notice. J'Nae squinted her eyes at him, then burst into a seductive smile, and said, "Dang, Baby Ray why you be gettin' at me like that? I thought you was my lil boyfriend," cooed J'Nae ostensibly.

He winked at his sidekick as if to say *I tol' ya*, then stuck out his little chest and pretended to pop his collar. "I'm cool on you now. I gots me another girlfriend."

"What...who? Unt-uhn, Baby Ray," said J'Nae, screwing her face in fake displeasure.

"Yep, and she look way better than you too."

"That's messed up, Baby Ray. I was gon' show you my new tattoo."

"Girl," he shooed her away, "nobody wanna see yo' stinkin' tattoo!"

"Uh huh," she said syrupy, "it's right here," and turned around, pulling away the tight elastic of her waistband.

Baby Ray and Carl exchanged wide-eyed glances. He stretched his little neck and said, "Lemme see then."

"Unt-uhn, not out here on front street; come over here by the car, this ain't everybody business, lil daddy."

He glanced at Carl suspiciously. Carl nudged his chin up, like, *go ahead, fool.*

Baby Ray got off his bike, and pimp daddy'd his way towards J'Nae, and they went around the side of the car. Head ducked down low, Carl rolled his bike into view, just as J'Nae leaned against the car and eased down her shorts.

"You see it, Baby Ray?"

"I don' see nothing."

J'Nae clicked her tongue. "Boyyyyyy, it's right there."

Baby Ray squatted a little closer and leaned his head in some. Just then, J'Nae reached back and grabbed his head, mashing it against her wiggling buttocks, while she ripped a loud, wet fart.

"Lemme go!" screamed Baby Ray.

"You see it now little punk! Ahhhhh...how ' bout that, fart face!" she said, stuffing his nose between her crack.

Carl bent over and laughed hysterically then jumped on his bike and peddled off, howling, "Baby Ray got the dooky's y'all!"

He hit a wheelie, and then piped, "Dooky Ray!"

Finally, she released his little head, and stepped back and grinned. He was hyperventilating, his little fist balled at his sides. He trembled in anger. J'Nae put her hands on her hips and said, "Awwww, Baby Ray. You mad?"

Baby Ray's bottom lip jutted forward, and tears squeezed out the corners of his eyes and he wailed, "You fat bitch! I'ma tell on you!"

"Go ahead, fart face."

At that moment, four neighborhood kids pulled up on bikes, chanting, "Dooky Ray! Dooky Ray!"

Baby Ray whirled around and spat, "Shut up! My name ain't no Dooky Ray!"

"Yeah it is!" said one of the more malicious kids, as he pointed towards Baby Ray. "Ya got a wet dooky stain on ya face, huh y'all?"

"Ugggh, he sho' do!" they chimed and then peddled off, yelling, "Dooky Ray! Dooky Ray!"

"I'ma beat yo' ass, Carl, watch!" screamed Baby Ray before running to J'Nae's house to bang furiously on the front door.

J'Neane came out fast with a look of concern painting her face; she looked down and saw Baby Ray boohooing relentlessly. She bent down and hugged him.

"Wassamatter, Baby Ray?" she said, motherly like.

He sniffled uncontrollably, wheezing so hard, he couldn't get it out.

"Calm down now and tell me what happened."

He tried to speak, while wiping his eyes with the back of his hands.

"He out here callin' people bitches, Mama!" snapped J'Nae.

"What you do to this boy, J'Nae?"

"I didn't do nothin'."

"Ye-ye-yes she did!" croaked Baby Ray.

"What she do, baby?"

"Sh-she farted in my face."

J'Neane had to turn her face to hide her laughter. Somehow, she found her voice and said, "J'Nae, did you fart on this chile?"

"Heck naw, Mama, he just lying," said J'Nae, barley containing a smirk.

"Uh-huh, now the kids callin' me Dooky Ray," he cried.

"Get in this house right now, J'Nae!" scolded J'Neane.

However, J'Nae knew she wasn't upset, they had their secret codes down pact. "Dang Mama, shooo, he lyin'!" spat J'Nae and eased by her mother, lifting her shoulder instinctively and defensively as she went into the house.

J'Neane gave J'Nae the eye and then bent back down to hug Baby Ray.

"Don't worry, Ms. J'Neane gon' take care of it."

J'Neane looked up to see Preston walking towards them.

"'Sup J'Neane, everything, everything?" asked Preston.

"Yeah, J'Nae just pickin' on my baby."

"Ain't nobody pickin' on him, he shouldn't be calling people out dey names, shoo!" yelled J'Nae from inside the house.

"Hush it fo' I bust it, J'Nae!" snapped J'Neane over her shoulder. Then she reached into her pocket and pulled out a few dollars and put it in Baby Ray's hand. "Here baby, go buy you something."

"Thank you, Ms. J'Neane."

"And wipe your face, baby."

He lifted the bottom of his shirt and wiped his face before running to his bike and peddling off.

"Yeah Carl," he shouted, "I'ma get you punk, and you betta not ask fo' none of my ice cream either!"

Chapter 20

It just so happened that T.G.I. Friday's was the restaurant of choice for their Friday meetings. Three months had flown by like a bullet train and J'Neane was just about complete with the edits; so much so, that this meeting, for all intents and purposes, was basically a quasi-date. As usual, the posh restaurant was bristling with activity; ballers, ball players, corporate execs and payday playas, accompanied by divas, professional eye candy, well-to-do hood rats, and gold diggers alike, all stylin' and / or posturing. At their favorite table, J'Neane nibbled on her salad and watched Preston devour a plate of tiger prawns, when a cute petite waitress approached for the umpteenth time; her eyes sparkled with obvious interest, clearly on Preston.

"Can I get you anything else?"

Preston flashed the dimple.

Why does he always have to show off that one funky dimple? thought J'Neane.

"Yeah, as a matter of fact, can you bring me another bottle of Tabasco sauce? This one seems to be just about empty," said Preston, handing over the near empty bottle.

"Sure. I'll be right back," she said, extra bubbly and spun off without bothering to address J'Neane. If J'Neane's eyes had been guns, the vivacious waitress would have had more holes in her than Swiss cheese. *Skinny ho!*

"Excuse me, wait bitch. I mean waitress!"

"Oh, I'm sorry. Can I get you anything ma'am?"

"Yes, Ms. Thang," said J'Neane snidely, "You can either get us another waitress or the manager. Thanks."

The waitress rolled her neck with a stank expression twisted on her face. J'Neane fired back with that "Girrrrrl, you know you don't want it", look, as the waitress smartly sized up the situation and scurried off.

Preston munched away, with smiling eyes.

J'Neane took a deep breath, and then rolled her eyes. "Preston, it isn't funny."

"Whaa?" he said, mouth full of prawns.

"Every time we come here, that lil tramp does that shit, and you just think it's so cute."

He chewed his food down and washed it back with water. Struggling in vain against the smirk on his face, he then said, "The only thing I think is cute is you."

"Whatever, Preston."

"But you do be goin' hard on skinny chicks, J, admit it."

She couldn't help but laugh, because he was on point. She said, "Preston, you don't understand; sistah-girl ain't never been a skinny minnie. I've been voluptuous..." she smiled and wiggled sexy-like in her seat, "And I swear, it's always the lil broomstick built tramps tryna run up on my man."

"So I'm ya man?"

"You is if you havin' dinner with me!"

"Thanks for the verbal memo."

"Whatever. I'm serious, Preston. That shit just, eeewww, it irks me when they do that shit."

"I think she realized that and cut her losses."

The new waitress walked up, her eyes gleaming.

"Tabasco sauce."

"Thank you," said Preston.

She stayed an extra second, and her body language rang like a church bell. J'Neane bugged her eyes out and the waitress spun off, tossing her ass this way and that way. Preston forced himself not to look.

"Umm-mmph... that must be that tramp's friend. Preston, we're not coming here no damn more!" snarled J'Neane, eyes following the departing waitress.

He reached across the table and caressed her hand, then stole her eyes and said, "Forget about them, focus on me. Knawmean? You said you had some questions you wanted to ask, now's the time."

At that moment, the restaurant slowly ceased to exist; his hands were strong and warm, and they sent chills down her spine. She stuck the tip of her finger in her mouth and threw him a provocative pose, then said, "Okay, let's see...ummm, what's your sign?"

"Gemini."

"The twins, huh? Two personalities."

"Somethin' like that."

"Which one should I trust?"

"Both."

"Why?"

"Cuz I say what I mean, and mean what I say. I and I. Get it? Twins..."

"I guess..." she smirked.

He grinned and loosened up some.

"What's your favorite book?"

"The Count of Monte Cristo."

Her eyebrows furrowed, and then she asked, "Why? Isn't that more along the lines of the ultimate revenge?"

"Yeah, but I gravitated to the protagonist's evolution, in prison, as opposed to his thirst for revenge. Moreover, I was empowered by the fact that the author, Alexandre Dumas, was a brotha."

"I can feel that...favorite movie?"

"The Five Heartbeats."

She smiled brightly and said, "I love that movie."

Preston screwed up his face and began to sing gruffly, "Nights like this, I wish that raindrops..." then he coughed like the washed up Eddie Kane.

She put her hand over her mouth and laughed feverishly. "Oh my God, you're so crazy."

"Next question," he said, smiling, his dimple peeked. She noticed and rolled her eyes.

"You and that damn dimple..." she exhaled sharply, "you only got one, why you be tryna wear it out?"

He smiled again, this time the dimple indented deeply, he said, "Here," and pretended to twist it from his cheek. "You want it? I'm tired of it, it attracts too much attention."

She sucked her teeth, and then pursed her lips. He blew her a kiss; she caught it and smiled.

"Favorite color?"

"Green."

"Favorite singers?"

"I feel Lauryn Hill and Musiq Soulchild, but I breathe Jay-Z."

"Well put. Okay now, besides monetary aspirations, why do you want to be a published author?"

His eyes drifted upwards and he rubbed his goatee as if in deep thought, then said, "Because somebody has to be the voice for the people who get lost in the system. Feel me? You see, J'Neane, those kids who grow up in the system don't want to be there, their choices lead them there. And sometimes the choices they make are the only ones they know or the only ones available, knawmean? But if they knew better, they'd do better. Yet you have to have a voice they respect or admire if you want them to evolve."

"And you have that voice?"

He lowered his eyes to slits and said, "I have their words, their voice and their pain...niggahs just want to be loved."

She studied his face intently. His eyes blazed with so much passion and he held her eyes hostage, until she forced herself to look away. "I think I just met your twin."

"Next question."

"Okay now, this is the billion-dollar question."

"Hold up!" he said, and then lifted his right eyebrow.

"What?"

"You didn't ask me my favorite food."

"Okay, what's your favorite meal?"

"Pussy!" Now both his eyebrows raised.

"Preston!"

He shrugged. "Ay, ya got to mix it up a little. Throw some kinky stuff around, ya know?"

"Whatever. Billion-dollar question. Ready?"

He nodded.

"Do you still, like...umm, love your ex? I mean you told me it was over, but you didn't go into detail...But do you still...I mean, do you think you'll ever get back with her?"

There was an awkward pause. Then he leaned back and folded his arms across his chest. "You listen to Frankie Beverly and Maze?"

"I do."

"You know the song 'Joy and Pain'?"

She nodded.

"Okay, get that beat in your head." He waited a few seconds then said, "Got it?"

Her eyes were closed, she said, "Yeah."

He crooned, "Made some changes in my head, I don't feel the same no more... Does that answer your question?"

She opened her eyes. "Pretty much…by the way, you have a nice voice."

"Thank you." He looked for a waitress. "Let's go, J." He waved for the check and left a nice tip.

J'Neane screwed up her face and cut her eyes at him like he was crazy, then snatched the tip and pocketed it. "Unt-uhn. NO! They ain't got nothin' comin' but gumbo and shit, and I'm fresh out of gumbo."

As they walked out, the waitresses smiled alluringly at Preston; he could feel J'Neane's eyes crawling on him and he forced an ice grill.

J'Neane waved at them then said, in fluent French, "Mange merde."

They looked at each other, baffled.

"J, what does that mean?" asked Preston on the way out the door.

"Eat shit!"

****

Minutes later, they strolled hand in hand under Lake Merritt's necklace of lights. The air was heavy with the scent of wild flowers and redwood trees. The moonlight swam across the murky water and the weekend traffic circled them. The scenery was majestic. Just before they stopped at a bench, Preston picked up a rock and side armed it into the lake; it skipped four times.

"Yes!" he said, channeling a Tiger Woods fist thrust. "I still got it!"

"Boys will be boys, huh?"

He grinned and slid next to J'Neane. "It's beautiful out here, huh J?"

"It is."

He took a deep breath, and then glanced into her honey colored eyes. "So, Ms. J'Neane, tell me about you."

"It's not really that much to tell."

"Come clean, dope fiend."

"What?"

"It's a joke. Come on, J, you know all about me, all my innermost thoughts and everything."

"What do you want to know?"

"What I need to know?"

"Well...can you at least sit a lil closer? It's getting kind of nippy."

"Sure, Thickem's." She pushed his shoulder playfully before they cuddled up.

"Where do you want me to start?"

"From the beginning."

She inhaled deeply and leaned her head on his shoulder. "Well, let's see...umm. I was born in Baton Rouge, Louisiana. My mom and dad owned an upscale seafood and gumbo restaurant. I guess that's why I've always been so voluptuous, because of my seafood diet." She giggled, and then said, "I saw food and I ate it."

"I'm glad you did, cuz I'm a thickaholic."

"Shut up," she said playfully.

"Okay keep it coming, J," he urged.

"'Kay...now, I went to Catholic school all the way up through high school, and I was a virgin all the way until my freshman year at LSU."

"I'll buy that for a dollar," said Preston sarcastically.

"Naw, for real; my parents were super strict and they kept me busy. If I wasn't at school, I was helping out at the restaurant, and if I wasn't doing that, I was reading or writing poetry and corny stuff like that."

"Poetry isn't corny."

"Yeah well. You know what I'm saying. I wasn't in the 'in' crowd. I was in the big boned crowd."

"I thought you said you was voluptuous?"

"Yeah, well that too."

He kissed her cheek, her skin was as soft as smoke. She said, "I met my husband in college. He used to bang those sticks in the band. You know, like the movie, *Drumline*?"

Preston nodded.

"Well yeah, I thought he was sooo...fly. And, anyways we was in love, I guess...whatever you wanna call it, but umm, we graduated the same year; he got his BA degree in economics and was offered a position with the marketing company he'd interned with in New Orleans. We got married and like that," she snapped her fingers, "I became pregnant with Wayne Jr. Then," she said somberly, "it went all downhill from there."

"How come?"

"Well...because...umm. This is kinda embarrassing."

"No more embarrassing than me doin' damn near a decade in prison," Preston countered.

"That's different."

"How so?"

"Because...well...what happened was I had a hard labor with Wayne Jr."

"Hard labor?"

"Yes, that big head boy nearly pulled my pussy out." Preston barked a laugh.

"It's not funny, Preston!"

"Well ya makin' me laugh the way you sayin' it."

She sucked her teeth and continued. "Well anyways, I was stitched up for real, and afterwards, when Wayne and I had sex, he-he..." She began to cry.

He held her close. "Ssshh, J, it's okay. You don't have to continue. It's not that serious."

She sniffled back tears, then gasped, "No, I made you answer difficult questions, so it's only fair..."

He kissed her forehead and rubbed her thighs. "Come on now, ma, it's good, don't trip. We'll talk about it another time."

"No...I'm okay, just give me a second," said J'Neane, wiping her eyes.

He moved his hands up and massaged her shoulders, he couldn't believe how soft and warm she was.

"So anyway," she huffed, "that lil punk gon' have the nerve to tell me that when we had sex, he can't feel nothin'."

Preston grimaced then said, "He can't feel nothin'! What the hell that s'pose to mean?"

"That's what I said. Then he gon' say…" J'Neane put bass in her voice like a man, "fuckin' you is like shakin' my dick out the window!'"

Preston exploded in laughter. She punched his shoulder.

"Or, he'd say, 'Stickin' my dick in you is like throwin' a tic-tac in the mouth of a whale'."

"Stop it —" Preston held one hand out, and the other clutched his stomach.

"See! Why you laughin'? It ain't funny."

"I-I'm sorry J," he said, "just let me get it all out and I promise you, I'll never laugh again." He laughed until tears rolled down his face. She stuck out her bottom lip and got up as if to leave.

He grabbed her in a hug.

"Let me go, Preston."

"I'm sorry J, come on, let's start love over," he said smoothly.

"Whatever."

He pulled her back down on the bench. "Okay, what happened next?"

"Nothin'!"

"Come on, J."

"Preston, I swear if you laugh one more time—"

"Okay, okay."

She continued. "Well, even with us having infrequent sex, I still managed to get pregnant with J'Nae and he really wouldn't come near me now. I ended up gettin' stressed and depressed and ballooned up to almost three hundred pounds."

"Whaaat?"

"Yes! So one night, this niggah comes home smelling like rotten fish, with scratches on his back, and lipstick on his boxers! So when I confront the sonuvabitch, he starts a fight and jumps on me, but his lil scrawny ass couldn't whip me. So you know what this little roach does?"

"No…what, J?"

"The punk goes and gets my journals and composition books, where I kept all my poems, essays, and notes that I'd had since junior high! He locks himself in the bathroom, rips 'em to shreds and flushes them down the toilet. Now ain't that some faggot shit, Preston?" She paused, the skin around her eyes tightened as she fought back tears.

"That niggah is a high powered coward," said Preston, shaking his head.

"Preston, I swear to God that shit hurt me more than him cheating on me. It felt like he raped my soul...Oooh, I hated him after that!"

"I don't blame you. I can't imagine what I'd have done if somebody threw away the only copies of my manuscripts."

J'Neane was visibly furious, but continued her story. "So this fool leaves and comes back four in the morning, pissy drunk!"

"You let him in?"

"Yeah, I let him in, and you know what I did?"

"What did you do, J'Neane?"

She gritted her teeth and said, "I let him lay down and just as he was about to nod off, I sat on him, and beat his ass!"

Preston laughed so hard, he started coughing. "Whew J, girl, you ain't nothin' nice, huh?"

"Shit, he lucky, cuz I was one malicious thought from hittin' him wit' den Al Green grits."

"Whoa."

"But guess what this lil punk does?"

"What he do?"

"He calls the police on me!"

"Did you go to jail?"

"Yeah, I went to jail, but the police laughed they asses off all the way to the precinct. And you know what was so funny?"

"What J?" asked Preston, still on the chuckle.

"I was interviewed by a lady cop. And I mean I cried up a storm, jack...I'm tellin' you. I mean, Preston, I put it on thick! So when I got through tellin' her what went down, she gave me a high five and said, 'You go girl'! And guess what happened then, Preston."

"What?"

"I was in the papers the next day and people wanted me to go on talk shows and everything."

"You kiddin' me."

"No I'm not. I went on this one talk show and they paid for me a personal trainer and that's how I got a job offer in California."

"That's crazy!"

"And I ain't looked back!"

"That's wassup."

"But ain't that a punk ass niggah?"

"Naw, that's what you call a poodle ass niggah on the verge of hamsterity."

She fell out laughing then said, Yeah. Ol' poodle ass niggah with his lil hamster dick."

Preston kissed her neck, but she was still caught up in her story.

"Preston," she said, punching the air, "you should have seen me. I was wailing on that lil Gary Coleman lookin' ass niggah."

"J, when he woke up, did he say..." he cocked his face to the side, "whayoutalkinboutWillis?" quipped Preston.

She slapped her thigh and laughed hysterically.

Chapter 21

"Mama, you losing your booty," said Dannielle with a look of concern.

"Stop lookin' at it then!" snapped Marie.

Marie closed the bedroom door behind her. *I'm losing my booty? I heard the fuck out of that.* Marie undressed then stepped in front of her full-length mirror. She cupped her breasts with both hands and jiggled them. "Puppies still ripe and firm." She let them loose, and they held. Next, she eyed her stomach; it was reasonably in good shape, albeit it was freckled with a few stretch marks here and there, but overall, not bad. Her eyes fell on her hips. "Hips let's see," she said, and then did the ReRe wiggle and popped one out to the side and sat her hand on it. "Uggh." Disappointed she twisted her lips, then turned around and stood on her tippy toes and peered over her shoulder to look back at her butt.

"Dang," she brooded, "it is kinda shot-out. I betta start eatin'. I'm still hot though," she said, and then bounced up and down to make her booty shake and sang, "*I think my butt's get'n big.*"

Yet, even that, which once used to make her smile and preen proudly, produced lackluster results. "Shoo!"

Her cell phone rang. It was her cousin, NeNe.

"Hello bitch."

"Hey ho," Marie replied dryly, "and it's Ms. Bitch."

"Marie," said NeNe, ignoring ReRe's obvious attitude, "Fly ass-fresh-to-the-flo'-Marie-Williams, you betta snap out this weak-ass, sucka fo'love, moody, mud duck, bum bitch, rat head—"

Okay, okay I got a visual," said Marie, pulling the cell phone away from her ear.

"Well bitch, did you get the memo? Cuz boss bitches don't crumble when some clown ass niggah who's been rottin' in prison fo' God knows how long, is actin' all stank. Sistah-cuzz, fuck dat niggah!"

Marie sucked her teeth and rolled her eyes; she could clearly picture her cousin's weave, weaving and hands gesticulating.

"NeNe, shut up, okay? Bitch, you prolly got a black eye right now. You got yo' nerve tryna to counsel me, when G-Man stay dog walkin' yo' ass."

"Oh, no you didn't!"

"Did that. Said that!"

"Mmmph.... Yeah sistah-cuzz, the G-Man might beat a bitch ass every now and then, and most of the time I starts the shit, but least we make up. *And please believe, the makeup do be worth it.*"

"Well, Preston don't hit on me. He don't get down like that."

"He don't get down like that?"

"No."

"Bitch please. You don't know how dat niggah gettin' down, you ain't slept wit' him in damn near a decade. For all you know, he coulda been in there poppin' booty, hittin' that man-gina."

Marie chuckled then said, "Whateva NeNe, nothin' you say gon' make me stop lovin' my man."

"ReRe, how's that yo man when after you put yo life on hold fa damn near ten years, and cuz you was gettin' yo liver shoved around a lil by the young neighborhood dick-down artist, he gon' leave you?"

"He caught him in the *house*, NeNe!"

"So!"

"He caught him coming out the house again."

"And!"

"NeNe, fa-real fa-real. You don't think he got the right to be mad? Come on now."

"ReRe, all bullshit to the side, girl, I never said he didn't have the right to be mad. All I'm sayin' is that you deserve a chance to be forgiven and to make up fo' dat shit."

"But—"

"But nothin'! Do you love whatthefuckhisname?"

"Rico. No."

"Didn't you tell me that when he was comin' out yo house the second time, he was just there to get his Xbox?"

"Yeah."

"Well don't you think you deserve some sorta opportunity to explain yo side? Cry, pout, shout, then fuck and make up. I mean, we fuckin' humans, that's what we do."

"NeNe I got cold busted though."

"Sistah-cuzz. What bitch don't get her shit beat up from time to time when a niggah go to jail? Shiiit, Winnie Mandela cheated on Nelson! And what you think he woulda been doin' if you was in jail…you think he woulda tied his little ass dick in a knot?"

"Big dick, bitch…real big," giggled Marie, then said, "and I'm more Coretta Scott King than Winnie."

"Big, long, thick, curved, what-the-fuck-ever! It don't matter. The most a niggah got comin' is a bitch be there fo' they ass knawmean? And fo' the record, Coretta was gettin' her shit nailed to the mattress too, after them crackas stole ol' Martin's dreams."

"Whatever, NeNe. I don't believe she was fuckin' after he got assassinated."

"ReRe stop being so naive. How many kids they have, like five? Ain't no woman gon' go cold turkey after a dick-a-day diet."

Marie doubled over with laughter. "Bitch, you stupid. Who do you think it was? That guy with the perm and the slick words? What's his name?"

"Al Sharpton. Nah, it was prolly Jesse beatin' them guts up; he was fly back in the days. But ReRe, back to what's really real. Don't you think that you should be given the benefit of the doubt? I mean, what about all those lonely, empty, and miserable nights you endured? What about those high ass phone bills? What about those long bus rides to see him every fuckin' weekend? And what about all the times you spent yo last dime to send him a package?"

"We s'pose to do that."

"No the-fuck-we-don't! We have an option to do that. You didn't rob that bank and get caught."

"NeNe, this is gettin' boring. Can we talk about something else now?"

"Why? Cuz you know I'm tellin' the truth?"

"Whateva."

"And why in the fuck is this niggah sneakin' up on you? What kinda shit is that? I rather a niggah black my eye, and then fuck me so good that I don't even remember what planet I'm on, let alone he hit me; then a niggah to creep up on me after I done rode fo' him fo' a thousand years, passin' up good dick left and right. I mean what kinda weirdo shit is that? That ain't love, that's mistrust."

"I dunno, girl. I dunno what it is," said ReRe gloomily.

"Is he workin' fo' some detective type shit, or is he tryna love you and yo daughter? Is that how he repay you?"

"NeNe, I'm 'bout to hang up."

"Well bitch, is you goin' out, wit us tonight or what? You need to get out, sistah-cuzz, seriously."

Marie clicked her tongue then said, "Bitch, I ain't got nothin' to wear, my hair ain't done, and I ain't really feelin' it."

"ReRe, if you don't pull that nappy shit back in a ponytail, piece somethin' together and come drop that big ol' dooky booty real low, and hope some big dick niggah—"

"Bye bitch." Marie ended the call, and then shook her head.

NeNe was her favorite cousin. They were inseparable all through childhood, up until she met Preston. The moment Preston laid eyes on ReRe it was all bad, and the two women drifted apart. However, when Preston went to prison, in a flash they were two peas in a pod again.

Her phone rang again and it was a text message from NeNe:

I'm just sayin', sistah cuzz. If he really loved you, I mean fa-real fa-real. he'd find it impossible not to forgive you. I mean, if you can say I love you, what's so hard about sayin' I forgive you! Cuz the most important element of love is being willing to forgive and look beyond your own pain and see the pain of the person you claim to love.

Marie lay down and thought deeply. *You know what, NeNe....you're absolutely right*, she mused. Then she responded to NeNe's text message:

ReRe: Thank you Dr. Phil-esha. U r right. Sistah-cuzz 4 life

NeNe: I'm always here for you. Even when ya niggah ain't. So is u goin' out wit us or what?

ReRe: Let a bitch rock that Gucci skirt.

NeNe: Negative.

ReRe: Versace dress?

NeNe: Never.

ReRe: Eat me! :-)

Chapter 22

"I could have left yo ass a thousand times! Hey hey heeeyyy, but you're not worth my tears..."

"Sing it, girl!" shrieked Marie, shakin' her fist and fighting back tears, as Mary J. Blige boomed out her house speakers, soulfully willing Marie to declare war on her pain. She gathered herself, wiped her face and applied her makeup. Ten minutes later, she did the ReRe neck roll and paused for effect. "Watch out nah, not bad...not bad at all."

She smiled. Her spirits were climbing. Today had been a turning point. Marie decided to live her life with or without having *any* man, dictating her happiness or co-writing her existence. Dannielle's love would just have to be enough.

"Dannielle!" she yelled towards the living room.

"What Mama?"

"Don't what me, I'm the Mama. Come here for a minute!"

Dannielle stepped into her mother's room, and her mouth dropped.

"How do I look?" said Marie, and did a little Beyoncé shimmy, then poked out her butt.

"I'm 'bout to cry...Mama, you look so pretty."

"Muah," she kissed Dannielle on her forehead. "Girl, you betta not, you know yo mama is the bounce back queen."

Just then Kelly Rowland's hit song, "Motivation", featuring Lil' Wayne, subbed out their speakers.

"Oooooh, that's my shit right there, Dannielle!" Head roll. Finger snap. Hip wiggle. "Now come on girl, sho' Mama that new dance, watch me get it in one take."

On cue, Dannielle swung into rhythm, at one with the beat; killin' it; all the little facial expressions goin' on, and some.

"Go Danni, it's ya birthday..."

A little while later, NeNe called, and she had her speaker phone on.

"Bitch, is you ready, cuz it's ladies night. Free drinks befo' ten o'clock."

"I'm ready, girl, I just can't figure out what earrings to wear."

"I knew you wasn't gon' be ready, ho."

"That tramp ain't ready?" somebody yelled in the background.

"Who dat?"

"Kiiillla Crew ho!"

"Aw, hell naw, 'sup Stacy?"

"Hey ho."

Stacy was the homegirl from NeNe and ReRe's high school days, when they had a clique of rough and rumble girls called the Killa Crew. They all hustled, carried razors, and would jump a niggah, if and when the need arose.

"Where you get that ho at, NeNe?"

"Shiiit, we ought to be askin' NeNe where she got yo ass at. *Click-Clack. Lock down, bitch!*" said Stacy in the patent Killa Crew twang and drawl. All the girls had the same twang in their speech and it was especially prevalent when they got together.

"Stacy, you still got that 'stache, bitch?" snickered ReRe.

"Fuck you."

Stacy was a big bitch with a mustache that fought like a dude.

"What you got on, ReRe?"

"NeNe, I got my dick-me-down daisy dukes on, with my hair pumped in the front like Janelle Monae."

"Uh-uh, bitch! I wouldn't be caught dead wit' no doo-wop lookin' bitch in some daisy dukes. We out!"

"Girl please, I'm just playin', I'm fly as usual. I got on this Bebe dress with the spaghetti straps that shows my back and shit. I was s'pose to wear it for Preston."

"That's wassup girl, don't waste style on no jailhouse niggah." She and Stacy chimed, "Okaaayyy. Then NeNe said, "And don't you still got them hoop earrings I been tryna steal from you since fo-fuckin-ever?"

"Yeah."

"Well bitch, that's wassup. Slap them hoops in and let's be out."

"A'ight, I'll be right down."

On her way out the door, she stopped and waved her index finger at Dannielle.

"Danni, I don't want nobody and I mean nobody in this house, you hear me?"

"Okay Mama. Dang. Just go and have a good time."

She smiled and hugged Dannielle and walked towards the door, then whirled around.

"Danni, you sure I look alright? My hair—"

"Mama, you're fine, stop worryin' and go get it poppin'."

Marie sucked her teeth and dropped her hands on her hips. "You ain't my mama."

"Bye Mama."

****

"Hey Stacy, I ain't seen you in hella long."

They did the Killa Crew air kiss thing, both cheeks.

"How do I look, sistah-cuzz?"

NeNe looked over her shoulder from the driver's seat, rolled her eyes and said, "Smirkishly-Skankish."

"Come on now fa-real, don't be hatin'..."

"Bitch, you look fly, okay? You happy?"

"Yep, 'specially comin' from you." She heard Chris Brown's hit song, "Look At Me Now". "Heeeyyy......, turn that up, Stacy."

Stacy turned up the music as NeNe pulled into traffic, then passed ReRe a spliff of Kush. "Fire this up, tramp."

ReRe put fire to the chunky blunt, took one drag and passed it back.

"Still ol' 'One-hit-ReRe', huh? NeNe, this bitch fo'eva takin' one hit and she cool."

"I know, huh?"

ReRe blew a trail of smoke in NeNe's direction, and noticed a tripled up Styrofoam cup in NeNe's hand.

"Shit, that's all a bitch need is one hit. My eyes too pretty to be all bloodshot red and what's in that cup, ho?"

"Bo," they said at the same time.

"Aw, unt-uhn, y'all on dat shit too?"

"Bitch this shit go! Want some?" said Stacy.

"Hell naw."

NeNe made a goofy ass face and sang, "*Sippin' on some sizznurrp,*" and took a swig, then a puff of the blunt.

"Bitch, you besta keep yo eyes on the rizzznoad, shoo! And I can't believe you let G-Man have you sippin' on that shit."

"It wasn't G-Man, it was bo-head ass, Angel, fo' yo information, shit."

"Do it matter?"

"Whateva."

They were at Angel's in a hop, skip and a jump, honkin' the horn.

"NeNe, watch this bitch start lyin' the minute she get in the car," said Stacy.

"I know, huh?"

"Killlla Crew bitch," said Angel, climbing in the back of the SUV. Now the Killa Crew twang and drawl was workin' double time.

"ReRe, when you get out of jail, gurrrrl?" Air kisses passed among them, both cheeks.

"Fuck you, A.G."

"I'm just saaayyyin', a bitch ain't seen you in like ten years' worth of conjugal visits, thooough."

ReRe flipped her the bird and rolled her eyes.

Angel licked her lips and said, "You promise? Oow oow! Guess what the fuck happened last night, hmmph."

Glances exchanged. Lips twisted.

"What A.G.?" said Stacy.

"You know that niggah, Low Key?"

"Dat niggah wit the Harley?" asked NeNe.

"Yep, that's the ooonnne."

"What happened, bitch?"

"That niggah motored a bitch pussy straight-the-fuck-up...I mean poppin' wheelies and throttlin' a bitch shit all night." Then she twisted her wrists and scooted in her seat. "Rrrmmm Rmmm."

"Bitch, you stupid...I heard that niggah had pipe though," said NeNe.

Angel spread her two index fingers apart, about a foot wide.

"That long."

"Uh-unh."

"Unh-huh. And he had a bitch ass tooted up, pullin' my fuckin' hair, grippin' my hips so damn tight and slammin' that shit in me. Uh-uh-uh," Angel grunted and grimaced and made like she was fuckin' the dog shit out somebody. "And girrrl, he started slappin' the cheeks, then all a sudden, he cracked my ass cheeks open, and bitch..." she paused for effect.

"What happened?" said ReRe.

"I had an accident."

"An accident?"

"Bitch, how come I pooted?"

They laughed, even though the bitch was probably lying, they laughed.

"Oooh, you dooky bitch, you gon' ruin our rep!" howled NeNe.

"And that ain't the half of it."

"What's the other half, ho?" asked Stacy.

"Y'all bet not say shit!"

"Bitch, jus' spill the beans, shit!" said ReRe.

"How come that shit felt like it had a lump in it?"

"Whahaddawho?"

"The poot, bitch."

ReRe's hand flew to her mouth and she said, "Bitch, you stuuupid, so you shit on his dick, ho?"

"Nah, false alarm, but he sho' fucked the shit out of me."

"Kiiillla Crew bitch, pass the bo, hoooo."

By the time they made it to their usual hole in the wall, the club was already yellow taped. Police were everywhere.

"Whatdafuck?"

"Oooh, somebody prolly got killed…it look like they loading somebody in the meat wagon," said Stacy.

"Come on, let's go fo' they start pullin' people over, a bitch got warrants," said Angel warily.

"This bitch ReRe, is jus' bad luck, y'all."

"I know, huh?"

"Nah, uh-uh, NeNe, don't blame that shit on me, shoo!" ReRe retorted, folding her arms across her chest.

Angel said, "Well, let's just go downtown y'all, and shine on them uppity ass hoes."

NeNe sucked her teeth then said, "I hate goin' to The Liege, dey be waterin' up a bitch drank."

"That's why we got our own drank. Pass the dirty Sprite, dyke...."

They were at Jack London Square in no time at all, and the joint was jumpin' and poppin' the most. Bitches in skimpy, and come-fuck-me-now clothes made their way from car to car, and to baller and wannabe baller; expensive cars were bumper to bumper and the line was damn near down the block.

"Ooh, bitch, it's poppin'!" said Stacy.

Angel's head shot up like a gopher out its hole.

"NeNe, there go yo Samoan friend workin' the door, go tickle his nuts and get us up in this bitch."

Head weave, finger snap, hip twist, NeNe said, "Watch a boss bitch do her thang."

They waited five feet away while NeNe sauntered toward the hulking Samoan.

"Can them mothafuckas even fuck?" spat ReRe.

"I know, huh; that'll be a damn shame, that damn big wit' a lil ass dick," said Angel.

Just then, NeNe signaled for them to come on.

"Ooh, bitch, we in, let's go," said Stacy.

Chapter 23

E-stro bobbed his head to the pounding bass line pumping from the candy apple red, '73 Chevy Impala, on 26-inch Dub Bellagios. He was pushing southbound on 23rd Avenue. It wasn't his car, but he was enjoying himself all the same because the whip was showroom floor clean. The passenger and owner, however, glanced about panning the streets intensely, then he glared at E-stro. *This niggah is having too much damn fun driving my shit.* Choppa Ken frowned, before abruptly turning down the music. E-stro whipped his head towards Choppa Ken, face on the screw, and said, "'Sup my niggah?"

"Slow this bitch down, bruh!"

E-stro blew air between his gold grill. "Man, stop being so fuckin' p-noid my dude...I got L's, insurance, all the shit!"

"Fuck what you talkin' 'bout," Choppa Ken tapped his chest, "I got dumb ass warrants, knawmean?"

"Ai-ight, ai-ight, my niggah, that's wassup...calm you ass down though."

Square ass niggah ain't never been to jail, he ain't feelin' me though, thought Choppa Ken.

Onward they pushed, until E-stro lit up like a light bulb.

"Ay, Chop."

"'Sup?"

"We might as well slide through the weed spot and snatch up some trees...maybe that'll calm yo nerves."

"You buyin'?"

"Yeah man, I got it,"

Choppa Ken glanced at his Gucci watch. "Niggah, you prolly got a lil bopper over there you wanna highside on."

"So what niggah, I'm buyin'...lean back."

"Don't be all day, blood."

"Bet. In and out like yeee!" yelped E-stro, he grinned and turned the music up.

E-stro bent a few blocks and a half a song later, they were pulling up to the purple spot. Sure enough, it was a few boppers prancing about; they eye fucked the candy paint and swayed to the subbin' bass.

"That mothafucka hella wet, huh bitch?" one of them said.

"I know, huh," said another.

"Kisha, ain't that yo dude?"

"Somethin' like that," she said, poppin' her gum; she primped her hair, stood up and poked her ass out.

E-stro released his shoulder length dreads form the hair tie and let them hang loose, got out and bounced towards the young ladies.

Choppa Ken twisted his lips, and shook his head. "This ol' sidebustin' ass niggah", he mumbled under his breath. Then he rolled down the window and barked, "Niggah, don't spend less than fifty either, niggah!"

E-stro waved him off and slid up on the young thick Kisha, putting his arm around her as they disappeared around the side of the building.

"Tsss, ol' bootsy ass niggah," hissed Choppa Ken, before bending down to adjust the music; satisfied, he bobbed his head to CeeLo's hit song, "Fuck You", put on his Prada shades and lightweight flirted with a few hoodrats; until once again, he grew impatient. He hit the horn.

Bommmp! Bommmp!

"Come on, niggah."

E-stro peeked his head from around the building and threw up his index finger like, *hold up*.

"Hold up my ass, hurry up, niggah!" bellowed Choppa Ken.

Choppa Ken knew he was playing it close. He had a bullshit warrant for slappin' the dog shit out his baby's mama, after she scratched "hoe" in giant letters on the hood of his car. Furthermore, he was on parole, and Detective O'Reilly and Limbaugh, also known as Beavis and Butthead, would jack him on sight. This was why he sprayed the Impala candy apple red; he even switched the Lexani rims, giving his whip a complete makeover.

Still, he was worried about Beavis and Butthead; just yesterday, they'd kicked in his mother's front door looking for him as if he'd killed somebody. Yeah, it wasn't looking good for the home team.

He glanced at his watch again; it was only 1:15.

"Shit!" he knew usually Beavis and Butthead changed shifts at 2:00 p.m.

At that moment, E-stro came bouncing from behind the building. He got in and they pulled off as the boppers blew kisses at them.

"Wipe that lipstick off yo face, clown."

"Aw, cuzzin'," he smiled, "I had to sweet talk the bitch to get a few extras, nah mean?"

"Wa'cha get niggah?"

"Lil bitch gave me five dub sacks fo' fiddy."

"Lemme see."

E-stro handed over the fluffy bags of purple Kush, and Choppa Ken opened one, sniffed it, and made a fuck face.

"Whew, this is that yadadamean," said Choppa Ken, examining the purple Kush buds.

"I tol' you, my niggah."

Instantly, Choppa Ken was back in the snarl. "Niggah you ain't tol' me nothin'…let's just get off these streets, fo' Beavis and Butthead fuck around and jack a niggah."

"Man, they always fuckin' wit' you, Chop."

"Man, cuz, you know that niggah, Skully G?"

"Yeah, the niggah from Sobrante Park they say yo twin?"

"Yeah…well that niggah shot up they car, and them mothafuckas don't know if it was me or him, and prolly don't give a fuck, but they put word on the street…we dead," replied Choppa Ken and glanced back behind them.

"That's why you be so damn p-noid, huh?"

"You mothafuckin' right…Fuck!" An unmarked squad car sped towards them.

"That's them, my niggah, smash off!"

"Ma-man…Chop, I ain't tryna get in no high speed, blood," whimpered E-stro.

"You bitch ass niggah, next corner, jump out."

"What….you trippin' man," whined E-stro, "I'm pullin' over."

"Pow!"

Choppa Ken fired right to the jaw. E-stro let go of the wheel and covered up.

"Aww fuck, blood, why you hit me?"

Choppa Ken grabbed hold of the steering wheel, just before they sideswiped a parked car.

"Next corner, get out, bitch!"

BOOM!

They were suddenly jolted forward as Beavis began to ram the back of the Impala.

"Man, they tryna kill us!" cried E-stro, furiously trying to regain control of the car, while Choppa Ken intuitively and quickly buckled up.

BOOM!

Again, they were slammed forward, this time the car fishtailed and lost control.

"Ahhhh!"

BAM!

The cops slammed into the Impala again; this time, it spun 360 degrees before wrapping around a light pole. E-stro flew through the windshield like a rocket, smack dab, headfirst into the streetlight.

SPLAT!

His head burst like a watermelon, and brain and skull chips splattered the pole.

"Oh my God!" screamed a bystander, cupping her mouth and turning her head as E-stro's body crumpled to the ground headless. Blood spurted gruesomely in successive squirts out the gaping hole in his neck, and pooled around his lifeless body.

Beavis and Butthead jumped out the police car, side arms aimed at the wreckage.

Choppa Ken popped out the car and staggered momentarily.

"Get down, get down!" screamed the detectives in unison.

Choppa glanced at the detectives; his were eyes wide with fear, and then he took off. Beavis gave chase.

"Stop motherfucker, or I'll shoot!"

Butthead jumped back into the cop car.

Adrenaline rushed through Choppa Ken's body, eating away the effects of the car crash and he began to leave Beavis in the dust, but suddenly, he stumbled and slid face-first.

"I got you now, scumbag!" howled Beavis, almost upon him, but Choppa Ken jumped to his feet and was off again. He made it to a residential area with Beavis hot on his heels and he hit the first fence he saw, clearing it with no problem. He heard the scuffling and pounding footsteps behind him. He looked over his shoulder and Beavis was gaining.

"Fuck!" he grunted and dug deep, pushing his legs to the limit. He thought quickly; he figured Butthead would be waiting on the next block; his heart was beating like a war drum. He began to double back, the same way he came.

"Stop runnin', punk, you ain't gettin' away!"

That's what you think, white boy.

Choppa Ken hit another gear on some Usain Bolt type shit; he leaped over a large fence, and ran through a wooden one, and just as he was about to hop into another yard, he was tackled so hard, it briefly knocked the wind from him.

"Fuck man, lemme go!" grunted Choppa Ken as he kicked and squirmed from beneath Butthead; he hopped to his feet and took off again.

Butthead stumbled up and staggered to brace himself against the house, he touched his head and looked at his hand, covered with blood; somehow, he had banged his head.

"Shit!" he yelled, swiping the blood spilling down his face.

Choppa Ken had one leg over the fence, when at the last second, he saw the hulking blue nose pit. It charged at him, ears pinned to its large head and snapped off several grisly barks, "Ruff, Ruff! Ru! Ru!" Saliva flew from its ferocious jaws as it leaped at Choppa Ken's dangling leg.

"Ooh shit!" gasped Choppa Ken, snatching his leg back just in time.

"On the ground now!"

The pit bull barked in an insane circle and leaped again.

"Ru-Ru-Ru-Ru-Ru! Grrrrrroowwl!"

Choppa Ken was stuck on the fence between a pit bull and a hard place; his eyes frantically searched for an escape route. Out the corner of his eye, Beavis appeared, gun drawn. Beavis took one look at his injured partner and screamed at the escapee. "Put the gun down now!" Then he squeezed off multiple rounds at the terror stricken Choppa Ken.

BOOM! BOOM! BOOM! BOOM!

The first shot blew his brains out; the others were just window dressing. Choppa Ken fell into the next yard, dead on impact. Nevertheless, the pit bull locked onto his neck and shook Choppa Ken's bloody body like a rag doll.

Chapter 24

Kobain's hands flashed over the turntables, cutting and scratching at the beat blaring from the club's state of the art sound system. The joint was packed; three divas to every young don, and they were all loose and fly; on the dance floor stylin' and profiling.

FreshKidd hopped onto the stage and grabbed the mic, Kobain killed the music, and the club's patrons gravitated towards the makeshift stage. FreshKidd paused and postured on some uber cock and swag shit; he was the king of this hip-hop shit in the Bay. Strobe lights flashed on him, he wiggled the gold toothpick in his mouth with his tongue, and then tucked it in his shirt pocket.

"Gee-gee-geyeah, how y'all feelin' tonight?"

"We good, FreshKidd," yelled one of his many female fans and admirers.

"Geyeah, that's wassup...y'all ready for his real fly thug shit, huh?"

"Hell yeah!" the crowd screamed, picking up on his energy and swagger.

"Nah...nah, y'all too quiet. I mean y'all act like I ain't Roc-a-wear-the-fuck-down tonight. Y'all act like my chain ain't froze like fuck, knawmean?" He let his iced out medallion hang low. "I'ma ask y'all one mo' again, y'all ready?" He pointed the mic at the crowd, and he knew he had them.

"Hell yeah!" roared the hip-hop heads.

"A'ight, that's wassup…but before we get started, I wanna introduce my boys," he jabbed his finger at the DJ booth behind him and said, "That's D.J. Kobain."

Kobain turned on the music and scratched the beat, swung his dreads real quick and stopped, then posed.

"Geyeah…ge-yeah," FreshKidd continued his edgy prance, and then put his arms around Drixxx. "This pretty boy right here, is my hype man and atomic beat maker, Drixxx." Drixxx nodded, eyes slanted like he was in a trance.

"And I'm…" Kobain cued the music; a pre-recorded cheer crawled from the speakers, in a rolling crescendo. "FreshKidd FreshKidd FreshKidd"…

"Y'all ready?"

"Hell yeah!" screamed the audience, camera phones and lighters up.

"Come on, FreshKidd, wit' yo fine ass!" said a female with major, crazy, cleavage for days, clicking away with her phone. He blew her a kiss, and she almost fainted.

"That's wassup, then…drop that fresh beat, Kobain!"

A powerful bassline rumbled throughout the club. FreshKidd got the neck thing going, ala T.I., and moved back and forth, adding his own personalized swag to it, gettin' amp'd with every step. Drixxx swung his long blond mane, rock star style, and FreshKidd pulled his Oakland A's fitted cap real low, before exploding into the Bay Area's hustlers' anthem, "CUT".

> *"Aaayyyyee…I'm slangin' in the cut.*
> *Niggah say what?*
> *Keep ya mouth shut or you'll get cut*

I'm King Tut
Ripped and cut
Diamonds, clear and cut
Bitch say what?
Listen to this cut
Swang that butt
Say I-don't-give-a-fuck!"

He pointed the mic at the crowd and they roared, "I don't give a fuck!"

"Countin' this doe..." He threw a wad of money in the crowd. "I gotta paper cut!"

****

In a jam packed area of the club, NeNe stood on her tippy toes, poppin' her fingers, enraptured by FreshKidd's stage performance and she said, "That niggah, FreshKidd, goin' bananas up there, huh Stace?"

"He ai-ight, he ain't all that tho', bitch!" Stacy replied dryly.

"Hater! Where them hoes at with our drinks, shit? I'm tryna be all there wit' it tonight, okaaay."

Stacy stretched her neck and said, "Here dem hoes come now."

Angel and Marie dipped by and through the packed crowd, drinks in both hands, desperately trying not to spill a drop. They passed NeNe and Stacy their drinks.

"'Bout time, bitch." NeNe took her drink, but kept rubbernecking the stage. "Oooh, y'all missin' it."

"What's up?" Angel was on her toes.

"That niggah, FreshKidd, go!"

"Aw, uh-uh," Stacy uttered, while looking at her drink all stank, "I wanted a cutie, what's this shit?"

"They call that a *look bitch,*", said Marie.

"Look bitch?"

"Yeah, *look bitch*; you know you ain't gave me 'nuf money for no damn cutie. So you best be happy I brought yo ass that!" She pressed her lips together.

They all fell out laughing.

"And thank you very much," Marie added.

"Oh bitch, you got jokes tonight, huh?" Stacy's ass wasn't feeling it.

"Hoe, you know I'm just playing!" Marie said, as the laughter subsided. "It's a screamin' orgasm, slut. Taste it, go 'head, taste that orgasm hoe, shit, that's what you like, ain't it?"

"Aw hell-to-the-naw!" yelped Angel.

"What?"

"Ain't that G-Man's baby's mama, Farrah?"

"Where?" asked NeNe, weaving her head around bodies.

Angel sipped her drink and then nonchalantly tossed her chin in Farrah's direction. "And ooh, why the bitch got on yo dress, NeNe?"

"Stop lyin'!" said Stacy.

Angel cocked her neck to the side and said, "Lyin'! Bitch hol' up." Then she turned and yelled over the crowd, "FARRAH!"

"Don't call that bum ass bitch over here!" spat NeNe.

"Too late, here she come," said Marie.

"Killlla Crew," mocked Farrah, mimicking the girls' widely known clique call.

All four ladies pushed out their breasts and sucked in their stomachs. Farrah stepped up with her two sidekicks posted at her sided on some uppity shit. Farrah was a six foot, redbone stallion, with a pretty face, small waist and bangin' hips. To top it off, the bitch had the nerve to wear two-inch heels that made her tower over NeNe and them.

"Heeeyyy," she said in her bullshit voice, "Y'all mob on anybody lately?"

"Girl, we grown now, recognize!" Marie said, and then rolled her eyes.

Farrah snaked her neck and turned her attention to NeNe. "Shit, the only thing I recognized is this rat-head bitch with my dress on."

Her two sidekicks cackled. "Oh no, she didn't!"

"Yo dress?" NeNe rolled her eyes. "You big foot bitch, yo money ain't paid for this."

"You know what tramp?" Farrah smirked, "I'ma give yo bootsy ass a pass this time."

Before NeNe could pop off at the mouth, Farrah spun around and made her massive backside wobble and jiggle. She looked over her shoulder seductively and said, "Too bad yo shit didn't come with this, huh?"

"Oooh shit, my niggah, that bitch got ridiculous booty," said a niggah standing near them.

"Caked the fuck up, dizzam!" added his homeboy, grabbing his crotch.

Farrah arched her back, stood on her tippy toes and made that ass clap harder, and stared off into the ceiling. Then she whipped her neck back towards NeNe and winked.

Stripper par excellence.

Stacy's pussy got wet, and she rubbed her mustache.

NeNe rushed forward, but Marie grabbed her arm. "Uh-uh, NeNe!"

"Lemme go, shit!"

"Ciao, ciao." Farrah smiled and waved. "She know she don't want it."

Pushing off, she swung her ass, as her cohorts fell in line and swung their backsides in kind.

"Ooh, I can't stand that Charles Barkley lookin' hoe!" hissed NeNe, watching them.

"Uh-unh, NeNe, you gon' let that bitch style on you?" Angel was on some egg-on shit.

"Hell no! Fuck that, where them hoes go?" NeNe tried to look over and through the packed crowd.

"There they go," Marie pointed.

"Where?"

"They going in the bathroom."

"Come on." NeNe reached for her purse. "I got somethin' for that hoe."

"Killa Crew!" declared Angel as she trailed NeNe. "We gon' show these hoes who don't want it."

In a matter of seconds, they bum rushed the bathroom and startled a few ladies, who exited quickly. NeNe surveyed the bathroom and saw the two cackling sidekicks hunched over the sink, snorting powder off a small mirror. Angel tapped NeNe on the shoulder and nodded her head towards the bathroom stall, only one was occupied. The two cacklers lifted their heads off the sink; one of them rolled her eyes at NeNe and them, then called out, "Farrah the birds are back in town," then sniffed and wiped at her nose.

"What?" Farrah sounded angry. "Hold the fuck up—"

NeNe slid into the stall beside her. "Shut the fuck up, bitch." She climbed on the stool.

"Say what?" Farrah was rushing to wipe her privates. "Ooh, we finna see, hoe."

"What I say?" NeNe peered over the stall, raised her Taser and fired.

Pow!

The tethered dart stuck Farrah in the neck.

"Stupid bitch!"

"Owwwww!" screamed Farrah, as she collapsed, convulsed, then flopped on the floor, striking her head on the toilet in the process. The Taser gun buzzed and crackled sinisterly.

"Oooh shit, they electrocutin' hoes up in this bitch!" said a woman patron and she broke out the bathroom.

At that moment, Big Stacy, Angel and Marie rat packed the sidekick cacklers.

"Get them hoes, y'all!"

"Stop!" one cried, "What y'all doin'?"

"What we do?" screamed the other one. All that cocky shit was gone. "We ain't got nothin' to do with that shit!"

"Shut up, bitch!"

Pow!

Big Stacy smacked a cowering sidekick upside her fake weave-wearin' ass head. "Hoe!" She kicked her in the ass and snatched off the girl's fake ponytail.

"Aw, hell naw," quipped Angel, "and I straight thought that shit was real."

Slap! Pow!

Weaves ripped off, and clothes tore to tatters. Miraculously, the cacklers ducked and squirmed from under their attackers and burst out the bathroom, beat the fuck up. Meanwhile, Farrah on the other hand, kept flopping, the Taser gun kept crackling, and Farrah kept screaming.

"Aaahhh!"

"Yeah bitch, who you stylin' on now, hoe?"

"Aaahhh!" howled Farrah in mid-flop.

Big Stacy busted into the cheap, rinky-dink stall, stepped over Farrah, and tore the flimsy dress off. Farrah's juicy titties spilled out, her latte-colored, silver dollar-sized areolas and meaty nipples on full display.

"Wake yo' game up, hoe! And stop tryna impersonate boss bitches!" said Big Stacy, lickin' her lips.

"Come on y'all!" Marie warned, damn near out of breath, "Let's go!"

They made it out, just as security rushed into the bathroom. Minutes later, security and the club manager escorted a half-conscious, battered Farrah out, jacket barely covering her gorgeous body.

"You ai-ight, Farrah?" called NeNe snidely from the crowd. "I'ma call the G-Man and tell 'em you had an accident, okay?"

****
****

Love...I mean, like, what the hell is in that shit? You know like Kool-Aid, for instance; we all know it's basically artificial flavoring, food coloring, water, sugar and BAM: Kool-Aid. But what the hell did God put in love, huh? A pinch of passion, a dash of jealousy, a smidgen of fantasy, and a pound of ecstasy? You see, just about everybody has felt love or has been in love, and some of everybody has their own theories on love; but has anyone actually got the formula right down to a precise science? 'Cause love, I'll tell ya, makes people do some of the damnedest things. Makes you kinda think he might have spit a little hate in the recipe, just to spice it up, and make it all come together..."TOOUAHH!"

Jeremih and 50 Cent's hit song, "Down On Me", pounded throughout the club, sending partygoers into a frenzy.

"Ooooh, bitch, that's myyy sooonnng!" crooned NeNe, poppin' her fingers and swaying her hips salaciously. "Come on y'all, let's let these hoes know we in the house."

"Bitch, I'm right behind you," said Angel.

"Watch our drinks, Stace," warned Marie.

"Go on and get that monkey funky, I gots this."

"And don't be sneakin' no sips off my shit, either. I don't know where yo damn mustache been," teased Marie.

"Fuck you, hoe!"

Marie smirked, stuck her tongue out and followed the stampede of bodies to the dance floor. She two-stepped with NeNe and Angel for a minute, but quickly they were pulled and soon they were all tearing the dance floor up. Marie glanced at NeNe, the girl was already on one; straight up freakin' a tall, light-skinned cat. Angel, the best dancer out the clique, was lettin' her dance partner have it, but he was one of those Disco Danny catz; limber, light on his feet, givin' her a good run for her money.

Marie smiled, and then was startled when the guy she was dancing with, whispered in her ear, just above the music, "So is you gonna dance or sight see?"

She rolled her eyes in mid-step, and then took a real good look at him; her mouth watered. He had the curly thing goin' on with his hair, ice in both ears, and his eyes looked like they were glowing in the dark.

"Ooh, you got some pretty eyes!"

He smiled.

Ooo...that damn smile, she thought.

The record changed and all hell broke loose on the dance floor when "Back That Azz Up" came on.

"Drop it like it's hot!"

"Drop it like it's hot!"

Angel and Marie were side by side, putting their moves down on the young cats. They even switched dance partners and got low, on the dime. Marie threw her head back and laughed.

"These hoes crazy! Fuck it; I'm 'bout to get turnt up too, shit."

Marie backed up on Green Eyes and swayed, and swerved her backside seductively, keeping up with the beat. Green Eyes grinded on her then started smackin' her ass, and she went wild. She got low, popped back up, whipped her head back at him and bit her finger; then she threw him that "I been a bad girl" look and backed up on him again.

Green Eyes rocked up instantly.

"Girlm who is you playin' wit, back that azz up!" sang Juve.

Just then, someone snatched her off her feet, and everything was a blur. "Whadafuck!" she screamed, and when her feet finally touched the ground, she stumbled then spun around and snarled.

It was Preston.

She gasped and her hand flew to her mouth.

"Fuck is you doin"?" barked Preston, his angry scowl crawling over her face.

Her eyes dipped towards NeNe and Angel, but he grabbed her chin and yelled, "I'm talkin' to you, ReRe, not them!"

She smelled the strong odor of alcohol on his breath.

Angel and NeNe came rushing towards them; Marie saw them in her peripheral.

"I'm doin' me, niggah, same thang you been doin', shit!"

"Ay, my nigg, what kinda ole sucka shit you on?" spat Green Eyes.

Preston pushed Marie to the side and faced off with Green Eyes.

"On Mamas, niggah, you really don't want it."

Green Eyes was a well-known beast in the streets and it had been a while since he had been challenged like so.

"Niggah, do that tough guy shit s'pose to scare me, fool? This the A-Team, niggah!"

"What niggah?" Preston stepped closer, eyes screwed tight. "You need a team niggah?" Preston had his finger in his face now. "I'll compress yo bitch ass!"

"Aye, aye, hol' up!" Kenzo separated the would-be combatants.

"Matata, what's up my niggah?" he asked the green-eyed cat as he pointed to Preston. "This my dude, bruh."

"Well, you need to tell yo' dude 'bout invading my personal space, my nigg!"

"Preston, dude good peoples, blood," said Kenzo.

Preston continued to ice grill Green Eyes.

"Betta get yo' mans en 'nem, Zo, fo it get ugly," warned Green Eyes.

Preston had a few run-ins with some dudes claiming the A-Team in prison and he despised the niggahs, so this was a good excuse as any to tie up those loose ends.

Kenzo turned his attention back to the green-eyed cat named Matata.

"Matata, my niggah, you know me and ya man, M.A. is folks; my boy just came home, let's not let this get out of hand—"

"You ain't got ta explain nothin' to that niggah, Zo!" roared Preston.

Kenzo put a hand on each of Preston's shoulders and spun him around.

"Stand down, P. Straight the fuck up, blood!" His eyes bore into Preston, and then he turned to face Green Eyes.

"Let this one go, bruh. I owe you one, ai-ight?"

Green Eyes flicked his nostrils like a boxer, then simulated a gun with his hand and pointed at Preston. "Pow! Niggah, I had you." He nodded his head at the crowd and at least eight to ten young goons emerged, they mean-mugged Preston and followed their de facto leader off the dance floor.

"Oooh, he lucky, they was gon' get him..." said a girl, watching the entire play.

"I know, huh?" her girlfriend agreed, as they both eyed Preston.

Preston wasn't impressed or intimidated.

"All this ova a bitch, my niggah?" Kenzo jabbed his thumb over his shoulders. "Them niggahs fa'sho got heavy metal outside...come on my niggah, we here on some music shit, not no bitch shit!"

Preston spun on Kenzo, but he wasn't trying to hear it. "Money over bitches niggah, stick to the script!" bellowed Kenzo behind him.

Preston found Marie and them in the back of the club. Marie was crying on NeNe's shoulder, her back was to him.

"Marie, lemme holla at you."

"She ain't tryna talk right now, Preston!" snapped NeNe.

"Stay out my business, NeNe. Marie!"

Marie turned to face him. "What!" she snapped; she had tears in her eyes, her nostrils flared.

"Fuck you mean what!" He motioned with his index finger. "Bring yo ass here!"

"Fuck that, I useta be yo' bitch, but I wasn't neva yo' muthafuckin' dog!"

"Yeah niggah, you trippin up in here!"

"I ain't gon tell you again, NeNe, stay up out of mines!"

"And what niggah!" She rolled her neck. "I ain't nunna Marie, niggah!"

"You know what, NeNe, you got a big mouth."

"So, shit!"

"Preston, why don't you just leave, my dude," said Stacy.

"I ain't goin' nowhere without my woman!" He reached his hand out. "Come on, ReRe."

"No!"

"What?"

"You heard me. All of a sudden you see the next niggah on me, so now you wanna be wit' me, fuck that!" She folded her arms across her chest and looked away.

"Ay, ma, we really need to talk."

"Well talk, I ain't got nothin' to hide from nobody, and I ain't got too much to say."

"Stop bein—"

"Niggah, she cool on you, step, shit!"

"NeNe," Preston growled, gritted his teeth, and then punched his palm.

"NeNe, my ass." Her head was weaving like mad. "I'm tired of you tryna brainwash my cousin wit' dat bullshit."

"Bitch, shut up!"

"Bitch!" In a flash of motion, NeNe tossed her drink in his face. "I got yo bitch, niggah."

In no time, his hand was around her neck in an iron like grip, dragging her away from Stacy and Angel.

"Let her go Preston, shit!"

The club's patrons took notice and backed up.

Preston let go of her neck, but held her arms at her sides. She gasped for air.

"NeNe I tol' you 'bout that stupid shit, calm yo ass down."

She hawked and spit in his face. "Phew!"

Preston pimp-slapped her viciously and as she fell over a table, her legs flew in the air.

"Bitch, fuck wrong wit' you?" he roared, and wiped his face with the bottom of his shirt.

"Niggah, I'm callin' the G-Man!" she cried and struggled to her feet.

Stacy rushed at him, but by now, the bouncers were on the scene.

"Ai-ight break this shit up!" demanded a burly brother, grabbing Stacy.

Angel was struggling with Marie, trying to get the Taser gun.

"Uh-uh Angel, No!"

"Bitch, let go!"

"You dead, niggah!" NeNe pointed at Preston, "Watch."

Chapter 25

The G-Man ushered the midnight black Grand National through the streets of east Oakland; he'd been on his way to Jack London Square to address the situation with NeNe tazing the hell out of his baby's mama, Farrah. Although secretly, he laughed inside; he'd warned Farrah repeatedly about antagonizing NeNe, but because of her size, Farrah paid him no mind.

He, himself, was a quiet, little dude, but what he lacked in size, he made up for in heart and cunning. He was once known as the Gank-Man, a moniker he'd earned due to his skillful and numerous robberies, but it had been shortened to the G-Man after he scored a lick for fifty birds. Like many others who busted big moves of that magnitude, the G-Man didn't beat his chest or yank his nuts in the 'hood. He let the dust settle, played the shadows and became tactical, which was why most people thought G-Man was short for Ghost-Man, because he was invisible, but felt.

These days, he played the game only in win-win situations, and although he supplied his 'hood with drugs and pulled all the major strings, he was rarely ever seen.

Lil Wayne pumped out his speakers. "While ya pussy niggahs is sleepin, I'm thinkin'; deep in thought, the boy ain't even winkin'."

He bobbed his head and twisted the San Francisco Giants cap on his skull. Lil Wayne's music was his mind candy; most niggahs just listened to the beat, but the G-Man studied his lyrics and surmised that the shit Lil Wayne was spittin' had to come from his mentor, Baby.

I mean, how can you not listen to a niggah with over half a million dollars' worth of diamonds in his mouth, shit every time he breathes, it's passin' through a million, mused the G-Man.

His mind reshuffled to the present. Tonight, he'd received two hysterical phone calls from both his baby's mamas. Yet he wasn't moved none the least by their spearing emotions. Only bitches and suckas acted without reasoning.

His pops had taught him to always, "*Analyze the body of facts making up a war situation as a whole*!"

And a war situation, simply put, is life.

He pulled up to Stacy's house. NeNe, Angel and Stacy were already outside.

NeNe ran to him; her lip was busted and she was visibly heated.

"I want you to kill that niggah!" she raged, "that niggah punched me like I was a dude, and he said 'Fuck you'."

"Oh he did?"

"Hell yeah," She turned to her friends. "Huh, y'all?"

They nodded.

The G-Man leanded back on the car, squinted his eyes, and pulled down his fitted cap. "So, NeNe, what you do to start all this shit?"

"Fuck you mean what I do?" Her face screwed up. "That muthafucka hit me like I was a niggah, and you gon' interrogate me?"

"Watcha mouth."

"I ain't watchin' shit, G-Man, you gon' kill that niggah or I am!"

Dealing with NeNe was a fuckin' science; she was a woman, but she thought like a dude; truly a boss bitch. Nevertheless, he admired her spirit, but it was times like this he'd come to dread.

"Tol' you 'bout talkin' reckless!" He walked around to the driver's side. "Get in!" he ordered angrily.

"No, uh-unh." She took a step back.

"Come on y'all," whined Angel, "we done had enough drama tonight."

He ignored Angel. "NeNe, I ain't gon' say it no mo'," he said forcefully, "Get in the car!"

She tapped her foot on the ground, and folded her arms across her chest. "Shoo!" she clicked her tongue, "You bet not hit me either, niggah!"

"Be cool, NeNe," urged Stacy, her face etched with concern.

The G-Man got in the car, popped the locks on the doors, and begrudgingly, NeNe got in, and they pulled into the avenues.

It was several minutes before either of them spoke. He navigated through the sparse traffic and sorted through his thoughts.

Jay-Z's song off *The Dynasty* album, "Get ya Mind Right", slumped inside the Grand National.

The streets were quiet and the sky was dark and murky. He reached into the car's console and fished out a pre-rolled spliff of purple haze.

"Here, fiya this up."

"I'm cool."

"Fiya it up, NeNe; don't make me repeat myself again, ma."

"Give it here, shoo!" She snatched it and sparked it up.

"NeNe, why you got to test me like I'm some mark ass, niggah?"

"Shiiit, you made me this way." She inhaled and held the potent weed fog, then blew out a plume of smoke. "Boss bitch, for a boss niggah."

He shook his head and hit some back streets, eyes drifting to the rearview mirror every so often, as the cannabis clouds floated and swirled.

"Relax Mami, let the Belvee flow, inhale the dro," sang Memphis Bleek.

They passed the spliff back and forth until finally, he stubbed out a fat roach in the ashtray.

Then slowly, he was able to dislodge the series of events and reluctantly, she explained how after she tased the fuck out of Farrah, she ended up gettin' into the situation with Preston, and how she threw a drink on him, and further spit in his face.

"NeNe, how many times do I got to tell you, every action deserves a reaction?"

"Whatever," she sucked her teeth, "I don't feel like hearin' that bullshit philosophy, shit."

"So you want me to smash up there and blast that niggah?"

"Yep."

"Okay, say for instance, I go rushin' up to the club and shoot it up? What you think gon' happen?"

"That niggah gon' be dead, cuz I know you don't shoot into no crowds."

"You don't know what I do," he corrected her, "but who do you think they gon' come gaffle?"

"Me and you."

"No, me," he said as he tapped his chest, "you gon' be back in the club shakin' yo ass, when I blow trial and get that kickstand."

"Uh-uh. No, I'm not," she said, "I'ma ride 'til the wheels fall off."

"Yeah, right."

"Well, shit, let me go blast his ass." She rolled her neck. "I'll do it too, shit."

"I know you will, but then I'll lose a boss bitch, and Lil G-Man will lose a good mother."

"So you just gon' let that niggah get away with slappin' a bitch?" She wasn't trying to hear his logic.

"Did I say that?"

"That's how you actin', shit." She looked out the window. "You prolly just mad, cuz I tased the fuck outta Big Foot."

He chuckled.

"And I had that Big Bird lookin' bitch, beggin' fo' mercy too, stupid bitch!"

He changed the subject. "Where's Marie?"

"That dumb bitch stayed with that punk ass niggah, they prolly up in the VIP section with that niggah Kenzo and them."

"Kenzo?"

"Yeah that niggah, Kenzo, think he some kind of fuckin' don or somethin'."

The G-Man flashed back to his Juvenile Hall days when he and Kenzo squabbled over some bullshit that he'd now forgotten, but he'd never forget how that niggah stomped him out while he was on the ground. He sucked his tooth. "Kenzo, huh?"

"Yeah, he got some fuckin' record label thing goin', and I think that niggah FreshKidd fuckin' wit' 'em...you ain't seen all them posters up everywhere?"

"Yeah, but I ain't know it was the niggah, Kenzo, behind it."

"Hmmph," she sucked her teeth, "well it is, and that's that niggah's best friend. So I feel like he slapped me too, shit!"

"I do too, Ma," he turned towards her, "And ya know, he just may have to pay for that shit, in more ways than one."

Chapter 26

The streets were all but silent; his window was cracked just a little, just enough to tickle his face. The slight buzz for the Patrón bubbled timidly, losing its strength by the second. Yet still, he drove cautiously, with Marie in the passenger seat in her own world as Smokey Robinson's smooth voice filled the car, "*Quiet storm, blowin' through my mind...*"

He snuck peeks at her foxy brown face; she'd lost a little weight, but she was still beautiful. He wondered if his decision to move on was an emotional decision as opposed to a rational one. It was obvious that he still loved her; or was that just an emotional impulse from seeing her dancing with another man? All these things floated in his mind, vying for attention.

"*Through my mind...*"

"Where are we going, Preston?"

"You tell me."

"You're the one driving in circles, shit." She sucked her teeth. "Take me home, Preston."

"I am."

"When?"

"When?" His eyebrows lifted, he turned slightly towards her. "Soon as I speak my peace."

"Speak, shit."

"I will." He turned onto the freeway and they slid across the Oakland-Alameda Bridge, and soon, they arrived at the Alameda Beach.

"Come on," he said, getting out the car.

"No."

"Get out my car fo' I drag you out!"

"What?" She rolled her eyes. "You don't har'lly scare me." Reluctantly she got out. "It's kinda nippy," she said, rubbing her hands up and down her arms.

"Here, take my jacket."

"Oh, so now, all of a sudden you wanna be chivalrous." She slipped on his jacket. "Straight up Dr. Jekyll and Mr. Hyde."

"Nope, just a Gemini."

"Same shit." A picturesque full moon dominated the sky, and brilliant scores of stars twinkled and winked on the dark, velvet-like backdrop.

"Look at the moon, ReRe," he said and pointed, "ain't it beautiful?"

"Damn, it is, huh?" Then she caught herself. "I'm still mad, so don't think all that Smokey Robinson shit, beaches, and full moons—"

"Ssshh…" He put his finger to his lips. "You killin' the mood."

"Whatever."

They walked the beach and watched the waves lick the shores repeatedly, while the moonlight slow danced on top of the water. He reached for her hand, but she snatched it away.

"Nope, it ain't happenin'."

He shook his head and led her to their familiar haunt; a place where they shared fond memories. They stopped and plopped in the sand, facing each other Indian-style.

He gazed into her eyes.

She stuck out her tongue.

"I don't care what you do, Preston, it ain't gon' work."

"Do you remember when we first came here?"

She stuck her thumbs in her ears. "La-la-la-la-la-la."

He pulled her hands down. "Stop playin'."

"I ain't playin', shoo!" she pouted, "you ain't finna play me, shit. I done cried my heart out, lost weight, man..."

A big wave splashed near them.

"Shit, you telepathic or somethin'?" said Preston, watching the big wave ebb.

"Nope, God just got his angels all around me."

Their eyes dueled and danced.

He took a deep breath and exhaled. "Look, ReRe, I know you been hurtin', ma..." he stabbed his chest with his finger, "but you don't think I hurt too?"

"Pul-lease..." She ticked off points on her fingers. "You been out here fuckin', partyin', and drivin' yo new whip...ah, let me see, oh yeah, fuckin' and partyin'."

"ReRe—"

"And stop callin' me that shit." She looked away, "Only time you call me that shit is when you want some pussy or when you want to intimidate me, shit."

"Baby, can we just talk things out, find some common ground?" he pleaded.

"Common ground?"

"Yeah."

She lowered her eyes. "Let me slap you."

"What?" He blew air through his teeth. "Getdafuckouttahere."

"Yeah, let me slap you as hard as I can."

"You crazy."

"No I ain't, let me slap you and we'll be on yo damn common ground." She picked up some sand and threw it at him. "Cuz this shit sho' ain't it!"

"You got to be out yo rabid ass mind!" he said, dusting himself off.

"Yeah…" she tossed her head, in the typical sistah-girl fashion.. "I got to be out my rabid ass mind fo' ridin' fo' yo ass all dem damn years too, huh niggah!"

"No!" He pointed in her face. "You lost yo' rabid ass mind havin' some young punk diggin' yo guts out, while a niggah was on lock."

"So!"

"So?" He shook his head. "You sho' know how to hurt a niggah."

"Preston, that lil niggah wasn't nothin' to me!"

"So how long was you fuckin' with him?"

She frowned. "Is that what this is about?" She sucked her teeth. "Man, please don't get to askin' me no dumb ass questions like," she changed her voice to a masculine pitch, "How many times you fuck him? Did you suck his dick?" She rolled her eyes. "Take me home! I thought you wanted to talk about us!"

"You had him in our house, that's what I want to talk about!"

"Okay yeah, I fucked up, and Preston, I truly regret that shit." Her eyes were watery now. "But if you loved me...loved us, we coulda worked that shit out, nah mean?"

"I was tryin' to, but you had the niggah in the house again!"

"Preston, he just came to get his damn Xbox!"

He twisted his lips, on some "yeah, whatever", shit.

"And if yo' ass wouldna been tryna play top cop, with all that sneaky shit, none of this shit wouldna happened, shit!"

"What's in the dark always comes out in the light," muttered Preston.

"What?"

"I ain't stutter."

"And I ain't fuckin' stutter when I accepted all yo' damn collect calls either, niggah!" She started finger ticking again. "I ain't stutter when I agreed to send you yo' damn quarterly package, did I? Shit, sometimes I sent yo' ungrateful ass two! I ain't stutter when you asked me to give that ol' dusty triflin' ass bitch a ride, so yo' homeboy could have a visit. I ain't broke my stride not one damn time!"

He jabbed his finger against her forehead. "You sound like yo dumb ass cousin, NeNe, wit' dat hoodrat ass shit! You s'pose to ride fo' a niggah."

"No I don't!" She slapped his hand down. "It's an option! I ain't put yo' damn ass in prison, shit!"

"Option?" He rubbed his palms through his hair. "Ah man, you on some bullshit."

"No, you on some bullshit!"

His eyes blazed and he shook with anger, yet he controlled his voice, loading each word in his mind with his pain. "You made a commitment to me, we made mutual promises no lesser than wedding vows. And not one damn time did you mention some fuckin' option, Marie. I ain't make you say, 'Preston, I love you, I ain't goin' nowhere'. You said that."

"But—" she tried to interrupt.

"Be quiet," he demanded, "let me finish."

She blinked back tears.

"You know why you made that commitment? I'll tell you why, 'cause you knew my love was true. And you knew how hard I tried to bring some food to the table. You knew that these clear people set all these traps fo' niggahs in the hood." He got his ticking game going. "Gang injunctions, no jobs, bullshit schools, liquor stores on every corner, guns and dope flooding the 'hood. Do we make that shit? Nah, but miraculously, it appears in the ghetto. You knew it's way harder on a niggah than it is on y'all. This is why they have thirty-three prisons for men, and only two, or something like that, for women." He pointed to himself. "And you knew I'm a good man, a muthafuckin'," he pounded his chest, "Warrior! That's why you promised me you'd hold me down!"

POW!

She slapped him.

He grabbed her wrists and mounted her. "Don't do that shit no mo' ReRe!" he growled.

"Shut up and fuck me!"

Chapter 27

Kevin O'Reilly was in deep shit; still, he drummed his fingers on the interrogation room's table defiantly, and glared at Detectives Green and Grim of Internal Affairs.

The ash blond, Senior Detective Green, said crisply, "We have two dead bodies and multiple witnesses who claim you were at fault, or at least reckless, and you have nothing to say?"

Blank stare.

"Come on, Kevin," barked sidekick Grim, "Give us something to work with, help us clean up this mess."

Finger drumming.

"So, that's it?" Green shook his head cynically. "If that's the case, it doesn't look too good."

The finger drumming ceased.

"Detectives," said Kevin finally, just above a whisper. The detectives leaned closer. "If you listen closely, you'll hear the sound of me not giving a fuck."

BAM!

Detective Grim slammed his fist on the table.

"Two dead, a city in an uproar, and you got jokes!"

"I just did my fuckin' job, okay!" Kevin shot back.

"Protect and serve is your job!" roared Grim, "Not hunt down and kill!"

"That's bullshit and you know it!"

"How do we clear you if you lawyer up, Kevin?" pleaded Detective Green, his voice calm and reassuring. "Talk to us."

Kevin's eyes danced back and forth between the two veteran detectives.

"Look guys," Kevin offered bluntly, his attitude hard-edged, "They were scumbags, they sped off, we pursued. They crashed. Scumbag-one isn't wearing a seatbelt and rockets out the windshield."

He shrugged and continued, "Scumbag-two rabbits, we give chase. I get to the scene, my partner's bleeding like a stuck pig, and scumbag-two points his gun. I fire. End of story."

The detectives exchange glances, briefly.

"That's the problem," said Green, turning his pen end over end, before pointing it at Kevin, "It sounds like a story, but not a very good one..."

"So why don't you take us to the beginning?" added Grim.

"Do I look like I got stupid—"

The interrogation room door opens, all heads turn towards the entrance. A studious middle-aged man in an expensive suit enters, and cuts his eyes at Kevin.

"I'm not stupid—"

"And," the newcomer announced; his voice demanding and his tone sharp, "you're not without representation." His eyes now on the detectives, he says, "Gentlemen, this interview is officially over. I'm—"

"We know who you are, Mr. Mason," sneered Grim, cutting the attorney off, "and trust me, he's gonna need your entire office."

Not to be outdone, Attorney Michael Mason straightened his tie, and then placed his hand on Kevin's shoulder.

"Well, if that's the case, Detective," he said, with a razor-lipped smirk, "my office is the best money can buy."

The two detectives headed for the door.

"Too bad money can't bring those two boys back," said Green over his shoulder.

****

Later that night, Kevin called Tamala. "Whatdayamean you can't talk to me, Tamala?"

"Kevin, you're on administrative leave and you may very well be charged with a serious felony," said Tamala into the cell phone.

"So are they sayin'—"

"That's exactly why I can't talk to you; it's a conflict of interest. I'm hangin' up now, Kevin."

"But, you can fuckin' talk to ex-cons you *claim* as your family," he said snidely.

"What does that have to do with you being responsible for two deaths, huh Kevin?"

"I'm not responsible for shit!" he yelled indignantly. "A cop can't so much as fart too loud in this city, without being accused of some sorta brutality."

"Two young men died, Kevin, and died brutally."

"They were criminals, and I was doing my job."

"They were human beings and you're not God."

"Tamala—"

"Bye."

Chapter 28

She lit the last candle and stepped back to appreciate her creativity.

"Ummm-hmmm," she clapped her hands softly. "Perfect," whispered J'Neane.

"Oops," she exclaimed as she reminded herself, "Lemme light this Black Loooovve." Smoke from the long stem incense curled into the air, she waved her hand through the smoke and sniffed. "Hmmph, hmmph, hmmph," she slapped her meaty hip. "It's gonna be erotic city up in herrreee tonight."

The phone rang and she rolled her eyes; she knew without looking at the caller ID who it was. She answered the phone, "What Paula?"

"Girl, you gon' get that dick, huh?" Aunt Paula teased in a hushed voice.

"Paula..." J'Neane said bashfully.

"See, what you do is when he hittin' it from the back," coaxed Aunt Paula excitedly, "reach up underneath and play with them big ole balls-—"

"Paula, you don't have to hold my hand."

"Woooo-weeee," Paula giggled, "'Kay, I'ma quit, but shit, I'm the one hooked you up with Nutzilla. I at least should be able to put my two cents in."

"You just a freak."

"Freak?"

"Freakazoid."

"I heard-the-hell-outta-that," said Paula, "but you the one write that ole porno-put-it-in-my-booty stuff, shit."

"As a profession, thank you."

"Oh well, you write it. I live it." Paula chuckled. "And love it. Thank God."

Laughter echoes through both phones.

Aunt Paula started in on J'Neane again. "Well did you at least fix the man some food? You gotsta feed them big ole balls, if ya want 'em to bust fat and lava-like on ya."

"Paula please…"

"Sticky-wicky," Paula kept teasing, then eased up a bit. "What you cook?"

"I made some Louisiana fried chicken, and the meat is so juicy, it just falls off the bone."

"The bone? Woo, now ya talkin'."

"Mashed potatoes, corn on the cob—"

"Corn on a cob…shit, I can deep throat a raw cob, peel it and bust every kernel, in one bob."

"Paula," laughed J'Neane, "woman, you is crazy."

"What about the candles, got 'em goin' girl?"

"Yep."

"Whatchu gon' wear?"

"A lil something I picked up from Victoria's Secret."

"J'Neane, I don't give a damn 'bout Victoria's Secret, you besta have them big ass titties right in his face, like, *BAM*!"

"You think I should?"

"Hell yeah, you shoulda seen the way he was lookin' at 'em."

"He was?"

"Yeah."

"I don't know..." J'Neane cupped one of her voluptuous, massive breasts. "I think they startin' to sag a lil."

"What?" Aunt Paula sucked her teeth, "Girl, if them damn things ever sag, you gon' be steppin on 'em."

J'Neane giggled and plopped her wide ass on the couch. "Leave my titties alone, and what my baby doin'?"

"J'Nae's lil hot ass in there with Five."

"Tell her—" A car pulled into the driveway, and she peeked out the window.

"That's him, I'll call you back."

"Play by play."

"Yeah...yeah...girl!"

"One last thang."

"What?"

"Swallow."

"Hush it."

J'Neane rushed into the bedroom to make some last minute adjustments.

Preston bounced out the car feeling like shit. He'd been avoiding J'Neane's calls all week, because he'd spent every waking moment in Marie's arms. However, today was unavoidable, because he had to pick up the manuscripts J'Neane edited, as well as pay her for her services, and on top of all that, he knew it was only right to come clean about him and Marie. Just how he was gonna do it, he hadn't the slightest idea.

He rang the doorbell. The door opened slowly and the velvet vocal of Teena Marie's, "Portuguese Love", floated out sensually. "*I ain't gonna let you go that easy. You've got to say you love me too...*" J'Neane stepped into view and pulled him inside.

"J'Neane—"

"Ssshhh."

The aroma was exotic; candles waved small fires underneath the dimmed lights, and just as his eyes adjusted, J'Neane dropped her robe from her shoulders. The biggest, ripest pair of black watermelons stood before him, each capped by large, pointed, meaty nipples. Her hips were wide and luscious, and the red silk lingerie set her curves off. She beckoned him with a finger. "Come on," she murmured, with glazed and pouty lips. "I got some good gushy-gushy for you."

He rocked up.

"Ummm Hmmm," she purred, "Come get it..." She lifted a big pillow of flesh and sucked on its nipple erotically. "Oooh, I'm so hot and horny, I'm 'bouta explode," she cooed.

He licked his lips and looked behind him. Part of him wanted to break wide, but the big part of him had him stuck. Seconds later, he was on the couch, his stiff manhood betraying him of his original intentions. *Fuck it,* he thought, *you only live once.*

"Owww...oh...daaammmn," he groaned, his hand guiding her bobbing head. She had his meat missile lodged between her huge breasts, slurping the bell shape of his dick head seductively, and then her head dived and bobbed.

"Oooooh, you like that?" Her voice was small and rich with desire.

"Shiiit yeah."

"Ooooh, this dick is soooo big and juicy." She put her wrist next to it. "Ohmigod, it's thicker than my wrist."

"Keep sucking, we'll talk later."

She did, and sweet, wet sucking noises filled the room.

SLURP. SLURP. SLURP.

He grabbed her head with both hands, and pushed his meatcicle deep down her throat.

She gagged, choked, but kept sucking and slurping. She lifted her lips off it briefly and stroked him, running a finger over the pre-cum leakage. Then she jacked it and kissed the bulbous dick head. "Muah," she smacked and put it back between her deep cleavage. "Ummm, big daddy, you can bust it in my mouth, call me bitch, put it in my ass, whatever you like, 'kay?"

"Ooooh daaammn," he sucked air through his teeth. "Sssss, you turnt up, huh?"

She resumed a greedy, wet, nasty bob. "Ummmmm..." she moaned as she spit, slobbered, and slurped, "hmmmmph."

"Yeahhhh, that's wassup," he rasped, "go dumb on that dick, girl."

She tossed her head up and down madly.

SLURP. SLURP. SLURP. SLURP. SLURP.

Teena Marie crooned a high note, in the background, "*Oooooh...*"

J'Neane made like *Deep Throat* in front of him. "Ummmm.."

He was all tingles and shakes.

"Ooooh, big daddy," she whispered, and looked up at him, "looks like you 'bouta bust."

"Oh shiiit, yeah get it," he urged and fondled her heavy, warm breasts.

He watched her reach beneath herself and flick her fingers frantically and spasm. She came up for air.

"Oooooh," she convulsed and made a fuck face, "Oooooh big daddy, see what you made me do...?"

He threw his head back and groaned. *Damn, this big bitch is a freak,* he thought.

She bobbed on his dick wildly, and slurped loudly, then squeezed his pulsating giant penis in between her large titties.

"Oooooh yeah big daddy, gon' ahead and bust it on mama's big tits, 'kay?" she purred, and then milked the bloated tip of his member with her soft, wet lips.

"Get it, get it," he moaned, "I'm 'bouta blow."

Her eyes relay from his face to his big dick as she sandwiched it in between her warm, jiggling mammaries. "Go 'head big daddy, I got it," she drawled as he fucked her titties. "Give it to me."

He shuddered and released a powerful. milky white jet of jism, followed by a few lesser spurts. "Owww...oh...shhhiiit..." he spasmed and moaned as his toes curled. His dick flopped and throbbed, and then spurted again.

"Oooooh, big daddy..." Her fuck face flashed wet puckered lips. "That was a phat one."

She rubbed the cum in like lotion across her nipples and areolas. "I betcha it's just rich in vitamins, huh?" Her big pretty eyes looked up at him, full of lust.

He was speechless.

"Nutzilla..." She smiled with a thin, silky rope of cum dangling off her lips.

"Huh?"

Chapter 29

He threw back four drumsticks and a breast, gobbled down the side dishes, and washed it down with two large glasses of orange juice. All under the smiling eyes of J'Neane, the dick fiend.

He licked his fingers, pushed back from the table and rubbed his stomach.

Then J'Neane's ole country ass gon' have the nerve to say, "Was it good?" She twirled her finger in her weave. "I mean, did you like it?"

"Horrible." He rubbed his stomach some more.

"Horrible?" She screwed up her face and pouted, "But you—"

"Horrible, cuz I ain't got another stomach," he belched, "excuse me, but shit, I wish I was a three hundred pound clown right now, cuz that shit right there," he pointed at the big bowl of chicken on the table, before snatching up another drumstick, "is the type of shit that make a niggah envy fat people."

Then he took a big bite out the drumstick.

She smiled from ear to ear.

He knocked the drumstick down to the bone like a starving Ethiopian, dropped it on his plate, and wiped his greasy lips.

"Boy you ain't playin', huh?"

"Nope."

"Well when you get through with that..." She dropped her hands on her curvaceous hips. "I got something else I wanna see you eat." Her voice was syrupy and sexy.

"Iz that right?" He licked his lips. "Woman, you ain't tired? You done pulled like fo', five nuts outta me."

"Hell, I'm backed up." She bit her finger seductively.

Well, this is as good a time as any to break it down to her. "J'Neane," he said as his face became all business-like. "Look, we need to talk."

She frowned.

"What's wrong?"

"Nothin'...but a lot."

"What's that s'pose to mean, *Mr. Man?*"

He got up from the kitchen table. "C'mere." He pulled her into the living room, on to the couch. "J'Neane..." He shook his head. "How can I say this?"

"What?" her voice was tiny and pleading, as she fastened her robe tightly. "Wha-what's wrong?"

He closed his eyes and exhaled slowly. "J'Neane..." He turned to face her and held her hands, "Look, you a beautiful woman feel me, but—"

"But what?"

"I don't know how to say this—"

"Say what?" She pulled her hands away and placed one on her chest. "You scaring me."

"I'm sorry." He rubbed her thick thigh. "But you remember what-when I tol' you about my ex?"

Her eyes instantly watered. "You know what, Preston?" She got up. "You need not say anymore, cuz I done heard this song before."

He pulled her back down on the couch and massaged her hand. She pulled it back and crossed her arms over her full breasts. "J'Neane..." he tried to hug her.

"Mooovve."

"C'mon girl."

"I said mooove." She pushed him away. "Lemme hear yo fake ass jive, so I can hurry up and heal, shit." She rolled her eyes and folded her arms.

"J'Neane, look...I swear a niggah wasn't playin'—"

"So y'all all a sudden back together," she turned to face him, "huh?"

He nodded.

"So you just gonna come fuck the shit outta me, get your manuscripts and bounce, huh?" It was her turn to shake her head now. "Wham-bam-thank-you-ma'am..."

"It ain't even—"

"I oughta delete yo shit, like you tryna delete me."

"Go 'head, I prolly deserve it!"

She rolled her eyes in disgust. "I shoulda known it was too good—" she broke down in sobs. "Wh-why I always gotta be the fat bitch that gets dumped, huh?" Tears fell freely now.

He really felt dumb ass shitty now. "Come on, J."

"C-co-come on m-m-my ass, Pr-Preston," she cried, "Women feel shit! It's what we do best, an-and right now,

Preston," she put her hands in her palms, "I feels fucked up..."

"I'm sorry, J'Neane, I came here to tell you before you...before we...you know."

"Like that's s'pose to make me feel better," she sniffled, "I see you're real good at this."

"I-I," he looked up at the ceiling, "I don't know what to say."

She sniffles, and then there's silence. "Preston."

"Wassup?"

Her voice was calm, but slightly cracking. "You wanna know what'll make me feel better?"

He was eager.

"Just say it, J'Neane, and I'll do it."

She dropped her robe, turned around and pressed her voluptuous breasts against his face. "Fuck me," her voice was barely a whisper, "and fuck me some mo'."

He rocked up again. All night and into the next day, he nailed her juicy pussy to the mattress.

When they woke up, she fixed him a big breakfast and they went over the final edit of both manuscripts.

He was ecstatic; she'd done a marvelous job. It flowed better, and there wasn't a single typo to be found. He kissed her on the cheek and pulled some bills out his wallet.

"Keep it, Preston." She leaned back and spread her legs wide. "Do it one mo' time fo' mama, 'kay?" she purred.

He did. As he dug her back out, she rocked, while her legs shook high in the air on either side of him. *Shit, ain't no need of crying when it's raining, she thought.* Then she wiped the sweat from his face, and stuffed a titty in his mouth. "Get it big daaadddy..."

Chapter 30

Marie was steaming, yet a wee bit worried. She'd been calling, texting and leaving messages on Preston's phone all night, then all morning, and well into the afternoon, and he hadn't returned a single call.

A car cruised by, music bumpin', as she rushed to the window and yanked back the shades. It wasn't Preston.

"Damn," she chewed her bottom lip, "This niggah got a bitch on window watch like a crackhead," she said aloud. *Where this niggah at?*

"Danni!" she yelled towards her daughter's room.

"Hol' up Mama," she called back, "I'm on the phone."

"Hold up nothing Wendy Williams, bring yo butt here, you can gossip later."

"Uggh...seeee," mumbled Dannielle and pushed out her room, face on the scrunch.

"And fix yo face!"

Dannielle twisted her lips and was about to add an eye roll.

Marie unleashed on her, "I'm dead serious."

Dannielle gave her a head roll and saucer eyes.

"I swear, Dannielle, you best not test me today, girl!"

"What I do, Mama?" she broke that shit down real quick, "Wassa matter?"

"Nothin'."

"What then?" her voice was tiny and timid.

"Go on Facebook and pull up that rapper name FreshKidd's profile."

"That's all?"

"Yeah."

"Oh, I thought I was in trouble or somethin'."

"You gon' be if you don't hurry up and get on that computer, gossip girl."

"'Kay Mama, dang."

Dannielle hottailed it to the desktop and in a flash, FreshKidd's page was up. Marie hunkered behind her and locked the numbers in.

"That's all, Mama?"

"Yep, now bounce."

"Oh, so now you done used yo' daughter up," she pursed her lips, "It's bounce now, huh?" She rolled her eyes. "I'm just so unappreciated."

She kissed her daughter on the cheek.

"Awww, poodah-doodah, you know you my supa girl."

"I guess..." She teased Marie with a head weave and smirk, then said, "Lookin' fo' Daddy huh?"

"Stay outta grown folks' business."

"You...sooo...spruuuuuung..."

Marie jabbed a finger towards Dannielle's bedroom. "Room."

Dannielle giggled and dipped off, singing, *"I'm sprung... got me doing things I'll never do..."*

"A'ight now," Marie warned playfully. After a few dry runs, she finally hit pay dirt.

"Speak."

She recognized his voice off the bat. "Damn Zo, you ain't har'lly professional."

"Who this?"

"Marie, who you want it to be?"

He grunted. "Yeah, wassup?"

"Dang, it's like that?"

He blew air. "You a cold piece of work, you know that?"

"What?"

"What?" he said incredulously, "you squeeze my boy's heart, twist his brain, then damn near cause World War III, and now you callin' my line uninvited, lookin' for him? Man...like I said, speak and speak fast!"

"Zo, stop trippin'; relationships be complicated, shit."

He had to chuckle on that one. "What you want Re-to-the-Re?

"Where my man at?"

Zo started laughing.

"What you laughin' at niggah, shit, ain't nothin' funny."

"You."

"Me?" she heard a car outside and peeked out the window again. "Joke on me, huh?" It wasn't Preston.

"Yeah," Kenzo said, losing a fight with the funnies. "P musta crushed yo coochie to powder, now ya dick sick huh?"

"Whatever."

"How you get my number anyway, tramp?"

"Fakeplayas.com, so don't feel special," she retorted, "now, have you seen Preston?"

"Nope."

"Come on, Zo, stop playin'," she pleaded, "he ain't callin' me back…is his phone broke or somethin'?"

"Not that I know of."

"Well, if you see him, tell him to call me, it's important."

"I'll think about it."

"Stop playin', Kenzo."

"Why should I do anything for you, cheater?"

"I ain't no cheater, shit."

"Oh, you just accidently fell on ol' boy's dick, huh?"

"Whatever, Zo," she said heatedly. "Me and my man done worked things out, so fall back dude, shit."

"You know what…I'ma do that, cuz I know the niggah love yo stankin' ass."

"So is you gon' tell him to call me?"

"Nope," he said teasingly, "That's what I ain't gon' do, I ain't 'bout to get in y'all business."

"You ain't shit, Zo."

"And I ain't yo watchdog either."

"Hmmph," she smacked her lips, "Well, see ya later, hater!" She ended the call. "Ol' punk ass niggah," she clicked her tongue, "he make me sick!"

The phone rang. She answered quickly. "Hello?"

"Is this dumb hoes chat line?"

"Fuck you, hoe, what you want?"

It was NeNe.

"Bitch, we gotta make up one day, so it might as well be today."

"Hmmph."

"And! Don't nobody care 'bout yo lil stank attitude, girl!" said NeNe.

"Girl, I really ain't in the mood right now, okaaayyy."

"You should be, you been gettin yo pussy stuffed like a stocking, shit."

"Whatever."

The line clicked. "Hold up NeNe." She clicked over. "Hello."

"Bitch, where my man at?" the caller snapped.

Marie wasn't the only one looking for her man.

"Who in the fuck is this?"

"You old washed up, bitch; you know who in the fuck this is!"

It was the boy toy's lil girlfriend; they'd had words before, but Marie, the mature adult, always shined her on. Then she chastised boy toy for giving her phone number out to some stupid young bitch, but he claimed she got it out his phone when he was sleep.

"Ahem…look little girl, I don't fuck with your boyfriend, okay, so why don't you go down to Mickey D's and get you a happy meal, okay?"

"Bitch, don't try to play me," the young girl popped back, "He said he still fuckin' yo stale ass, and you cashin' him out, dumb bitch!"

275

"Look, little girl, he's lyin', but you know what? I ain't finna be too many more of your bitches!"

"What bitch!" young girl was hyped now, "Bitch, I know where you stay at, don't have me come beat yo' old ass!"

"You bring yo stupid ass over here if you want to, hoe, but I'll tell you this much, you'll come walkin', but you'll leave crawlin', dirtbag bitch!"

"Bitch what! I'm on my way!"

Click.

Marie's heart began to beat fast, replaying those words and the way the young broad had said it. She had that certain distinctive tone. *She wasn't playing*, Marie thought as she stared at the phone.

NeNe had hung up, so Marie hurriedly called her back.

"Boss Bitch Incorporated."

"NeNe, that was Rico's lil punk ass girlfriend, callin' me with that bullshit."

"What bullshit?"

"She think her lil punk ass niggah over here, now she talkin' 'bout she on her way."

"Bitch, you stay in some shit, huh?"

"Whatever, NeNe, that bitch just called my house out the blue. I don't even speak to that young niggah no mo'."

"Where she from?"

"I think she from the Bottoms."

"West Oakland?"

"Yeah, I think so."

"Well bitch, I'm 'bout to come over there, cuz them West Oakland hoes be on that bullshit, and if she say she coming, her little ass on her way."

"I'll mop that hoe up, let her come," she was trying to pump herself up. "Let her come."

"Well bitch, grease up, cuz she comin'."

Marie's heart beat faster.

Chapter 31

He activated the FaceTime feature on the iPad. Kenzo's face appeared. "Where you been, my niggah?"

Hol' up, lemme pull over."

"Yeah niggah, do that."

Preston slipped out of traffic and parked. "'Sup?"

"Niggah, yo' girl just called, worried to death."

"Damn."

"Where was you?"

"Man," he burst into a Colgate smile, "I got clobbered by some titties the size of a monster truck, and fell into a cum coma."

"The wannabe Zane bitch, huh?"

"Yeah."

"Was it good?"

"Niggah, it was yum-yada."

"Yum-yada, huh?"

"Yesssirrr."

"Well, you betta zoom-yada yo ass and go check on yo' girl fo' she call yo' parole agent or somethin'," he laughed. "Hold up for a second."

He yelled for Ramona. She came and sat down next to him and he pulled off her shirt.

"What you doin', my niggah?" asked Preston.

Kenzo pulled Ramona's bra off and pushed her huge breasts towards the camera, the round bosses of her nipples and juicy breasts filled the screen.

"Stop Kenzo'," Ramona protested mildly.

"Damn!" It escaped his mouth. Kenzo jiggled her titties.

"Was they bigger than these?" asked Zo in the background.

"Yep."

"Stop lyin' niggah and go check on ya girl, you poodle."

"I'm on my way, titty-bo."

"One."

"One."

Chapter 32

"Stace, wassup?"

"Nothin', why?"

"Look, I'm on my way, Marie got beef!"

"Whaaat…with who, NeNe?"

"Some young West Oakland bitch."

Well hurry up, where Angel?"

NeNe pressed the loudspeaker button.

"Right here! Killa Crew, bitch!" piped Angel. "Them young hoes don't know who they fuckin' with!"

Chapter 33

They were parked discreetly, right outside Marie's apartment complex, waiting on a way in.

"Oh she want it, huh Tish?' said boy toy's fat ass, shit-starting sister, and as usual, she was on her bullshit. "You betta beat that punk bitch down too, ho!" she egged from the driver's seat.

"Mmm-hmm," the young broad nodded frantically, tying her weave in a ponytail, and slipping off her earrings. "I'm 'bout to drag this ho, watch!"

She tucked her cellphone in the glove compartment and then peered out the window, anxiously, bouncing in her seat.

"I got yo back, Tish, shit," chimed another pump-up artist in the back seat, "I'm tired of these ole suga mama ass hoes, just buyin' the dick, let's dog walk this bitch, show her what that lower bottom like."

"Yeah."

"That's wassup."

The other girl was very quiet, but her eyes darted back and forth around the car excitedly.

A car pulled up and buzzed the gate.

"Oooh, bitch, we in," said the young broad from the passenger's seat, "Come on go. Go!"

Chapter 34

Marie paced back and forth in the living room, every so often peeking out the window.

Her thoughts turned inward. *Where is he at?*

She tucked her lips over her teeth, and then hollered, "Danni!"

"Huh, Mama?"

"Call Preston from your phone and see if he answers."

"'Kay Mama, what's the number?"

"777-9311."

After a minute or so Dannielle yelled back, "Straight to voicemail!"

She walked over to her purse and fished out a Newport, and sat back on the couch puffing away. She smoked it damn near to the filter, before laying it in the ashtray without bothering to put it out. The smoke wormed its way up from the butt in a silky, fluttering, and winding dance, and then disappeared before it hit the ceiling. She put the butt out briskly, and then called Preston again. This time when his voicemail came on, she left a message. *"Preston I don't know where you're at, but you could have at least returned my calls, I know you see all those missed calls..."* she paused briefly, *"but on second thought, that's alright, don't even bother. Stay where-ever-the-hell you been at. Bye!"* She slammed the receiver down. "Hmmmph." She was still mad, but for the moment, it felt good to release some steam.

Chapter 35

Preston was halfway to Marie's house when he realized he'd left his phone back at J'Neane's.

"Damn", he glanced in the rearview, then made an illegal U-turn and sped back towards J'Neane's house.

From parts unknown a prickle of alarm tingled the back of his neck.

He drove faster.

Chapter 36

"Wassamatter, Mama?" Dannielle's eye followed Marie intensely. "Why you so nervous?"

"Ain't nobody nervous!" she said in a nasty, snapping sort of way, "And I done tol' you 'bout bein' in my business any damn way!"

"Mama, why you yellin' at me?" Dannielle sulked and slumped teary-eyed on the couch. "I ain't even do nothin' but ask what's wrong."

Marie's motherly instincts subdued her uneasiness momentarily, and she sat next to her daughter. "I'm sorry baby," she hugged her and tousled her hair. "I shouldna yelled at you, 'kay?"

Dannielle sniffled and nodded slowly. "But what's wrong, doe?"

"Nothin' but Rico's girlfriend callin', here playin' on my phone."

"Tisha?"

"That her name?"

"Yeah Mama," her eyes got big, "What she say, cuz Mama, them broads is stupid rowdy."

"Ain't nobody worried—"

CRASH!

Glass exploded, and a rock smashed against the wall, knocking down several pictures.

"Bring yo' ass out here, bitch!" the voice shrieked and challenged, "I wanna see you make me crawl, ho!"

Marie rushed towards the door.

"Hold on, Mama, wait fo' me," Dannielle kicked off her house shoes and slipped on her tennies, while her young eyes looked for a weapon.

"Come on, Danni," Marie was antsy. "Hurry up!"

Suddenly, another rock came flying and this time, it smashed into the entertainment center.

"Aww hell-to-the-naw!" Marie jumped back, as a collection of CD's collapsed to the floor.

"Come downstairs, ho!" threatened the voice and Marie knew it couldn't be anybody but young broad's. "Talk that shit now, bitch!"

Young broad glanced at fat ass shit starter, who was bending down looking for another rock to chunk.

"Fuck that!" Marie tore out the house.

By this time, people stretched their necks outside apartment doors, trying to figure out where the ruckus was coming from.

Marie was barreling down the stairs, two at a time, and it didn't take her long to figure out which of the four girls was Rico's girlfriend, cuz she stepped up, bounced on her toes, and then threw her dukes up like a dude.

"Come on, bitch!"

She had about ten pounds on Marie, all in the ass and legs, but this made no difference to Marie, none whatsoever. Marie had that crazed look in her eyes and she charged at young broad with such ferocity, that the other girls, lightweight backed off.

Young broad started swinging wildly, but Marie didn't break her stride. "Bitch..." A few blows glanced off young broad's head. "I tol' your stupid ass..."

She rushed young broad straight to the dirt and young broad's head banged viciously on the ground.

BAM!

Marie mounted her and began to pummel her face.

BAM! SLAP!

"Oowww," young broad was dazed, and now she realized she'd bitten off more than she could chew. "Get her off me, y'all," she begged.

Shit-starter grabbed a handful of Marie's hair.

"Oouch!" yelped Marie, "Lemme go!"

"Let her up, bitch!"

Somebody kicked Marie in the face. "Ooof," she grunted as she tasted blood.

This was when shit-starter's fat ass saw a flash of movement out the corner of her eyes; she threw her hands up.

WHAM!

It was too late.

"Bitch, get off my mama!"

Shit-starter somersaulted forward; her skirt flew way up and over, exposing her massive, fleshy buttocks. The two chunky half-moons were littered with cellulite, and several shades of rashes colored the crevasses of her ass cheeks. Fat ass came to a sliding halt; face-first. She was knocked-the-fuck-out.

Now it was a small crowd of onlookers.

"Oooh them hoes killin' shit out here," someone said.

"Awww naw," an onlooker pointed, "that bitch straight snoring."

"Aye, somebody cover her nasty lookin' ass fo' I throw up," another added.

"I'll hit that shit," countered his partner, he grabbed his crotch. "Late night, though."

"Uggh."

"You bitches..." *WHOOSH!* The air whistled as she swung the big stick. "Back up!" Dannielle shouted and the ax handle she wielded, bobbed and weaved above her head for another strike.

They spread out backing up, eyes darting back and forth to one another, then at Dannielle.

BOOM!

Dannielle hit the ground and rolled, clutching her jaw. "Owww," she screamed, her eyes searching for the culprit.

"Bitch!" It was Rico and one of his homeboys. "Don't be hittin' my fuckin' sister, lil ho!" He snatched the stick from underneath her.

"Watch niggah," Dannielle yelled, still writhing in pain, "My daddy gon' beat yo' ass again, punk!"

Now all three girls rat packed Marie like wild dogs. One kicked her, the other yanked her hair this way and that way, while young broad ripped her clothes off. Marie's shapely breasts swung and jiggled for all to see.

"Uh-unh," pleaded a woman resident, "hell naw, somebody help her!"

287

Dannielle shook the cobwebs out her head and jumped to her feet. Quiet-girl peeped her and she and Dannielle squared off. They were evenly matched.

"Get that bitch, Dannielle," urged a bystander, "help yo' mama girl!"

Quiet-girl charged at Dannielle, and Dannielle snatched her shirt over her head and rode her to the ground.

"Get her, Dannielle!" bystander yelled excitedly, "Get her!"

Titties swinging their beefy tips, Marie was still fighting wildly, two against one. However, her energy was waning; she'd rush young broad only to be blindsided by the other broad, and vice versa.

"Rico, break that shit up!" someone barked.

Rico was attending to fat ass shit-starter, who was bleeding about the head and face.

"Fuck that!" he scowled, "Let them hoes chunk 'em!"

"Come on, you washed up bitch," taunted young broad, "You got lucky the first time."

"Why you need help?" Marie puffed and wheezed, sucking air fast; her eyes darted back and forth between the two girls stalking her. "You can't handle me by yo'self, stupid bitch?" She made no move to cover herself. She just didn't have the energy.

A Good Samaritan came and stood in between Marie and the two assailants; he handed Marie a shirt. Hurriedly, she slipped it over her head and gulped in as much air as she could.

"Moooove niggah," the two girls tried to push through Good Samaritan, but he held them off.

"Y'all go 'head up!"

Rico and his homeboy punched Good Samaritan from both sides, and his good ass fell and curled up. They stomped him. "Stay up outta muthafuckas..." The sound of boots smashing against flesh arose in the air with a sickening sound. "Business!"

Young broad's cohort ran to help her homegirl fend off Dannielle.

Marie had her second wind now and she chased her down, socking her about the head and face.

WHAM!

"Bitch, get off my baby!"

POW!

Young broad took this opportunity to grab a handful of Marie's hair, wrenching her neck back brutally.

BAM!

She socked her, "Where you goin' bitch!"

"Killla Crrreeewww!"

The crowd parted.

"Ooh shit, here come the cavalry!" someone yelled.

"Get them hoes!"

Big Stacy, amazingly light on her feet, led the charge. She snatched young broad by her neck and tossed her to the ground like a rag doll, and commenced to booting her in the ass.

BOOM!

"Killa!"

POW!

"Crew!"

FLUME!

"Stupid ho!"

"Put them fif-fo' D's on then hoes y'all!" an O.G. yelled, and then turned to a youngsta. "That's what we used to say in my days."

Angel and NeNe was all over the other two girls like flies on shit. "Killa Crew, bitch!" they shouted, letting loose a serious flurry of kicks, slaps, and punches on those two girls, wherever they could connect with flesh, skin, or bone.

"Fuck you think this is!"

Rico ran up on NeNe and swung wildly.

Dannielle screamed, "Watch out, NeNe!"

NeNe ducked at the last moment and backed up; then reached into her jacket and whipped out a chrome .380. She cocked one in the chamber.

CLICK-CLACK!

"Run up on me again, young punk!" She walked towards him. "You wanna hit on bitches, huh?" She turned it sideways. "Come on, hit me now, niggah!"

He took off running and his homeboy ran off with him.

"You busta ass niggahs," she called out after them. "Got lifted by a bitch!"

Marie was now mounted squarely on top of young broad, she had two fists twisted in young broad's hair, banging her head on the ground, ministering in the process.

"Bitch..."

BAM!

"Didn't…"

"BAM!

"I tell you…"

BAM-BAM-BAM!

She still held young broad's head. "You was gon' leave here crawling ho!"

BAM!

Suddenly, Angel screamed, "Ahhhhw!" She fell and clutched her stomach, as the quiet cohort ran towards Marie.

"She got a knife!" somebody screamed.

"It's always the quiet ones you gotta watch," one bystander whispered to another one.

"Maaammmaaa!"

The large butcher knife came down hard and fast like a guillotine. "Ahhhhhh!" Marie's piercing scream penetrated the air and her eyes bulged in agony and shock.

"Oh my God!" an onlooker covered her face.

The butcher knife was impaled in the middle of her back to the hilt.

Pop! Pop!

"Bitch!" NeNe fired, striking Marie's butcher in the neck and shoulder.

She fell and flopped in convulsions, next to Marie.

The crowd instantly scattered like roaches.

Dannielle pulled her mother gently into her lap. "Mama!" Dannielle's young eyes were full of tears, pain, and gloom. "Oh Mama, just keep yo' eyes open!"

Marie's eyes flickered strangely and blood creeped out the sides of her mouth, as she tried to speak. However, death was calling.

"Mama, don't talk, just hold on 'kay...just hold on. I'm right here."

Valiantly, Marie fought off death. "D-D-Danni", she gasped, and then coughed up blood.

"Huh Mama?" she cried. "Don't go Mama, please!"

"I-I-I love you, 'kay?"

Dannielle felt it right then, the eerie vibration when the body shivers as life slides away.

"Mama, nooooo...Mama!"

So far away.

"Tell him, Danni," she said with her last breath, "tell him I love him." Her eyes waved goodbye and she was gone...

Chapter 37

"*I'm goin' up yonder...I'm goin' up yonder!*" sang the choir.

In the background, organ chords merged with the heavenly voices harmonizing and galvanizing spirits. Old ladies rocked and fanned their faces. The children were wide-eyed; some curiously peeked at the casket up ahead, while others stretched their necks to and fro, watching and weighing the silent tears and sporadic wails.

"Maaammma!" screamed Dannielle, as someone tried to console her.

Marie's pearl white casket was decorated with several colorful wreaths.

"Whhhyyyy?" she shrieked louder; then tried to run towards the casket. They held her. "Don't leave me, Maaammma!"

"That's so sad," murmured a parishioner, as she wiped a tear. "So, so sad..."

"Whhhyyyy?"

The choir clapped and swayed, "*To be with my Looorrrd!*" several had tears streaking down their cheeks, arms held up high, as they hit their last rising note. "*YONDER!*"

The music ceased as he preacher stepped up to the podium. He was in his late 30's, well groomed, with captivating light brown eyes. The church became silent. He shook his head and spread his Bible out before him.

"Praise the Lord," he said; his voice was a trained, smooth, boom. "Amen."

"Amen," chimed the congregation.

Praise the Lord, O my soul, and forget not His benefits, who forgives all your sins, and heals your diseases; who redeems your life from the pit and crowns you with love and compassion." He raised his head. "Psalms 103, verses 1 through 4," he said softly.

"Wellll…" someone added.

He closed his Bible and shook his head again, then said, "You know, when the Williams family asked me to speak today," his eyes swept over the crowd of mourners, "I stayed up all night to search…" he paused, "to search my Bible, and my memories, to find something meaningful to say."

"Amen."

"See, 'cause I knew Marie too…she grew up in this church!"

"Mmm-hmm."

"I've seen her smile!"

"That's right."

"I've heard her laughter!"

"Say it."

"Such a beautiful young woman." He shook his head.

"Amen."

"And because I failed to find anything that *I* felt was spiritually poetic enough, to articulate what I wanted to convey, I just decided to speak from the heart."

"Speak."

"Why?" He glared at the crowd. "Why is it so much hate?" He closed his eyes briefly "Why do we love to hate one another?" He wiped his head with his handkerchief.

"Mm-hmm."

"When it's so many reasons to love."

"Say it."

"But that's okay, 'cause God got her back now," he raised his voice dramatically and waggled his finger. "It ain't gon' be no stabbin's in the back in Heaven!"

"Praise Him!"

"It ain't gon' be no more jumpin' people!"

"Preach."

"Lyin' in wait!"

"Welllll..."

"Ain't gon' be no more crews of killa's!"

"Praise the Lawwd."

"Not for her," his voice became as calm as still waters, "So dry your eyes, 'cause she's safe now...ohhh yessss...God got her back now." He pointed up above.

The choir rose.

"She's with my Lord now."

They sang again.

"Yonder!"

"Maaammma!" wailed Dannielle, kicking and screaming.

When it was over, Preston filed out the church with Kenzo at his side, his footsteps were heavy with guilt and shame. His head hung low, face shrouded by sunglasses to mask bloodshot eyes, and bloodshot pain. Kenzo rubbed his shoulders, as they shuffled down the church steps. It felt like every eye in the crowd burned holes through his spirit.

Just ahead, he caught sight of Dannielle and NeNe holding onto each other, struggling towards the awaiting limo.

He raced forward and grabbed Dannielle's arm. "Danni," he croaked.

She spun around, her face a mask of agony. Her eyes crawled over him. "Where were you!?" she spat, "When have you ever been there for us?"

"Come on, Dannielle," NeNe said, shooting daggers at him.

"Where were you when we needed you, huh?" she raged, her eyes, her sorrow, her pain, paralyzed him.

He dropped his head...

BOOK

III

Chapter 38

Kenzo peered into the trashed room, shook his head in disgust, and then pinched his nose.

"Eeewww," he said.

The room was straight trashed, half-eaten Chinese food on the floor peppering a minefield of pizza crusts, and on the dresser, a mad legion of ants were having their way with a discarded candy bar. In the center of it all was a body, tucked head to toe, underneath a heavy comforter.

He kicked the bed. "Get up sucka!" There was no movement, so he kicked it harder. "Get up!"

"Lemme alone, blood," the voice underneath the comforter moaned.

"Fuck that!" roared Kenzo, "you on some weirdo shit, bruh!"

He kicked the bed again, and then snatched the comforter off. "It's been three weeks, get yo ass up!"

Preston jumped to his feet in a teary-eyed scowl. "I'm tellin' you, blood..." He balled up his fists at his sides. "Backdafuckup!"

"Or what, niggah?" Backing down was not on the agenda, as he said, "What you gon' do niggah, huh?"

"Dude, you cain't see," he pounded his chest violently, "a niggah hurtin'?"

"Nah," he rocked a finger in Preston's face, damn near touching his nose, "I see a niggah goin' through extras for nothin'!"

Preston slapped his hand down, and shoved him. As Kenzo flew backwards, Preston screamed, "Nothin'? You callin' my girl nothin', niggah?"

Kenzo regained his footing and shoved Preston back onto the bed. "Niggah, I ain't mean it that way, but you ain't make her fuck that young niggah, and if you ever touch me again, I'ma K.O. yo ass!"

"What?" Preston snatched off his T-shirt, and flexed his pecs. "Niggah, you don't want it..." he bit his lip, "I'm tellin' you, Zo—"

Kenzo fired to the jaw.

BAM!

BOOM!

BOOM!

Preston returned a two-piece combination.

BAM!

BAM!

"Zo, I'll molly-wop yo ass blood."

Kenzo stumbled, gathered himself, wiped the blood from the gash above his eye and tasted it. "Good one", he nodded, and then snapped a jab to the nose. *BOOM!* Then he followed that up with a crushing hook to the solar plexus. *BOOM!* "But not good enough."

Preston bent over like a dead plant.

Kenzo danced on his toes.

"This is what you want, weenie, this what you gon' get!"

"Ahhhhgh," Preston screamed and then rushed Kenzo like a Brahma bull.

Kenzo's eyes saucered.

"Niggggaahh," Preston yelled as he lifted him off his feet, high in the air, then slammed him. *BOOM!*

However, Kenzo jumped right back up, thumbed his nose, and fired another lightning quick jab, then immediately shot for Preston's legs and returned the body slam.

BAM!

Preston popped up instantly.

"You my niggah, P," said Kenzo, "And if I got to dust you off to bring you back to life—"

"Ahhhhgh!" Preston came charging again.

They collided like two rams, *KA-BOOM!* Then each man struggled and grappled for an opening or advantage.

The door burst open. It was FreshKidd, followed by Drixxx and Kobain.

"C'mon, break that shit up, y'all!" pleaded the wide-eyed FreshKidd.

"Yeah man!" added Drixxx.

"Stay outta this," grunted Kenzo and lifted Preston in the air, but Preston reversed the move, and they tumbled to the ground. They got up swinging.

BOOM! BAM!

"Aye, you muthafuckas trippin'!"

BAM! BOOM! More blows exchanged, and then they went back to grappling.

"C'mon you guys, break it up," pleaded Drixxx, "before someone gets hurt."

Kenzo caught Preston with a left hook. *BOOM!* "Niggah, I'm beatin' yo ass cuz I got love fo' you."

Preston countered. *BAM!* "You don't give a fuck 'bout me fool!" he fired again. "Never did!"

Kenzo crumbled to his knees and he got up wobbly.

"C'mon break it up."

"That's how you feel, P?" Kenzo walked up to Preston with his arms at his sides. "Go ahead and hit me then niggah, as hard as you want."

Preston pushed him. "Back up," He raised his fist and cocked it back. "Don't walk up on me again, niggah."

Kenzo put his arms behind his back, and marched back in Preston's face.

"Go 'head niggah, take yo pain out on me, blood."

Their eyes battled.

"Yo, yo," barked Kobain, "Why don't you guys take your pain out on some tracks, G?" He twisted a dread around his finger. "Let the fuckin' song cry, bro!"

They all turned towards Kobain.

Next, Preston eyed Kenzo and Kenzo smiled.

"You ready?" Preston nodded once slowly, then twice briskly. "Yeah man," he agreed as he rubbed his jaw. "Let's do it."

In the sound booth, Preston stepped up to the mic, lumped and sore, he could still taste the blood in his mouth. He adjusted the mic. "Kobain."

"Yo."

"Gimme something touchy, like Fiddy's '21 Questions', but ethereal like Goapele's 'Closer To My Dreams', a'ight?"

"Aye," Kenzo lit up, "Give 'em that track with that Harold Melvin & the Blue Notes, 'Miss You', twisted up in it."

"Got it," said Kobain. Kobain's fingers ran over the modules, and the track blazed through the studio speakers.

Preston closed his eyes, pressed the earphones to his head and nodded to the beat. "Ge-yeah, that's him right there," he nodded deeper into the rhythm. "Yeah...this is for the fallen angels floating throughout time and space, and for the souljahs, any souljah who's ever lost his soulmate...This is for the heart, from the heart..."

He sang...

"So near, yet so far away...
Your love was my soul food, your tears my soup
Your body...Um, hmm, my fruit."

"Aye, that niggah singin'," said FreshKidd.

"Singin' his heart out," replied Kenzo.

"Bittersweet, you set sail too soon
So far away...
You left me a sun, with no moon
A star with no light
So far away...
A souljah with no fight
You took my breath away
So far away..."

Kobain's jaw dropped. "You hear that shit?" He turned to Kenzo. "Hey Zo, man, you didn't tell me this dude could sing."

Kenzo blotted the cut above his eye with a wet towel and shrugged. "Never knew." He examined the towel. "But I know one thing, we got a hit."

"Damn sho' do," said FreshKidd, "just lemme bless it on the remix."

"Naw, don't touch it," said Drixxx. "Leave that shit just the way it is."

Chapter 39

Nine months later...

As he stared out the window of the courtroom lobby like an alcoholic fighting a losing battle with the bottle, his mind was pulled and twisted by the thoughts of his Marie.

Man... if I hadda just got there in time, I prolly coulda stopped it.

"And if your auntie had nuts, she'd be yo uncle!" countered a voice in his head, "here he go with that sucka shit."

"Nobody can outrun their destiny," said another voice, "so don't fall off the wagon."

He shook his head.

The courtroom doors opened and he heard his name. "Preston."

He turned; it was Tamala and a female assistant.

"Yeah?" His face was stoic as he answered, "What's up?"

"We're not gonna need your testimony," her voice was soft and sympathetic. "She's going to take the plea bargain."

Her assistant nodded her head gently.

"I wasn't gon' testify anyway!" he snapped. "I didn't see shit; when I came, it was all over."

"I understand."

"Apparently you don't, or you wouldna subpoenaed me."

Tamala turned to her assistant. "Sarah, can you excuse us briefly?"

"Sure," she drew a squinty smile, "no problem."

"Preston..." Tamala faced him as the assistant reentered the courtroom. "Look, I know this is difficult for you, and I know how much she meant to you—"

"You don't know shit...you're just the referee for these peckerwoods!"

"Preston..." She held his arm. "I'm sorry, okay?"

He looked away.

"Preston, c'mon now."

He took a deep breath then exhaled, and slowly calmed himself. "It's not your fault, Tamala," he grimaced, "Shit happens."

She caressed his arm. "It's gonna be alright, okay?"

"Yeah," he sighed, "I guess."

"So what was the deal?" he asked.

"Fifteen to life." She shook her head. "What a shame, she's barely eighteen."

"Like I give a fuck," he hissed, "What about NeNe?"

"She'll plea to the gun and receive probation."

"Good. I kept thinkin' they was gon' revoke her bail or up it," he said, "Lemme ask you this, T?"

"Go ahead."

"You think that lil bitch will ever get out?" His eyes narrowed. "Keep it one hunnid."

"Preston, she won't get out for a long, long time, and those bullets NeNe put in her ricocheted, and trashed through arteries, tendons, and muscles alike…she can barely walk, so no, she'll never make it out alive."

"Good," he scowled. "Well, I'm up outta here, I'll see you around…I guess."

He turned to leave, but she pulled him back.

"Preston?"

"Yeah," He gazed into her eyes. "'sup?"

"Look…if you need me…for anything…call me, okay?"

Their eyes danced.

"Okay", he said softly.

They embraced.

"You take care of yourself," she whispered. "And by the way, I love our song. I'm so proud of you."

"Thanks."

"But I'm not buying the book, unless you autograph it for me."

"Sure I'll sign it—to, Incognito Piss Girl, T." He smiled.

"Boyyy…" She punched his shoulder, and grinned. "Forget you."

On the way out, he ran into NeNe and Dannielle, with Stacy in tow, assisting a hobbling Angel, who was noticeably grimacing with every step. He felt bad for her; he'd heard that the knife wound was so wide and deep that they had to practically stuff her intestines back into her stomach, and staple the folds of her skin. They rolled their eyes and smirked as he walked towards them.

"Aye, they—"

"Uh-unh," NeNe gave him the "talk to the hand" signal. "Keep it movin', niggah!"

His eyes landed on Dannielle. "Danni," he pleaded.

She put her hand to her ear. "Y'all hear something?"

"Nah, we don't hear shit."

"That's what I thought!" Dannielle said sarcastically as she rolled her eyes, and they pushed on.

Chapter 40

They released the single "So Far Away" and the e-Book *Truality* on the same day on iTunes, and received rave reviews. His fans on Facebook, Myspace, and Google + increased exponentially, and the single was the most requested song on the West Coast. Preston was extremely excited, cuz now they were set to drop the album and the paperback together, the same way they'd done the e-Book and single. The album, titled, *Rated PG for Truality*, was primarily Preston to the head, with the exception of Kenzo and FreshKidd featured on one track. In addition, today he was set to open up the boxes containing ten thousand paperbacks, with the album neatly tucked into the sleeves of the books' jackets, in effect, cross promoting and cross marketing between the two industries.

He pulled in front of J'Neane's house; he wanted her to take pictures, as well as share this memory with him, because she'd done an extraordinary job of editing, everyone said so.

J'Nae opened the door and let him in.

"Where's…" his voice trailed off as he looked down and saw that she was half naked.

"Close yo' mouth for you get flies in it," said J'Nae, standing there in a pair of flimsy panties and matching bra; her young round breasts pushed at her bra, and her hips curved and flared. She smiled teasingly.

"Girl, put some clothes on!" He demanded and frowned. "Where yo' mama at?"

"I don't know," she said smartly, then shimmied towards her room. The thong threading her voluptuous butt cheeks was the size of dental floss; her ass cheeks swayed and jiggled with reckless abandon.

That's a damn shame, he thought as he moved to the couch and called J'Neane from his cell phone. In the last few months, they'd been kickin' it tough. She could never replace Marie, but she helped him ease the pain and move on.

J'Neane picked up. "Hey you."

"'Sup ? Where you at?" he asked.

"I'm on my way, wait for me okay?"

He glanced at his watch. "How long, woman?"

"You anxious, huh?"

"Hell yeah."

Okay...okay, give me like fifteen minutes."

"A'ight."

"If you're hungry, I left you a plate in the fridge."

"Woman...as much as I love yo' cookin', you know I can' t do no eating right now."

"Okay," she giggled, "see you in fifteen."

"Bet." He ended the call. "Yeah," he said, juiced up like, and then did a little shoulder shimmy. "It's a comin' together like black people did in the sixties." He chuckled.

"Preston."

"'Sup?" He turned to see J'Nae, seductively entering the room in a white, one-piece swimsuit. He wanted to turn his head, but he couldn't. His eyes trailed from her fat round breasts, to the puffy V between her legs; she hadn't trimmed her bikini line and wild pubic hairs peeked out the sides.

"Whatchu think about this swimsuit, you think it's too tight?" She turned around and wiggled her ample backside, then looked over her shoulder salaciously. "Or is it too cute?" She winked, "huh?"

His words got stuck in his throat. "It's a'ight," he found his voice, "now put on some clothes."

"I got clothes on."

"Put on something presentable."

She waved him off. "Man you trippin'. If we was at the beach, this is what I'd be wearing, so what's the difference?" She sat her hand on top of her wide hips.

He shook his head. "Little girl, you something else."

"Sho' is," she sassed as she walked towards him, switching her hips, "but I ain't no lil girl, is you blind or something?"

"Gon' play somewhere, J'Nae."

"I ain't playin'." She weaved her neck, smiled and stopped no less than a couple feet away from him. "Did I tell you I'ma cheerleader, though?"

"Naw."

"Well, I am...watch."

She raised her hands above her head and easily melted down into a wide split.

"Gimme a D," she purred and winked. She did the maneuver again, this time with her backside facing him. "Gimme an I." She leaned forward. "Gimme a C." The swimsuit hiked up into her young ass cheeks and they spread. "And..." She whirled her body around like a break-dancer. "Gimme a K." She pulled her leg high; the swimsuit looked like it was about to snap off. "You see it?"

He was speechless.

The skimpy fabric of the swimsuit was being chewed and camel toes by her vagina folds.

"What does that spell?" She put her finger in her mouth. She wasn't finished. "Plus..." she added as she threw her leg behind her head, "I'm double jointed," she cooed, and her heart shaped glutes bulged and cracked open before him. "Yep," she said, wet and nasty like. *"Double jointed."*

He burst from off the couch.

"J'Nae!" he roared.

"What?" This wasn't what she was hoping for. "Don't act—"

"Put some damn clothes on!" He threw on his ugly face. "I ain't with that weak shit!"

"Man, you trippin'."

"Naw you," he scolded and lifted her off the ground, "you trippin'!" He tilted her chin and stole her eyes. "Look J'Nae," he said sternly, "I got way too much respect for your mother, and too much respect for your body to be sittin' here gawking at you...I ain't that type a niggah."

"Man—"

"Man nothing," he cut her off. "Any niggah that will take advantage of your naïveté and innocence ain't no fuckin' man!"

"I ain't naïve," she pouted, "I know what I'm doin'."

"If you knew what you was doin', you woulda knew I ain't biting."

"Lemme go!" She snatched away from him.

He backed off.

"You prolly just scared I'ma tell." She cocked her head. "I ain't gon' say nothin', I can keep a secret," she said conspiratorially.

"Naw...naw," he answered as he furiously shook his head, "Ain't gon' be no reason to keep a secret, baby girl."

"What, you think I cain't hang or somethin', Nutzilla?"

"W-what?" He was shocked she knew about the nickname.

"Yep, I heard all about it." She rolled her neck. "Just cuz I'm young, don't mean I can't handle a grown man. Mannnn, I'll drown..." she pointed at his crotch, "that shit," she said sassily.

He shook his head. "J'Nae," he walked up closer, speaking softly. "Look, you're a beautiful young lady, but if that's all you got to offer a man—"

"I gots lots to offer, hmmph!" She crossed her arms defiantly.

He spun off and went into her room.

"Get out my room!" she yelled.

He came out with a pair of pants and a T-shirt. "Put 'em on!"

"You ain't my damn daddy, shit!" She snatched them out his hands and reluctantly did so.

He pulled her to the couch.

"Lemme go, shit," she yelped. "I said you wasn't my daddy, you deaf?" Arms crossed, she sat next to him but looked the other way.

"J'Nae", he said softly.

"What!" she snapped.

"Okay, say like if you had a daughter—"

"I ain't got one."

"Say if you did, would you want your boyfriend to take advantage of her?"

"No."

"Would you want him to be tryna to sneak and watch her undress, or touch her?"

"No."

"Then why would you want me to disrespect your mother or take advantage of you, huh?"

"I dunno," she said and pantomimed a yawn, "can we change the subject, this is getting boooorrrrring."

"See J'Nae," he pressed on, "there's a lot of weak niggahs out there who would love to get up in you, and you may feel like that's what it is to be a woman, but baby girl, sex ain't womanhood."

"I know what sex is."

"Maybe you do, J'Nae, but do you know—"

"Don't lecture me, okay?" She faked another yawn. "I know about sex, STD's, blah, blah, blah."

He squinted his eyes and nodded slowly. "How old are you, J'Nae?"

"Fifteen," she huffed through another yawn. "Age ain't nothin' but a number."

Look, J'Nae, it's like this, I'ma real niggah. I been there and back, just to see how far it was, feel me? And, I'm tellin' you, if I was a dirty niggah, I'da took advantage of you and I'da kept takin' advantage cuz you gave it to me. And since you didn't have no respect for your moms, or your body—"

"I got res—"

"Shut up!"

"Don't be yellin' at me!"

"You don't respect shit; you think you know every fuckin' thing already and..." He jumped up. "C'mon," he ordered.

"Unt-unh," she protested, "Where?"

"I got something I wanna show you."

"What?"

"You'll see, c'mon."

Chapter 41

It wasn't long before they were cruisin' eastbound down International Boulevard, formerly known as E. 14th Street, one of the longest and roughest streets in East Oakland, and home field for many a prostitute. Today, like most days, the hoe stroll was alive and crackin'. Broad daylight and the prostitutes were active, like pimples on a teenager.

"Wanna date?" asked a girl as young as J'Nae and tried to flag him down.

On the next block, a tall transvestite blew him a kiss, then turned around and promptly mooned him.

"Uggh," said Preston, "I'm about to be sick."

"Ohmigod," said J'Nae, astonished, "that was a dude."

"Yeah, it's wild out here, J'Nae, but this is a ho's world." He nodded. "Whatchu see is what you get."

Her young eyes scanned the hoe stroll.

"But you know this already, right?"

She was quiet.

"Look at her..." He nudged his chin at a young streetwalker in skimpy clothes, no more than thirteen. "You think she know what she doin'?" He rubbed his chin. "I doubt if she do."

"How you know?"

"How I know, J'Nae?" He arched his eyebrows. "Open yo' eyes."

He rounded the block and pulled up behind a tricked-out Caddy.

"Hol' up for a minute."

He got out and walked towards the man standing next to the Cadillac, givin' a white prostitute an earful of pimp verbs. The pimp noticed Preston coming and reached into his waistband. Preston raised his hands, and called out, "Hol' up, bruh."

"P?" The pimp hiked an eyebrow. "That you, mayne?"

"Yeah mayne," Preston smiled. "What's good, pimpin'?"

"Whathefuck, I know you ain't come to buy no pussy, bruh-bruh?"

"Nah, bruh, I just need yo' expertise for a second."

The pimp frowned inquisitively, then said, "A'ight, give a pimp a sec." He spun on his heels and released a verbal avalanche on his white whore. "Bitch, go get that doe; you don't hear it callin' you?"

"I'm tired," she complained, "Daddy, my feet hurt."

"Bitch, I'ma throw yo ass," he stabbed his finger above him, "up on that telephone wire like them tenna shoes, ho!"

"But——"

"Go, snow, and get me some doe!" he snarled.

She scurried off, looking up at the tennies hanging off the wire.

Preston chuckled and shook his head.

He'd met Prince the Pimp in prison and they had established a mutual respect, and as usual, he had a way with words.

"What can I do for you, P?" asked the pimp.

Preston ran it down to him.

The pimp stretched his neck to look past Preston. "That's her in the car?"

"Yeah."

"C'mon." A few seconds later, Prince was in the backseat, glaring at J'Nae. "What's your name?"

"J'Nae", she wasn't intimidated.

"J'Nae, I'm a pimp."

"I know," she retorted and did a mock shiver, "and ooooh, I'm so scared…where yo pimp cup?" she smirked.

"Oh, you one of them huh?" The pimp smiled. "I got it, I see you."

"See what?" She rolled her eyes.

"Aye, P?" He ignored J'Nae. "I see you got an iPad in this bitch."

"Yeah, a lil somethin', ya know."

"Aye, punch up that song 'Olivia' by The Whispers."

"A'ight." Preston punched through his iPad, found the song and it thumped through the interior.

"Yeah…see, J'Nae," said the pimp, "I see all types out here on these streets."

"So?"

"So… I wanna tell you a story 'bout this girl name, Olivia."

The Whispers harmonized, and the speakers rocked and subbed.

"O-li-via the slave... got distracted..."

"P, bend a few corners right quick," said the pimp.

Preston started the car and they patrolled the hoe stroll.

"Yeah...so, J'Nae, I knew this chick named Olivia and she was young and fine, just like you. See what I'm sayin'?" His head weaved in the backseat, searching the streets intently. "And yeah, you couldn't tell her nothin'; had that spunky thang goin' on, just like you."

"And!"

"Okay stop, P." He let his window down, and hollered, "Olivia!"

A beat-down looking prostitute stopped in her tracks. "Who's that?' she peered at the car, rubbing her arms up and down as if she was freezing.

"It's Prince, c'mere!"

She sauntered over. She would've had pretty eyes if they weren't dead, and she would've had a pretty face if it wasn't so hard and haggard. "What?" She looked scared. "I ain't did nothin'—"

"I ain't said you did."

"Whatchu want then?"

How old is you now, Olivia?"

"Dude, why you—"

"Bitch, shut up! When a pimp talks, a hoe listens!" Prince barked, "Now, how old is yo' dumb ass?"

"Nineteen, shit." Her nose was running. "And can you please turn that song off? I can't stand it!"

Lost and turned ooouuut...

"Fuck that hoe!"

"Prince, why you fuckin with me, man?" she whined, "I'm sick, dude. I gotta make some doe—"

"Lemme see yo' tracks."

"What?" She scowled. "You trippin', Prince."

He crumpled up a twenty-dollar bill and threw it at her. "Bitch, I said lemme see yo' tracks."

She stuffed the money in her bra, squatted down, shoved her sleeves up and thrust out her arms.

"There...see, shit!" Both arms were spotted and pitted with needle marks.

The song began to send chills down J'Nae's spine.

"How you end up hoeing, hoe?"

"What up, you finna make a damn documentary or some shit?" she complained, then sniffled.

"Bitch, gimme my money back!"

"Okay, okay dammit," she sucked her teeth, "I'ma give you the short version."

She started scratching her neck. "You know, I was tryna be grown and shit, and started fuckin' wit' this older cat."

"Who was he?"

"Prince, shit...c'mon, dude!"

"Bitch, just tell it!"

"My mama boyfriend, okay, you happy?" She rolled her eyes. "Shit."

"Wasn't you a track star or something?"

"Yeah, all that, but um..." She looked at Preston. "Dude, can you please turn that song off?" Her eyes pleaded. "I hate it."

"Hell no, hoe!" interjected Prince. "Why you stop runnin' track?"

"I started fuckin' wit this shit." Her bottom lip began to tremble and tears welled up in her eyes. "Can I go now?" she whimpered.

"Get up outta here and stay outta trouble."

"'Kay."

"You got condoms?"

"Yeah."

"Lemme see 'em."

She reached in her pocket and pulled out several. "See?"

He nodded.

Preston drove off, but he was visibly disturbed, and so was J'Nae.

The pimp turned his gaze to J'Nae. "So yeah, J'Nae, she's nineteen years old, lost and turned out, and HIV positive."

"What?" said J'Nae; all that tough shit was gone now. "She got AIDS, too?"

"Yeah, the dude gave it to her and her mother."

"How you know?" She was scared now and it reflected in the tremor in her voice.

"She's my cousin," he said, "but bloodlines, it don't count in these streets, blood is just blood."

"Ohmigod!" She covered her mouth. "But—"

"But nothin'!" his verbals fired rapidly. "You gotta let a hoe be a hoe. I look out for her and that's it, but it ain't no love out here, see what I'm sayin'?" He popped his collar. "Look lil mama, it's a cold, cold world out here, so don't rush to get old, and stay in yo' muthafuckin' lane, seewhatI'msayin', cuz if you don't..." He tossed his thumb towards the mean streets. "That's how you gon' get treated. No love, no respect, you'll just shitted on 'til you rot away, seewhatI'msayin'? From a track star to a hoe track," he snapped his fingers, "Just like that."

She nodded, teary eyed.

Preston dropped Prince off at his Caddy and pushed into traffic.

Neither of them said a word.

"Preston."

"'Sup?"

"You ain't gon tell my mama is you?"

"Nope, then I would be violating yo' trust, feel me?"

"Thanks," she said in a hushed tone.

"Don't trip," he said, "just remember that the most important part of a man, as well as a woman, is what's inside their minds and heart, not what's between their legs."

She nodded.

He pulled up at Marcus Bookstore. "Hol' on, I'll be right back." A minute or so later, he came back and handed her a bag.

She reached inside the bag.

"What's this?"

"*The Coldest Winter Ever*, by Sistah Souljah."

"Oooh, I heard about this book."

"And the fifty dollars in the bag is for the book report you're gonna do. If you want the matching fifty, when you complete it."

She hugged him. "Thank you."

"Just respect yo'self and don't de-value yo'self, a'ight?"

"I got it Preston, believe me, I got it." She hugged him tighter. "It's too cold out there on them streets; I'd rather be somewhere warm, man...I'ma stay on the right track."

Chapter 42

"Huh, daddy?" the voice sleepily answered.

"Y'all get over here and bring my toy," Kenzo said.

Toy?" Yawning, the voice asked, "What toy?"

"Cocoa," he said impatiently, "Put Ramona on the phone."

There were some ruffling sounds, and then Ramona answered, "Hey babe." She was half-sleep, too, but she knew the business.

"You up?"

"I am now."

"I need you to bring my toy."

"Right now?" she asked incredulously.

"Nah," he turned it up a bit, "right damn now!"

"Okay," she yawned.

"You know what I'm talkin' bout, right?"

"Yeah," she sucked her teeth, "duh!"

He got on her helmet real quick. "What I tell you 'bout playin' wit me, huh?"

"'Kay, boo," she broke that shit down, "I—"

"Just hurry up and smash over here!"

He fed her the click, and then went over to the studio where he found FreshKidd knocked-the-fuck-out, on the couch snoring like a five hundred pound, funky fat man. Shit sounded like a battle to the death, between a lawnmower and a jackhammer.

How can a muthafucka not wake himself up snoring that damn loud, and more importantly; how can you keep a bitch? thought Kenzo. "FreshKidd!" Kenzo shook him awake, but he knew it wouldn't be easy, 'cause FreshKidd was a notoriously hard sleeper. "FreshKidd get up!" He shook him again.

"I'm up, bruh!" He made a fucked up face, kicked his leg violently, and then curled up in a ball like a potato bug.

"Okay niggrow," Kenzo said, "I got somethin' that a wake yo' game up."

He wheeled on his heels, snatched up a 2-gallon water pitcher, filled it up with cold water, then stood over FreshKidd and poured.

"Grow niggrow," Kenzo said in amusement, "Take root."

FreshKidd slapped at the water dousing his face, and then flapped frantically before jumping to his feet.

"Maaannn," he screamed, wide awake now, "whatdafuck!"

"C'mon, blood, we gotta hit the road."

"You trippin', bruh," FreshKidd complained, glancing at his wet clothes and then grilling Kenzo.

"I tol' you last night we was pushin' first thang manãna, but you wanted to serenade some bucket mouth bitch all night," Kenzo said.

"What time is it?"

"Five a.m."

"Shit."

Chapter 43

Just outside, two men dressed in all black, with ski masks fitted over their murderous faces, crouched low on either side of the studio, pistols at the ready.

Chapter 44

Kenzo smelled blood. While the economy was jacked, he mimicked the cash fat corporations, and Hedge funds: letting the weak leak, then gobbling up property and equipment at the cheap. He'd been scouring the internet, hoping to find some poor schmuck twisted in debt or divorce and find a steal of a deal on a tour bus. Bingo! A week ago, he'd found one, and yesterday the purchase inspection was completed. Then the owner threw in another incentive; he'd knock off an additional two grand, if Kenzo would pick up the bus by today. The ever frugal Kenzo wasn't about to pass on a win-win situation.

"Why in the fuck can't we just fly, bruh?" asked FreshKidd, now dressed and ready.

"Cuz I'm John-the-Fuck-Madden, I hate flying, that's why!"

"That's crazy," FreshKidd muttered, and then licked the Dutch.

"And niggah, hurry up and burn that shit, cuz you know it ain't no smokin' in my whip."

"Yeah, yeah, yeah." FreshKidd waved him off. "Blah, blah, blah."

"A'ight niggah", Kenzo warned, and then dialed Ramona's cell phone. The call went straight to voicemail.

'How this niggah 'spect me to be fly if I ain't high," mumbled FreshKidd, barely above a whisper, then pulled out his phone and got to texting.

Fuck it, I'm pushin', Where them bitches at though? *thought Kenzo.* Something just wasn't right.

He glared at FreshKidd.

FreshKidd's thumbs sped across his cellphone, the blunt bobbed at the corner of his mouth.

"You got about five minutes and we out."

FreshKidd nodded.

Chapter 45

His breath vaporized and floated from the mouth of his ski mask, his anxious eyes surveyed the surroundings. He ran his finger along the trigger guard of the .9mm he was clutching. He twisted with evil intentions. "C'mon niggah, c'mon and drink this soup," he whispered.

At that moment, the door opened.

Chapter 46

When Preston's book and soundtrack started selling like crack in the early 90's, it also caused a spike in interest and sales of the entire record label. Concert promoters all over the country contacted Kenzo, hoping to pencil them in at gigs all throughout the U.S., so the tour bus became an absolute necessity. Yet that wasn't the main reason for the drive to Los Angeles that morning. He also needed to get a secret stash spot cut into the new Chrysler 300 he recently purchased, as getting it outfitted with a stash spot in the Bay Area was a no gooder: the cops were keeping close watch on all the known auto body shops specializing in stash spots.

It was a no-brainer. Los Angeles is where he was moving and grooving to. In addition, while both the Chrysler and the tour bus were being fitted with new sound systems and stash spots, he and FreshKidd were going to shop and network for a few days.

FreshKidd headed out the door and blew out a cloud of Newpimp smoke.

It was still dark; the streets were damp with morning dew, and the crickets...

"You hear them fuckin' crickets, Zo?" He took one last drag and thumped the Newport; it bounced and sparkled.

In a blur of motion, something flew past his leg. "Whoa!" He jumped back. "Whatdafuck?"

It was a big black tomcat. It stopped, turned and gazed at FreshKidd, its creepy eyes glowed eerily. "Meow," it hissed and scampered off.

FreshKidd placed his hand on his chest. "Scared the fuck outta—"

That's when he felt the cold steel on his neck.

"Don't move!" the sinister voice spoke, "Or I'll splatter the fuckin' crickets with your thoughts."

FreshKidd gulped noisily.

Chapter 47

Kenzo buttoned the black Banana Republic pea coat, tugged the matching colored Raiders fitted cap low, slung the soft leather Davek Messenger bag over his shoulders, and headed out the door.

"Naw, niggah, I don't hear no fuckin' crickets," Kenzo snapped, still pissed the fuck off his girls weren't answering his calls.

BAM!

A ski-masked man smacked Kenzo with a pistol.

"Ahhhh!" He fell to his knees stunned and dazed.

"You hear this, niggah?"

Click-clack.

"Huh, niggah?" growled the ski-masked jacker. "Don't make this a murder, ya heard?"

Kenzo nodded, as he felt blood crawling down the nape of his neck.

"Man, I got almost a hundred racks in the bag…take it," Kenzo pleaded.

In front of him, he saw FreshKidd snatched up on his tippy toes by a large, masked man. A pistol was jabbed into FreshKidd's neck, and he was cowering and shaking like a snitch in a gangsta party.

"Awww naw, niggah," snarled Kenzo's assailant, "I don't want yo' chump change."

He snatched Kenzo up by his collar. "Bring yo' bitch ass inside!"

FreshKidd's nerve broke. "They gon' kill us!" He tore loose from his surprised assailant, screaming like a muthafucka, "Help! Help!"

"Niggah!" FreshKidd's assailant squeezed off two shots.

BAK! BAK!

FreshKidd's head burst open like a smashed pumpkin. He crumpled to the ground like dirty clothes.

At that moment, Kenzo flung his head back with all his might and smashed the jacker's nose.

"Owwww!"

Kenzo pivoted quickly and rocketed a knee to the jacker's nuts.

BAK! BAK!

"Ahhh!" he screamed as a bullet tore through Kenzo's shoulder and another one slammed against his back.

He was knocked to the ground face-first. Seconds later, he could feel them standing over him. "Take the money, man," he pleaded, "Don't—"

"Shut up, stupid ass niggah," growled one of them.

BOOM! BOOM!

Two more shots slammed into him. "Ahhhh!" Kenzo hollered in agony.

Then came a staccato of gunfire.

Tacatacatac!

Both ski-masked men were raked down in a hail of gunfire.

A bullet ricocheted off the ground and ripped through Kenzo's leg, just as one of the assailants fell on top of him.

A grotesque gurgling sound emitted from the ski mask, directly on the side of Kenzo's face. It took all his power not to freak out. As the gurgling hissed in his ear, Kenzo played dead.

Footsteps came close. *Please God, don't let me die,* he prayed silently.

"Kenzo! Daddy please!" It was Ramona. "Please don't be dead!" she screamed.

He opened his eyes and rose up.

"You okay, daddy?" She was cradling the mini-MAC machine gun pistol.

He made the sign of the cross over his chest and looked at the sky. He threw the bag off his shoulder.

"FreshKidd! Ohmigod!" Cocoa vomited violently over FreshKidd's semi-headless body. "Ohmigod!"

Kenzo struggled to his feet with Ramona's assistance. He grabbed the gun from out Ramona's hands, stood over FreshKidd's killer and sprayed him.

Tacatacatac!

Then he squatted down and lifted the ski mask. He didn't recognize him. "Rest in piss, faggot!" spat Kenzo. He squatted over the other assailant and ripped the mask off the still gurgling face. Blood flooded from the man's mouth, his eyes were golf balled, but he was still alive, barely. "Mmm-humph, gotcha," Kenzo said menacingly. He recognized the man. "I knew you was gon' try me one day, G-Man," Kenzo snarled as he beat his chest. "That's why I kept this vest on, faggot!"

"C'mon daddy," Ramona said nervously, while trying to calm the shocked and sobbing Cocoa. "People coming outside, baby."

"Just bounce, ma."

Her eyes danced around skittishly. "You sure ?"

"Go!" Kenzo demanded, without ever taking his eyes off G-Man.

Ramona and Cocoa got ghost.

The G-Man had a bullet the size of a plum in his neck, which was the cause of the gurgling. The G-Man's eyes followed Kenzo's movements, terrified. Kenzo stabbed two fingers into the wound. It felt like raw hamburger meat. He twisted and hooked his fingers, then yanked. The G-Man began to choke and convulse. "Yeah niggah," Kenzo said looking deep into G-Man's dreadful eyes. "Look atchu now, niggah!"

The G-Man continued to choke as his neck began to spasm and his body violently jerked.

"You the D-Man, now...the Dead Man!" Kenzo whispered in his ear.

The G-Man's body relaxed as the last gram of his life slid away into another world.

Kenzo rose up, and then spit on the dead man, before punting his head.

"That's one for the road..."

Chapter 48

Six months blew past since the ambush attack at his studio. All type of shit was in the mix since then. FreshKidd had a large, sad, yet well-publicized funeral. Kobain and Drixxx were scared shitless and became unreliable, and Cocoa ran off. Yeah, it was lookin' rather ugly. He could only count on Ramona and Preston while he was cooped up on the super max section of the County Jail.

They'd slapped him with a triple murder indictment; the two ambushers and incredibly, they also included FreshKidd's murder, because he had refused to cooperate. This was a typical ploy used by prosecutors: throw as much shit at a defendant as you can and see what sticks. Only one body was needed to wash him; but three bodies would make him seem like a monster, fit to be slayed and in California, a multiple homicide charge qualified an accused to be fitted with special circumstances—the death penalty.

In light of all the hoopla and publicity surrounding the incident, the District Attorney himself, one Thomas Orloff, initially headed the case. That is, until the skin of the evidence was pulled off. It just so happened that the G-Man had a criminal history, dating back to his early teens, and his cohort, Timothy "Technine" Simpson, was wanted for a double murder at the time of his demise. When this was brought to light, Thomas Orloff slid the case around the office like a bowl of hot shit. It stunk, and nobody wanted it.

The bullpen was crowded, noisy, and funky. Kenzo had claimed a coveted spot close to the wall to prevent being smashed between two musty men.

He stared off into space and tried to block out the bullshit blabbering. A youngsta rocked next to him, pounding a bassline on his chest, and rhymed to the beat. Kenzo had furtively tried to tune in, but the kid's breath was hummin' so tough, he scooted as close to the wall as possible, and covered his nose.

"Aye," somebody said, "Lil Weezy new shit is hot."

Not as hot as this lil niggah's breath.

"Man, that niggah can't fuck with me!" declared the youngsta. "All he fuckin' talk about is Baby and Martians."

"Oh yeah, why you ain't signed, my niggah?" someone challenged.

"I was, fool," he lied through funky breath and a smirk, "I was fuckin' with FreshKidd and 'nem, but you know my boy got murked."

Kenzo cut his eyes at the dude and frowned.

"Izat right?"

"On Mamas, niggah!" He was bouncing in his seat now, getting hyphy, he had everybody's attention. "Yeah mayne, they got my niggah, Kenz,o on a bum rap, nahmean, but he gon' beat that shit."

"Yeah?"

"Fuck yeah. And—"

The bailiff opened the courtroom door and the noise subsided.

"Kenzo Warfield," the bailiff called, "you're up."

Several inmates eyed the youngsta's lying ass, pointed, and shook with laughter, and then the entire bullpen exploded. They'd all read the newspapers, and some of them even knew Kenzo in passing, but had sense enough to see that the man didn't feel like being bothered.

"Quiet down!" bellowed the bailiff over the laughter, as Kenzo got up and walked into the courtroom. He glanced into the crowd looking for Ramona; she waved and caught his attention, then blew him a kiss.

He smiled and mouthed, "I love you."

"I love you, too," she mouthed back.

As he took a seat, his attorney leaned close and whispered, "You got a new D.A."

"That's nothing new," he shrugged, "Good or bad this time?"

"See for yourself." Kenzo leaned forward and looked over at the D.A.'s table just as Tamala had swung her eyes nervously in his direction. His mouth dropped.

Tamala felt queasy. She was caught in between three conflicting energies. One was her duty as an officer of the court; two, her familiarity with the accused, and three, her empathy to the 'hood. Nevertheless, she had every intention of removing herself from the case.

"You Honor," she addressed the court.

"Yes, Ms. Davis?" said the judge, peering over his glasses.

She stole a glance at Kenzo's pleading eyes, and then the butterflies in her stomach turned into dragons.

She paused awkwardly.

"Ms. Davis?"

Another glance at the defendant's table and this time, she saw Preston. She subtly shook her head to clear it.

"Ahem...Judge Goldberg, we'd like to reschedule this case 'til later on today. That is, if the court doesn't mind."

The judge turned to Kenzo's attorney. "Counselor?"

"We have no objections."

"So be it," said the judge, "add Mr. Warfield to the afternoon calendar."

Chapter 49

Immediately following court that afternoon, Kenzo placed a frantic call to Preston.

"You have a collect call from," droned the automated operator.

"Kenzo!" he screamed through the receiver.

The robotic voice added, "Please press five to accept—"

Preston accepted the call. "Aye, 'sup blood?"

"You, my niggah! Man," Kenzo said excitedly, "get down here, we need to holla!"

"Today visiting?"

"Yeah."

"I'm there."

"One."

"One."

∎∎∎

Preston gazed at Kenzo through the thick Plexiglas window of the County Jail's broom closet-sized visiting booth. The Plexiglas window was smeared and streaked with God knows what, and there were several small pen holes drilled at the base of the window frame to allow visitors and inmates to talk. Nevertheless, they tried to keep their voices down and talked in riddles, 'cause niggahs was forever getting caught up talkin' reckless, either on the phone or at visiting. And the D.A. wasn't past sliding a jailhouse snitch in a visiting booth next to an accused. Therefore, Kenzo left nothing to chance.

He was hunkered over a piece of paper, scribbling furiously and sneaking glances over his shoulder every so often. When he was done, he placed the paper on the glass for Preston to see.

"Aye, fool. Tamala is the D.A. on my case now. Man, go holla at her my niggah!"

Preston's right eyebrow hiked up. "What?"

Kenzo nodded and balled the paper up and ate it. "Feel me?"

"Whatcha want me to do?" Preston asked.

"Whatdahellyoumean? Niggah, you know what to do…kinda question is that?"

"Blood, you don't know T; that broad loves that job, she ain't—"

"No!" He shot a finger at Preston. "That broad loves you!"

"Fuck that gotta do with it, bruh?"

"Fuck you mean?" snapped Kenzo. "She'll do *anything* for you, niggah!"

"Stop barkin' at me like I'm some sucka, bruh!"

Kenzo calmed himself. "My bad, P…a niggah stressed the fuck out, mayne." He massaged his temples and sat down. "But look, P, if she loved her job so much, she woulda stepped down."

"How you know she ain't already did?"

"She was about to...I saw it in her eyes, my niggah, but she didn't."

"I'll see what I can do."

"What?" Kenzo unhinged and launched from his seat, eyes afire. "Niggah, they tryna give me the death penalty and you gon' see what you can do!"

Preston eyed his best friend. Kenzo had lost weight; he was gaunt, pale, and bags decorated his eyes. He was right, though, Preston knew he had to do whatever it took.

"You look like shit," he joked. "Ol' needy ass niggah."

"Eata dick, Mark." Kenzo frowned. "This shit ain't nothing to laugh at, man."

"Bruh-bruh you right." Preston became serious-like. "Whatever I gotta do; I'll do it."

Kenzo's eyes welled up. "Man, P..." He ran his fingers through his hair. "You gotta make it do what it do..."

Preston nodded.

Chapter 50

"What are you doing here Preston?" Tamala asked as she opened the door to let him in, shooting nervous glances behind him.

"Don't worry; I parked five blocks away,"

She closed the door and turned to face him. Her hair was wrapped in a scarf, and she wore nothing but an oversized T-shirt.

"It's past ten o'clock, and I have to be at work early," she whined, "what do you want?"

She knew exactly what he wanted.

"I need you, T-baby."

"Need me?" she played dumb. "Need me for what?"

"Don't play, T-baby, I've seen yo piss stains…you can't hide nothing from me…you know why I'm here." He smirked and produced a perfect dimple.

"Kiss my ass, Preston," she said, and rolled her eyes. "And stop calling me T-baby; you only call me that when you wanna use me."

"Seriously" He slid closer to her. "Tamala, you know that's my boy."

"Your boy?" She gave him a blank expression. "Your boy, who?"

"T-baby, stop playin', ma."

"I'm not playing." She turned around and walked towards the kitchen, her backside swayed tantalizingly beneath the tee. "Do you want something to drink?"

He caught up with her and pulled her to the couch.

As soon as he touched her and electric tingle shot through her.

"Mooovvve," she protested meekly, "lemme go, Preston."

His hand slid up her thighs restlessly, yet expertly, as he whispered in her ear,

"T-baby, c'mon ma,. They tryna kill my niggah." He kissed her neck.

"Ssss...ooooh..." she moaned, "don't so that, stoooppp."

He eased down and sprayed soft kisses in between her thighs.

"Preston..."

He cocked her legs back and spread them as wide as ecstasy.

"Preston, no..." she purred.

Her pussy peeked out like the first cupcake out the Hostess package, and he licked small fires around it until it literally creamed up before his eyes, producing a small pearl of nectar stirring from her sugar walls and oozing atop her pussy lips.

"Ooooh..." she whimpered and palmed his head.

Just as he was about to taste her juices, she sprang up.

"No!" Her tone was sharp, and her face was business. "It ain't happenin' captain."

This wasn't gonna be a cakewalk. He threw up his hands, in mock despair. "T-baby—"

"Stop calling me T-baby!"

He hit her with the dimple again. "Tamala..." he sighed, "I ain't tryna play you or use you...I'm tryna save my boy's life...an innocent man's life at that."

"Innocent?" she said in disbelief, "he stood over them and fired round after round into their bodies while they were down."

"But—"

"But my ass Preston," she cut him off. "He kicked them, ripped at gunshot wounds, he massacred them. Shit, he might as well have ate 'em—"

"C'mon ma..." He was up off the couch now, "You puttin' way too much on it! *They* ambushed him, murdered his artist, and then shot him repeatedly while *he* was down!"

She knew the circumstances better than he did; nonetheless, Kenzo's overkill, as far as the District Attorney's office was concerned, had sealed his fate. "If he'd cooperate and tell us who the other shooter was, maybe—"

"It's not gonna happen."

"Then I'm sorry, Preston."

"So..." He began to pace. "You tellin' me that a muthafucka wanted for a double murder, and another dude with a criminal record longer than E. 14th Street, can lie in wait for a businessman, kill his damn artist, and shoot him multiple times? Then miraculously, he's saved, but just 'cause he's protecting the identity of his savior and added the same coup de grâce that was applied to him, you're sanctioning his death?" He turned towards her and shot a heated glare. "You need to *give* him a parade, not parade him to the gas chamber!"

"I don't make the laws, Preston—"

"But you know ways around them!"

"My job isn't helping criminals find loopholes in the law, Preston—"

"But your 'job' is to represent the people, right?"

"Yes."

"But I take it Kenzo's kinda people ain't good enough for your goddamn representation..." He wagged a finger at her, "Huh?"

"What the hell is that s'pose to mean?"

"You know goddamned well what it means," he said. "I mean, here it is, a law-abiding citi—"

"Spare me, Preston." She weaved her head, "they just haven't caught Kenzo dealing his fuckin' drugs, and do you call having automatic weapons and bulletproof vests law-abiding?" she shouted.

"In-fuckin-credible!" he said rigidly, "A 'man' and his 'employee' are attacked, one brutally murdered by two known killers, the surviving victim gets charged for it, and you're standing there tryna justify it?"

"It was overkill, Preston!" she emphasized.

"Well charge him for the damn overkill," he countered, "not for defending his life!"

"I can't justify charging him for that," she gasped, "I can't—"

"Dammit, Tamala, does a college education eat away at your conscience?"

She folded her arms across her breast and stamped her feet. "No dammit," she fumed, "a college education, allows me to view the facts according to the law!"

"I'm not talking 'bout the damn law, Tamala," he lowered his voice, "I'm talking about what's right and what's wrong, okay?"

"But—"

"No buts, 'cause your same office justified several officers killing a buncha unarmed black men in the past, and chalked it up to 'just in the line of duty'. But my niggah gets ambushed and you guys tryna send him to the gas chamber?"

"You're twisting the facts, Preston," she said softly.

"Am I?" he leaned closer and pulled her to him. "Tamala, c'mon ma, what good will it do to take another life, huh babe?"

He clasped his strong hands around her wrists and placed her arms around his neck.

She gazed into his eyes. "I'll lose my job," she sobbed.

"He'll lose his life..." He stroked her hair. "Besides you can always become a defense attorney...you ain't got to work for them damn clear people, ma."

He raised her chin and looked deep into her honey brown eyes; her body was warm, and getting warmer. He kissed her pretty lips.

"Preston."

"'Sup?"

"I'll do it," she kissed him hungrily, "on one condition."

"Just tell me what it is ma, and I'll do it."

"Marry me."

"Huh?"

She searched his eyes. "Yep," her eyes twinkled, "Marry me." She unfastened his belt and released his massive sex shooter, then stroked it 'til it was rock hard. "Mmm-hmm....deal or no deal?"

****

"Well?" asked Kenzo anxiously.

Preston shrugged.

"Izit cool, I mean—"

Preston sighed.

"You wanna hear the good news or the bad news?"

"Gimme the bad news."

"The bad news is you gonna have to sit for a couple years in the County, and 'bout five more in the pen."

Kenzo smiled and nodded. "Okay, okay, I think I can manage that. What's the good news?"

"The good news is that I'm gettin' married."

"What?" He couldn't believe it. "No way, blo—" Then it dawned on him, and Preston nodded his head. "Getthefuckouttahere."

"Unless you wanna staythefuckinhere."

"Congratulations."

"That's what I thought."

Chapter 51

"Graaammma!" shouted Dannielle out her bedroom door, "Grammmaaa!"

"She at bingo, dammit!" yelled Uncle Buster from downstairs.

"Shoo!" she stamped her foot violently.

"And don't be stomping up in here, girl. What the hell wrong wit you?" He added, "You don't own nothin' in this house."

"Neither do you, shit!"

"Don't you get—"

She slammed her door so hard that the walls shook. "I can't believe this shit," fumed Dannielle. Another pair of her jeans was missing, these still had the tags on 'em. "I'm tired of mufuckas stealin' my clothes, shit!"

Shortly after her mother's funeral, Dannielle had moved in with her grandmother on her father's side. It was either that or a group home.

Grandma Terry was a lively woman, but unfortunately, her house was filled bumper to bumper with deadbeat family members, depending on her for their survival. A retired nurse; she took it all in stride. Grandma Terry tried her best to make Dannielle feel at home, but Dannielle still felt like an outsider. Mainly because the minute she dropped her bags in the six-bedroom, two-story house, she created an enemy in her cousin, Dyshay, who had long been the apple in her grandmother's eye.

"Hmmph," Dyshay had rolled her eyes, and said, "She don't look like nobody in this family!"

That was the opening salvo to a wicked smear campaign.

Dyshay was ingeniously manipulative and in no time, she had succeeded in turning everyone in the house, except Grandma Terry, against Dannielle. She didn't stop there; at school, and in the neighborhood, she whispered vicious rumors about Dannielle.

One week it was, "You know the bitch got dem herpes."

"Hell naw!"

The next week it was, "They say her stepfather robbed her booty."

"Robbed her booty?"

"Yeah...sodomized her."

"Whaaaat?"

On top of all that, Dannielle had long suspected Dyshay had been stealing her clothes.

"Fuck that!" Dannielle tipped out her room and peered down the hallway. She needed proof, 'cause Dyshay was just too damn slick. She eased up to Dyshay's door and turned the doorknob, and to her surprise, it came open. Dyshay usually kept it locked tighter than Fort Knox.

Dannielle thrust open the closet.

"Well, whadayaknow," Danielle exclaimed; sure enough, half the closet was filled with stuff Grandma Terry and NeNe had purchased for her. "Thievin' lil bitch!" Dannielle said aloud.

"What the hell you doin' in my room?"

Dannielle damn near jumped out her skin, but quickly got her mojo back and started snatching her clothes out the closet. "Repo, hoe!" She tore a pair of pants off a hanger. "What it look like I'm doin', bitch!"

"Uh-uhn!" Dyshay scrambled over to her closet, pushed Dannielle out the way and guarded the door with her body. "You got me fucked up."

Dyshay was charcoal black, with a pretty face, small waist, and super wide hips.

It was an even match.

"I'ma give yo' crispy-ass one second to un-ass my shit," Dannielle balled up her fists. "You ratchet mouth bitch, or I'ma—"

"Or you gon' do what? Huh?" Dyshay stepped to Dannielle and poked a long manicured finger in Dannielle's face.
"Ain't...nobody...har'lly...scared...of...yo...ol...orphan...An—"

WHAM!

Dannielle snuck one to the snotbox.

"Ouch!" Dyshay covered her bloody nose and crouched over.

Dannielle socked her again, twirled a fist around Dyshay's three hundred dollar weave, and rammed her head to the ground.

"Uncle Buster!" screamed Dyshay, loud enough to wake the dead.

When they finally pulled her off Dyshay, the whole house was in an uproar, yelling and screaming at her, and not a single soul took her side.

She couldn't take it anymore, so she grabbed her jacket and smashed out the door.

"You get back in this house!" ordered Uncle Buster's wife, Mattie.

"Fuck you!" cried Dannielle.

"See," someone said, "straight problem child."

As she stomped down the street wiping at the tears streaming down her face, she called NeNe, but the call went straight to voicemail. Ever since the G-Man's death, she'd been missing in action. Rumor was, she had all the dead man's money and jewelry. She tried her grandmother, but got the same results.

"Shit," she sniffed and tried to gather herself. "I ain't got nobody, and this shit is sooo not cool."

Out the corner of her eye, a pearl white Corvette hit the corner behind her, and a rumbling bass engulfed her as the car rolled up. The driver gave her a double look, passed by, and then suddenly he stopped and backed up expertly right next to her.

The passenger window slid down, unleashing Steel Pulse's classic reggae song, "Throne of Gold".

She's my queen...And I'm her king...

Dreams of sunshine, got my head spinnin' around...

"Hey lil velvet," said the handsome, dreadlocked driver as he lowered the volume, "you good?" He had on a pair of Armani aviator glasses.

"Huh?" She wiped her face and found herself slightly nodding to the beat, sorta disappointed he'd turned it down.

"Why?" she asked with a little attitude.

"I mean, you look a little shook up." He pulled on a long silky dread and smiled, as a mouth full of sparkling bling winked at her. "And you too fine to be out here lookin' all twisted."

And fine she was. In the two years since her mother's passing, Dannielle's young, ripe breasts had ballooned to a 38-C, and her backside had exploded curvaceously and deliciously. No doubt about it, she was a straight stallion. Moreover, NeNe kept her fresh to death; hair, nails, facials, the works. At the moment, even though it was a bit nippy, she was workin' a tight Gucci skirt that showed off her thick Beyoncé bronze thighs, and she was rockin' her real hair: lyed, dyed and laid to the side, on some Keri Hilson type shit.

"Twisted?" She cocked her neck and gave him a dirty look. "Ain't nobody twisted."

Mr. Corvette tossed his hands in the air, suave-like, in mock surrender.

"Palms up," he said, ultra pimpishly, "I'm just sayin' doe, don't kill pimpin'."

"Pimpin'?" She rolled her eyes. "I heard the hell outta that." She kept it movin', and added, "I'm cool," as she tossed up the peace sign.

"Hol' up..." He glided alongside her, and then called out from the car, "What's yo' name doe, lil velvet?"

She ignored him.

"It's like that, huh?"

She turned to face him. "Would you leave me alone?"

"I will if you tell me yo name."

She stammered briefly, "It's uh…Destiny, okay, now push."

"Destiny, huh?"

"Yep." She hugged her arms.

"How old is you?"

"Eighteen," she lied.

"Destiny…eighteen, huh?"

"That's what I said."

"Well, my name is Future, so get in and lemme read yo' palms, ma."

"You and yo' damn palms." She cracked a small smile. "And yo name ain't no damn Future."

"And yo' name ain't Destiny," he said, "so we got something in common."

"What, lying?" She bit her lip and rocked her neck from side to side, "'Cause I damn sho' ain't no hoe."

I got one, she a stunna and got spunk; let's play ball.

He eased the Corvette into an open slot against the curb and popped out the car. She stepped back and gave him the once over from head to toe.

He was tall, nut-brown, and undeniably gorgeous. He took his shades off. "Look, lil velvet," he said and she found herself looking up into a pair of stunning, light brown, hazel eyes. "I ain't no monster…I simply provide proper management."

This niggah gon' have the nerve to have pretty eyes too, hmmph.

"And it's by choice, not force, but that don't mean I don't appreciate a beautiful young lady when I see one."

"You prolly say that to everybody." She had to tear her face from those eyes. "Is that yo' favorite line or something?" She looked away.

I know she ain't eighteen, shit! If she wasn't so young, I'd wife her!

I ain't got no lines, lil velvet," he said, "I say what I mean, and mean what I say...but look," he changed subjects smoothly, "Where you goin'?"

"Why?"

"'Cause I'll take you there."

"Uh-uh," she smirked, "Negative." NeNe had schooled her on not jumping in the car with just any niggah, not smoking weed that she hadn't rolled up herself or seen rolled. Dannielle was far from a dumb bitch.

Mr. Corvette eyed Dannielle momentarily, licked his lips, then tossed her the keys and got in the passenger's seat. "Okay lil velvet, you take us there."

She was stunned. "How you know if I can even drive, huh?" She could, she even had a permit. *There's no way he coulda known that.*

"I ain't worried, I can upgrade you." He smiled and the diamonds waved at her.

"Is that right?"

Fly niggah, fly car; the temptation was just too irresistible. She swung the keys on her finger for a second, then sashayed over to the driver's side and pulled off into the fast lane in more ways than one.

Chapter 52

"Married!" She gazed at him with a pained expression. "You gotta be kidding, right?" said Five, her eyes moistening by the second.

"Five..." Preston reached for the teary-eyed young tender, "C'mere girl."

"No!" She stomped out the room. "I'm too through with you now, hmmph!" She slammed the door behind her.

"Girl, I know one damn thang," A.P. yelled, her voice booming through the door. "You best stop slammin' my damn door, huzzy!"

Then she turned to Preston and smacked her lips. "Don't even trip off that lil school girl crush that girl got on you." Her eyes dipped towards the door. "That girl got wall to wall niggahs sniffin' at her stankin' tail." She shrugged off Five's tantrum. "Now tell A.P. the business." She patted a spot on her bed. "C'mon, sit down, Nut."

He sat next to her. "This is between me and you, right?"

Aunt Paula crossed her plump puppies. "Cross my tits and hope to smell like shit."

He chuckled. "Okay, A.P., you know they was tryna give Kenzo the death penalty, right?"

"Yeah."

"Well, you remember my friend, Tamala, from back in the days?"

"Not really..." She squinted. "I don't think so."

"Anyways, she works for the D.A's office."

"Okay."

"Well...outta the blue, she got assigned to Kenzo's case."

"Okay..."

"And... that's my soon to be wife."

"Ooohhh," said Aunt Paula, "I see, said the blind hooker."

"Yeah, but J'Neane prolly gon' trip out, just like Five, nahmean?"

"Boy," she rolled her eyes, "she can trip all she want 'til she bust her damn head, shit!" declared Aunt Paula. "Sometimes people gotta do what the hell they gotta do."

"But—"

"But, my wide, wet ass, shit!"

Laughter bubbled up from both of them, until they were almost in tears.

She twisted her finger softly in his dimple then said, "Look here, you fine, long donkey dick, young man," she hugged him, "Kenzo is my nephew, and your best friend...to hell with what she gon' go through. She'll get over it, Nut." Her light perfume floated from her round bosom. "Besides, how y'all say it? Bro's befo' hoes."

He chuckled again. "A.P. you crazy, you know that?"

She grabbed his privates. "Crazy 'bout Nutzilla." She shot him a sneaky look. "Gimme some, Nut."

"C'mon A.P.," he protested through a smile.

"Mama!" It was Five at the door; he was saved by the bell.

"Damn, Nut!" fumed Aunt Paula, "do she got a goddamn radar on yo' dick?" She rolled her eyes. "What Five?"

"I need to ask him something," she sounded like a little girl.

"Lawwwd." A.P. shook her head as Five entered the room.

"'Sup Five?" said Preston, he guessed Five had calmed somewhat.

"I just wanna know if you can hire me, promoting or something, I need a job." Her lips pouted.

"Girl, first you wanna kill him, now you wanna work for him? Is you losin' you r damned mind or somethin'? Mama," she whined, "I meant to ask him before he got to talkin' 'bout gettin' married and stuff."

"Well, you shouldna been ear hustlin'."

Preston interjected, "Yeah, sure Five, it's all good."

"Fa real?" She was glowing now. "Don't be playin' wit me."

"Fa-real, fa-real," said Preston.

"Oh thank you, Preston!" She jumped in his lap and kissed him in the mouth. *MUAH!*

He blushed. "C'mon now, Five."

"Get yo'—" A.P. hollered.

She was up and on her way out the door, swinging her hips like *America's Next Top Model*, and she turned around and looked at her mother. "Don't hate, Mama, " she smirked and blew Preston a kiss. "See you later, boss." She said it with her body just as much as she said it with her lips. Then she was out the door.

"Boy what you gon' do with her, huh?"

"I don't know, A.P., she...I think of her like a lil sister."

"Whatcha think 'bout me, Nut?' she asked, forever freaky like.

"Well, I think you're the most beautiful lady in the whole wide world, A.P." He smiled, dimple peeking, and said, "And the sexiest."

"Oooh," she gushed and fanned herself, "I'm gettin' hot flashes, watchit now!"

"But, A.P., you know I really like J'Neane and she gonna be hurt when she finds out I'm gettin' married."

"I know, hun." Aunt Paula was serious now. "I'll try to talk to her, but that girl is sprung on you."

"I know, I feel crummy, too."

"But, wouldn't you feel crummier if Kenzo got the death penalty and you didn't save him, knowing you coulda?"

"Yeah."

He thought about his boy, Squeaky, and how he felt leaving his partner, knowing he'd never see the streets again.

"Yeah, A.P., you're right...it's still win-lose, ya know?"

"Hell, that's life, Nut...somebody's gotta win, and somebody gotta lose." She fondled his johnson again. "But wit a dick like this, Nut, you ain't gon' do too much losin'..."

Chapter 53

It was sheer pandemonium in the limo as they floated across the Bay Bridge, headed to San Francisco.

"Pop that mu'fuckin' bottle, P!" hooted Brandon, shaking the bottle of Armand de Brignac. "Strip club here we come!" he hollered, as he placed the bottle on his privates, simulating a penis. "Tits and pierced clits!" he yelped, "I, Brandon J. Square Extraordinaire, am gon' be the new Tupac of porn in that bitch...All ass on me!" Then he segued into a champagne spray war with Kobain and Drixxx.

"Hell yeah!" shouted Kobain, above the free-flying foam, "booty, booty, booty, booty, rockin' everywhere!"

"RIP Freshkidd!" howled Drixxx.

"Man, dawg...I wish I was out," Kenzo muttered somberly into the cell phone.

"It's goin' down tonight!" whooped Brandon in the background, "I'm leaving with two bitches tonight, watch!" He beat his chest and yanked his nuts.

"Don't trip, my niggah," Preston said, "Oops, my bad. You prolly can't say niggah no mo', huh?" Preston teased, "Against prison politics, huh?"

"Fuck you."

"Aye, my ninja," mocked Preston, "When you get out, leave that prison shit in there, 'cause I'm tellin' you right now, that shit don't work out here."

"Fuck you, again."

"I'm just fuckin' with you, blood," Preston said, "You gon' be right here with us, mayne! I mean, how many catz in jail gotta fuckin' iPhone, bruh-bruh?"

Preston had ingeniously secreted an iPhone and charger in the soles of a pair of orthopedic shoes, and had the heels modified, so that they could clip on and off and would be impossible to detect, unless you were privy to its function. Some straight James Bond shit. Because of the gunshot wounds to his leg, Kenzo convinced the doctor, with the help of a small bribe, to issue a chrono, granting him permission to wear orthopedic shoes. From there, Ramona just had to drop the shoes off at the County Jail, with a copy of the chrono, attached to the shoebox.

"Still ain't the same, dawg," Kenzo's voice was glum.

"Bruh, this ain't nothin' but a funky ass bachelor party, bruh. We gon' do it big when you touch-ten-toes-down, in the town."

"Yeah."

"You already know, bruh."

"That's wassup," Kenzo said, "we gon' do it B.I.G., P?"

"Bigger than big!" assured Preston, screaming and thrusting the phone in the air, "how we gon' do it when Zo hit the bricks?"

"We gon' get funky like a fat bitch!" shouted Brandon.

"Yeah…that's wassup!" they all chimed in.

Drixxx hit Preston with a blast of champagne foam.

"Hey!" yelped Preston, tucking the phone just in time. "Cut that shit out! Aye, Zo, call me back in like five, and we'll be inside the club."

"A'ight, blood," said Kenzo.

Preston passed out softball sized, G-stacks of one-dollar bills to all, and rubbed his hands together, scanning the half-naked ladies of lust.

Freak music pumped out the speakers in the club. It was chocolate Wednesdays, and most of the strippers were sistas: redbones, dark-chocolates, lattes, almond browns. There were wide hips, dooky bootys, apple bottoms, silicone, and perky-to huge round breasts; strolling, strutting, sashaying, and prancing all about.

It was VIP all the way for them as soon as the DJ announced, "A'ight ladies, we got special guests in the house; give it up for P-Styles and Liquid Traxxx!"

Within seconds, the club owner rolled out the red carpet for Preston and his boys.

They swarmed the men like bees on honey. "We 'bouta make it rain in this bitch!" Drixxx and Kobain got turnt up.

"Hol' up, hol' up!" announced Brandon J, and the women stopped in their tracks. "It's my boy's bachelor party, feel me? Show him some love to the utmost," said Brandon, pointing out Preston.

Preston smiled eagerly.

A platinum blonde stripper with hella ass and monster hips grabbed Preston's arm.

"I got this one y'all," she winked at the other strippers and they all acquiesced, except one, ghetto-booty redbone, wearing a short curly red 'fro, with her baby hairs slicked down and lined.

"Uh-uhn," she frowned with her hands stationed on her super hips. "She always tryna steal the show…fuck that!" she reached and yanked Preston's other arm. "I'm red and ready, that bitch is a rat head."

"Stop hatin', Queen Payless," snapped blondie.

"What?" She let go of Preston and her and Blondie stood titty to titty.

"Hol' it…" Brandon saved the day and tossed a blizzard of ones all over the redbone. "Baby, I love your redness," he grabbed her. "Lemme see redrum go dumb for Brandon J."

She couldn't help but drop her guards, although she still glanced over her shoulders, watching Blondie lead Preston away.

"Punk bitch!" spat redbone.

"Yo' mama, hoe!"

"Damn, I hit the lottery," said Preston, gazing down at the blonde stripper's wiggling, G-stringed butt cheeks swaying in front of him. "Bossy and beautiful, wit it."

She led him into a private booth. "These ol' tired ass hoes, can't cramp my style, handsome." She walked around him salaciously, as though he was the last big dick on Earth, caressing his shoulders and kissing his neck. "Umm-umm," she whispered in his ear, "what am I gon' do wit you, huh?" Blondie stepped in front of him and melted into a routine of limber splits and seductive gyrations. "Maybe, I'll do this..." She twirled her hips and cupped her succulent breasts. "And that, huh?" The more she danced, the more lust filled her eyes became.

"Ooooh...shiiiit..." hissed Preston, stroking his now swollen member. "Gaw deeezammm."

She turned around and shook her backside viciously; it was so close to his face, he could smell the slight musk of her natural scent underneath the tropical body spray. She looked back over her shoulder and made her buttocks clap.

Plap! Plap! Plap!

He tossed a cloud of greenbacks on her and she went wild.

"Get that shit, girl..."

She got low, low, low, low, low...

"Heyyyyy!" said Preston, his right eyebrow shot up. "Don't I know you?"

"Do you?" She gazed deep into his eyes.

"What's yo' name, ma?"

"Me?" She smiled.

"Yeah you...you the only one in here, right?"

She laughed. "Lauryn Hill."

"Lau...getthef—" he stopped short as suddenly it came to him. "Y-you're the girl I met on the Greyhound bus, the day I got out the one with the pretty lil girl."

"Busted." She continued to straddle him. Her breasts were firm and perky, nipples erect and meaty like giant Raisinets. "So are you marrying whassername?"

"Wasserwho?"

"You know, the girl that was waiting on you."

"Nope." He was becoming unbearably aroused, and he felt guilty.

"Why? What happened?"

"Long story."

"Well, would you look-a-here...Mr. Man," she purred and reached down and squeezed his love muscle. "Damn, is that all you, honey stick?"

"Something like that," he said dryly and bit the soft flesh of his lower lip.

"Oh, you not that into me no more?"

"I didn't say that..." He tried to change the subject, "How's Gabby, she hella big now I bet, huh?"

She smiled. "Awww, that's so sweet, you remembered her name."

"Yeah, I guess I did, huh?"

"Aye, I gotta confession to make," she said and squirmed on his lap, and placed his hands on her ripe breasts.

"What?"

"Squeeze 'em and I'll tell you."

He did.

"Ummm...I like that."

"That's it?"

"Nope," she wiggled, demanding, "now kiss 'em."

He did.

"Ummm...I bought your book and CD." She felt him growing hard beneath her.

"Thank you." He tried to adjust his pulsating member. "But that's nothing to confess."

"It is when my baby's daddy thinks I cheated on him…with you."

"How come he thought that?"

"'Cause, um…a lil birdie tol' him." She twisted a finger innocently against her cheek. "Tweet, tweet."

He laughed softly. "Why you do that, girl?"

""'Cause you're a good man, the type I wish he could—"

"Precious…" Two soft knocks came and another stripper entered. "Time's up—"

Out the corner of his eye, he saw a body that could have been Marie's twin, only curvier and younger. When he looked up at her face, his jaw dropped.

"Ohmigod!"

The stripper tried to cover her plump breasts in her tiny hands, but it was no use and she dashed out the room, high heels clicking the floor.

"What the fuck!" Preston pushed Precious off him and tore out the door. "Dannielle! Dannielle !"

Chapter 54

Mr. Corvette's real name was Maceo; he had no problem charming the young and vulnerable Dannielle right out her panties, and then banging her little coochie right out her back.

It wasn't even a match.

"Keep yo' legs up, girl," he barked lustfully, glaring down at Dannielle's fat round breasts and her trembling legs spread eagle at his sides.

"I can't," she whimpered through a moan and tried to let her legs down. "It hurrrts."

All the smart-alecky and sassy shit was gone, as he beat up her vagina walls with long, hammering strokes.

"I want 'em up," he huffed huskily; his pectoral muscles stretched and rippled as he watched his long, veiny penis become slickened with her juices. "Yeah, mmm…hmmm, I want all this young pussy."

"I'm…oowwww, tryin'." She tried to scoot back "You goin' too deeeppp."

"Mmm-hmmm." He was damn near slobbering; the pussy was piping hot and super tight; he couldn't believe his luck. He was a pro at the dick game so he switched gears, put her legs down and leaned over to whisper in her ear, "C'mon mami, be a big girl, and give daddy this pussy." Then he started working his hips in small, slow, circles.

"Maceo…oohh," she cried, "Oh please, baby."

"Fuck me back."

"Maceo!" She lifted her legs and tried to grind back. "Ooohhh...oowwww."

"Mmm-hmmm..." He wiped a sheen of sweat from his forehead. "There you go."

The small circles became big circles, and soon he was figure-eighting in the pussy and it opened wider with a wet plop.

"Oooohhh...Maceo."

"There it go, mami."

He paused briefly to slide a pillow under her fleshy butt cheeks, then propped her legs on his shoulders. His massive member throbbed right at her hungry, wet entrance. "Put that dick in girl, show daddy you want it."

"Ssssss...'kay," she whimpered and timidly reached down with her little hand, and guided it in slowly. "Ooohhh." She jerked as every inch filled her hot hole. "Oooh, Maceo, "she begged, "go slow, 'kay?"

He slid in and out slowly; it took all his power to restrain his hips, and his manhood was like an enraged Pitbull chasing after a pussycat. He rocked in and out her young, sweet thang and soon, wet slurping noises filled the room.

"Ooohhh, owwww, baaabbbyyy..." Her pussy muscles involuntarily milked at his engorged meat spear. Bravely, she lifted her hips to meet his nasty strokes. "Like that, daddy?"

"Yeeeaaah..." She became so wet that he almost slipped out. He latched onto her shoulders and began to pound at her pussy in a savage rhythm.

"Ooohhh," she cried, "You in my stomach, now!"

"Gimme this pussy!" He pounded her pussy out as sweat rained down his face, his biceps contorted and striated. Dannielle's face became a mixture of pain and pleasure as suddenly, a wave of sensations washed over her and she quivered uncontrollably beneath him. "Maceooohhh", she wrapped her thick, juicy legs around his body like snakes, and strangled his waist.

"Give it to me, bust it, baby!" He slammed his member in and out, and then switched to wide circles again.

She clasped his bunching buttocks. "Ooohhh, right there, Maceo!" her voice was erotically pleading, then she arched her back and trembled. Her lips formed a perfect O. "Oooohhhh..."

Minutes later, bent over slightly, she stumbled to the bathroom, holding her stomach. He watched as her buttocks bounced softly, causing his semi-hard penis to twitch on his thigh.

"You was tryna kill it," she pouted over her shoulder. "Meanie."

"Aye," he said, just before she entered the bathroom. "What?"

"Look."

She did.

He was waving a now monstrous sized penis at her, and then smiled. "It's his fault," he stroked it sensually, "When you get back, we gon' get his ass, okay?"

"Unt-uhn!" she giggled and closed the door behind her. "No!"

He stroked it as if it was a pet snake. "Mmmm-hmmm."

****

Maceo couldn't stay outta Dannielle's hot, tight cooch; thus, committing the cardinal sin in his line of business: he went tender-dick on the P-game, and let his "peter be the leader". His hawkeyed and jealous bottom bitch gave him an offhand warning about the time and money he was spending on Dannielle without turning her, before flying the coop, taking 70 G's and the bread-winning snow bunny with her. When he finally caught up with her, she was stylin' in a pair of Jimmy Choo's, alongside some two-bit street punk. He knocked them both out, breaking her jaw in three places, but she had enough jawbone to scream for the police, who promptly arrested him for strong-armed robbery, and assault and battery.

This left Dannielle in the impossible position of being responsible for the rent on his two-bedroom condo, and car note on the Corvette. Much to her relief, she tracked down NeNe, who was now living in the ATL running her own beauty salon, still sittin' on over two hundred grand of her deceased baby daddy's thug money.

After Dannielle gave her the rundown, she cried, "NeNe, what am I s'pose to do now, huh?"

"Fuck that niggah, drive down here to the ATL, I got you."

"Uh-uhn," she refused as she remembered how good Maceo's dick was and how he treated her like a princess. "I gotta have his back, NeNe."

She just like her mama, every time she cums, it blows up a million neurons. "Girl, don't be stupid, the niggah's a pimp!"

"So!"

"Girrrl," NeNe sighed audibly, "You got a lot to learn."

"NeNe," cried Dannielle, "I gotta learn my lessons regardless, so I might as well get it over with now."

"Okay, first lesson for a boss bitch. Possession."

"What?"

"Who got the car?"

"I do," Dannielle replied, "but they tryna repo it, 'cause he ain't paid the note on it this month."

"Okay, jewelry. Who got that?"

"I do, NeNe...I got everything."

"Okay, second lesson. Authenticity."

"What?"

"In other words, let's see if you got a real niggah or a clown. Go get his jewelry."

Dannielle went and retrieved his jewelry.

"'Kay, I got it."

"What kind of watch he got?"

"A Rolex."

"A Rolex, huh?"

"Yep," Dannielle said, "and it got diamonds everywhere."

"Dannielle, look at the second hand on the watch, so it ticks or do it glide?"

"It glides."

"Okay, it's prolly real," NeNe chuckled, "look like you his main chick; you must got that good gushy-gushy like yo' mama."

Silence immediately stifled the air, and then Dannielle sniffled audibly.

"I'm sorry, Danni..." NeNe knew it was still too early to bring up Marie so casually.

"It's okay."

"Danni, like you said, you gotta learn your lessons, so I'ma take the training wheels off you, but always remember you can reach out and hold onto me, okay?"

"I know, NeNe."

"Now look, I'm gon' blast you ten G's, pay off the car note if you can, put a nickel on his books, and then look for a job. But the minute it gets funky, call me and I'll send you a plane ticket, a'ight?"

"'Kay..." Dannielle breathed a sigh of relief. "Thank you, NeNe."

NeNe overnighted two cashier's checks for five grand apiece. Maceo owed $3700 more for the Corvette. Dannielle paid it off, and put $500 on his books.

However, within two weeks, she burned through the money, helping with Maceo's attorney fees. The following week, he was set to take a three-year bid, and because he was on parole, bail wasn't even an option. On top of that, he was hinting around that once he left County Jail, he wanted her to drop the car and jewelry off at his mother's house. She wasn't goin' out like that though.

Number one, she was sharper than he thought, and two, she wanted to prove to him that age wasn't nothing but a number, and she could pull her weight, just like any other woman.

Then Maceo's sister, Trina, started to come to the condo frequently. At first, she was suspicious, but after a few days, she looked forward to her visits. Trina told Dannielle all Maceo's business, and that she was a stripper.

"Girl," Trina bragged, "You need to come get this money wit me, I'm tellin' you wit all that ass and those big ass titties you got, you'll make a killin'."

"Trina, I'm only sixteen."

"Only who?" Trina was shocked. "Ohmigod, I thought you was at least twenty."

"Nope, sixteen."

"No wonder why that niggah, Maceo, sprung; you his baby."

"Fuck you, bitch."

Trina doubled over with laughter. "But look, don't trip, it's ways around everything, if you wit it."

"I gotta pay these damn bills, and ain't nobody hiring," said Dannielle.

"A'ight, this what we gon' do..." Trina hooked Dannielle up with a fresh set of fake ID and Social Security card, placing her at nineteen years old. Then she interviewed at the Golden Key strip club across the bridge, where Trina was also working. Dannielle was hired on the spot and soon, she was raking in six to eight hundred dollars a day.

From that moment forth, she was able to keep Maceo's book fat, and made sure she was at San Quentin every visiting day. Maceo was in love with his young stunna.

Everything was going smoothly, until she got busted by Preston and had to quit, but she easily found another strip club to work in. However, there was one problem; she quickly picked up a creepy customer, a white dude with eerie, piercing blue eyes.

Chapter 55

Ordinarily when a guy was due to be married in the morning, he'd be thinking about his bride. However, the only thing on Preston's mind was tracking down Dannielle; he just wasn't about to stand by and watch her get swallowed by the nefarious elements of the sex trade, 'cause in his eyes, stripping led to prostitution. She got ghost on him that night at the strip club, but every night since then, he showed up looking for her, and harassing the manager. He had even got into a tussle with security, which was why now he was strapped with the .9mm. He descended from the car and made his way toward the club's entrance.

"Psssst...pssst...hey handsome."

Preston pivoted toward the voice. It was Precious; he turned around and walked to her car.

"'Sup?" His face was hard.

"Damn, like that?"

"Yeah." He bounced his head. "My daughter's only sixteen, and she's working in a strip club...so yeah, it's like that!"

"Well, she's not working here anymore."

"Is that right?" He narrowed his eyes.

"Preston, I have no reason to lie to you."

He continued to ice grill her.

"But I do know where she works now."

"You do?" His eyes widened. "Where?"

"On the other side of town at the Crazy Horse."

He hopped in her car. "Take us there!" It was more an order than a request.

"I'm on in five minutes," she complained.

He peeled five crispy hundreds off his bankroll and slapped them on the dashboard. "You dancin' for me tonight!"

Chapter 56

Dannielle parked the 'Vette and grabbed her bag and jumped out. She was late and the manager was as asshole, especially if you didn't let him sneak a free feel or two.

As she walked briskly toward the club, the fine hairs on the back of her neck stood.

Shit, they need to do something 'bout the lighting in this damn parking lot.

She walked faster, almost at a trot, as the van door she passed suddenly slid open and she was snatched inside. It happened so fast, she didn't have a chance to scream. When she did, it was too late.

Chapter 57

"Lemme go!" Dannielle screamed and twisted in the iron grasp of her attacker. She opened her mouth to scream again, just as a rag was crudely shoved in her mouth, then duct tape was roughly strapped around it. Her eyes bulged as she tried to scream, but it came out a smothering muffle. Within seconds, she was handcuffed, with her arms stretched up above her, attached to some sort of customized hook. The assailant moved with precision and pinned her legs down, and clamped them wide apart to another set of clamps on the van's floor.

Her heart beat wildly and tears squeezed out her pleading eyes.

Even though her attacker had a hoodie pulled tightly over his head, she knew who he was. His sick blue eyes gave him away and his smell. He was the creepy guy. "Stinky", she called him. He had wanted a private show, but she denied him, 'cause he grossed her out with his stench, and he had creepy eyes.

"Don't cry now, you black bitch!" he ranted, his psychotic eyes darted right to left. "I fuckin' take what I want, whore! You hear me?"

She saw the huge menacing butcher knife in his hand. She nodded nervously.

"That's what I thought, whore!"

He cut her shirt open and her firm breasts sprung free. He trailed the sharpened edge of the knife against her skin with one hand, and fondled her chest cruelly with the other.

"You wanna die, whore?"

She flailed her head from side to side.

"Well bitch, pray!"

She did.

He licked his lips grossly, then bent down and sucked her breasts, slobbering all over them.

She closed her eyes tight and whimpered.

Then hideously, he bit down on a nipple and mauled at it with his teeth.

The pain jolted her and she arched her back and pulled against the restraints, and screamed horrifically into the rag.

He rose up and blood smeared his lips. He smiled sinisterly, before spitting half a nipple onto her face; it bounced off her forehead and rolled across her neck. She screamed so hard, she passed out.

Chapter 58

He sent her inside to scout it out.

"Her car is here, but they said she hasn't come in yet."

Preston scratched his head and panned the parking lot. Instinctively, he started walking toward the lot.

"Where are you going, Preston?"

"Which one is her car?"

"The Corvette," replied Precious.

Chapter 59

"Wake up, bitch!" raged the blue eyed sicko. He slapped her repeatedly.

SMACK! SMACK!

"I want you awake!"

SMACK!

She came to, only to glance down at her now completely naked body. She was bleeding profusely from her right breast.

"That's right, whore!" He licked his lips manically. "Eyes wide open!"

He bent down and slobbered over her breasts again, licking the blood and all.

She braced herself. *Please God. Pleeeeaaaasssse...*she prayed. *I don't wanna die like this. Mama! Oh God...*

At that moment, the passenger's window burst open and an arm forcefully thrust into the van and unlocked the door.

"Hey, what the fuck!" yelled the assailant.

Preston barreled into the van, gun drawn. His eyes saucered at Dannielle in her distressed state.

"You muthafucka!" He aimed the gun at the knife-wielding attacker. "Drop it muthafucka!" screamed Preston. "Drop the knife!"

In a flash of motion, the attacker lunged at Preston.

"Arrrggghhh!"

Preston fell backwards, yanking the trigger.

BOOM! BOOM! BOOM!

The shots tore into the attacker, blowing him backwards; he fell on the side of the terrified, prone, Dannielle.

Preston rushed to Dannielle's aid. Pulling the duct tape off and removing the rag, he choked out, "Oh my God, Dannielle!"

"Daddy, I'm sorry..." she moaned incoherently.

"It's okay, you're fine now. Daddy—"

"Arrrggghhh!" Hoodie discarded, the attacker sprung at Preston again, barely missing his jugular vein with the knife. In his attempt to defend himself, Preston dropped the gun.

"Daddy!" screamed Dannielle. They were almost on top of her.

The knife was hovering above him, held at bay only by Preston's brute strength. However, the attacker was just as strong as Preston, and what's more, he had leverage. He was using his legs, pushing off the side of the van. As Preston struggled underneath the attacker, he watched the veins snake across the attacker's forehead, and suddenly he realized who the attacker was. It was Tamala's ex-boyfriend, the cop.

"Sonofabitch!" grunted Kevin O'Reilly, as he recognized Preston. "I'm gonna kill you, nigger!"

"Fuck you!" roared Preston, and with a burst of energy, he reversed Kevin's mounted position and slammed two vicious head butts home.

"Ahhh..." groaned Kevin and he released the knife.

Out the corner of his eye, Preston saw the .9mm and in one lithe motion, he slammed an elbow to Kevin's Adam's apple, then swiftly reached for the gun and fired a shot at point blank range into Kevin's head.

BOOM!

The sound was deafening, as the Hydra-Shok bullet blew a hole out the back of Kevin's head, big enough to drop an apple in it.

Hurriedly, Preston searched the dead body and found the handcuff key; he released her, then covered her body with his jacket and carried her outside.

"Daddy..." she said groggily.

"Shhhhh..." he said.

A crowd was forming and Precious came running over to him, with two police cars skidding to a halt just behind her.

"Here, help me get her to the car." He didn't have time for the police; Dannielle needed medical attention.

"Daddy."

"Sshh..." he tried to calm her, "Daddy's got you."

"No, you don't understand, Daddy," said Dannielle, "h-he bit off my nipple, it's in the van."

"Oh shit!" Preston rushed back to the van, kicked Kevin's body to the side and searched the interior. Then he saw it; it looked like a piece of hamburger meat. He grimaced and placed it inside a tissue, and jumped out the van.

The cops were aiming their side arms at him now.

"Drop the gun!"

He forgot he still had the gun. "Okay." He went to lay down the gun with one hand, but he still had the other hand clasped around Dannielle's chewed-up nipple.

An overzealous rookie cop, yelled, "He's got something else in his hand!"

They opened fire.

Chapter 60

BLOOM! BLOOM! BLOOM!

The crowd scattered in all directions as bullets charged through Preston's shoulder and stomach. "Ahhh!" he screamed. Out of sheer reflex he fell to the ground and returned fire.

BOOM! BOOM! BOOM!

One cop went down. His partner saw him fall and fired wildly at Preston again.

BLOOM! BLOOM!

Instantly, he then rushed to his partner's aid.

However, Preston had already rolled underneath a car, and he blasted at the direction of the shots.

The cop fell in a heap.

Preston struggled to his feet, as his mind was reeling, frantically.

"Daddy!" screamed Dannielle, from somewhere. He stumbled toward her panicky voice. "C'mon Daddy!"

He found the car and fell against it. Precious got out and held him up.

"P-Precious..." He tried to give her the tissue. "Take her to the hospital."

"Pres-Preston!" She was distraught.

"Watch out, Daddy!"

Four cops fired at him from behind their squad cars.

Pop! Pop! Pop! Pop!

"Get down!" Preston shouted at Dannielle and Precious, and stumbled away at a crouch, ducking behind cars. He stuck the gun behind him and fired blindly, and the .9mm barked.

BOOM! BOOM! BOOM!

They returned fire.

Pop! Pop! Pop! Pop!

Windshields exploded all around him, and bullets whistled by his head.

He rose up and fired again.

BOOM! BOOM! BOOM!

Another officer fell, as a bullet gutted his neck and a gruesome crimson liquid splattered the police car.

BOOM!

The chamber slide reared back. Preston was out of bullets.

"Ahhh!" Frustrated, he threw the gun at the police, just as the bullets began to find their mark. Bullet after bullet crashed into him.

Pop! Pop! Pop! Pop!

He spun around as his body danced grotesquely with the hot metal.

Pop! Pop! Pop!

"Daddy!" was the last word he heard before he faded to black.

EPILOGUE

His eyes fluttered open as Marie dabbed the hot towel against his head. He quickly jumped back from her.

"Oh shit!" he blurted as his eyes bulged and he began to pat his body for bullet holes as if he was on fire.

"Stop being a little punk!" she said, "come here crazy ass man."

"You can talk like that in Heaven? Oh shit, this must be hell!"

"Heaven?" she wrinkled her forehead. "Hell?" she shook her head. "Boy, what you talkin' 'bout?"

"You-you-you got stabbed, and-and," he stammered, "the police shot me to death."

Marie's face wrinkled up as she howled with laughter. "Boy, the only thing happened is you jumped on that lil punk, Rico, and he had a gun and it grazed yo head, and I found you passed out in the street."

"What?" He couldn't believe it. "So we not dead?"

She kissed him deeply with her soft lips. "Does that feel cold?"

"Nope."

She put his hand underneath her oversized T-shirt. "How 'bout that, do it feel cold and dry?"

It was warm and wet, just the way he liked it. He shook his head no, to answer her question.

"Well then, crazy man, you've answered your own question."

"B-b-baby, I…"

She snuggled up close to him. "What? What mama's lil baby want?" she coaxed as she baby-talked him.

"Baby, I love you, and...and...I'ma do all I can to be—"

"To be what?" She kissed him. "A good man, huh?"

"Yep..." He held her tight. "That's what I'm gon' be..."

End

Made in the USA
San Bernardino, CA
23 May 2019